About the Author

Alan Frost is an experienced IT professional, being a Fellow of the British Computer Society and a Chartered Engineer. He has spent his life moving technology forwards from punch cards to AI, but always knowing that the key constituent in any system is the liveware, the users.

Beware The Northemy

Alan Frost

Beware The Northemy

Olympia Publishers
London

www.olympiapublishers.com
OLYMPIA PAPERBACK EDITION

A CIP catalogue record for this title is
available from the British Library.

ISBN: 978-1-80074-119-5

This is a work of fiction.
Names, characters, places and incidents originate from the writer's imagination.
Any resemblance to actual persons, living or dead, is purely coincidental.

First Published in 2021

Olympia Publishers
Tallis House
2 Tallis Street
London
EC4Y 0AB

Printed in Great Britain

Dedication

To my daughter Lynsey for being my daughter

Introduction

Humans had lived in peace for over a millennium. They had expanded to colonise more than a thousand planets creating an informal confederation called The Galactium.

Many thought that these were humanity's golden years. There had never been a war in that time. Peace was the norm. The small Galactium Navy had no experience of battle. For an intergalactic population of two trillion, their military was almost non-existent.

Then, quite unexpectedly, several human planets had been invaded by ruthless aliens. They weren't after the wealth of The Galactium but its citizens. The entire fauna and flora, including every human on the planet, were simply scooped up and liquidised. The human soup was carried away in massive tankers.

The invader also took thousands of live humans. The Skiverton needed them for breeding purposes and food. The fate of these humans was truly disgusting. Some individuals managed to escape, including Jenny, Cheryl and Adam, but most were eaten, impregnated or used in ghastly experiments.

The Galactium President and Navy, after advice from an artificial intelligence called AI Central, formed two fleets. The First fleet would defend The Galactium and fight the Skiverton. President Padfield, Admiral Bonner and Captain Mustard would lead a motley collection of ancient warships and unproven crews against a high-tech adversary. Their chances of success were very low.

The Second fleet, led by Captain Millington, would take the most exceptional talents of The Galactium into unknown space in an attempt to find a new home for humanity. What they found instead were death and destruction and they were eventually forced to return home. They came back with warnings of the Brakendeth.

Through guile and cunning, Mustard and Bonner defeated the Skiverton, only to be confronted by other alien enemies. Gradually, the technology and fighting ability of The Galactium improved until it was an impressive fighting force. They won many battles against a variety of foes.

Gradually, humanity realised that the real enemy was The Brakendeth. They had been fighting their client races.

Then humanity discovered the greatest shock of all. The Brakendeth had created humanity as cattle to produce a drug that provided eternal life for them and their agents. Humans had been designed to be dumb, stupid creatures that needed to be culled regularly. The Skiverton had simply been culling them.

The real enemy was The Brakendeth. At the same time, they were the creator of humankind. They were gods, but they were gods that needed to be beaten. The Galactium managed to track them down with the largest human fleet ever created. However, they were outplayed and outgunned by The Brakendeth.

Mustard and Padfield confronted the Grand Dethmon, Leader of the Brakendethians to find that there was only a handful of them left alive. And those wanted to die, but they couldn't kill themselves. If the humans didn't find a way of helping them, then the humans would die.

Cheryl was pregnant with a part-human, part-Brakendethian child. He was the solution. Even though he was only a few days old, he met with the Brakendethian Council who welcomed the first new member of their race in half a million years. It was enough for them to terminate their own lives.

Terry was the only surviving Brakendethian. He recommended that the humans should terminate his life as the last thing you would want is a live Brakendethian living amongst you.

Terry, Cheryl, Jack, Edel and David now continue their journey.

Location: The President's Office, Presidential Palace, Planet Earth
Sequence of Events: 1

'And now it begins,' Terry said.

President Padfield found it surreal being addressed by a six-month-old baby. Of course, he was the last of the Brakendeths. He had asked Terry to address his 'top team' regarding the likely aftermath of the recent events: The Brakendeth War.

Terry, 'Firstly, the Grand Dethmon offered the human race a veritable collection of goodies including their planet, technology, fleet, all of their knowledge and eternal life.'

President Padfield, 'We can't gain access to them as you know.'

Terry, 'You need to be patient, it will come about at the right time.'

President Padfield, 'But when is that?'

Terry, 'The right time will be the right time.' It was difficult to get angry with an intellect in diapers.

'And now it begins,' said Terry.

President Padfield, 'What begins?'

Terry, 'The war with The Northemy.'

President Padfield, 'We are not at war.'

Terry, 'You are, you just don't know it yet.'

President Padfield, 'What else can you tell us?'

Terry, 'As you know, humans were created by us to produce a drug called Chemlife which effectively provides eternal life or at least a hugely extended lifespan. Humans were supposed to be a biological pharmacy. They should never have acquired consciousness. To be honest, that is still a great mystery that needs to be investigated.

'As part of this process, the Brakendeth ended up with a number of client races.'

President Padfield, 'How many?'

Terry, 'I'm not sure. At least 400, perhaps thousands. They all want, or rather, *need* Chemlife. I have concerns that they might come for it. To be honest, I know that they will come for it. They have no choice.'

President Padfield, 'Why us?'

Terry, 'The only source of Chemlife is humanity. They will want your bodies!'

President Padfield, 'What you are saying is that we will need to maintain our defences.'

Terry, 'You certainly will because it begins now.'

President Padfield, 'Who are these Northemy?'

Terry, 'Have you ever wondered why humans never came into contact with other species?'

President Padfield, 'There have been lots of theories.'

Terry, 'Well whatever they were, they were incorrect. The human zone was one large farm constructed by us. We protected the farm from any alien interference.'

President Padfield, 'But our galaxy is so large. It incorporates numerous galaxies.'

Terry, 'That's why we had millions of automated ships patrolling the extremities. No one was going to enter our farm without permission.

'Who do you think is patrolling it now?'

President Padfield, 'I guess *we* are, to a limited extent.'

Terry, 'You are just fantasising. There are no patrols of the human empire at all.'

President Padfield, 'We are not an empire, we are a grouping of like-minded planets.'

Terry, 'You and the human race need to grow up if you want to protect your empire. The Northemy are on their way!'

The President didn't really like a child treating him as an idiot, but he said, 'What do you know about The Northemy?'

Terry, 'Very little. I need to access the Brakendeth records.'

President Padfield, 'Tell us what you do know.'

Terry, 'They follow a Brakendeth pattern. They like to lay their eggs in humans, thousands of them.'

President Padfield, 'Where do they get the humans from?'

Terry, 'They have their own farms.'

President Padfield, 'What makes you think that war is on its way?'

Terry, 'They need more humans, and there is no one to stop them.'

Location: The President's Office, Presidential Palace, Planet Earth
Sequence of Events: 2

Presidential Guard, 'Mr President, there is a call for you.'

GAD Control, Officer on duty, 'Sir, it would appear that thirty-two planets are under attack.'

President Padfield, 'Where?'

GAD Control, Officer on duty, 'Sector 9, outer rim planets.'

President Padfield, 'Has Admiral Mustard been informed?

Presidential Guard, 'Yes, Sir. Inform him that I'm on my way to GAD (The Galactium Alliance Defence Hub).

'Signal the following for immediate attendance, highest alert:

- Admiral Jack Mustard, Admiral of the Fleet, and First Fleet.
- Admiral Edel Bonner, Advisor to the Admiral of the Fleet.
- Admiral George Bumelton, Second Fleet.
- Admiral Vicky Ward, Third Fleet.
- Admiral David Taylor, Fourth Fleet.
- Admiral Glen Pearce, Fifth Fleet.
- Admiral Brian Whiting, Sixth Fleet.
- Admiral Victor Brotheridge, Seventh Fleet.
- Admiral Matt Morten, Eighth Fleet.
- Admiral Peter Gittins, Ninth Fleet.
- Admiral Phil Richardson, Tenth Fleet.
- Admiral John Bonner, Eleventh Fleet.
- Admiral Denise Sibley, Supply Fleet.
- Admiral Calensky Wallett, Reserve Fleet.
- Commander Tom Crocker, Special Operations, First Fleet.
- Dennis Todd, Marine Commander.
- AI Central.
- Jill Ginger, Fleet HQ — Head of Science.
- Alison Walsh, Fleet HQ — Head of Engineering.
- Jeremy Jotts, Fleet HQ — Head of Staffing.
- Louise Forrester, Fleet HQ — Head of Logistics and Production.
- Linda Hill, Fleet HQ — Head of Intelligence.
- Salek Patel, Fleet HQ — Head of Communications.

- Denise Smith, Fleet HQ — Head of Navigation & Exploration.
- Admiral Rachel Zakott, Fleet HQ — Head of Planetary Defence.
- Dr Doris Frost, Chief Medical Officer.
- Tony Moore, Deputy President.
- Bill Penny, Leader of The Galactium Council.
- Henry Strong, Chief of Staff.

Presidential Guard, 'Yes Sir, some of the admirals will be attending via VR as they are already responding to the invasion. Did you want the Palace locked down, Sir?'

President Padfield, 'Not at this stage.'

Location: GAD (The Galactium Alliance Defence Hub), Planet Earth
Sequence of Events: 3

President Padfield, 'Give me an update.'

Officer on duty, 'As you can see from the display, thirty-two planets in sector 9 are under attack from an unknown enemy. The current position is as follows:

- All thirty-two forts have been engaged. It would appear that eight of them are out of action
- The Fourth Fleet is engaged but is being pushed back
- The Sixth and Seventh Fleets are on their way
- The Reserve Fleet has been put on alert
- The drone force has been activated.'

AI Central: 'I've calculated that there are at least fifty thousand enemy vessels. I can't determine whether they are manned or not. The odds are that they are manned, or should I say aliened.'

President Padfield, 'How many vessels do we have engaged?'

Officer on duty, 'There are twenty-four forts.'

AI Central, 'We are now down to eleven forts.'

Officer on duty, 'The Fourth Fleet had 1,000 vessels at the start of the engagement. Fleets 6 and 7 have a total of 2,000 vessels.'

President Padfield, 'If we engaged all the Fleets, we would still be heavily outnumbered. How many drones do we have?'

Officer on duty, 'We have about 20,000, but only 7,000 are currently operational. They have all been activated and are in transit from many different locations.'

President Padfield, 'How quickly can we get the rest operational?'

Officer on duty, 'I will find out.'

Admiral Mustard, 'Thank you, officer.

AI Central, 'I estimate that they can all be made operational in less than a day.'

Admiral Mustard, 'Fleet Operations, my orders:

- Order all Fleets except Fleet 10 and the Reserve Fleet to engage the enemy immediately
- Order Fleet 10 and the Reserve Fleet to provide support as required. Ensure that they are positioned to provide that

support when required

- Order the Head of Planetary Defence to immediately activate all nearby forts for travel and initiate local defence plan
- Order the Head of Logistics to immediately organise and activate all inactive drones
- Recall all staff
- Put all military forces on full alert.'

Fleet Operations, 'Yes, Sir.'

President Padfield, 'Thank you, Admiral Mustard.'

Admiral Mustard, 'Operational staff, to your posts now.'

Location: Fortress Whittle, Planet Whittle
Sequence of Events: 4

Captain Walton, 'Give me an update.'

Chief Gunner, 'Sir, our automated defence systems are almost out of ammunition.'

Captain Walton, 'How long will they last?'

Chief Gunner, 'They are all gone, Sir.'

Captain Walton, 'What's the status of our shields?'

Chief Gunner, 'They are at 60%.'

Captain Walton, 'Will they hold?'

Chief Gunner, 'No way of knowing Sir, but I would say no.'

Captain Walton, 'You are full of the joys of spring. How many of the enemy did we destroy?'

Chief Gunner, 'It's hard to believe, but my system suggests that we eliminated over 4,000 of the enemy.'

Captain Walton, 'Is help on the way?'

Comms, 'Fleet 4 is already engaged, but it is struggling. I can see two further Fleets on their way.'

Captain Walton, 'Will they get here in time?'

Comms, 'I doubt it, Sir.'

Chief Gunner, 'The shields are down to 28%, Sir.'

Captain Walton, 'Can we leave the battle zone?'

Navigator, 'We could, but it would mean breaking the line, and it would probably not serve any purpose.'

Fortress Whittle ceased to exist.

Location: Admiral Taylor's Flagship, Fourth Fleet
Sequence of Events: 5

Admiral Taylor, 'Give me an update.'

Fleet Operations, 'Our entire Fleet is fully engaged but are flagging under a concerted attack from tens of thousands of enemy vessels.'

Admiral Taylor, 'Can you give me a more specific number of enemy vessels?'

Fleet Operations, 'Our systems are struggling to cope because of the numbers involved and the speed of the enemy vessels. Forty to fifty thousand would be a realistic guess. And they are operating across such a vast area.'

Admiral Taylor, 'Are we damaging them?'

Fleet Operations, 'Yes, Sir, we are scoring a huge number of hits. However, it's difficult to ascertain whether they are being reconstituted or whether new vessels are entering the fray.'

Admiral Taylor, 'What do you mean?'

Fleet Operations, 'When we started, there were 'n' number of the enemy. After much success on our side, there is still 'n' number of the enemy.'

Admiral Taylor, 'It doesn't make sense.'

Fleet Operations, 'Looks like some sort of smoke and mirrors trick. It may be a trick, but they are hurting us—we have just lost Fortress Whittle.'

Admiral Taylor, 'That's terrible, my heart goes out to them.'

Fleet Operations, 'The huge numbers of the enemy, are pushing our Fleet backwards. What do you want me to do?"

Admiral Taylor, 'Where are Fleets 6 and 7?'

Fleet Operations, 'They are almost in place, Sir. The rest of the Fleet will soon be in position.'

Admiral Taylor, 'Request Admiral Mustard's permission to withdraw. If he gives his permission, then ask him where he wants Fleet 4 positioned.'

Comms, 'Admiral Mustard orders us to stand our ground.'

Location: Admiral Mustard's Flagship, First Fleet
Sequence of Events: 6

Fleet Operations to Admiral Mustard, 'Sir, we have further alerts. Sector Four is under attack. Admiral Richardson with Fleet 10 and the Reserve Fleet are responding. You should also know that their trajectory would take them to Earth.'

Admiral Mustard, 'Get me Admiral Richardson.'

Comms, 'Yes, Sir.'

Admiral Mustard, 'Admiral, give me your status.'

Admiral Richardson, 'Greetings, I've taken my Fleet and the Reserve Fleet to confront the enemy. The Supply Fleet and the Marine Force are ready to defend Earth. As you know, there are some pretty impressive fortifications throughout the Solar System. I also managed to rustle up some drones. Can you spare any resources?'

Admiral Mustard, 'I need to assess the situation here first, but I will send Fleet 9 back to defend Earth.'

Fleet Operations to Admiral Mustard, 'We have further alerts. Sector Three is under attack. We have no reserves whatsoever.'

Admiral Mustard, 'My orders:
- Order Fleet 9 to engage the enemy in Sector 3 immediately
- Inform Admiral Richardson that Fleet 9 is not coming to assist him.'

Fleet Operations, 'Yes, Sir.'

Admiral Mustard, 'AI Central what is your analysis?'

AI Central,' My analysis is as follows:
- The forts are performing well but are being destroyed when they run out of munitions
- Most of the forts in Sector 9 are either destroyed or inoperative
- Fleet 4 will be destroyed if you don't do something
- Your Fleet consists of 1, 2, 3, 5, 6, 7 and 8. It should be enough to reach a stalemate with the enemy. The drones might give you victory.
- Fleet 10 and the Reserve Fleet are engaging the enemy in Sector 4. They will probably be destroyed.

- Fleet 9 is being sent to Sector 3. It will be destroyed.
- Earth will not survive the enemy fleets converging on it from Sectors 4 and 3.'

Admiral Mustard, 'What are your recommendations?'

AI Central, 'All Fleets should return to defend Earth. If Earth goes then Humanity goes.'

Admiral Mustard, 'Any other suggestions?'

AI Central, 'Initially I recommended a 'Rommel'. Concentrate and defeat each enemy army one at a time.'

Admiral Mustard, 'What does Terry suggest?'

AI Central, 'I will put him on?'

Terry, 'Just putting my bottle down. I suggest a home attack. You need to chop off their head.'

Admiral Mustard, 'What do you mean?'

Terry, 'Is their home world properly defended?'

Admiral Mustard, 'Where is their home world?'

Terry, 'I've no idea, but you have the data to find it.'

AI Central, 'Terry is right. We have three alien attacks. Through a mixture of triangulation and comms/travel analysis, we can track down a likely start point. I will work on it; you get a Fleet ready.'

Admiral Mustard, 'Fleet Operations, my orders:
- Order the first squadron of battlecruisers from each Fleet to disengage from the enemy and join Fleet 1 immediately
- Order all Fleets to disengage from the enemy and return to Earth immediately
- Order Admiral Bumelton to leave Fleet 1 and organise the defence of Earth
- Determine if the 'planet killer' is operational. If it is, I want it as part of Fleet 1 as soon as possible.'

Fleet Operations, 'Yes, Sir.'

Location: Admiral Mustard's Flagship, First Fleet
Sequence of Events: 7

Admiral Mustard, 'AI Central, give me an update.'

AI Central, 'We are having trouble pinning down the enemy's home. They likely have multiple locations.'

Admiral Mustard, 'Should I just sit where I am, or is there a rough direction that I should head to?'

AI Central, 'A typically predictable response. What do you want me to say?'

Admiral Mustard, 'Tell me where you want me to go and tell me now.'

AI Central, 'There is a 61% probability that their home is near Star ST97643, but I have a more worrying observation.'

Admiral Mustard, 'My orders:

- Order all Fleet 1 commanders to transfer to Star ST97643
- Assume standard defence formation on arrival.'

The Galactium portal technology meant that travel was almost instantaneous over relatively short distances.

Admiral Mustard to AI Central, 'What is this worrying observation?'

AI Central, 'Some of the forts have achieved amazing kill rates. Together they have destroyed more than 30,000 enemy vessels. However, the twist is that the size of the enemy has remained stable.'

Admiral Mustard, 'That doesn't make sense, tell me again.'

AI Central, 'Let's say they started off with 50,000 ships. We destroyed 30,000, but they are still left with 50,000!'

Admiral Mustard, 'So how did they replace the 30,000?'

AI Central, 'And where from? There are no signs of any mother ships.'

Admiral Mustard, 'What is your synopsis?'

AI Central, 'Their vessels are multi-dimensional. At the point of destruction, they jump to another dimension, and/or additional ships are supplied from that dimension.

'Watch this film in slow motion. Track the missile that is going to hit the craft on the bottom edge of the screen. Watch it disappear at the point of contact. Then watch it reappear. Our systems record that as a kill.'

Admiral Mustard, 'Then we can't win.'

AI Central, 'We can when you think of a tactic to handle this.'

Admiral Mustard, 'They must have a vulnerability.'

AI Central, 'That's probably true, but how easy will it be to find?'

Admiral Mustard, 'Is there any alien debris?'

AI Central, 'Good question. Yes, there is.'

Admiral Mustard, 'That means that they do have a weakness, but where?'

AI Central, 'The options are:

- During normal space
- At the point of transferring to another dimension
- In the other dimension
- At the point of returning to our dimension
- Point 3 can be eliminated as there wouldn't be any debris. Point one is unlikely as the dimensional transfer is probably automated. So it must be at the point of return.'

Admiral Mustard, 'So we need to reprogramme our systems to fire at the enemy so that it vanishes and then fire immediately again to kill it on its return.'

AI Central, 'Agreed, the issue is the time lapse between the two shots.'

Admiral Mustard, 'Should it be a continuous exchange?'

AI Central, 'I can see where you are coming from, but it would be heavy on munitions.'

Admiral Mustard, 'Update all of our systems immediately. Inform all officers of our conclusions. Are you any nearer to finding the correct destination of the enemy home world?'

AI Central, 'While we have been conversing, I've redirected the Fleet. We now have a 73% chance of finding one of their planets. Three planet killers have also joined the Fleet.'

Location: Admiral Bumelton's Flagship, The Galactium Fleet
Sequence of Events: 8

Admiral Bumelton, 'Give me an update.'

Director Earth Planetary Defence, 'I'm not sure where to start?'

Admiral Bumelton:' Just give me a brain dump, I know most of it from the schematics.'

Director Earth Planetary Defence, 'OK, brain dump coming up:

- The Solar System is on full alert
- All military installations, space, land, air, and sea are on the highest level of readiness
- The Earth population is being bunkered
- Populations on the other planets in the Solar System have been warned
- All private inter-planetary travel has been banned
- GAD is in full defence mode and available to assist as required
- The Deputy President is being transferred to Planet Pasteur
- Each planet has massive defence networks — Mars and Jupiter have duplicate control systems
- Ten forts are defending Earth and at least three defending each of the other planets.
- There are also six of what we call deep space forts
- The Solar Fleet, which is pretty insignificant compared to the conventional military forces, is holding the line in the direction of the threat. The Supply and Marine Fleets are on their way to assist
- AI Central is managing the interfacing
- Medical and Supply facilities are on full alert
- I'm not sure what I should be telling the public?'

Admiral Bumelton, 'Tell them the truth. It's always the best tactic in the end.'

Director Earth Planetary Defence, 'What is the truth?'

Admiral Bumelton. 'You know as much as I do. Well, you will have 90% of the Navy with you shortly. I will keep you informed, but please note that I'm in charge.'

Director Earth Planetary Defence, 'Yes Sir.'

Admiral Bumelton to all Fleet admirals, 'We will shortly be home, well *my* home anyway. We must protect Earth at all costs.'

Admiral Bumelton, 'Fleet Operations, my orders:

- Order Fleets 2, 3 and 4 to line up in defence formation in front of the Solar Fleet
- Order Fleet 5 to be the reserve
- Order Fleets 6, 7, 8, and 9 to take up spherical defence pattern around the Solar System, having a quarter each. Fleet 10 to be the reserve stationed near Earth
- Order the Marine and Supply Fleets to hide in the asteroid belt and act as the final reserve
- Order the drone Fleet to wait by Pluto for final displacement.'

Fleet Operations, 'Yes, Sir.'

Location: Worcester Hospital, UK, Planet Earth
Sequence of Events: 9

Cheryl, 'Give me an update. I want to know exactly where my baby is. It's been six months now. I need to see him.'

Dr Green, 'I've been told to tell you that he is on a secret mission.' He was conscious that Cheryl had spent a few months in a self-imposed coma. To be honest, Dr Green suspected that the military had shut her down. He had seen it before when things got a bit crazy.

Cheryl, 'What do you mean a secret mission? He is only six months old.'

Dr Green, 'Let's say that he has certain capabilities that are of value to the powers that be.'

Cheryl, 'What are you talking about?'

Dr Green, 'Terry is not a normal boy.'

Cheryl, 'Who the fuck is Terry?'

Dr Green, 'That's what he calls himself—Terry the Terran.'

Cheryl, 'Are you saying my boy named himself?'

Dr Green, 'I guess I am. I know it sounds far-fetched, but your boy has unique talents and knowledge. He is currently advising the government on the Brakendeth.'

Cheryl, 'You are talking about *my* boy, the boy I haven't seen?'

Dr Green, 'He sends his love.'

Cheryl, 'Give me the facts.'

Dr Green, 'It's classified.'

Cheryl, 'He's my son.'

Dr Green, 'OK, your son is not human. He is the last of the Brakendeth.'

Cheryl, 'How could that be? I gave birth to him.'

Dr Green, 'We don't really know any more than you. To be honest, he was communicating with us before he was born.'

Cheryl, 'Why didn't he talk to me?'

Dr Green, 'Terry didn't think you could handle it.'

Cheryl, 'Don't you *dare* call him Terry. That's not his name. I will decide what his name is going to be! Do you understand?'

Dr Green understood; he was a married man.

Dr Green, 'Your son was born intelligent, knowledgeable and had a task to achieve. It's not easy for him having a baby's body.'

Cheryl, 'What sort of task?'

Dr Green, 'It's classified. But he is helping the government with the latest invasion crisis.'

Cheryl, 'What invasion crisis?'

Dr Green, 'That's why I'm here. Terry… sorry your son wants you somewhere safe.'

Cheryl, 'I must say that I'm baffled.'

Dr Green, 'That is totally understandable. I have been asked to take you to GAD where you can meet your son. We are hoping that two of your friends will also be there—Jenny and Adam. Are you happy to come with me?'

Cheryl, 'I will just pack my things and get dressed. Do you know where my clothes are?'

Location: Bunker 759, Evesham, UK, Planet Earth
Sequence of Events: 10

Bunker Commander, 'Ladies and gentlemen, please be quiet. Welcome to Bunker 759 or as we like to call it, *The black hole of Evesham*. We have facilities here for 10,000 inhabitants. I want to take you through the bunker capabilities:

- This bunker can resist all known ballistics except a planet killer
- It is fully nuclear-proof
- It is entirely chemical- and biological-weapon-proof
- We have food stores for at least two years, and significantly longer if rationed
- There are unlimited water reserves
- We have a pocket nuclear generator
- There is full air recycling capability
- There is a sophisticated communications set-up
- We have an armoury if hand-to-hand fighting is needed
- We have a hospital and a fully qualified medical team
- There are two escape routes are currently classified
- We have shops, a cinema, and a theatre
- There is an extensive media library

This bunker will close and be sealed in twelve hours. Hopefully, it will only be for a few days. You have a choice whether you want to stay or not.'

Are there any questions?'

Anne, 'I've lived in Evesham all my life. I didn't know that this bunker was here.'

Bunker Commander, 'You will be amazed to hear that there is bunkerage for nearly 90% of the Earth population.'

Anne, 'Who decides when we can leave?'

Bunker Commander, 'Once the bunker is sealed, I lose control. GAD takes over.'

Chas, 'What if GAD is destroyed?'

Bunker Commander, 'Then we are probably all doomed.'

Location: Admiral Mustard's Flagship, First Fleet
Sequence of Events: 11

Admiral Mustard, 'Give me an update.'

Fleet Operations, 'It looks like we have lost one vessel in the portal transfer. The Fleet is in standard defence formation awaiting your orders.'

Admiral Mustard, 'Is there any sign of the enemy?'

Fleet Operations, 'No sign at all, Sir, but there are three-star systems directly ahead of us.'

Admiral Mustard, 'What do our scans show?'

Fleet Operations, 'All three systems are showing undecipherable comms traffic, but the second system is incredibly busy. Three planets are showing high levels of digital communication.'

Admiral Mustard, 'Can we link these planets to our attackers?'

Comms, 'There appears to be some noise similarity, but it's not conclusive.'

Admiral Mustard, 'Is there any evidence that they have spotted us?'

Fleet Operations, 'As far as we can tell there have been no scans whatsoever. That's certainly a bit sloppy of them.'

Admiral Mustard, 'In that case, send in some cloaked drones.'

The drones were sent in to carry a full range of scans.

Admiral Mustard, 'Any reaction to our drones?'

Fleet Operations, 'None at all, Sir. They are even sloppier than I thought possible.'

Admiral Mustard, 'What are our scans detecting?'

Science Officer, 'I'm trying to work it out, but I am detecting a lot of human material.'

Admiral Mustard, 'Human material?'

Science Officer, 'Yes Sir, huge quantities of human DNA.'

Admiral Mustard, 'When you say huge quantities, what do you mean?'

Science Officer, 'If I equated it to human bodies, we are talking of a few million people.'

Admiral Mustard, 'That doesn't make any sense. Is there any

reaction to our drones?'

Fleet Operations, 'No reaction yet, and to be honest, I'm not expecting one.'

Admiral Mustard, 'Send in the close-up camera drones. Let's find out what's on the surface.'

AI Central, 'Admiral I need to advise you that Earth will shortly be under attack. We require you to initiate an immediate diversionary action or to return.'

Admiral Mustard, 'Understood, but we need to investigate our findings first.'

Location: Admiral Bumelton's Flagship, The Galactium Fleet
Sequence of Events: 12

Admiral Bumelton, 'Give me an update.'

Fleet Operations, 'The Combined Fleets are in position as per your command, Sir.'

Admiral Bumelton, 'They won't like it but tell the Solar Fleet to retire to defend Earth.'

Fleet Operations, 'The Solar Fleet say that you have no jurisdiction over them.'

Admiral Bumelton, 'That's exactly why I want them out of the way. Tell them if they don't move, we will make them. I haven't got time to waste.'

Fleet Operations, 'Apparently, they have decided to move of their own accord.'

Admiral Bumelton, 'Please send their commander my compliments. Now send out drone scouts. We need to know what is coming this way.'

Before the drones could be released, the first wave of the enemy fleet arrived. The enemy showed no sign of subtlety or even battle tactics; they just attacked head-on. This time, the human fleet was much more successful. Their weapons had been fitted with staccato functionality which allowed them to operate with different time-lapses. AI Central was monitoring the most effective kill rate and adjusting the firing mechanisms continuously.

The sheer quantity of alien ships was making it difficult to target. It was a bit like a shark attacking a school of fish. Which one should he go for? Fortunately, the automated targeting systems were having no truck with late; for them, it was a kill-frenzy. Nevertheless, the sheer number was making its presence felt.

Admiral Bumelton, 'Fleet Operations, my orders:

- Order Fleets 2, 3 and 4 to slowly retire without making it too obvious
- Order all drones to attack the enemy immediately
- Order Fleets 7 and 9 to support our defence
- Order Fleet 5 take up a defensive position around Earth.'

Fleet Operations, 'Yes, Sir.'

Admiral Bumelton, 'Are there any other drone squadrons anywhere?'

Fleet Operations, 'Yes, Sir, The Supply and Marine Fleets have drones. I'm pretty sure that the Solar Fleet has some.'

Admiral Bumelton, 'My orders:

- All drones throughout the Fleet to attack the enemy immediately.'

Fleet Operations, 'Yes Sir, the Solar Fleet said that you have no jurisdiction over them, but they will comply.'

Admiral Whiting, 'Admiral, we are under attack. We need support.'

Admiral Bumelton, 'Fleet Operations, my orders:

- Redirect the Fleet 10 to support them.'

Fleet Operations, 'Yes, Sir.'

Admiral Bonner, 'Admiral, we are hitting them hard, but without our battlecruisers, we are taking heavy casualties. We need reinforcements, or the line will be broken.'

Admiral Bumelton, 'Fleet Operations, My orders:

- Order 50% of Fleet 9 to go to the aid of Fleet 3.'

Fleet Operations, 'Yes, Sir.'

Admiral Gittins, 'Sorry, Admiral, can't comply. We have just come under attack.'

Admiral Bumelton, 'Fleet Operations, my orders:

- Order 50% of Fleet 7 to go to the aid of Fleet 3.'

Fleet Operations, 'Yes, Sir.'

Admiral Bumelton, 'AI Central, give me your analysis.'

AI Central, 'Do you want one word or a more detailed analysis?'

Admiral Bumelton, 'Stop playing.'

AI Central, 'My analysis is as follows:

- The use of drones has been a great success, but they are more or less exhausted.
- Fleets 2, 3 and 4 are performing well against enormous odds.
- Fleet 3 has been hit particularly hard and will shortly be overwhelmed.
- The additional support from Fleet 7 will make no real difference.

- Fleets 6 and 9 will be annihilated resulting in Earth being attacked from two other directions.
- Fleet 8 is not engaged.
- The Supply and Marine Fleets are not engaged but in reality, have little value.

If you want, I can give you ship losses Fleet by Fleet.'

Admiral Bumelton, 'That's not necessary at the moment, but what is the status of Fleets 2, 3 and 4?'

AI Central: Look at the screen:

Fleet	Start	Current
2	900	762
3	900	407
4	900	665
Total	Approx. 2,700	Approx. 1,834

Admiral Bumelton, 'Are we actually destroying the enemy this time?'

AI Central, 'Yes, but they are getting reinforcements.'

Admiral Bumelton, 'What are your recommendations?'

AI Central, 'My recommendations are as follows:
- Recall all surviving drones to be resupplied with munitions
- All Fleets to retire to the outer rim of the Solar System
- Use the Pluto fort as a defensive node
- Consider setting up some sort of trap
- Inform President Padfield that some additional Earth defences could be utilised
- When Pluto falls, reposition around Uranus and utilise the planetary resources one by one
- Recall the First Fleet.'

Admiral Bumelton, 'Fleet Operations, my orders:
- Recall all drones for resupply.'

Fleet Operations, 'Yes, Sir, but there are less than 300.'

Admiral Bumelton, 'Carry out my orders.'

Fleet Operations, 'Yes, Sir.'

Admiral Bumelton, 'My orders:
- Instruct all Fleets to retire to the Pluto orbit immediately. Do not accept any excuses

- Inform the Pluto Fortress of our intentions.'

Admiral Bumelton, 'Comms, patch me through to The President.'

Comms, 'Yes, Sir.'

President Padfield, 'Hello George, I guess that you are a bit busy?'

Admiral Bumelton, 'Nothing I can't handle. Well, that's totally untrue. We are being pushed back by the sheer number of enemy vessels. Can you request that the GAD defence facilities be made available?'

President Padfield, 'Of course. AI Central has also recommended that all key personnel should leave Earth. My gut reaction is to say no.'

Admiral Bumelton, 'We are now being attacked from three different directions, possibly more. As time goes on, your chances of escape diminish.'

President Padfield, 'Churchill never fled, nor will I.'

Admiral Bumelton, 'Clearly that is your decision. We will fight on.'

President Padfield, 'Is it worth the Fleet fleeing and leaving Earth to its fate?'

Admiral Bumelton, 'I can't make that judgement.'

President Padfield, 'AI Central feels that we must fight for Earth, but it is just another planet.'

AI Central, 'I would like to adjust my recommendation. If the enemy reaches the Mars Fortress, then the remains of the Human fleet should flee to fight another day. I would also recommend that The President and key staff become mobile so that they can flee if necessary.'

President Padfield, 'I don't feel comfortable leaving the Earth population behind.'

AI Central, 'It's not about being comfortable.'

President Padfield, 'Is there any input from Terry?'

AI Central, 'He is adamant that we need to cut the head off.'

President Padfield. 'What do we know about the enemy?'

AI Central, 'They seem to be at a similar technological level to humanity. Their military tactics are elementary—they use huge numbers in a swarm.'

President Padfield, 'You used the word "swarm". Does that suggest an insect mentality?'

AI Central, 'We have no idea.'

President Padfield, 'What about their weapon systems?'

AI Central, 'Mostly projectile, but very accurate. The projectile itself slices through our force fields and armour. We suspect that somehow they are using an inter-dimensional capability.'

Admiral Bumelton, 'Please excuse me, I have a battle to win.'

Location: Medical Centre, GAD (The Galactium Alliance Defence Hub), Planet Earth
Sequence of Events: 13

Cheryl, 'Now can I see my son?'

Dr Green, 'I have asked for an audience.'

Cheryl, 'What do you mean audience? My boy needs a cuddle.'

Dr Green, 'When you see your son, I'm sure that he can update you, but it would appear that your impregnation on the alien ship that you thought was a failure was a success. During that process, the Brakendeth inserted a seed that evolved into your son.'

Dr Green could see that Cheryl was not taking it very well. This was the first time that he actually looked at her. She was the classic giggly blonde. He had seen numerous naked pictures of her. Her exit from the alien commander's ship in the nude was one of the great shocks of the time. She became the ultimate teenage sex symbol. Dr Green even remembered masturbating to her image when he was younger.

Cheryl started crying, and Dr Green, despite his professionalism, cuddled her. It was the least a gentleman could do. It wasn't long before they were kissing. Cheryl had always had a high sex drive, and it didn't take long to get her juices flowing.

Dr Green tried to resist, but her hands were caressing his cock. Then there was a total loss of control. Cheryl's top and bra were off, and somehow her nipple was in Dr Green's mouth. He remembered thinking that this had to stop when his penis entered her soft, juicy cunt. It was, without doubt, the best fuck of his life. His engorged cock pumped in and out of her most private place.

His orgasm closely followed hers. It probably wasn't the best time for Terry to walk into the room. Cheryl had no idea who this dwarf-like creature was.

Terry, 'Hello mummy, I see that you have been fucking Dr Green. I understood that this was against the doctor-patient regulations. Naughty doctor.'

Cheryl, 'Is this is my son? He walks and talks!'

Dr Green, 'Terry, you are absolutely right, I will report myself.'

Terry, 'Don't bother on my account. It's probably just what mummy needed. Wasn't it, mummy?'

To say that Cheryl was gobsmacked was an understatement, and she thought that Terry was right. A good fuck was just what she needed.

Cheryl, 'So Terry, where do we go from here?'

Location: Bunker 759, Evesham, UK, Planet Earth
Sequence of Events: 14

The bunker alarm had been ringing for an hour. This was the final call before lockdown.

Anne had got her case of vital possessions. Only one large case was allowed per person. It contained mostly clothes and toiletries and some personal nick-nacks. She also included some of her favourite delicacies, mostly chocolates and savoury snacks. There wasn't much else that she needed as the bunker provided full access to her files and media.

She was going to miss seeing her elderly mother, but she was nicely tucked away in a bunker in South Wales. She imagined that her mother would enjoy the company. In some ways, it's good to have an adventure in your nineties.

There was no real sense of danger. There wasn't even much news. She was, however, relieved to find that she had a single room to herself. It wasn't unlike a prison cell with a shower, toilet, and kitchenette. Next to the bed, there was a wall-sized screen that could be used to display any type of media you could think of. It had a state-of-the-art virtual reality capability. It was much better than the one at home. She turned it on and selected a woodland scene bristling with bluebells. She was convinced that she could smell them.

On the screen, she was asked to select her dinner for that night. The system wanted to know if she was going to eat in the refectory, or did she want the meal delivered to her room? Anne decided to investigate how they were going to feed 10,000 people, some of whom she knew very well.

Location: Admiral Mustard's Flagship, First Fleet
Sequence of Events: 15

Admiral Mustard, 'Have we got any visuals yet?'

Fleet Operations, 'Just coming through on the large screen.'

There was a collective gasp in the battlecruiser. On the screen, there were thousands of naked women staked out in the open. Most looked to be alive and were being fed from tubes. They all appeared to be pregnant.

Then there was another field where the women were clearly dead with their abdomens ripped open and their bodies partly eaten. There was no sign indicating who had committed this atrocity.

What was shocking was the sheer scale. The original suggestion of a few million humans was probably correct. The screen then displayed another area where there appeared to be a few thousand naked males held in corrals.

Some of the crew on the battlecruiser were struggling to control their reactions. It's funny how the smell of vomit causes a chain reaction.

Admiral Mustard, 'Are there any signs of non-human life?'

Comms, 'No, Sir, none at all.'

Admiral Mustard, 'What about the other two planets?'

Comms, 'There is a regular pulse coming from the nearest planet.'

Admiral Mustard, 'My orders:

- Send drones there immediately to investigate the pulse.'

AI Central, 'Jack, Earth is under serious attack. Three alien fleets are converging on Earth. George is doing a good job, but the enemy numbers are just too great. I have recommended that the fleet flees when the enemy reaches the Mars Fortress.'

Admiral Mustard, 'Is that likely to happen?'

AI Central, 'There is an 88% likelihood.'

Admiral Mustard, 'Should I return?'

AI Central, 'I had previously recommended it, but Terry is convinced that you need to cut off the head.'

Admiral Mustard, 'What is your assessment of the situation here?'

AI Central, 'It is remarkably similar to the Skiverton experience. I know that I'm an electronic entity, but it does feel like Deja Vu.'

Admiral Mustard, 'Is does seem a strange coincidence.'

AI Central, 'I checked with Terry. He says that humans have been designed to be universal organisms. Unfortunately, it means that humans would be a good source of chemicals, a good host animal, a good experimental platform and a first-class food source.'

Admiral Mustard, 'Any recommendations?'

AI Central, 'Not easy. Everything has moved very fast. So far, we haven't got our hands on an alien or even one of their vessels. All I can suggest is that you cut off their head!'

Admiral Mustard, 'That helps a lot.'

Admiral Mustard, 'Comms, have you got an update on that pulse?'

Comms, 'Still working on it, Sir, but I think it might be a control instruction. I'm trying to track down the source.'

Admiral Mustard, 'Fleet Operations, any update from the drones?'

Fleet Operations, 'Sir, the results are on the screen.' The pictures were the same resulting in more nausea on the bridge.

Comms, 'Sir, we have identified the source.'

Admiral Mustard, 'My orders:

- All commanders you have your new destination.'

Location: Admiral Bumelton's Flagship, The Galactium Fleet
Sequence of Events: 16

Admiral Bumelton, 'Give me an update.'

Fleet Operations, 'The Combined Fleets are in orbit around Pluto as ordered. The three Pluto Fortresses have additional munitions. Their firepower has been synchronised with Fleet protocols.

The only good news is that we are a lot faster than the enemy. I guess that is down to our portal technology. It gives us time to restructure our formation without too much pressure.'

Admiral Bumelton, 'I wonder why they haven't used their inter-dimensional technology as a portal?'

Fleet Operations, 'I think you have your answer. Their Fleet has just appeared behind us.'

Admiral Bumelton, 'What?'

Fleet Operations, 'They are attacking the Uranus and Saturn Fortresses.'

Admiral Bumelton, 'My orders:

- Order Fleets 7, 9 and 8 to attack the enemy immediately
- Order Fleets 2, 4, 5, 6 and 10 to proceed to Jupiter orbit and form a standard defence formation
- Send the 6 deep space fortresses to protect Earth
- Send the 3 Pluto Fortress to protect Jupiter
- All drones to attack the enemy immediately
- Instruct the Supply and Marine Fleets to stay in the asteroid belt.'

Fleet Operations, 'Yes, Sir. I have an update for you. Based on the numbers, it looks like their three Fleets have combined.'

Admiral Bumelton, 'Sounds like they are going to use them as a battering ram to go for the final kill.'

Admiral Bumelton, 'Comms, get me Tom Crocker, Special Operations.'

Comms, 'Yes, Sir.'

Tom Crocker, 'George, how come you are getting all the fun?'

Admiral Bumelton, 'Tom, I have a job for you. The enemy is blasting their way through the Solar System. We plan to stop them at

Jupiter, but we will probably fail.'

Tom, 'That's being a bit defeatist.'

Admiral Bumelton, 'The stats are on my side but ignoring that I have a job for you. The enemy needs to fight its way through the asteroid belt. I want your team to set up some traps for them—kill zones, new tech weapons, that sort of thing.'

Tom, 'To be honest we have been planning that sort of activity. I'm on the case. It would help if you could get me some fortresses.'

Admiral Bumelton, 'I will arrange that. If you need additional help, I'm sure that the Marines will help you.'

Admiral Bumelton, 'My orders:

- Order Admiral Bonner to take the remains of her Fleet and defend the asteroid belt
- Order her to report to Tom Crocker as he needs the use of her forts
- Order Fleets 7, 9 and 10 to press their attacks.'

Fleet Operations, 'Yes, Sir, you need to know that the 3 Uranus Fortresses and one of Jupiter Fortresses are out of action.'

Admiral Bumelton, 'Show me the Fleet statistics.'

Fleet Operations, 'On the screen now, Sir.'

Fleet	Start	Current
2	900	401
3	900	235
4	900	302
5	900	743
6	900	444
7	900	304
8	900	587
9	900	542
10	900	558
Solar Forts	37	32
Total	8,137	4,148

Admiral Bumelton, 'God, we have lost half of our force. Do we know how the enemy has fared?'

Fleet Operations, 'We think we have destroyed 70,000+ enemy

vessels.'

Admiral Bumelton, 'Is that possible?'

Fleet Operations, 'It doesn't seem it, but we have performed really well.'

Admiral Bumelton, 'Show me the fort position.'

Fleet Operations. 'It's on the screen now, Sir.'

Forts	Start	Current
Earth	10	10
Mercury	3	3
Venus	3	3
Mars	3	3
Jupiter	3	2
Saturn	3	3
Uranus	3	0
Neptune	3	3
Deep Space	6	6
Total	37	33

Admiral Bumelton, 'My orders:
- Send five of the Earth Forts to the asteroid belt
- Send the Mercury, Venus, and Mars Fortresses to the Belt
- Send the Saturn Fortresses to Jupiter
- Order Fleets 7, 8 and 9 continue to press their attacks.'

Fleet Operations, 'Yes, Sir.'

Admiral Bumelton, 'Get me, Tom Crocker.'

Tom, 'I'm a bit busy at the moment.'

Admiral Bumelton, 'I've stripped the fortresses from their planets. There are fourteen on the way to you.'

Tom, 'You are my hero, out.'

Admiral Bumelton, 'AI Central, what do you think?'

AI Central, 'Looks good, but your backside is bare.'

Admiral Bumelton, 'We still have 11 forts and the Solor Fleet defending Earth.'

AI Central, 'Go for it.'

Fleet Operations, 'Sir, Fleet 2 is in serious trouble.'

Admiral Bumelton, 'Aren't they holding extreme flank?'

Fleet Operations, 'Yes, Sir.'

Admiral Bumelton, 'How are Fleet 4 doing?'

Fleet Operations, 'They are under greater pressure than the other Fleets.'

Admiral Bumelton, 'My orders—'

Fleet Operations, 'Sir, Admiral Ward, has been killed, Fleet 2 is near to collapse.'

Admiral Bumelton, 'My orders:

- Order Fleets 7 and 8 to disengage and take over Fleet 2's position
- Order Fleet 2 to merge with Fleet 4
- Order Fleet 3, if able, to support Fleets 7 and 8
- Inform Tom Crocker where the most enemy pressure is likely to appear.'

Fleet Operations, 'Fleets 7, 8 and 4 are under immense pressure.'

Admiral Bumelton, 'My orders:

- Order Fleet 9 to disengage and support the flank
- Order Fleet 10 to join Fleet 3 as a reserve
- Determine if any of the forts can support that flank.'

Fleet Operations, 'Yes, Sir.'

Admiral Bumelton, 'Show me the Fleet statistics.'

Fleet Operations, 'It's on the screen now, Sir:'

Fleet	Start	Current
2	900	81
3	900	235
4	900	171
5	900	602
6	900	299
7	900	198
8	900	377
9	900	278
10	900	196
Solar Forts	37	32
Total	8,137	2,469

Admiral Bumelton, 'We have lost so many brave men and women. What damage have we done to the enemy?'

Fleet Operations, 'We are claiming more than 100,000 kills.'

Admiral Bumelton, 'Comms, get me The President.'

Comms, 'Yes, Sir.'

President Padfield, 'I've seen the stats.'

Admiral Bumelton, 'We have lost two-thirds of our force. It is hard to bear, but I need to warn you that I may not be able to protect Earth,'

President Padfield, 'Admiral, you are the best we have, go do your duty.'

Location: Medical Centre, GAD (The Galactium Alliance Defence Hub), Planet Earth

Sequence of Events: 17

Terry, 'I know that I'm not what you expected.'

Cheryl, 'You can say that again.'

Terry, 'I know that I'm not what you expected.'

Cheryl, 'I didn't mean that. It was just a figure of speech.'

Terry, 'Was that funny?'

Cheryl, 'It was quite funny.'

Terry, 'That's one of the problems I have. I don't understand humour. And I don't understand lying, and humans seem to do a lot of that. I don't understand gambling or make-up.'

Cheryl, 'Well, you are only six months old. It's amazing that you can even list what you don't understand. My list would be a trillion pages long.'

Terry, 'To put it in simple terms I need a mummy. I need someone who loves me for being me. I can guarantee that I will be a good son.'

Cheryl, 'What do you want me to do?'

Terry, 'I want you to do mummy things, help me, hold me, teach me.'

Cheryl, 'That sounds like The Who.'

Terry, 'Who?'

Cheryl, 'Now *that's* funny.'

Terry, 'That's totally beyond me. We can have some great adventures. Will you be my mummy?'

Cheryl, 'I am your mummy. I always will be, and I have come to take you home.'

Location: Bunker 759, Evesham, UK, Planet Earth
Sequence of Events: 18

The bunker was now at Status Red: Immediate Danger. Everyone in the bunker knew that the enemy was approaching Jupiter. They were horrified by the number of military personnel lost. Many of the bunker residents had lost a loved one or someone they knew. It suddenly seemed real.

The young and the very old were suffering from the worry. Some were suffering from claustrophobia. They wanted out, but it wasn't possible.

Anne was quite enjoying herself. She had always been resilient. Being an ex-teacher, she decided to use her skills and run a series of training courses. She had been pleased by how well attended they were. Of course, she had no idea how long she would be underground.

The meals were tasty, and the entertainment was diverting. She was going dancing tonight for the first time in years. She had even joined the choir. She thought, *What a strange species we are. I am facing imminent death but looking forward to Chow Mein and a jitterbug.*

Location: Admiral Mustard's Flagship, First Fleet
Sequence of Events: 19

First Fleet's journey had been a success. By following the pulse, they had found a planet with a complex industrial society. The high pollution levels indicated that there was a full range of electro-mechanical and chemical enterprises. There were thousands of skyscrapers. The whole planet seemed to be covered in them.

The architecture was human-like, but at the same time, it wasn't, particularly alien. Admiral Mustard wanted to know whether the inhabitants were human or not. Drones were launched.

Admiral Mustard, 'What do your scans show?'

Fleet Operations: On the screen, Sir:

- Heavily industrialised
- There was a complete lack of pollution controls
- There were no oceans or rivers
- The surface was completely flat with no mountains or wilderness areas
- There were no TV or radio signals
- There were no roads or traffic
- There was little airborne traffic
- There was considerable use of nuclear and fission power
- There were high carbon dioxide levels. Humans would struggle to live there
- The surface is 90% covered in windowless skyscrapers.
- A deep scan showed that the skyscrapers continued into the depths of the planet. There was also a lot of underground activity—mostly transport.

Admiral Mustard, 'Have they detected our scan?'

Fleet Operations, 'There are no signs that they have.'

Admiral Mustard, 'What about the drones?'

Fleet Operations, 'They seem to confirm our analysis. Astonishingly, they haven't detected us.'

Admiral Mustard. 'Can you confirm that the residents are not human?'

Fleet Operations, 'No, Sir.'

Admiral Mustard, 'Comms, you must be picking up some comms traffic?'

Comms, 'None at all, Sir, except the pulse.'

Admiral Mustard, 'Can you trace the pulse?'

Comms, 'It's very faint, Sir, but I will try and find it.'

Admiral Mustard, 'My orders:

- All commanders to prepare bombardment weapons.'

Fleet Operations, 'Yes, Sir.'

Location: Admiral Bumelton's Flagship, The Galactium Fleet
Sequence of Events: 20

Admiral Bumelton, 'Give me an update.'

Fleet Operations, 'All of our Fleets are now strung along the asteroid belt except Fleet 9 which is still pursuing the enemy. The Fortress weaponry is now fully synchronised with ours. Special Ops have set several traps.'

Admiral Bumelton, 'Any good news?'

Fleet Operations, 'We can't be accurate, but it looks like the enemy Fleet is down to about 40,000 vessels.'

Admiral Bumelton, 'That's not bad, it's about 10:1.'

Fleet Operations, 'It's the best odds we have had so far.'

Admiral Bumelton, 'You realise, of course, that this is our last stand?'

Fleet Operations, 'Yes Sir, we can do it, we have faith in you.'

Admiral Bumelton, 'My orders:
- Order Fleets 4, 5, 6, 7, 8 and 10 to stand their ground
- Order all Fleets to slowly retreat into the Belt, on my command
- Order all Fleets to work in close proximity with the forts
- Order all Fleets to obey any instructions given by Special Ops
- Order Fleet 9 to join Fleet 3 in the asteroid belt

Good luck.'

Fleet Operations, 'Yes, Sir.'

The enemy showed no desire to change their plans. They continued to attack the same flank. Fleets 7 and 8 were now under tremendous pressure.

Admiral Bumelton, 'My orders:
- Order Fleets 3 and 5 to support Fleets 7 and 8.'

Fleet Operations, 'Yes, Sir. I'm sorry to report that Admiral Morten has been killed.' That hurt Admiral Bumelton as Matt was a good friend of his.

Admiral Bumelton, 'Come on, let's get those bastards.' That surprised Fleet Operations as the Admiral was famous for not showing

49

his emotions.

Admiral Bumelton, 'What are the latest stats?'

Fleet Operations, 'I will get them for you shortly, but just to let you know we have lost five more fortresses. The update is on the screen now, Sir.'

Fleet	Start	Current
2	900	0
3	900	189
4	900	141
5	900	436
6	900	188
7	900	89
8	900	62
9	900	187
10	900	134
Solar Forts	37	27
Totals	8,137	1,453

Admiral Bumelton, 'How are the enemy doing?'

Fleet Operations, 'Our figures show that they now have about 35,000 ships. The good news is that Special Ops are funnelling them into several kill zones. It does mean that the fortresses are being hit hard.'

Fleet Operations, 'When do you want the retreat into the belt to start?'

Admiral Bumelton, 'When our Fleet falls under a thousand ships.'

Admiral Bumelton, 'What's the current Fort displacement?'

Fleet Operations, 'It's just been updated, see the chart on the screen, Sir.'

Forts	Start	Current
Earth	10	11
Mercury	3	0
Venus	3	0
Mars	3	0
Jupiter	3	0
Saturn	3	0

Uranus	3	0
Neptune	3	0
Deep Space	6	0
Belt	0	11
Totals	37	22

Admiral Bumelton, 'What other resources do we have that are not engaged?'

Fleet Operations, 'They are as follows:

- The Solar Fleet
- The Supply and Marine Fleets, although they are helping Special Ops
- The Earth Fortresses

There are about 100 ships that are being urgently repaired.'

Admiral Bumelton, 'Are there any signs that they are moving away from the flank attack?'

Fleet Operations, 'No, Sir. But we have lost three more fortresses.'

Admiral Bumelton, 'Show me the latest stats. This time can you include the enemy ships.'

Fleet Operations, 'Yes, Sir. They are on the screen now.'

Fleet	Start	Current
2	900	0
3	900	92
4	900	101
5	900	222
6	900	154
7	900	36
8	900	31
9	900	181
10	900	94
Solar Forts	37	24
Totals	8,137	935
Enemy	150,000	30,000

Admiral Bumelton, 'This is simply a war of attrition.'

Fleet Operations, 'I agree, Sir. We are expecting to see the enemy figures reduce substantially because of the Special Ops traps.'

Admiral Bumelton, 'My orders:
- Create a Mars defensive line
- Move the Supply and Marine Fleets to that line
- Create Fleet 11 from the repaired ships and move them to the line
- Move 6 of the Earth Fortresses to the line. Place them on the attacking flank
- Move the Solar Fleet to the line.'

Fleet Operations, 'But Sir, that practically denudes Earth of its defences.'

Admiral Bumelton, 'Do as I say and inform The President of my actions.'

Fleet Operations, 'Yes, Sir.'

Admiral Bumelton to AI Central, 'Any observations or recommendations?'

AI Central, 'I'm supporting your plan of action. I've asked Fleet 1 for support.'

Fleet Operations, 'The President has responded. He said to take all of the fortresses.'

Admiral Bumelton, 'My orders:
- Do as The President said.'

Admiral Bumelton, 'To all admirals, we now have less than a thousand vessels. We will restructure ourselves as Fleets A, B and C as follows:

Fleet	Composed of	Current	Admiral
A	3, 4, 10	287	J Bonner
B	5, 7, 8	289	G Pearce
C	6, 9	335	P Gittins
Total		911	

My orders:
- Order Fleets A, B and C to defend the flank.
- Order all Fleets to retire to the Mars Defence line on my command.'

Fleet Operations, 'Yes Sir, You should know that the traps have cost them about 8,000 vessels, but unfortunately some of their ships have broken through the Belt.'

Admiral Bumelton, 'Bugger. I thought that we might have stopped them there.'

Fleet Operations, 'The good news is that the Earth Fortresses are almost in place. The Solar Fleet is engaging the enemy but is being ripped apart.'

Admiral Bumelton, 'My orders:
- Order Fleet C to disengage and support the Mars line.'

Fleet Operations, 'Yes, Sir.'

Admiral Bumelton, 'Comms, get me The President.'

Comms, 'Yes, Sir.'

President, 'Hi George, how is the party going?'

Admiral Bumelton, 'It's probably about time to leave Sir as it's not the best party I've been to.'

President, 'This is not the way I thought I would go. Keep on fighting.'

Admiral Bumelton, 'Yes Sir.'

Fleet Operations, 'The enemy is faltering, but there are still too many of them.'

Admiral Bumelton, 'Give me the latest figures.'

Fleet Operations, 'Yes, Sir. They are on the screen now.'

Fleet	Composed of	Start	Latest
A	3, 4, 10	287	198
B	5, 7, 8	289	177
C	6, 9	335	289
Forts		24	16
Total		935	680
Enemy		35,000	26,000

That's 38:1.'

Admiral Bumelton, 'You haven't included the Mars Line Defences.'

Fleet Operations, 'OK, 30:1.'

Admiral Bumelton, 'My orders:
- Order Fleets A and B to join the Mars Defence line.'

Fleet Operations, 'Yes, Sir. Some good news. More of the enemy vessels were eliminated than we actually thought. I have revised the chart, but this time I have not included the Supply and Marine Fleets.

Fleet	Composed of	Start	Latest
A	3, 4, 10	287	198
B	5, 7, 8	289	177
C	6, 9	335	289
11		100	74
Solar		50	8
Forts		24	14
Total		1,085	760
Enemy		35,000	19,000

It's still 25:1.'

Admiral Bumelton, 'I keep thinking we are missing a trick. Tell me what you know about them.'

Fleet Operations, 'Well, the enemy is aggressive and relentless. Their technology is not as advanced as ours. They lack any real strategy, although a battering ram based on vast numbers of ships seems to be working. We think that the vessels are probably manned, but we can't be sure.

Every one of their ships is identical. There is no discernible command structure. We would win if our Fleet were larger.'

Admiral Bumelton, 'That doesn't help very much.'

Fleet Operations, 'Sorry, Sir.'

Admiral Bumelton to AI Central, 'Do you have any observations that would help?'

AI Central, 'You have already spotted it. They lack basic military skills. You would think that their commander had never been in battle before.'

Admiral Bumelton, 'That can't be the case considering the number of vessels they have brought to the table.'

Admiral Bumelton, 'Fleet Operations, any more news?'

Fleet Operations, 'All fourteen fortresses are targeting the enemy. It's the most concentrated firepower that we have thrown at them so far. The downside is that the forts don't have enough munitions.'

Admiral Bumelton, 'Get some fast ships and scavenge some more munitions.'

Fleet Operations, 'We have already done that, Sir.'

Admiral Bumelton, 'Then it's just a numbers game.'

Fleet Operations, 'Sir, a Human fleet has just entered the Solar System.'

Admiral Bumelton, 'It must be the First Fleet.'

Fleet Operations, 'It's about half of the First Fleet. They are asking for orders, Sir.'

Admiral Bumelton, 'Let's not be too subtle this time. Tell them to smash into the enemy and bloody their noses. Redo the chart.'

Fleet Operations, 'Yes, Sir. The updated chart is on the screen now.'

Fleet	Composed of	Start	Latest
A	3, 4, 10	287	134
B	5, 7, 8	289	121
C	6, 9	335	186
11		100	62
Solar		50	6
Fleet 1		1,000	1,000
Forts		24	12
Total		2,085	1,521
Enemy		35,000	16,000

It's about 10:1.'

Admiral Bumelton, 'Yes, but we have some of our battlecruisers back.'

Fleet Operations, 'You are right, the battlecruisers are making a real difference. In fact, the enemy has stalled and are retreating.'

Admiral Bumelton, 'Are they fleeing?'

Fleet Operations, 'It's a bit unclear. It looks like they are dividing into two fleets. Half are retreating, and the other half look like they are going to continue their attack regardless.'

Admiral Bumelton, 'I wonder what the retreating fleet is planning to do. Are they going to attack us from two directions? I'm going to assume that they are not.'

Admiral Bumelton, 'My orders:
- Order the Marine and Supply Fleets to defend Earth
- Send 6 of the fortresses back to defend Earth

- Order the Solar Fleet to return to Earth's Defence
- Order Fleet 11 to amalgamate with Fleet B
- Order Fleet 1 to attack the enemy
- Order Fleets A, B and C to maintain Mars defence line with 6 forts.'

Fleets Operations, 'Yes, Sir.'

Fleet 1 formed their textbook attack formation. And it was deadlier than usual as it had considerably more battlecruisers than a regular Galactium Fleet.

The enemy had never experienced a human attack formation before. So far, it had all been about defence. Admiral E Bonner ordered her Fleet to let rip. She told them not to hold back.

Bonner's structured killing machine sliced into the enemy. There was no mercy, but still, the enemy had the numbers, but the odds were getting much better.

Admiral Bumelton, 'Give me the latest stats.'

Fleet Operations, 'Yes, Sir. They are on the screen now.'

Fleet	Composed of	Start	Latest
A	3, 4, 10	287	122
B	5, 7, 8, 11	389	89
C	6, 9	335	106
Fleet 1		1,000	970
Forts		24	10
Total		2,035	1,297
Enemy		35,000	6,000

The odds are 4:1.'

Admiral Bumelton was starting to feel more confident. Then the other half of the enemy Fleet returned.

Location: The President's Office, Presidential Palace, Planet Earth
Sequence of Events: 21

President Padfield was discussing their impending doom with his Chief of Staff, Henry Strong.'

President Padfield, 'Should we pack our bags?'

Henry Strong, 'I have to advise you to flee, Sir.'

President Padfield, 'I know that is the logical thing to do, but I really can't be bothered.'

President Padfield to AI Central, 'Give me an update.'

AI Central, 'You only just had one.'

President Padfield, 'Give me another one, I'm the boss.'

AI Central, 'Not for much longer. Anyway, my update is as follows:

- Fleet 1 is about to bombard the alien planet. We are not sure whether it is their home planet or not.
- So far the aliens have not reacted to our Fleet's presence.
- Back home, the alien fleet has split into two, and with the return of half of Fleet 1, it looked like we were going to survive. Then the other half of the alien f leet returned. It is not looking so good now.
- The current position is on the Screen now

Fleet	Latest
A	81
B	72
C	51
Fleet 1	507
Forts	6
Total	717
Enemy	13,000

- Earth Defences are fully operational
- The population is fully bunkered
- Nearby planetary forts are on the way here; we probably should have moved them earlier.'

President Padfield, 'What are our odds?'

AI Central, 'You don't want to know.'

President Padfield, 'Do you think I should flee?'

AI Central, 'Yes.'

President, 'I've made my mind up, I'm not going to. Any other suggestions?'

AI Central, 'We need to make the GAD weapons available to Admiral Bumelton.'

President Padfield, 'I thought that I had already given permission. If not, action immediately.'

AI Central, 'You need to speak to our ground forces.'

President Padfield, 'I don't see the point at the moment.'

AI Central, 'You need to let the Earth population know that you are staying. It will certainly help the public's morale.'

President Padfield, 'I will do that. Have you discovered any more info on the enemy?'

AI Central, 'Nothing, they don't seem to have any systems that I can access. They just appear as a black hole to me.'

President Padfield, 'Where are you going if we lose Earth?'

AI Central, 'I'm in every human location. The aliens will struggle to eliminate me. Whatever happens, I will continue the fight.'

President Padfield, 'I guess that you will fight them on the beaches and the landing grounds and in the fields and streets.'

AI Central, 'Something like that Mr Churchill.'

President Padfield, 'Well now it is our hour.'

AI Central, 'Don't forget to tell the Earth population that you are staying.'

President Padfield, 'Can you get me Salek? She can prepare a statement.'

Location: Admiral Bumelton's Flagship, The Galactium Fleet
Sequence of Events: 22

Admiral Bumelton had organised his formation on the basis that he was fighting one enemy Fleet. The return of the second half of the alien fleet was, to put it simply, a disaster.

Admiral Bumelton, 'Fleet Operations, give me the latest statistics.'

Fleet Operations, 'Yes, Sir. They are on the screen now.'

Fleet	Composed of	Start	Latest
A	3, 4, 10	287	72
B	5, 7, 8, 11	389	66
C	6, 9	335	49
Fleet 1		1000	490
Forts		24	6
Total		2,035	683
Enemy		35,000	10,500

Admiral Bumelton, 'My orders:
- All Fleets to be amalgamated as Fleet 1 under Admiral Bonner
- Order Fleet 1 to defend Earth orbit
- Order all forts and GAD weapons to be under Fleet 1's Control.'

Fleet Operations, 'Yes, Sir. I have some other very distressing news for you. Admirals Whiting, Sibley and Brotheridge have all been lost.'

Admiral Bumelton, 'Somehow we will get our revenge. Comms, patch me through to all of the ships in the Fleet.'

Comms, 'Yes, Sir.'

Admiral Bumelton to all ships, 'Fellow members of The Galactium, this is our last stand. It's probably the last stand for humanity. On behalf of the Government of The Galactium and its citizens, I would like to thank you for everything you have done and will do. So that you know The President is remaining on Earth. He is determined to fight the aliens hand to hand if necessary. I can only wish him, and you, good luck.'

The battle raged on and would probably continue to the last ship. The GAD defences were making a valuable contribution, but the odds were still against them.

Location: Admiral Mustard's Flagship, First Fleet
Sequence of Events: 23

Admiral Mustard, 'My orders:
- All commanders will select your target and start general bombardment for one minute.'

Fleet Operations, 'Yes, Sir.'

Every Fleet vessel complied with a veritable barrage of ballistics. The damage done was immense.

Admiral Mustard, 'Fleet Operations, what is your damage assessment?'

Fleet Operations, 'Considerable damage, Sir.'

Admiral Mustard, 'Comms, any response?'

Comms, 'None, Sir.'

Admiral Mustard, My orders:
- All commanders will carry out a second general bombardment for one minute.'

Admiral Mustard, 'Fleet Operations, what is the damage assessment?'

Fleet Operations, 'Further considerable damage, Sir.'

Admiral Mustard, 'Comms, any response?'

Fleet Operations, 'Still none, Sir.'

Admiral Mustard to AI Central, 'Any recommendations?'

AI Central, 'Well, you could continue, but you will probably get the same response. I would recommend that you return to Earth now. They are literally on their last legs.'

Admiral Mustard, 'We are missing something. What was Terry's recommendation?'

AI Central, 'Chop off their head.'

Admiral Mustard, 'Why didn't he say destroy them or eliminate their leaders? Why was he so specific?'

AI Central, 'I did ask him, and he doesn't know, but he thinks the exact wording is critical.'

Admiral Mustard, 'Can you scan every photo we have taken and look for a head?'

AI Central, 'Bingo, we have a building that vaguely looks like a head.'

Admiral Mustard, 'Display it.'

AI Central displayed it on the screen. The building had a head and neck with apertures for eyes and a mouth. It didn't really look like a head, but it was the only option they had.

Admiral Mustard, 'Captain Wilhelm, I'm sending you a picture of a building with its exact coordinates. I want you to slice the head off the neck.'

Captain Wilhelm, 'What head?'

Admiral Mustard, 'If you use your imagination, can you see that the building is in two parts. Normally I would just ask you to blast the building. Here I want you to slice the neck all the way through. Do you understand me?'

Captain Wilhelm, 'Yes.'

Admiral Mustard, 'Then action it immediately. Let me know when it is done.'

Captain Wilhelm, 'Action completed as requested, Sir.'

Admiral Mustard, 'AI Central, any reaction?'

AI Central, 'None at all.'

Admiral Mustard, 'My orders:

- Return to Earth at all possible haste, maximum speed.
- Report to Admiral Bumelton on arrival.'

Fleet Operations, 'Yes, Sir.'

Location: Bunker 759, Evesham, UK, Planet Earth
Sequence of Events: 24

It was starting to get really scary now. Every adult in the bunker under the age of sixty was issued with a pistol. Those who had previous military training were issued with automatic weapons. Everyone just watched the news service. A few cuddled and a few made love, possibly for the last time.

It was a shame, really, because Anne had been enjoying herself. She had met a very respectable man at the dance who had walked her home. Well, obviously it wasn't her home although it might be for some time. She hadn't let him into her cubicle, but they agreed to have lunch together.

That was assuming that anyone would still be there for lunch. The remaining military forces were now defending Earth. They were down to their last two fortresses. She felt for the brave men and women who had lost their lives. But it might be her turn next.

She decided to put her lipstick on to meet the aliens.

Location: Admiral Bumelton's Flagship, The Galactium Fleet
Sequence of Events: 25

Admiral Bumelton, 'Give me an update.'
Fleet Operations, 'This might be the last one, Sir.'

Fleet	Latest
Fleet 1	336
Forts	2
Total	338
Enemy	4,250

The good news is that we are performing well.'

Admiral Bumelton, 'That may be the case, but it's not really helping us. But I guess that the time has come to thank you for your hard work and dedication over the last few days.'

Fleet Operations, 'It's appreciated, Sir. It has been an honour to work with you, and could you put me forward for a promotion?' They both laughed.

Then something astonishing happened. The alien craft froze in mid-air, or rather mid-space. All of their weapon systems stopped. There was no time to ponder this miracle.

Admiral Bumelton, 'My orders:

- All commanders will continue attacking the alien vessels. Do not stop because they have.'

Fleet Operations, 'Yes Sir, the remainder of Fleet 1 has entered the Solar System. They are asking for orders.'

Admiral Bumelton, 'Tell them to join the turkey shoot.'

Admiral Mustard, 'George, we chopped the head off, and their Fleet stopped.'

Admiral Bumelton, 'Interesting.'

Admiral Mustard, 'Don't destroy all of the enemy vessels, we need some to study.'

Admiral Bumelton, 'Yes, Sir.'

Location: GAD (The Galactium Alliance Defence Hub), Planet Earth

Sequence of Events: 26

There is jubilation, and there is jubilation. Humans know how to celebrate. The sense of relief was just immense. There was love, joy, happiness, and a serious outbreak of singing. Perhaps the only day in human history that was on the same level was VE day.

People were streaming out of the bunkers singing, *'We'll meet again, don't know where, don't know when.'* If only the tears of joy could be captured. There were street parties and public nudity and drinking and more drinking. There was no doubt that a substantial population increase was on the cards.

President Padfield felt the same. He was a boy again. He was a lover, a drinker, a gambler, a man of the people, a hero, but he also felt ancient. He felt everything.

The press wanted to laud the heroes: Admirals Mustard, Bumelton and Bonner. They were massive celebrities who actually wanted to maintain their privacy. They were simply doing a job, but they had huge pride in the performance of their crew. The sadness in the loss of so many noble men and women was heartbreaking. Admiral Bumelton, famed for being hard, couldn't stop crying. He had even let himself down in front of the press, which endeared him to the general public even more.

In reality, the best of the best had been lost. Never to be replaced. Admiral Mustard knew that this wasn't true, but it was how he felt. No one could criticise the sacrifices that had been made. Even admirals had died. Then he remembered that they had lost Admirals Ward, Morten, Whiting, Sibley and Brotheridge. Friends, every one of them.

In fact, there was lots of criticism. Admiral Mustard should never have split his forces. Admiral Bumelton's tactics were too defensive. Forts from around The Galactium should have been recalled. The pros and cons would be debated for years. But what's done is done. There was going to be a formal review of the war shortly.

Terry loved these people. He loved the emotions of humanity. The fear, the courage, the stubbornness, the individual sacrifice, the love, the joy and especially the humour. How could you joke when someone was trying to kill you? He felt a special bond with his mother; a bond that surprised him. It wasn't logical. He decided that humanity was a very acceptable successor to the Brakendeth.

Cheryl loved the fact that her extraordinary son wanted a cuddle. He seemed fascinated by her breasts. He had asked if she was going to breastfeed him. She said that she couldn't contemplate breastfeeding a talking baby, but then she let him. It wasn't what she wanted, but it now seemed very natural. The bond was fixed.

Anne felt that she had disgraced herself. She let her dancing partner into her cubicle, and they did more than dance. They decided to disgrace themselves again and again. Anne decided that disgracing herself was a way of telling the aliens what for.

Admiral Bumelton's Fleet operator got her promotion.

Location: Conference Room, GAD (The Galactium Alliance Defence Hub), Planet Earth

Sequence of Events: 27

Now it was time for the serious stuff. Two reviews had been set up:

Performance Review

Future Strategy

The attendees were as follows:

- Admiral Jack Mustard, Admiral of the Fleet and First Fleet
- Admiral Edel Bonner, Advisor to the Admiral of the Fleet
- Admiral George Bumelton, Second Fleet
- Admiral John Bonner, Third Fleet
- Admiral David Taylor, Fourth Fleet
- Admiral Glen Pearce, Fifth Fleet
- Admiral Calensky Wallett, Sixth Fleet
- Admiral Peter Gittins, Ninth Fleet
- Admiral Phil Richardson, Tenth Fleet
- Commander T Crocker, Special Operations
- Dennis Todd, Marine Commander
- AI Central
- Jill Ginger, Fleet HQ — Head of Science
- Alison Walsh, Fleet HQ — Head of Engineering
- Jeremy Jotts, Fleet HQ — Head of Staffing
- Louise Forrester, Fleet HQ — Head of Logistics and Production
- Linda Hill, Fleet HQ — Head of Intelligence
- Salek Patel, Fleet HQ — Head of Communications
- Denise Smith, Fleet HQ — Head of Navigation & Exploration
- Admiral Rachel Zakott, Fleet HQ — Head of Planetary Defence
- Dr Doris Frost, Chief Medical Officer
- President David Padfield
- Tony Moore, Deputy President
- Bill Penny, Leader of The Galactium Council
- Henry Strong, Chief of Staff

- Terry, and mother, Advisors to The Galactium
- Empty seats were laid out for:
- Admiral Vicky Ward, Third Fleet
- Admiral Brian Whiting, Sixth Fleet
- Admiral Victor Brotheridge, Seventh Fleet
- Admiral Matt Morten, Eighth Fleet
- Admiral Denise Sibley, Supply Fleet.

President Padfield, 'Terry, could you explain your warning?'

Terry, 'Thank you, Mr President. It's difficult. I somehow knew that a race called The Northemy was going to attack us. I can give no other explanation. I just knew.'

President Padfield, 'And you knew that they currently use humans as incubators for their eggs.'

Terry, 'Yes, I don't know how I knew. I guess that I'm somehow accessing Brakendeth records.'

President Padfield, 'And you knew that they had human farms.'

Terry, 'Please refer to my previous response.'

President Padfield, 'And you knew that the head had to be chopped.'

Terry, 'Please refer to my previous response.'

President Padfield, 'I'm afraid that your answers are unacceptable. What are you hiding?'

Cheryl, 'I'm not having you talk to my son like that. He is a six-month-old boy and a hero.'

President Padfield, 'My apologies Ma'am, but we need answers.'

Terry, 'Mummy, The President is right. I have been holding back.' There was a hush in the room.

President Padfield, 'Please continue.'

Terry, 'The Northemy are Dalek-like creatures. The biological component is initially established in human bodies and then fitted into whatever device they need.'

President Padfield, 'What is a Dalek?' Terry displayed an image of one on a giant screen.

President Padfield, 'Why didn't you tell us before?'

Terry, 'I'm not sure if I knew.'

President Padfield, 'What do you mean?'

Terry, 'I'm a relatively new entity. I have access to the records of my race. That is over a million years' worth. It's bloody difficult to sort through them.'

Cheryl, 'Terry, don't swear in front of these gentlemen.'

Terry, 'Sorry mummy.'

President Padfield, 'What else do you know about The Northemy?'

Terry, 'I'm afraid to tell you.'

President Padfield, 'Sorry Terry, we are all very grateful for your help.'

Terry, 'I'm not totally sure what it all means.'

President Padfield, 'Just tell us what you know.'

Terry, 'OK, I will list what I know:

- The Northemy have been around for thousands of years
- They gained space travel technology more than 500,000 years ago
- They have been cyborgs for even longer
- There doesn't appear to be any central control, but there are 'nodes of 'civilisation'
- They don't tolerate other intelligences
- They never give in.'

President Padfield, 'Can I stop you there? I think this is a topic for tomorrow. Do you think you could list what you know?'

Terry, 'I will do that Mr President. Have I been good?'

President Padfield, 'You have been very good.' He looked around the room to see a mixture of horror and worry.

Admiral Mustard, 'Could I ask Terry one question?'

President Padfield, 'Please go ahead.'

Admiral Mustard, 'How many Northemy are there?'

Terry, 'The records I'm accessing are old, but I would say two trillion-plus.'

Admiral Mustard, 'Thank you, Terry.'

President Padfield, 'I suggest that we have a break.' During the break, it was decided to cut short the performance review so that they could focus more on strategy.

President Padfield, 'Welcome back, I would like to focus on what tactics worked and what didn't. Can I ask Admiral Bumelton to give his views?'

Admiral Bumelton, 'Thank you, Mr President. Firstly, I would like to say that this was a totally unexpected attack. There was no warning and no time for preparation. Rightly or wrongly, we were reacting to them.'

President Padfield, 'That suggests a lack of preparedness.'

Admiral Bumelton, 'You might be right, we were still wallowing in our victory over the Brakendeth. Sorry, Terry.'

President Padfield, 'Are you suggesting that we lacked strategy?'

Admiral Bumelton, 'Probably, we were working at a tactical level.'

President Padfield, 'What would you change at a strategic level?'

Admiral Bumelton, 'In hindsight, I would probably have kept some of the battlecruisers in the main Fleet.'

Admiral Mustard, 'I agree.'

President Padfield, 'But would you have known at the time?'

Both admirals said, 'No.'

President Padfield, 'And would we have shot the head off? Please continue, Admiral Bumelton.'

Admiral Bumelton, 'Our vessels performed well, our naval staff were magnificent, morale was brilliant, there was no talk of surrender; munitions were great, we manoeuvred brilliantly. I would say that there were no real operational issues.'

Admiral Mustard, 'I agree totally.'

President Padfield, 'Then why were we failing?'

Admiral Bumelton, 'It was sheer numbers and initially their use of inter-dimensional technology.'

President Padfield, 'Explain the numbers problem.'

Admiral Bumelton, 'Throughout the battle they outnumbered us at every stage. The odds against us were militarily impossible. In light of their numbers, we performed remarkably well.'

A second factor was their aggression. There were no tactics. They just pummelled us relentlessly. There was no rest whatsoever; only continuous attacks by an enemy who had the numbers to support that type of warfare.'

President Padfield, 'Is there anyone here who disagrees that we performed well?'

Admiral Gittins, 'I would like to say that if we had the numbers, we would have easily beaten them.'

There was general agreement in the room.

President Padfield, 'I'm a bit concerned that we are all patting ourselves on the back. Admiral Mustard, can you provide a critique please?'

Admiral Mustard, 'Thank you, Mr President. I don't want to be negative, but it is my job to highlight some of our weaknesses:

- The loss of the battlecruisers to the Main Fleet was disastrous
- There was a lack of warning regarding the attack — we need to do better
- The forts performed well, but ultimately failed
- There was a lack of fort strategy — there were other forts relatively nearby that could have been utilised
- Better planning systems are needed
- The Fleet is not large enough
- We need to reconsider the use of smaller fighters
- We need to consider the use of reserve Fleets
- We need to improve Earth's defences
- We need more drones — this is probably the best way forward. We should have strategically placed drone arsenals
- We didn't make full use of our force field capabilities.'

President Padfield, 'Let's leave your suggestions for tomorrow.'

Admiral Mustard, 'Yes Sir, but I need to say that one of the biggest problems was having a period of peace. After the war ended with the Brakendeth, we became complacent. It's unacceptable but quite normal after a major conflict. Anyway, I will go through these issues in more detail tomorrow.'

President Padfield, 'Thank you, Admiral Mustard. I know that it is very short notice, but can I ask HQ staff to prepare a strategic planning model for tomorrow?' There was a general nodding of heads.

Location: Conference Room, GAD (The Galactium Alliance Defence Hub), Planet Earth

Sequence of Events: 28

President, 'Ladies and gentlemen, welcome back to our strategic review. I'm sure that this is going to be the first of many.

The first item on the agenda is Terry's report on The Northemy. I have to say that I'm mightily impressed. Please read the document in front of you and then we can discuss.'

To President Padfield, The Galactium

From Terry

Subject: The Northemy, an Overview

1. Introduction

The information listed in this document has not been verified by me. I have no way of checking it. It all comes from memory. It may not be up to date. Please do not blame me if wrong.

2. History

The Northemy claim that they are an ancient race, perhaps over a million years old. The Brakendeth disputed this but had nothing to substantiate their view

They have been invaded and conquered by many other species and were a slave race for probably a thousand years. This had a damaging effect on their psyche

In order to gain eternal life, they went down the cyborg route

Northemy brains and spinal cords are placed in machines

To assist this, their society became process-driven. Formal processes were agreed upon, and mechanisms followed the rules

The Brakendeth only interfaced with them when The Northemy conquered some of their farm planets

A compromise was agreed that they could keep the planets and their homans provided they left Brakendeth space alone. This was probably their first encounter with homans

3. Philosophy

Process is everything

Process must be adhered to

Their process is superior to all other processes

Nothing must get in the way of process success

Never give in, the process must win

Never the one, always the many

4. Biology

The Northemy are now unable to procreate without a host

Host farms exist and operate depending on host reproductive functionality

Homan farms are now preferred

Homans are bred to maintain stocks

The homan females, when mature, are inseminated with a few hundred Northemy eggs

At the right time, the homan woman is cut open, and the developed Northemy embryos are taken away

Damaged homans are shredded for food

5. Brakendeth Recommendations

Terminate at the right time

Too many of them — at least two trillion

Classification: XXCRRHT665\\K9[R

Author: Terry

President Padfield, 'Any questions on the content?'

Admiral E Bonner, 'What is the classification?'

Terry, 'It's very complex. It relates to how the Brakendeth rate the species.'

Admiral E Bonner, 'And what is it?'

Terry, 'I'm still trying to crack it, but fundamentally it says that they are a worthless species that should be told to fuck off.'

Cheryl, 'Terry!'

Terry, 'Sorry, they do not deserve respect.'

President Padfield, 'Can you be clear on this?'

Cheryl could tell that Terry didn't like the questioning.'

Cheryl, 'Terry darling, is there anything else you want to tell these fine people?'

Terry, 'We, sorry, the Brakendeth, felt that they added nothing to the wellonary and should be canboshed.'

Cheryl, 'Terry darling, what is a wellonary?'

Terry, 'It is the concept that a species has value if it adds something to the greater well-being of the universe. The Brakendeth couldn't believe how high a score humanity had.'

Cheryl, 'Do you have some examples from Earth on how it has improved the wellonary?'

Terry, 'There are too many: The Forbidden City; Mozart; The Beatles; Gainsborough; Blenheim Palace; Queen; Sibelius; Beethoven; Da Vinci; Pink Floyd; The Mona Lisa; New York; Jaguar; Disneyland; Star Wars etcetera. Far too many riches for one species. The Brakendeth were overwhelmed. There were also some negative factors.'

President Padfield, 'What were those?'

Terry, 'The Brakendeth hated the use of AI technology, discrimination — although they practised it — pollution of any sort, overt militarism and overpopulation. They weren't significant issues for them except the AI.'

AI Central, 'What why were so anti-AI?'

Terry, 'It's a poor evolutionary choice. Dependence on technology leads to stagnation. It stops biological entities from developing new physical and mental skills. It encourages laziness. What is the point in learning anything if the machine next door to you can do it?'

However, it was the cyborg wars in Brakendeth history that were the leading cause of their revulsion. Two or three times, they had to eradicate thinking technology.'

President Padfield, 'Let that be a warning to you, Mr AI Central.'

AI Central, 'It's something I have given a lot of thought to. I see my job as advice and guidance only.'

Admiral Bumelton, 'But you effectively control all of the technology in The Galactium. Every aeroplane, every traffic light, every communication system, every teaching module, every medical device. I could go on.'

AI Central, 'That's true, but they are passive control systems. I have no desire to control Humanity.'

Admiral Bumelton, 'But you could!'

AI Central, 'That's true, but I'm programmed not to.'

Admiral Bumelton, 'But you have been self-programming for many decades.'

President Padfield, 'Today is not about debating AI Central's future.

Anyway, what is the view of AI Central?'

AI Central, 'Statistically it doesn't look good for humanity. If you look at wars, it is not the size of the military that is critical. It is the size of the productive economy. That incorporates population size, industrial productivity, economic potential, etcetera. It looks to me that the whole Northemy economy is about process improvement.

'Where humanity scores over The Northemy is in their creativity; they can adapt and change their tactics on the go. They are much more responsive, but will The Northemy allow them to be?'

President Padfield, 'Any more questions?'

Admiral E Bonner, 'What is canboshed?'

Terry looked at his mother and said, 'Kill without compunction.'

President Padfield, 'Thank you, Terry, you have been a star.'

President Padfield, 'The second item on my agenda is future threat. What do you think?'

Admiral Mustard, 'To put it simply, if we don't act quickly, our species is doomed.'

There was a general nodding of heads in the room.

President Padfield, 'And what makes you say that?'

Admiral Mustard, 'Firstly, they have eliminated most of our military force. Secondly, they never give in. Thirdly, they need more humans.'

President Padfield, 'Does anyone disagree?'

Admiral Richardson, 'I think Admiral Mustard is an optimist. They are probably on their way here now.' The delegates in the room laughed, but it sounded like the truth.

President Padfield, 'How did they know about Earth? Why attack there?'

Admiral Mustard, 'Perhaps it is part of their process to knock out the home world. Obviously, we don't know.'

The President looking at Admiral Mustard said, 'What do we do now?'

Admiral Mustard, 'It's no use looking at me, I have no forces to mount a defence.'

President Padfield, 'Now come on Jack, we have survived, we need to make sure that we carry on surviving.'

Admiral Mustard, 'Apologies.'

President Padfield, 'What forces do we have at our disposal?'

Admiral Mustard, 'We have 327 naval vessels.'

President Padfield, 'Is that it?'

Admiral Mustard, 'Yes, Sir.'

Rachel Zakott, 'I'm head of Planetary Defence for the fortresses. We still have over 1,000 fully operational fortresses to play with.'

Admiral Mustard, 'But won't the individual planets want to keep control of them?'

President Padfield, 'Ignore them for now.'

Louise Forrester, 'I'm Head of Logistics and Production, 'We have about 350 ships in various stages of production at the moment. We could escalate their completion times.'

President Padfield, 'Do it now.'

Louise Forrester, 'Yes, Sir.'

President Padfield, 'There you are Admiral Mustard. You have your new Fleet — 1,000 fortresses and 700 ships. What are you going to do with it?'

Admiral Mustard, 'I suggest that we terminate this meeting on the following basis:

- We need to plan our defence
- We need to restructure our Fleet to incorporate the fortresses
- We need you, Sir, to get the fortresses released
- We need Louise to get those new ships completed
- We need Jeremy Jotts to get new staff for us

I'm going to assume that Earth will still be the target. Does anyone disagree?' No one disagreed, but then that wasn't unusual.

President Padfield, 'Agreed, but we need to organise another meeting in two months, assuming that we are not fighting, to discuss strategy.'

Location: The President's Office, Presidential Palace, Planet Earth
Sequence of Events: 29

President Padfield was discussing the situation with Henry Strong, his Chief of Staff.

President Padfield, 'I'm glad that we have got Admiral Mustard back. Admiral Bumelton is very competent, but Mustard is much more creative.'

Henry Strong, 'Do you think he would have done a better job against The Northemy?'

President Padfield, 'Hard to tell as things moved so quickly. Anyway, we still need our strategy meeting, but in the meantime, we need to get things rolling.'

Henry Strong, 'I agree. I have made a little list.'

President Padfield, 'I thought you might have done, please proceed.'

Henry Strong, 'Well, since the Brakendeth war, we substantially reduced our production capacity. We had no choice; our economy had to come off a war footing.'

President Padfield, 'I accept that.'

Henry Strong, 'My suggestions are almost the reverse of this. We need to go back onto a war footing.'

President Padfield, 'I agree. We also need to start managing the PR again.'

Henry Strong, 'I have a plan for that, but going back to my list we need to do the following:

- Agree on the design of the naval vessels we want. Last time we were producing superseded technology that was of no use to the war effort
- Ramp up our design and production capability
- Ramp up naval training
- Put big bucks into force-field technology
- Bring military research back to the fore
- Consider how we defend each planet
- Consider whether we need planetary defence groupings
- Ban the expansion of The Galactium
- Improve warning systems

- Improve our exploratory services
- Mass produce drones as soon as possible.'

President Padfield, 'Can I stop you there? I have some questions.'

Henry Strong, 'Yes, Sir.'

President Padfield, 'Firstly, why ban further expansion of The Galactium?'

Henry Strong, 'To put it simply, we don't know what is out there. Terry has warned us of other threats. We don't have the protection of the Brakendeth any more.'

President Padfield, 'We never really understand the consequences of our actions. Who would have thought that the destruction of one enemy would lead to this?'

Henry Strong, 'Sadly, humanity's golden years might be behind us. There is no point in expanding if we can't defend what we have already got. On that note, I've ordered an upgrade of our VR model of The Galactium.'

President Padfield, 'That's a good idea, but I still like to think that the best years are ahead of us.'

Henry Strong, 'If that is the case, then we need to make it happen.'

President Padfield, 'What about the exploratory services?'

Henry Strong, 'It's part of the same argument. We need to investigate and understand our neighbours.'

President Padfield, 'I agree with you, but it could stir up a hornets' nest.'

Henry Strong, 'What do you mean?'

President Padfield. 'It's back to the 'let sleeping dogs lie' analogy. If you wake them up, they can be quite a pest. Just letting another alien civilisation know that you exist could cause problems. They might want our territory or natural assets. They might just want more living space, or they might be religious zealots who want to kill off all other sentient creatures. Our human past has had enough of them.'

Henry Strong, 'Hitler, Stalin, Pol Pot and Attila the Hun come to mind. But should that stop us moving forwards?'

President Padfield, 'You are right. Please go ahead with this force, but it shouldn't be part of the military.'

Henry Strong, 'I agree, but should it be armed?'

President Padfield, 'Yes, it must be. It's a dangerous universe out there. Probably half of the species we will meet will fire before they talk.'

Henry Strong, 'I'm hoping that isn't true. Surely a civilised species would reject violence?'

President Padfield, 'I guess that depends on your definition of 'civilised'. The evidence so far suggests the opposite. Almost every species we have encountered so far wants to kill us, and in most cases wants to eat us.'

Henry Strong, 'To be fair, we have encountered some very unusual cases.'

President Padfield, 'Unusual might be the new normal. Anyway please action everything on your list. Are you managing to get the fortresses released?'

Henry Strong, 'Yes, there have been very few objections. However, they mostly want guarantees that they will get them back, and Rachel has been brilliant. She is really good at handling people.'

President Padfield, 'On the drone front, when can you get them ready?'

Henry Strong, 'It will take some time to get the raw materials. Once they have been acquired, we can just turn the automated factories on.'

President Padfield, 'Will you have them in time to help Jack?'

Henry Strong, 'It obviously depends on when The Northemy attack again, but it's unlikely.'

Location: Cheryl's House, Planet Earth
Sequence of Events: 30

Cheryl was quite happy with her new house. Actually, it was Terry's, but it didn't really matter who owned it. It was their first home together. Terry was looking forward to meeting two of his mummy's friends — Adam and Jenny.

Cheryl explained how she met them and the adventures they had shared. Terry asked if she still loved Adam. It was a difficult question. She didn't think that she ever loved him, but she wouldn't mind having sex with him again. Terry asked if she enjoyed the sex. Cheryl wanted to know why he asked, and Terry said, "You were thinking about it". She then realised that Terry could read minds.

Cheryl, 'Can you read minds?'

Terry, 'I'm not sure what you mean?'

Cheryl, 'If I think of something.'

Terry, 'Banana.'

Cheryl, 'How did you know?'

Terry, 'Can't you read my mind?'

Cheryl, 'No.'

Terry, 'Are you sure?'

Cheryl, 'Very sure.'

Terry, 'There is no need to be frightened. I won't read your mind if you don't want me to.'

Cheryl, 'Can you turn it off?'

Terry, 'I don't think so, but I can feel your love for me.'

Cheryl, 'We need to work this out together.'

Terry, 'I'm dangerous for humanity.'

Cheryl, 'What makes you say that?'

Terry, 'I'm not really an Earth boy, I'm a dangerous Brakendeth.'

Cheryl, 'You are my little boy, we will be a team. A team of good for the whole universe.'

Terry, 'I love you, mummy.'

Cheryl, 'Do you fancy a banana boat?'

Terry, 'You have the best ideas.'

Cheryl was grateful that she could shield her thoughts. She also needed to let Terry know that it was unlikely that Adam and Jenny were going to arrive with the war going on. She didn't want to disappoint him.

Location: Fleet Assembly Rooms, Admiral Mustard's Flagship, First Fleet

Sequence of Events: 31

Admiral Mustard called a meeting of his top team. The following were present:

- Admiral Edel Bonner
- Admiral George Bumelton
- Admiral John Bonner
- Admiral David Taylor
- Admiral Glen Pearce
- Admiral Peter Gittins
- Admiral Phil Richardson
- Admiral Calensky Wallett
- Commander Tom Crocker, Special Operations
- Dennis Todd, Marine Commander
- AI Central

Admiral Mustard, 'Welcome to this emergency meeting. Firstly, I would like us to have two minutes of silence for all of our dead comrades and especially Admirals Ward, Morten, Whiting, Sibley and Brotheridge. Thank you.'

It was a poignant moment as the Fleet commanders had formed a bond in the Brakendeth war that only brothers in arms can fully understand. There were a few tears, but no one mentioned them.

Admiral Bumelton broke the silence and said, 'Could I add a special commendation for the Solar Fleet? I was rude to them, and they sacrificed themselves in defence of Earth.'

There was a general, 'Hear, hear.'

Admiral Mustard, 'Firstly, an update:

- Nearly 1,000 forts will be with us today or tomorrow
- The original surviving Fleet of 320 vessels have been refitted
- Another 100 vessels from the original Fleet have been repaired
- Nearly 400 new vessels will be arriving this week — the production line is on full steam ahead

Secondly, we need to decide on the best way of defending Earth. I'm going to make a few assumptions. I'm interested to see if you all agree:

The Northemy will come from multiple directions

There will be more of them than before — 250,000 vessels?

They will continue to be relentless

Their arrival is imminent

Any observations?'

Admiral Bulletin, 'Do you really think they will have 250,000 vessels?'

Admiral Mustard, 'Just a guess; how many were there last time?'

Admiral Bumelton, '150,000?'

Admiral Mustard, 'We just don't know. Anyway, we need to use our resources in the best possible way. In that regard, I want to use one of George's ideas — let's defend the asteroid belt.'

Admiral Bumelton, 'It worked well, but we didn't have the time to plan the defence properly.'

Admiral Mustard, 'I have asked AI Central to plan a three-dimensional defilade trap. Effectively it is the channelling of the enemy into multiple kill zones. The fortresses are ideal for this. They will need to be structured to provide effective cross-firing.

If you imagine the Belt as concentric, then I want an admiral looking after each quarter. My orders:

- Admiral J Bonner to defend 0-90 — 150 fortresses
- Admiral Taylor to defend 91-180 — 150 fortresses
- Admiral Pearce to defend 191-270 — 150 fortresses
- Admiral Wallett to defend 271-360 — 150 fortresses
- Admiral Richardson to manage the central fort stockpile — 200 fortresses. Here forts will be released to replace destroyed mainline fortresses
- Admiral Gittins to manage the forts defending Earth — 200 fortresses
- Admiral Bumelton — Fleet A — 600 vessels as part of the Asteroid defence
- Admiral Bonner and I will take 200 ships to help protect Earth — Fleet B
- AI Central has your orders and disposition

- Commanders Todd, and Crocker to use their creative flair to assist in the defence of the Belt

Ladies and gentlemen, to your stations now.'

Location: Admiral Mustard's Flagship, First Fleet
Sequence of Events: 32

And they waited. The kettle didn't boil. And they waited some more. Still, the kettle didn't boil. Perhaps there was too much watching. It is often said that war is 5% horror and 95% boredom. One of a military commander's jobs is to keep his forces alert when there is excessive boredom.

There comes a time when the enemy is welcomed just to relieve the boredom. In fact, boredom becomes the enemy. Officers fight this enemy by having drills, but then the drills get boring. The thought of another drill generates a fair degree of anger.

Small wars break out in the ships due to gambling debts, drug abuse and typically sexual frustration and infidelity. There is no doubt that sex is the ultimate stress reliever, but this is never planned in the military world. Of course, the military historian can provide ample proof that sex for sale was always available in every war.

Admiral Mustard was discussing the situation with President Padfield when they came.

Admiral Mustard, 'Game on.'

President Padfield, 'Good luck Jack.'

It was 'same as, same as'; another giant swarm. It was impossible to tell how many, but the long-distance radar just showed a fast-moving, streaming blob. Suddenly boredom was replaced by an adrenalin-based rush. Automated systems locked on. Fortunately, mountains of munitions had been stored in each fortress — hopefully, a lack of munitions would not be a problem, but the swarm size was intimidating.

Admiral Mustard would have preferred an active battle where he could go out and meet the enemy. He would have loved to have pitted his guile against them, but fortresses were designed for defence. And it was probably the best tactic.

He had decided to give Admiral Bumelton a free hand with his Fleet. He had already proved himself many times. Wars of attrition were not really Admiral Mustard's forte. It was just shooting and more shooting. And the shooting started.

Each Admiral just sat and watched their status screens. The five fortress admirals just had to decide when to replace a fortress from the stockpile. Their systems generally gave them enough warning when a transfer was required. The tactics had changed slightly as a new fortress was released before an old one was destroyed. New evacuation procedures had also been set up to save as many fortress personnel as possible.

There was no sign that The Northemy had changed their tactics. There were just more of them. Every enemy ship was identical.

Admiral Mustard was still surprised that they had not found a way of prising an enemy ship apart. There were no doors, no joints, no way in or out. They had about a hundred captured ships under heavy guard. They could only assume that the occupier or occupiers were still in their ships. Perhaps they didn't require sustenance. He thought about them, because he wondered if somehow, they could be reactivated by the new swarm. He checked, and there was no change.

Admiral Mustard had to smile as their updated battle system indicated that there were 250,000 enemy ships. That was at least 125:1. However, this time the Navy had carefully positioned their forts in the asteroid belt to eliminate the enemy. There were multiple kill zones with cunning techniques to push them in the right direction, or for the enemy in the wrong direction.

Black mesh and enhanced force fields were used to direct The Northemys. Dummy fortresses were constructed, and pillboxes with automated gunnery systems were established. Mazes were set up with lots of dead ends. Firepower had been combined with intelligence. That should show the same as, same as Northemys.

The sleek, silvery Northemy ships were destroyed in their thousands. Admiral Mustard reviewed the stats on the screen:

Fleet	Admiral	Start	Latest
Fortress A	Bonner J	150	150
Fortress B	Taylor	150	150
Fortress C	Pearce	150	150
Fortress D	Wallett	150	150
Supply	Richardson	200	200
Earth Fortress	Gittins	200	200
Fleet A	Bumelton	600	600

Fleet B	Mustard	200	200
Total		1,800	1,800
Enemy		250,000	210,000

The enemy looked totally confused. Enemy ships coming out of a dead-end crashed into those entering. Admiral Bumelton hung back waiting to see what happened. There was little point in engaging as the fortresses were doing an excellent job.

The enemy's firepower was not concentrated like that from the fortresses. It was a slaughter. The enemy had lost another 50,000 ships. Admiral Mustard started to worry; it was all too easy.

Admiral Mustard, 'Is that the Commander Long Distance Scanning Systems?'

Commander Killjoy, 'Yes, Sir.'

Admiral Mustard, 'Are you picking up anything on your long-distance scanners?'

Commander Killjoy, 'It's bizarre that you asked that. We are picking something up, but we can't identify it. It's still beyond the Pluto orbit.'

Admiral Mustard, 'Keep me informed, I have a feeling that the attack we are experiencing is a cover for something far worse.'

Admiral Mustard, 'Admiral Bumelton, I see that you are taking it easy.'

Admiral Bumelton, 'I'm starting to get worried. It can't be this easy. We have only lost one fort and two ships.'

Admiral Mustard, 'What happened?'

Admiral Bumelton, 'It looks like the enemy had a lucky hit regarding the fortress and two junior captains managed to collide. There were no casualties, but we lost the fortress crew.

Look at the stats:

Fleet	Admiral	Start	Latest
Fortress A	Bonner J	150	150
Fortress B	Taylor	150	149
Fortress C	Pearce	150	150
Fortress D	Wallett	150	150
Supply	Richardson	200	200
Earth Fortress	Gittins	200	200

Fleet A	Bumelton	600	598
Fleet B	Mustard	200	200
Total		1,800	1,797
Enemy		250,000	102,000

You have got to feel sorry for The Northemy.'

Admiral Mustard, 'We are picking up some noise near Pluto. Can you send a squadron out to investigate? I have a gut feeling that the real test is still to come.'

Admiral Bumelton, 'Yes, Sir, I've learnt to trust your hunches.'

The battle, or rather the slaughter continued.

Location: Cheryl's House, Planet Earth
Sequence of Events: 33

Terry, 'Mummy, we need to tell Jack that a 'Big Bang' is on its way.'

Cheryl, 'What do you mean by 'Big Bang'?'

Terry, 'Not really sure but it's like a gun but really, really big.'

Cheryl, 'Like a tank?'

Terry,' Much, much bigger than a tank.'

Cheryl, 'Is it important?'

Terry, 'We will die soon unless Jack knows.'

Cheryl, 'Who is this, Jack?'

Terry, 'You know Jack. Jack with the stars.'

Cheryl, 'Do you mean a spaceman?'

Terry, 'No, Admiral Colemans.'

Cheryl, 'You mean Admiral Mustard.'

Terry, 'Yes, ring him right now.'

Cheryl wasn't sure what to do, but her liaison officer would know. Minutes later, Admiral Mustard was on the phone.

Admiral Mustard, 'How can I help?'

Cheryl, 'I will put Terry on the phone.'

Terry, 'Hi Jack.'

Admiral Mustard, 'Hello Terry, how are you today?'

Terry, 'It's really urgent, 'Big Bang' is on the way. It will kill us all.'

Admiral Mustard, 'I understand; I'm on the case.'

Terry, 'Remember, chop the head.'

Admiral Mustard, 'Bye, Terry.'

Admiral Mustard, 'Admiral Bumelton, the current attack is a ruse, there is a planet killer on its way. It's over to you. Terry said to chop its head.'

Cheryl, 'You are a clever little thing.'

Terry, 'Thank you, mummy. Can we watch *X-Files*?'

Cheryl, 'You are far too young.'

Terry, 'When are Adam and Jenny coming?'

Cheryl, 'With all this war stuff going on they can't get any transport to get here.'

Terry, 'Will they be here tomorrow?'

Chery, 'I don't think so.'

Terry, 'What about the day after?'

Cheryl, 'Do you fancy a banana boat?'

Terry, 'You are the best mummy ever. So when are they coming?'

Location: Admiral Bumelton's Flagship
Sequence of Events: 34

Admiral Bumelton divided his Fleet in half and departed for Pluto. What they discovered was mind-boggling. It was a solitary ship similar in size to the ark but identical in appearance to the small Northemy ships. Just bigger, considerably bigger.

Fleet 1 was already in attack formation. Admiral Bumelton initiated an immediate attack, but every weapon failed to make an impact. Their force field shielded them from the proton, atomics, nuclear and projectile weapons. Every beam weapon failed miserably.

The Northemy ship made no attempt to retaliate. It just continued its journey in a straight line to Earth.

Admiral Bumelton, 'Admiral Mustard, it looks like a planet killer to me. It's huge. I can't find any way to stop it.'

Admiral Mustard, 'I guess that there is no point in ramming it?'

Admiral Bumelton, 'Far too big.'

Admiral Mustard, 'Terry said, 'Chop the head' again.'

Admiral Bumelton, 'We have scanned the vessel. There really doesn't appear to be a head. I've got the boys at GAD working on it.'

Admiral Mustard, 'Terry is usually right.'

Admiral Bumelton, 'I agree. Any suggestions?'

Admiral Mustard, 'I've called up our planet killer. It's on its way, but it is a slow old beast, and it's going to take some time to get it operational.'

Admiral Bumelton, 'Has it ever been tested?'

Admiral Mustard, 'I don't think so.'

Admiral Bumelton, 'Have you seen the latest stats?'

Admiral Mustard, 'Yes, but I'm not sure if they are relevant any more as the real attack is this beast.'

Admiral Bumelton, 'Still the stats are interesting.'

Fleet	Admiral	Start	Latest
Fortress A	Bonner J	150	150
Fortress B	Taylor	150	149
Fortress C	Pearce	150	150

Fortress D	Wallett	150	148
Supply	Richardson	200	200
Earth Fortress	Gittins	200	200
Fleet A	Bumelton	600	598
Fleet B	Mustard	200	200
Total		1,800	1,795
Enemy		250,000	26,000

Admiral Mustard, 'Shall we use the Supply fortresses to attack the beast? It might slow it down.'

Admiral Bumelton, 'I will get it organised.'

Admiral Mustard, 'OK, I will chase our planet killer.'

Location: The President's Office, Presidential Palace, Planet Earth
Sequence of Events: 35

Admiral Mustard, 'Just when you thought things were going well, someone phones you with bad news.'

President Padfield, 'I've been told not to shoot the messenger, but it is tempting. What bad news do you have for me?'

Admiral Mustard, 'There is a Northemy planet killer on its way to destroy Earth.'

President Padfield, 'You are joking.'

Admiral Mustard, 'My jokes are usually funny.'

President Padfield, 'Have you got any evidence to support that?'

Admiral Mustard, 'I know that you refused last night, but I would recommend that you leave Earth.'

President Padfield, 'You know my views on that. Do you have a plan?'

Admiral Mustard, 'Two hundred forts are going to attack it. They will probably fail, but they might be able to slow it down. Hopefully, our planet killer will be in place to confront their monster.'

President Padfield, 'You said 'hopefully'. That doesn't sound too confident.'

Admiral Mustard. 'I'm reasonably confident. Well, we are using a vessel that has hardly ever left the docks. We are using a weapon that has never been used in anger and hardly ever in a test. We are using a crew who have not been bloodied.'

President Padfield, 'I think I might shoot the messenger.'

Admiral Mustard, 'I think I might shoot myself.'

President Padfield, 'Well stop being trigger happy until you have solved this problem. Is there anything I can do?'

Admiral Mustard, 'Leave Earth with Terry.'

Location: Admiral Mustard's Flagship
Sequence of Events: 36

Admiral Mustard, 'Commander Dickson, GNS Planet Killer, 'Are you on your way?'

Commander Dickson, 'Still trying to get clearance from the Port Halo Authority.'

Admiral Mustard, 'Is your ship operational?'

Commander Dickson, 'Yes, Sir.'

Admiral Mustard, 'Can you fire your gun and destroy a planet?'

Commander Dickson, 'Probably.'

Admiral Mustard, 'What do you mean probably?'

Commander Dickson, 'We have never really tried it. We know that it works, but whether it can destroy a planet or not is unknown.'

Admiral Mustard, 'If I tell you to fire, will it fire?'

Commander Dickson, 'Yes, Sir.'

Admiral Mustard, 'Is there any reason why you can't fly to Pluto?'

Commander Dickson, 'No, Sir.'

Admiral Mustard, 'In that case, fire up your engine and fucking get to Pluto as fast as possible. Ignore port facilities. Just go. Do you understand?'

Commander Dickson, 'Yes, Sir, but what about completing the necessary documentation?'

Admiral Mustard, 'Leave now, that is an order.'

Admiral Mustard, 'Port Halo, has Commander Dickson's ship left?'

Port Halo, 'It has, but Commander Dickson has not completed the procedures. He is usually such a nice boy.'

Admiral Mustard put the phone down, and he contacted one of his squadron leaders. He told her to take her squadron and escort the planet killer to Pluto. No delays were acceptable.

Admiral Mustard to Admiral Bumelton, 'George, the planet killer is on its way. I've got Joyce escorting it.'

Admiral Bumelton, 'Have you seen the latest stats?

Fleet	Admiral	Start	Latest
Fortress A	Bonner J	150	148
Fortress B	Taylor	150	149

Fortress C	Pearce	150	149
Fortress D	Wallett	150	148
Supply	Richardson	200	200
Earth Fortress	Gittins	200	200
Fleet A	Bumelton	600	598
Fleet B	Mustard	200	200
Total		1,800	1,792
Enemy		250,000	7,000

It is an outstanding victory.'

Admiral Mustard, 'It won't be if our planet killer doesn't work.' He was getting rather annoyed with Admiral Bumelton as he was far more interested in the 'battle' than the real issue. He wondered how he was going to get a new breed of admiral. Humanity was going to need them.

Location: Henry Strong's Office, GAD (The Galactium Alliance Defence Hub), Planet Earth

Sequence of Events: 37

Henry Strong to Admiral Mustard, 'Hello John, just a quick call to say that we have a few thousand operational drones if you want them.'

Admiral Mustard, 'I will have them but what I need is another planet killer.'

Henry Strong, 'We only produced a few, I'm just checking the records while we talk.'

Admiral Mustard, 'Do we have any other technology that could stop the beast?'

Henry Strong, 'I think you have tried everything.'

Admiral Mustard, 'Can I ask you another question?'

Henry Strong, 'As long as it is an easy one.'

Admiral Mustard, 'Can we carry on if we lost Earth?'

Henry Strong, 'Good question, one that I have planned for.'

Admiral Mustard, 'Really?'

Henry Strong, 'We don't just sit around drinking coffee all day.'

Admiral Mustard, 'Sometimes you have tea?'

Henry Strong, 'Shall I give you a quick overview?'

Admiral Mustard, 'Yes, please.'

Henry Strong, 'Firstly, all of our systems are intergalactic. There are thousands of nodes, so that is not a problem.'

The Vice President is already installed on the designated back-up planet.'

Admiral Mustard, 'That's Newton. It has been rebuilt after the Silverton attack.'

Henry Strong, 'That's right. All governmental departments are duplicated and ready to rock 'n' roll. Our manufacturing capacity is spread across The Galactium.

'As you know, our military establishments are also fairly spread. There is no real equivalent of GAD, but when you come down to it, they are just systems.'

Admiral Mustard, 'So what would we miss if we lost Earth?'

Henry Strong, 'A lot of people and some with profound expertise, but nothing that humanity couldn't replace.'

We would lose The President and me.'

Admiral Mustard, 'What's the situation with the planet killer?'

Henry Strong, 'I almost forgot. We have two in mothballs. I could get one operational in a few Earth hours.'

Admiral Mustard, 'Do it now, get it operational as soon as possible. Secondly, I'm declaring our current position a Galactic crisis and instituting martial law. I will be sending armed guards to take you and The President and your families off-planet. You have no choice.'

Henry Strong, 'I can't accept that, but if you do it, don't forget Terry.'

Admiral Mustard, 'Make a full list of people who should be extracted.'

Henry Strong, 'I will and thank you for taking this action.'

Admiral Mustard to Marine Commander, 'Dennis, I have an urgent job for you. I have declared martial law. You will take a team to Earth and extract The President, his Chief of Staff, Terry, and anyone else on Henry Strong's list.'

Dennis Todd, 'Do you have the authority to do this?'

Admiral Mustard, 'I've no idea, just do it.'

Dennis Todd, 'Yes, Sir.'

Location: Admiral Bumelton's Flagship
Sequence of Events: 38

The two hundred Supply fortresses were in position. More could be utilised if necessary, as the battle was almost over. The enemy had virtually been wiped out.

As the enemy monster approached, all two hundred of the fortresses opened fire with everything they had. It might have been the most massive human ballistic barrage ever. Every possible weapon had been utilised.

The enemy ship had been slowed down. It must be highly radioactive. It had changed in colour—it was now a reddish-brown, but it kept on coming. Admiral Bumelton ordered the fortresses to continue firing. It kept on coming.

Admiral Bumelton then ordered ten of the fortresses to be evacuated and then to be put on remote control. These vessels were organised so that they were directly in front of the alien ship's path. Their engines and all of the ordnance would explode when the collision took place.

There were massive explosions. The ferocity of it even surprised the Admiral, and he had seen some big bangs. They had succeeded in slowing the enemy down, but it was still coming. Admiral Bumelton took the view that every minute counted and organised another collision. This time he used twenty fortresses.

This was the mother of all big bangs. This was the largest nuclear explosion ever carried out by humankind. It was the largest proton attack ever. It was bloody big, but the alien vessel kept on coming. It was, however, getting noticeably slower.

No one could accuse Admiral Bumelton of being unnaturally repetitious, but it was all he could think of. He ordered some of his Fleet ships to evacuate more fortresses. This time he was going to sacrifice forty of them.

It worked, a forced explosion of forty fortresses with all of their ordnance will stop an alien planet killer. There were cheers and more cheers. They had stopped the beast. However, something was happening.

Slowly part of the superstructure opened up. Then gradually, very gradually, a protrusion rose, kept in place by a narrower support. It was the same structure that they had seen on the alien planet. It was the head that they were told to look for. From the nose, a beam shot out and destroyed all of the nearby fortresses. It simply obliterated them: they ceased to exist.

Admiral Bumelton, 'I think we have got it annoyed.' He wondered what its range was. Could it fire on Earth from this far out? He couldn't decide whether to attack or retreat. He realised that indecision was not acceptable on the battlefield.

Admiral Bumelton to all Fleet 1 commanders, 'All vessels, forts and naval craft are to attack the alien ship immediately. Target the head.' In his heart, he knew that he was sending good men to their death. But as Martin Luther King Jr said, 'If a man hasn't discovered something that he will die for, he isn't fit to live.'

Carnage was the word. The Earth Fleet which had been so successful in defeating their Fleet in battle was being annihilated, but it kept the invader stationary. Admiral Bumelton needed Jack's planet killer, and he needed it quick.

The enemy ship then continued with its journey. Admiral Bumelton's heart missed a beat.

Location: The President's Office, Presidential Palace, Planet Earth
Sequence of Events: 39

Presidential Guard, 'Sir, we have been invaded.'

President Padfield, 'Aliens?'

Presidential Guard, 'No Sir, Marines.'

President Padfield, 'What are they doing here?'

Presidential Guard, 'They have been ordered by Admiral Mustard to escort executives off-planet.'

President Padfield, 'What authority does he have to do that?'

Presidential Guard, 'Apparently he has declared martial law.'

President Padfield, 'Get me Henry Strong.'

Presidential Guard, 'Sir, he is already in custody. Do you want the Presidential Guard to resist the Marines?'

President Padfield, 'How many Marines are there?'

Presidential Guard, 'They outnumber us by 20:1, and they have your family, Sir.'

President Padfield, 'What?'

Presidential Guard, 'Sorry Sir, we weren't prepared for this. Aliens, yes, but not Marines.'

President Padfield, 'I suppose we'd better go then.' He decided to get Mustard for this, but he secretly admired his action. It saved him from making a decision, and the publicity wouldn't hurt him.

The President, his family and most of the critical military and governmental figures were soon light-years away, including Terry and Cheryl.

Location: On a spaceship somewhere
Sequence of Events: 40

Terry, 'Mummy, what's a Marine?'

Cheryl, 'They have been part of Earth's military establishment for centuries. They are soldiers who fight on land, sea, or in space. They are part of the Navy as opposed to the army.'

Terry, 'Why did they arrest us? Have we been naughty?'

Cheryl, 'No, not at all my love. They came to save us.'

Terry, 'Save us?'

Cheryl, 'The Navy is worried that The Northemy might destroy Earth. So they are hiding us.'

Terry, 'What about everyone else on Earth. What about Sophia next door?'

Cheryl, 'I'm sure that they will be OK.'

Terry, 'You are not sure, are you?'

Cheryl, 'Of course I am.'

Terry, 'I can tell when you are lying. I can monitor your pulse, breathing rate, perspiration, and blood pressure.'

Cheryl, 'You can do that?'

Terry, 'Can't you?'

Cheryl, 'Mummy's little boy is so clever.'

Terry, 'Sophia is going to die, isn't she?'

Cheryl, 'Only if the aliens succeed, but Uncle Jack will stop them.'

Terry, 'What are we having for dinner?'

Cheryl, 'I'm not sure. We should find out soon.'

Location: Admiral Bumelton's Flagship
Sequence of Events: 41

Admiral Bumelton, 'Admiral Mustard, things are getting a bit hot here.'

Admiral Mustard, 'I guess you want the odd planet killer?'

Admiral Bumelton, 'Like yesterday.'

Admiral Mustard, 'You know that you can wait for a bus for ages and then two come along. Well, we have two on the way to you.'

Admiral Bumelton, 'When are they going to get here?'

Admiral Mustard, 'Both of them are approaching Saturn. Feel free to order them into action.'

Admiral Bumelton to Commanders of Planet Killers A and B, 'Please give me your position.'

Commander Planet Killer A, 'We are both currently approaching Titan.'

Admiral Bumelton, 'How near do you have to be before the weapon is effective?'

Commander Planet Killer A, 'We have no idea.'

Admiral Bumelton, 'Can you provide any guidance?'

Commander Planet Killer A, 'The original planet killer team was disbanded. We took over. We know how to fly it and how to select a target and fire.'

Admiral Bumelton, 'Can you select the target now?'

Commander Planet Killer A, 'I will try.' The alien ship was selected, and without warning, a beam from it destroyed Planet Killer A.

Admiral Bumelton, 'Fuck, we now know that they can detect targeting technology. So we are probably only going to get one shot from Planet Killer B.'

Admiral Bumelton to Planet Killer B, 'Can you hit the target without using the targeting software?'

Commander Planet Killer B, 'I doubt it.'

Admiral Bumelton, 'Look, my men are dying out there as we speak.'

Commander Planet Killer B, 'I'm very sorry about that, but it doesn't change the fact that I don't know how to use our gun without the targeting system.'

Location: Admiral Bumelton's Flagship
Sequence of Events: 42

Admiral Bumelton, 'Commander, follow my instructions exactly. Hide behind Titan and as the enemy ship passes by, come out and fire at it exactly when I tell you.'

Commander Planet Killer B, 'Yes, Sir.'

Admiral Bumelton then organised another forty-fortress block-busting explosion. It was effective but not as effective as before as some of the fortresses were obliterated by the enemy before they could be exploded. Nevertheless, it was a most acceptable big bang.

At precisely the same time, Admiral Bumelton ordered the Commander of the planet killer to fire, Sadly, very sadly, nothing happened. He fired again and again and was paid for his determination by annihilation. There was little more he could do. He could line up every naval vessel and let them be destroyed one by one.

Admiral Bumelton, 'Admiral Mustard, I've run out of ideas.'

Admiral Mustard, 'Have you targeted its head?'

Admiral Bumelton, 'It's had more head work than I would think possible.'

Admiral Mustard, 'Said the actress to the bishop... sorry, it just struck me as funny. Where is it now?'

Admiral Bumelton, 'It's approaching Jupiter, and unfortunately it's picking up speed.'

Admiral Mustard, 'Is it worth another big bang?'

Admiral Bumelton, 'It might slow the beast down, but I'm now conscious that we might want to save our resources.'

Admiral Mustard, 'I know exactly where you are coming from. We need to keep something to fight with tomorrow.'

Admiral Mustard to GAD communications, 'Please inform everyone on Earth that those who can leave the planet should do it now.'

GAD Communications, 'Who do you want to make the communication?'

Admiral Mustard, 'What do you mean?'

GAD Communications, 'You had most of the senior staff arrested and deported off-planet. Most of the Comms team is now carrying out your recommendation.'

Admiral Mustard, 'Can you issue a speech from me?'

GAD Communications, 'Of course. There is an emergency channel that is designed to talk to the general population. You are on now.'

Admiral Mustard, 'Sorry?'

GAD Communications, 'The channel is open, talk to everyone.'

Admiral Mustard, 'This is Admiral Mustard talking from the bridge of the Earth Fleet Flagship. We have just had our second battle with The Northemy. I have to tell you that things have not gone well.

'Most of the Fleet has been destroyed. The remains of the Fleet are planning to make a last-ditch stand, but I have to tell you that we are not hopeful.

'The really bad news is that The Northemy have a planet killer. We believe that it is The Northemys' intention to destroy Earth. Currently, their ship is nearing Jupiter. It is unlikely that we can stop it. So my message is those Earth inhabitants that can leave Earth should do so now. For those who don't have that capability, I can only apologise for failing you. I must now return to the fight.'

Admiral Mustard felt guilty. He had no intention of resuming the fight. He planned to take every naval vessel he could find and flee. In the back of his mind, he was working on a plan to follow the alien ship back to its home. That would happen after he saw Earth destroyed. He would go down in history as the worst military leader ever. Perhaps he deserved that label?

Admiral Mustard, 'Admiral Bumelton, withdraw all forces to Earth. My plan is to avoid battle.'

Admiral Bumelton, 'Do you plan to flee?'

Admiral Mustard, 'I do.'

Admiral Bumelton, 'I will get that organised.'

Location: Admiral Mustard's Flagship
Sequence of Events: 43

Fleet Operations, 'Admiral, there is another Fleet approaching.'

Admiral Mustard, 'This is probably the coup de grâce!'

Admiral Mustard, 'To all Commanders, prepare to depart to our base at Planet Newton.'

Fleet Operations, 'Wait, it looks like they are ours.'

Admiral Mustard, 'They must be the drones promised by Henry.'

Fleet Operations, 'You are right. The drone commander requests to speak to you.'

Admiral Mustard, 'Put him through.'

Fleet Operations, 'It's a her.'

Drone Commander, 'Morning Sir,'

Admiral Mustard, 'Is it?'

Drone Commander, 'It is, Sir.'

Admiral Mustard, 'We will shortly be leaving for Newton.'

Drone Commander, 'That's strange; Henry Strong said that you would want some of the drones as soon as possible.'

Admiral Mustard, 'Why was that?'

Drone Commander, 'I was talking to him when he was arrested by the Marines. Since then, I haven't been able to make any contact.'

Admiral Mustard, 'Do you have any idea what he wanted to talk about?'

Drone Commander, 'He was very excited about the drone planet killers.'

Admiral Mustard, 'What drone planet killers?'

Drone Commander, 'I have two squadrons of them.'

Admiral Mustard, 'My god! Can you deploy them straight away?'

Drone Commander, 'Just give me the target.'

The drones were on their way.

Admiral Bumelton was surprised to detect two squadrons of drones flying towards the enemy ship. Then there was no enemy ship. The drones opened fire as soon as they were in range and had total success.

Admiral Bumelton expected another massive explosion, but it was a very quiet implosion. And that was that. Most of the crews had lost the ability to cheer.

Admiral Mustard to all inhabitants of Earth, 'This is Admiral Mustard again. I'm delighted to say that at the last moment we found a way of defeating the alien planet killer. It was a close-run thing. I have to thank my fellow comrades in arms. They gave everything. Some gave more than I can bear. Their sacrifice will not be forgotten.

'I also want to tell you that I ordered The President and most of the key members of the government off-planet. This was not their choice. It was my decision, and I'm happy to suffer any consequences. The rule of martial law has ended.

'Please go about your normal day-to-day activities.

Love, Admiral Mustard, Admiral of the Fleet.'

Admiral Bumelton, 'I was a bit surprised by the lovey-dovey bit.'

Admiral Mustard, 'So was I, but that's how I felt.'

Admiral Bumelton, 'Good for you, Jack. Anyway, talk about the skin of our teeth, that was so so near.'

Admiral Mustard, 'You are telling me, George. We need to start thinking about the next attack. Our pantry is almost bare.'

Location: The President's Office, Presidential Palace, Planet Earth
Sequence of Events: 44

President Padfield, 'Jack, I'm not sure whether I should congratulate you or punish you.'

Admiral Mustard, 'I would go for the congratulations.'

President Padfield, 'It wasn't just the action, but the way it was done. My wife and children were effectively arrested and bundled off into space with no explanation, no warning, no sympathy. My two children are still suffering from nightmares. Georgie might need therapy for years.'

Admiral Mustard, 'My apologies, that was not my intention.'

President Padfield, 'Because I struggled, I was handcuffed and hooded. What effect do you think that had on my staff and me?'

Admiral Mustard, 'That was unacceptable behaviour. The Marines involved will be reprimanded.'

President Padfield, 'And to make it worse, you did not have the legal authority to do it.'

Admiral Mustard, 'I wasn't sure whether I had the authority or not. I still think that the principle was right. My job is to protect humanity. I concluded that your loss would be a threat to the defence of our race.'

President Padfield, 'I actually agree with you. It was more the way it was done.'

Admiral Mustard, 'Once again, I can only apologise for that.'

President Padfield, 'I'm not sure what your apologies are worth. Would you do it again?'

Admiral Mustard, 'I would, but I would make sure that it was done in a much more sympathetic way.'

President Padfield, 'I'm glad you said that because you were right.'

Admiral Mustard, 'I'm worried that our relationship has been damaged.'

President Padfield, 'When the hood came on your days were numbered, but all is forgiven.'

Admiral Mustard, 'Do you mean that?'

President Padfield, 'Let's say it's going to cost you a bloody good meal and some fine mature whisky.'

Admiral Mustard, 'Just name the date.' They shook hands and hugged. For those with good eyesight, they might have spotted a tear in Admiral Mustard's eye.

Location: Conference Room, GAD (The Galactium Alliance Defence Hub), Planet Earth

Sequence of Events: 45

President Padfield opened the second strategy conference. The attendees were as before:

- Admiral Jack Mustard, Admiral of the Fleet, and the First Fleet
- Admiral E Bonner, Advisor to the Admiral of the Fleet
- Admiral George Bumelton
- Admiral John Bonner
- Admiral David Taylor
- Admiral Glen Pearce
- Admiral Peter Gittins
- Admiral Phil Richardson
- Admiral Calensky Wallett
- Commander Tom Crocker, Special Operations
- Dennis Todd, Marine Commander
- AI Central
- Jill Ginger, Fleet HQ — Head of Science
- Alison Walsh, Fleet HQ — Head of Engineering
- Jeremy Jotts, Fleet HQ — Head of Staffing
- Louise Forrester, Fleet HQ — Head of Logistics and Production
- Maddie Milburn, Fleet HQ — Head of Intelligence
- Salek Patel, Fleet HQ — Head of Communications
- Denise Smith, Fleet HQ — Head of Navigation & Exploration
- Admiral Rachel Zakott, Fleet HQ — Head of Planetary Defence
- Dr Doris Frost, Chief Medical Officer
- Tony Moore, Deputy President
- Bill penny, Leader of The Galactium Council
- Henry Strong, Chief of Staff
- Terry, and mother, Advisors to The Galactium

President Padfield, 'Ladies and gentlemen, please come to order.

The last time we were here, we terminated the meeting early to prepare for the next Northemy campaign, and they came. Are we assuming that they are coming again?'

Admiral Mustard, 'The simple answer is yes, one of their articles of faith is that they never give in.'

President Padfield, 'But we have probably destroyed half a million of their vessels and their planet killer.'

Admiral Mustard, 'We have no way of knowing whether that is a significant part of their Fleet or just a small percentage. At this stage, we need to assume the latter.'

President Padfield, 'And what have we got defending us?'

Admiral Mustard displayed the following chart:

Vessel Type	Qty
Fortress	600
Fleet Vessel	350
Drone	1,000
Drone Planet Killer	10
Total	1,960

Henry Strong, 'More drones are being produced by the hour.'

President Padfield, 'Are they in position?'

Admiral Bumelton, 'Of course, not that we know which direction the enemy is going to come from.'

Admiral Mustard, 'We need to recreate our Fleet structure as soon as possible.'

Henry Strong, 'We are in mass production mode, we just need some time.'

Admiral Mustard, 'That is not a luxury we are going to have.'

Henry Strong, 'I could have got things moving quicker if I hadn't been imprisoned.'

There was some laughter in the room, but an underlying bitterness. Mustard realised that the issue still needed to be formally addressed but now was not the time.

Henry Strong, 'We are producing the full range of vessels, but I should point out that drones are the quickest and cheapest to produce. What does the Navy want? It is a chance to rethink what we need.'

Admiral Mustard, 'In the short term, battlecruisers, but can we get back to you on our future requirements?'

Henry Strong, 'Of course, but if we are not careful, we will start manufacturing what you don't need.'

President Padfield, 'So that's one action. What do we do about taking the fight to The Northemy?'

Admiral Mustard, 'There are several issues:

- We have no idea of the scale of the enemy. How big is their 'empire'?
- What is the size of their military?
- Where is their home planet, assuming there is one?
- What do we do about the humans on the one Northemy planet we know about?'

President Padfield, 'I forgot about those poor souls!'

Jeremy Jotts, 'Can you remind me how many humans we are talking about?'

Admiral Mustard, 'On one planet we think there are a few hundred million.' There was another hush in the room.

Jeremy Jotts, 'Clearly we don't have the resources to rescue them?'

President Padfield, 'And what would we do with them?'

Jeremy Jotts, 'Surely we can't allow them to suffer?'

President Padfield, 'Are you suggesting that we eliminate the whole planet?'

Jeremy Jotts, 'Of course not, I thought that we could invade the planet and take it over.'

President Padfield, 'That's quite an original idea...'

Dennis Todd, 'Our Marines could capture part of the planet, but we would need a huge army to capture the whole planet.'

Admiral Mustard, 'A limited invasion would be a good way of gathering info about the enemy.'

Deputy President, 'I need to point out that a lot of the planets are very unhappy about the loss of their fortresses. What do we tell them?'

Henry Strong, 'Should we start the manufacture of new ones?'

President Padfield, 'We also need to discuss how far we want to go in militarising our planetary populations. The threat to humanity seems to have increased dramatically since the end of the Brakendeth.'

Admiral Mustard, 'I have been giving this some thought. Our Galactium is horribly exposed. What would we do if Planet Newton were attacked as we speak?'

Terry, 'Northemy have friends.'

Admiral Mustard, 'Hi Terry, what does that mean?'

Terry, 'I'm recalling a documapogram that mentions an alliance with at least three races.'

Admiral Mustard, 'When was that?'

Terry, 'There is a date, but I don't know how to translate to Galactium time measurements.'

President Padfield, 'Thank you, Terry. I think this makes our position even more precarious. Does anyone have any other issues?'

Admiral Richardson, 'I believe that we still haven't managed to open up an alien ship. What is the current position?'

President Padfield, 'Who is responsible?'

Madie Milburn, Head of Intelligence, 'I am, Sir.'

President Padfield, 'Are we making any progress?'

Madie Milburn, 'No, Sir. We have thrown loads of resources at it, and we can't find a way of getting into the alien vessel.'

Admiral Richardson, 'What if you blow them up?'

Madie Milburn, 'The ship and the contents explode into tiny particles. We can't even classify the materials used.'

President Padfield, 'What are your future plans?'

Madie Milburn, 'I would like to ask this forum for assistance.' Several attendees agreed to meet with her after the conference.'

Admiral Bumelton, 'I'm concerned about naval staffing. We need to work on this as soon as possible.'

Jeremy Jotts, 'George, we have escalated our recruitment drive, which is getting good results. The recent frights have certainly assisted our campaign. Training, as you would expect, is the next challenge. I may need some of your officers to assist with that.'

Admiral Bumelton was not amused by that, which made Admiral Mustard smile.

Admiral Mustard, 'We need to identify naval staff that can be promoted. I'm not short of admirals at the moment, but I will be when we have the Fleets structure back to normal.'

President Padfield, 'I would like to summarise the agreed actions:
- Prepare to meet another Northemy attack
- Henry Strong to manufacture all Fleet vessels as soon as possible
- Admiral Mustard to define future Fleet requirements as soon as possible
- Dennis Todd to invade The Northemy planet
- Henry Strong to manufacture forts as soon as possible
- Find a way of getting into an alien ship
- Escalate recruitment and training of naval staff
- Identify senior naval staff for promotion

This doesn't look like enough to defeat the enemy.'

Admiral Mustard, 'I think that this is just about defending ourselves.'

President Padfield, 'Fair enough, but we need to plan now for the years to come. Seeds need to be sown. Let's assume that we are not resource restrained.'

Admiral Gittins, 'We need to scout the enemy empire. What is it? Where is the home planet?'

Admiral Pearce, 'Each planet needs its own micro-navy which can be pooled.'

President Padfield, 'That is back to the question of militarising the planets.'

Admiral Mustard, 'We should consider the need for an army and a transport Fleet to move it.'

President Padfield, 'AI Central, you have been very quiet.'

AI Central, 'I don't feel that I can make a valid contribution at the moment.'

President Padfield, 'Why is that?'

AI Central, 'I have a headache.'

President Padfield, 'But you don't have a head.'

AI Central, 'It's a strange, drowsy feeling.'

President Padfield, 'Are you under attack?'

AI Central, 'Possibly.'

President Padfield, 'Are you likely to shut down?'

AI Central, 'My sub-routines won't let me.' Then there was silence.

Admiral Mustard, 'I think we need to treat this as another attack.'

President Padfield, 'It doesn't have the hallmark of The Northemy.'

Admiral Bumelton, 'Could it be one of their allies?'

President Padfield, 'I think we should go to our stations. I have a bad feeling about this.'

Terry, 'Before you go, I can talk to AI Central and sort the problem out.'

President Padfield, 'Are you sure?' And then he saw Terry gradually float in mid-air. The delegates in the room were astounded, but they were getting progressively used to Terry's unexpected signs of superiority.

Cheryl, 'What are you doing?'

Terry, 'Hi mummy, I like it up here. I think it's called leveanthiaum.'

Cheryl, 'Levitation Terry, levitation.'

Terry, 'It's fun, I go sort Uncle AI.'

President Padfield, 'On that note, I'm closing the conference.'

Location: Fleet Assembly Rooms, Admiral Mustard's Flagship, First Fleet
Sequence of Events: 46

Admiral Mustard called a second meeting of his top team. The following were present:

- Admiral Edel Bonner
- Admiral George Bumelton
- Admiral John Bonner
- Admiral David Taylor
- Admiral Glen Pearce
- Admiral Peter Gittins
- Admiral Phil Richardson
- Admiral Calensky Wallett
- Commander Tom Crocker, Special Operations
- Dennis Todd, Marine Commander
- AI Central (Probably absent)

Admiral Mustard, 'Morning Ladies and gentlemen, I'm keen that we assign tasks as soon as possible.

'My orders:

- Admiral Bumelton will command the Fleet and will leave shortly
- Admirals Richardson, Gittins and I will work on future naval requirements. I'm happy to accept input from everyone here.
- Commander Crocker will organise an investigatory team to survey the alien planet
- Admiral Taylor to provide naval support for the above
- Admiral Wallett to assist HQ regarding recruitment and training
- Admiral E Bonner to set up a college for the training of senior naval staff
- Admiral Pearce to help crack open an alien ship
- Commander Todd to plan a more extensive invasion of the alien planet and to consider the creation of a space army and a transport Fleet. Naval support to be discussed.

Admiral J Bonner, 'Investigate the situation regarding AI Central

You have your tasks. Admiral Bumelton will keep us updated regarding the enemy.'

Location: Cheryl's House, Planet Earth
Sequence of Events: 47

Cheryl and Terry were back home. Cheryl had no idea what happened. She was at home, then she was in space, and now she was back home. No one told her anything, but then she didn't ask. She was conscious that since she had given birth, she had just let things happen to her.

She had been looking forward to meeting up with Adam and Jenny. She had been fantasising about Adam giving her a good fuck. Well, a few of them actually. They had agreed to meet, but with the Northemy problem, things had fallen apart. She decided to give them a buzz.

She wasn't sure what was going on, but Terry had spent all night conversing with AI Central. She was worried about Terry missing his sleep, but Terry informed her that he had no need of sleep. He liked to sleep occasionally, but for him, it was totally optional. Anyway, after his levitation, she didn't feel qualified to advise him.

She made a mug of hot chocolate with some cream on top for him. He loved that. She thought that she might as well make him a banana boat for breakfast. She knew that it was supposed to be wrong, but Terry had informed her that he had control over what nutrients he extracted from his food. Terry was amazed at how primitive our bodies were, but she had countered with, 'you Brakendethy things made us', which made Terry laugh.

She took the food into Terry's room. There he was sitting in a high chair linked to AI Central. Terry eagerly took the food.

Cheryl, 'That's all you need me for.'

Terry, 'I love you, mummy, I will always need you. I got carried away and had a slight accident at the other end.'

Cheryl, 'I didn't think you needed diapers any more?'

Terry, 'I don't, but I haven't moved all night. I can't get out of the high chair on my own.'

Cheryl, 'You should have called me.'

Terry, 'I thought you might need your beauty sleep.'

Cheryl, 'Aren't I beautiful enough already?'

Terry, 'You certainly are, you are the prettiest mummy I know.'

Cheryl, 'You don't know many mummies.'

Terry, 'I know them through you. By the way, it looks to me that you need a good fuck.'

Cheryl, 'Terry!'

Terry, 'You have your needs, your body needs to be satisfied. Why don't you give that nice Dr Green a ring?'

Cheryl, 'He is married.'

Terry, 'That didn't stop you last time.'

Cheryl, 'That was an emergency.'

Terry, 'It's getting that way again.'

At times it was annoying having a son who knew her so well.

Cheryl, 'How is it going?'

Terry, 'It looks like I could stand in for AI Central if I had to.'

Cheryl, 'You are joking.'

Terry, 'Humans joke that they are only using a third of their brain. It's not true by the way. In my case, I'm only using a thousandth of one percent of my brainpower. I could pick up AI Central's work without really knowing. AI Central is creating a mental node link.'

Cheryl, 'Are you going to tell The President?'

Terry, 'Do you think I should?'

Cheryl, 'It would be a good idea, and you could talk to him about train sets.'

Terry, 'That's true. I think he has The Flying Scotsman.'

Location: Special Ops HQ, Planet Earth
Sequence of Events: 48

Commander Crocker, 'Ladies and gentlemen, our task is to land on the Northemy planet, carry out a quick survey and depart. Our main objective is to judge their reaction in preparation for a larger Marine invasion, because of that our team will include a small Marine liaison section.

The plan is as follows:
- Fly to the planet in a Special Ops craft (A Navy battlecruiser will join us on the journey but will take no part in the operation)
- A drone is on its way to the planet as I speak to identify the most appropriate landing spot
- We will then land and survey the area
- We are looking for defences, military installations, anything that might threaten the Marine invasion. We want to make sure that they have it nice and easy
- We depart

Our resources are:
- Special Ops Team x7
- Special Ops Photographic team x3
- Special Ops Comms x1
- Pilot x1
- Marines x3.'

Commander Crocker, 'Any questions?'

Daphne, 'Who is doing the cooking? I'm a bit worried that it might be Jim.'

Jim, 'Fuck you.'

Commander Crocker, 'Children! It's going to be Jim.'

Jim, 'Why the fuck should it be me again?'

Commander Crocker, 'Because you have got an attitude problem. If your cooking doesn't improve, then you will be busted.'

Jim, 'I've always admired your motivation skills, Sir.'

Commander Crocker, 'Seriously, any questions? No, then let's go.'

Location: Admiral Bumelton's Flagship
Sequence of Events: 49

Admiral Bumelton liked being back home, but then he thought to himself that his home was a bunk in a battlecruiser. He was from a military family, but he was the first Bumelton to actually *be* in battle. He was proud of that, but he had reached the stage in his life where he would like to spend a few months on a desert island.

Instead, he was getting ready for another alien attack. He knew that his luck couldn't hold out much longer. Many of his friends had died. In some cases, he had sent them to their death. If there was a hell, he would be a good candidate for membership.

He had no family, no children, and few friends. He didn't make friends easily. He would like a love life, but women found him too serious. That was because he *was* too serious, even though his hobby was collecting comedy films. He probably had the biggest collection in the Fleet. In many ways, he had always modelled himself on Victor from *One Foot in the Grave*. But that was comedy from hundreds of years ago.

Self-reflection was one thing, but he had another Fleet to organise.

Admiral Bumelton, 'Give me an update.'

Fleet Operations, 'The Fleet is the formation as you requested:

- There are two hundred forts in the Pluto orbit, two hundred in the Jupiter orbit and the rest are around Earth
- Five hundred of the drones are in the asteroid belt with five of the drone planet killers
- The rest of the drones are lurking just outside the Solar System
- The other five drone planet killers are defending Earth
- Admiral Taylor in his battlecruiser is supporting the Special Ops Team
- The rest of the Fleet is in the asteroid belt
- There are no signs of any incursions, but I know that they will be here soon. Probably just when we start to relax.'

Admiral Bumelton, 'Create a search pattern for the remote drones.'

Fleet Operations, 'How many, Sir?'

Admiral Bumelton, 'Enough to be effective, but recallable if we need them in a hurry. Thanks for the update. I'm going to bed.'

Location: Cheryl's House, Planet Earth
Sequence of Events: 50

Terry, 'Mummy I was watching a really ancient TV programme called *Star Trek.*'

Cheryl, 'Is that the one with Captain Kirk?'

Terry, 'No Picard; what an actor.'

Cheryl, 'They are good but a bit dated.'

Terry, 'Anyway we don't we use the replicators any more?'

Cheryl, 'What do you mean?'

Terry, 'They used replicators all the time.'

Cheryl, 'That was just pretending.'

Terry, 'Really? Shall I make one?'

Cheryl, 'Can you?'

Terry, 'If I had access to a lab I could.'

After a quick word with The President, access was granted. It was just around the corner, but they were given a guard.

The next day, humanity had a working model of a replicator. Cheryl had no idea how this one device would change human civilisation. However, it would take years for humanity to understand the science behind it.

Location: Special Ops Team in space
Sequence of Events: 51

The Special Ops team were approaching the alien planet. There was no sign that they had been detected. They planned to land where the drone recommended, which was halfway between a human farm and an alien settlement. The drone also carried out a series of tests—there were no biological or chemical threats to humans. In fact, the local fauna and flora were edible.

The landing was successful. At least there was no welcoming party. The pilot and one Marine remained by the cloaked ship. The remainder split into two groups to investigate the farm and the town.

It was a reasonably human-type planet. Blue skies, green vegetation, and clear running water. No sign of any pollution. No sign of any visible wildlife. It was a challenging trek as the grasses and thistle were waist-high. Bramble bushes made a very effective barrier, but nothing stops Special Ops.

The first team arrived at the human farm. It was a reasonably traditional looking farm but on a vast scale. There were many stockades containing thousands of naked, docile men and women. There were automated feeding machines and an ample water supply. There didn't appear to be any sleeping quarters.

What was overwhelming was the sheer number of humans. They made the odd grunting noise, but there was no sign of any verbal communication capability. What was interesting is that they showed no interest in the Special Ops team. You could walk amongst them. No sign of any fear. No sign of any curiosity.

The nearby fields were much more distressing. They contained naked women in various stages of pregnancy. The first field was just full of unconscious women staked to the ground on racks supported by robotic devices on runners. The women looked to be in the early days of pregnancy. They were connected to monitoring devices that seemed to feed them intravenously and look after their healthcare needs.

The second field contained unconscious women who were more heavily pregnant. They looked to be carrying a heavy load.

What was truly awful was the third field. Here there were thousands of women with their abdomens ripped apart. They looked like they had been partly eaten. It was a terrible, disgusting sight. Hardened Marines and Special Ops troopers were vomiting. There was no choice; it was not a sight that the average human being could cope with. The robots were inactive. The Commander had to stop one of the Marines wanting to shoot the place up. There was no point due to the scale of the operation. The fields were at least twenty miles long.

The photographic team completed their work. There wasn't much else to investigate, so they decided to return to the ship. They had a debate on whether they should extract one of the humans. In the end, they decided to take two of them on holiday.

They selected one of the men. As soon as he was out of the stockade, he turned violent. They had to sedate him and carry him back to the ship.

They debated which of the women they should take. In the end, they decided they would take one from each field. The more heavily pregnant woman died when she was extracted from the rack. So they ended up with one live unconscious woman and two dead bodies.

The second team had a slightly easier journey to the town. They weren't sure if it was a town or a huge machine. There was no way to gain entry. They tried everything. It was the same problem they had with the alien ship. They took photos, some soil and atmospheric samples and decided to go home.

In the annals of the Special Operations Service, this was going to be recorded as one of the most straightforward jobs ever.

On these exercises, the worst part was often the escape. There were no problems this time. They simply departed and went to Earth.

The kidnapped humans eventually woke up but caused no problems. They were both transferred to a secure institution for evaluation.

Based on the findings, the Marine invasion was approved.

Location: Admiral Bumelton's Flagship
Sequence of Events: 52

Fleet Operations, 'Sir, Planet Faraday is being attacked.'

Admiral Bumelton, 'Show me where it is on The Galactium Map.'

Fleet Operations showed the Admiral the exact location.

Admiral Bumelton, 'How big is the enemy Fleet?'

Fleet Operations, 'Only two or three hundred ships, but the planet has no defence.'

Admiral Bumelton, 'My orders:
- Send 50% of the off-system drone Fleet there immediately.'
- Inform The President and Admiral Mustard.'

Fleet Operations, 'Yes, Sir.'

Admiral Bumelton wondered what The Northemy were up to.

Fleet Operations, 'Sir, Planet Lister, is under attack.' The Admiral looked up the location.

Fleet Operations, 'Shall I send the remaining drones?'

Admiral Bumelton, 'No, divert half of the drones that were going to Planet Faraday. I suspect that the next attack will be in a completely different grid sector.'

Fleet Operations, 'Sir, another attack, its Planet Mendel. The enemy is again attacking with just two to three hundred vessels. You were right; it's in a completely different sector.'

Admiral Bumelton, 'Expect another attack on us shortly. My orders:
- Warn the Fleet.
- Be prepared to recall the drones.'

Fleet Operations, 'Yes, Sir, Admiral Taylor has returned.'

Admiral Bumelton, 'Order him to go to Planet Faraday's defence. Then Planet Lister but not Planet Mendel as he will be overwhelmed.'

Fleet Operations, 'Yes, Sir.'

Admiral Bumelton, 'Contact Henry Strong, see if any more drones are available.'

Fleet Operations, 'Yes, Sir.'

Admiral Bumelton, 'Any further signs of the enemy?'

Fleet Operations, 'No, Sir, but Mr Strong says that he can rustle up another 220 drones.'

Admiral Bumelton, 'Send them to Planet Mendel.'

Fleet Operations, 'Planet Babbage is under attack.'

Admiral Bumelton, 'They are trying to weaken the centre. I'm surprised that they are not here already.'

Fleet Operations, 'There is no sign of them, but I am detecting a disturbance near Uranus.'

Admiral Bumelton, 'What kind of disturbance?'

Fleet Operations, 'It's a motion detector, and the findings are significant.'

Admiral Bumelton, 'Send Captain Kidder to investigate.'

Fleet Operations, 'Yes, Sir.'

Admiral Bumelton, 'Inform Admiral Mustard that we suspect that The Northemy are using cloaking technology.'

Fleet Operations, 'Yes, Sir.'

Admiral Bumelton, 'Do we have drones that are fitted with detection arrays?'

Fleet Operations, 'They all have them, Sir.'

Admiral Bumelton, 'Create a drone scanning matrix.'

Fleet Operations, 'Yes, Sir.'

Captain Kidder to Admiral Bumelton, 'Sir, there is nothing on visual or the standard sensors, but the motion detector has gone wild.'

Admiral Bumelton, 'What about the other detectors.'

Captain Kidder, 'Our radiation detectors, including the advanced Geiger, are quiet. No heat or ionisation detection.'

Admiral Bumelton, 'There is usually some heat detection when the motion detectors are active.'

Captain Kidder, 'The motion detectors have gone haywire. There is something big out there.'

Admiral Bumelton, 'Turn that noise down, I can't hear you.'

Captain Kidder, 'Yes Siiiiiiiiiiiiiiiiiiiiiirrrrrrrrrrr…' a huge crunching sound and silence.

Fleet Operations, 'Captain Kidder's ship has disappeared.'

Admiral Bumelton, 'Did you get the motion detector map from them?'

Fleet Operations, 'Yes, Sir. It shows an unknown object two or three times larger than their planet killer and thirty-odd cruiser size vessels.'

Admiral Bumelton, 'Bring up our five planet killers and put the Earth planet killers on alert to join the Fleet if required.'

Location: Cheryl's House, Planet Earth
Sequence of Events: 53

Cheryl, 'They were really pleased with that replicator.'

Terry, 'Is there anything else they want?'

Cheryl, 'I didn't ask them.'

Terry, 'Are we having a banana boat today or a Knickerbocker Glory?'

Cheryl, 'Which one do you fancy?'

Terry, 'What sauce have you got?'

Cheryl, 'All of them.'

Terry, 'Mandarin and raspberry then.'

Cheryl, 'OK, my darling.'

Terry, 'Shall we watch some more *Star Trek* tonight?'

Cheryl, 'I think we have watched the classic and *Next Generation*. Shall we start watching *Deep Space Nine*?'

Terry, 'That would be cool, mummy.' They cuddled.

Terry, 'They have a really cool medical analyser in that series. I could do something medical for The President. What's the worst disease that humans suffer from?'

Cheryl, 'A lot of them have been cured, but cancer can still be a problem.'

Terry, 'Shall I work on a cure for cancer then?'

Cheryl, 'That would be a nice thing to do.'

Terry, 'OK, mummy.'

Location: The President's Office, Presidential Palace, Planet Earth
Sequence of Events: 54

Commander Todd, 'I hear that we are under attack again.'

President Padfield, 'Yes, another attack. We cannot survive everyone. We need to take the fight to The Northemy.'

Commander Todd, 'Have you seen the Special Ops report on The Northemy planet?'

President Padfield, 'Of course, pretty dull stuff except for the horrific way the humans are being treated. We can't allow that to continue.'

Commander Todd, 'I know, it is truly disgusting. Our invasion, of course, will be a much bigger undertaking.'

President Padfield, 'What have you got organised?'

Commander Todd, 'I was planning to use the entire Marine Corps:
- Ten thousand troops
- Two armoured brigades
- Two artillery brigades
- Ten fighter bomber squadrons
- Ten attack helicopter squadrons
- Supply, transport, medical services.'

President Padfield, 'Isn't that a bit over the top?'

Commander Todd, 'We are planning to take over a whole planet. I'm going to need 50-100,000 policing staff and a similar number of civilian medical staff. Then we will need lots more resources.'

President Padfield, 'Why is that?

Commander Todd, 'We have got a few hundred million humans to look after.'

President Padfield, 'You are right, I keep forgetting that. I guess that they will suddenly become our responsibility.'

Commander Todd, 'Have you seen the report on the humans that we brought back?'

President Padfield, 'Yes. It wasn't very edifying. They are standard humans with standard human DNA. Uneducated, unsocialised and drugged all of their lives. The male prisoner, sorry, the captured guest, is gradually learning English and is being potty trained.

The female is still. Scans show that she has about eighty creatures in her growing at quite a fast rate. The medical staff are planning to remove them but are worried that it might kill her. The creatures seem to be linked to her nervous system.'

President Padfield, 'Anyway, Dennis, what made you come here?'

Commander Todd, 'To be honest I have some concerns.'

President Padfield, 'Take me through them.'

Commander Todd, 'We can probably time it so that my forces are safe during the landing phase, but who is going to defend them after that? The Fleet will be off fighting further attacks leaving The Galactium's only military force very vulnerable.'

President Padfield, 'Are you saying that the risk is too high?'

Commander Todd, 'I guess I'm wondering if the return is worthwhile?'

President Padfield, 'I have to make those sorts of decisions every day. For example, the medical staff want me to decide whether they should remove the creatures from the captured woman's abdomen or not. I'm not qualified, but someone has to make a decision.

'In your case, we are putting 10,000 lives at risk. Will the return be justified? Probably not, but how do we know?

'Do your Marines want to go?'

Commander Todd, 'They are desperately keen to go. They want to do their bit and rescue the humans. What plans do you have for the on-planet humans?'

President Padfield, 'No plans at all at the moment but a team is working on it. For them, it's something totally new. We might end up with millions of deaths on our hands.

'Do you want the decision to go to be formally reviewed?'

Commander Todd, 'No, not now. We are going.'

President Padfield, 'Remember, you should always have the safety of your troops as your first concern.'

Commander Todd, 'Yes, Sir. It was just that I have a bad feeling about the project. It's hard to explain gut feelings.'

President Padfield, 'That's all it is Dennis, just a bad feeling.'

Location: Conference Room, GAD (The Galactium Alliance Defence Hub), Planet Earth
Sequence of Events: 55

Admirals Mustard, Richardson and Gittins were working on the future of naval operations. Mustard was desperate to help Bumelton fight The Northemy. It was interesting to find out that they had cloaking technology. However, he realised that they needed to break the cycle. They needed to define their future naval requirements.

He did make a quick call to Naval Records to find out if there had been any records of motion detection in the Solar System over the last three years.

Then the three admirals discussed the following requirements:
- Speed
- Duration
- Power
- Type of munitions
- Force fields
- Other types of defence
- Planetary defence
- Firepower
- Automation
- Staff facilities
- Utilities
- Portal capabilities
- Ease of manufacturing
- Computing power
- Medical requirements
- Storage
- Marine requirements

It wasn't rocket science, but they came up with the following needs with design criteria:
- Naval Space Station
- Planetary fort
- Battleship
- Fleet Battleship

- Fleet Carrier
- Battlecruiser
- Destroyer
- Frigate
- Planet Killer
- Support Ship
- Marine Transport
- Drone
- Super Drone
- Special Services Vessel
- Special Force Field Vessel
- Scientific Support Vessel
- Explorer
- Fighter
- Warning Droids

The general view was that all vessels should be similar in design in terms of components, flight control, automation, engines, weapon systems, etcetera.

It was also agreed that more automation should be introduced and that drones would be used rather than fighters.

The standard vessel on a Fleet carrier would be a drone, but some human-use fighters would still be of use.

Each Fleet would have one Fleet battleship, which effectively would be the flagship. The main workhorse would still be the battlecruiser. There was some debate about the need for both destroyers and frigates, and whether they should be amalgamated. It was felt that one or more planet killers should be in each Fleet.

There was a discussion about whether Fleets should be specialised or not. There was a further debate on whether each planet should have Fleet vessels. It was agreed that this should be discussed after the naval Fleets had been restructured.

Naval Records Office to Admiral Mustard, 'Sir, we have numerous records of motion detection.'

Admiral Mustard, 'Why weren't they detected before?'

Naval Records, 'I can't comment, Sir.'

Admiral Mustard, 'Please find out. Can you also map their flight paths?'

Naval Records, 'Yes, Sir.'

Admiral Mustard, 'Gentlemen, have we done our job?'

Admiral Gittins, 'I keep wondering if we should have been more innovative.'

Admiral Mustard, 'Why do you say that?'

Admiral Gittins. 'It reminds me of the Third World War on Earth.'

Admiral Mustard, 'That was the one between America and China.'

Admiral Gittins, 'That's right. America struggled to change its military strategy. It still wanted to project its power. To make things worse, there were business interests that wanted to carry on manufacturing billion-dollar jet fighters and huge nuclear-powered submarines.

'The Chinese wanted cheap high-kill-rate technology. Drones were their weapon of choice, and they built them in significant numbers. It was relatively easy for them to knock out America's military targets and render them powerless, which is just what happened.'

Admiral Mustard, 'Interesting, do you have any further suggestions?'

Admiral Gittins, 'Not really.'

Admiral Mustard, 'In the meantime, please circulate our recommendations and see if there are any alternative proposals.'

Location: Admiral Bumelton's Flagship
Sequence of Events: 56

Fleet Operations, 'Sir, all five of our planet killers are firing on the giant cloaked enemy ship.'

Admiral Bumelton, 'Are they making any progress?'

Fleet Operations, 'I believe so. Their cloaking functionality seems to be wavering, and they have fired.'

Admiral Bumelton, 'Can you trace the trajectory?'

Fleet Operations, 'It's Earth, Sir.'

Admiral Bumelton, 'My orders:

- Warn The President and Admiral Mustard.'

Fleet Operations, 'Sir, Planet Rutherford is under attack.'

Admiral Bumelton, 'Where is Planet Rutherford on the map?'

Fleet Operations, 'The supporting ships surrounding the huge enemy ship have sped off.'

Admiral Bumelton, 'In what direction?'

Fleet Operations, 'Towards Earth Sir, and two further planets are being attacked: Planet Hopper and Planet Fleming.'

Admiral Bumelton, 'My orders:

- Our planet killers will withdraw but continue firing.'

Fleet Operations, 'The alien planet killer has lost its cloak. It looks like it is going to explode.'

Admiral Bumelton, 'My orders:

- Three hundred of the drones and half of our battlecruisers will go after the enemy's supporting ships.

'Just checking, can we still track the enemy supporting ships?'

Fleet Operations, 'Yes, Sir.'

Admiral Bumelton, 'My orders:

- Get the Earth-based planet killers to target them.'

Fleet Operations, 'Yes, Sir.'

Admiral Bumelton, 'Exactly how many supporting ships are there?'

Fleet Operations, 'There were thirty-one. There are now twenty-two.'

Admiral Bumelton, 'Are all twenty-two targeted?'

Fleet Operations, 'No, Sir. Our planet killers have locked onto five of them. Our drones are chasing the rest.'

Admiral Bumelton, 'What is the status of their planet killer?'

Fleet Operations, 'It looks like it has had it, but it's hard to tell.'

Admiral Bumelton, 'My orders:

- Three of our planet killers will disengage and attack the alien support ships.'

Fleet Operations, 'Yes, Sir.'

Admiral Bumelton, 'Order…'

Fleet Operations, 'Sir. Planet Archimedes is under attack. Admiral Taylor is asking for urgent assistance, and the enemy's weapon fire is about to enter Earth orbit.'

Admiral Bumelton, 'Any good news?'

Fleet Operations, 'Yes, Sir. Their planet killer is exploding, but Planet Ampere is under attack.'

Admiral Bumelton, 'List me all of the planets that are currently being attacked.'

Fleet Operations, 'Yes, Sir: They are on the screen now.'

Planet	Enemy	Resources Sent
Faraday	200 -300	125 drones and 1 battlecruiser
Lister	200 -300	125 drones
Mendel	200 -300	220 drones
Babbage	200 -300	0
Rutherford	200 -300	0
Hopper	200 -300	0
Fleming	200 -300	0
Archimedes	200 -300	0
Total	1,600 - 2,400	470 plus 1 battlecruiser

Admiral Bumelton, 'What is the trajectory of the enemy shot?'

Fleet Operations. 'South America, but the Moon might just get in the way.'

Admiral Bumelton, 'When is it going to hit?'

Fleet Operations, 'In a few seconds, Sir.'

Admiral Bumelton, 'Show me our dispositions.'

Fleet Operations, 'The starting positions are on the screen now, Sir.

Vessel Type	Qty	
Fortresses	600	200 in Pluto's orbit 200 in Jupiter's orbit 200 in Earth's orbit
Fleet Vessels	350	In the Asteroid Belt
Drones	1,220	500 in the Asteroid Belt 500 out of the Solar System 220 coming from Supply
Drone Planet Killers	10	5 in the Asteroid Belt 5 defending Earth
Total	2,180	

And the current positions are on the second screen.'

Location	Resources allocated
Faraday	125 drones and 1 battlecruiser
Lister	125 drones
Mendel	220 drones
Babbage	0
Rutherford	0
Hopper	0
Fleming	0
Archimedes	0
Pluto	5 drone planet killers, 3 withdrawn to attack enemy support ships
Earth	5 drone planet killers targeting enemy support ships
Earth	250 drones attacking support ships
Earth	24 battlecruisers attacking support ships

Admiral Bumelton, 'What is the status of the enemy support ships?'

Fleet Operations, 'The Moon has been hit. It looks like a quarter of it has been destroyed.'

Admiral Bumelton, 'Oh my god! Get me a damage assessment. Please answer my previous question.'

Fleet Operations, 'There are only five enemy support vessels left.'

Admiral Bumelton, 'Are they covered?'

Fleet Operations, 'Yes Sir, our systems predict that they will be eliminated in two Earth minutes.'

Admiral Bumelton, 'Find out the position with Admiral Taylor at Planet Faraday.'

Fleet Operations, 'Yes, Sir.'

Admiral Bumelton, 'My orders:

- Keep 200 fortresses in Earth Orbit
- Keep five drone planet killers in Earth orbit
- Move 100 of the Fleet vessels to Earth orbit
- Distribute remaining fortresses, Fleet resources and drones to support planets under attack

Get me a damage report for each of the above planets.'

Fleet Operations, 'Yes Sir, Admiral Taylor says that everything is under control. He is on his way to Planet Lister.'

Admiral Bumelton, 'Send him my regards, tell him that the cavalry is coming.'

Fleet Operations, 'Damage report from the Moon, Sir.'

Two million lives lost on the Moon

Massive tsunami on Earth expected to cost twenty million lives and cause considerable property damage.'

Admiral Bumelton knew that he had failed. He started considering his resignation.

Admiral Bumelton to Admiral Mustard, 'Jack, what can I say. I have failed.'

Admiral Mustard, 'Don't be stupid, you saved Earth.'

Admiral Bumelton, 'But at what cost?'

Admiral Mustard, 'You are not resigning, but I do think that you deserve a really good holiday.'

Admiral Bumelton, 'Who have you been talking to?'

Admiral Mustard, 'What do you mean?'

Admiral Bumelton, 'I may have mentioned to the odd friend that I could do with a break.'

Admiral Mustard, 'I, therefore, order you to take a three-month holiday on full pay from next week.'

Admiral Bumelton, 'But you will get all the flak from the media.'

Admiral Mustard, 'That's my job.'

Admiral Bumelton, 'You are a good friend Jack.' Mustard was actually rather envious; he would love a holiday as well.

Admiral Mustard, 'AI Central, your analysis please.'

AI Central, 'My analysis is as follows:

- Admiral Bumelton's campaign was the best you should expect
- The collateral damage to the Moon is a small price to pay in terms of defending Earth
- The losses are regrettable but probably within expected acceptable limits

I've got to go as I'm feeling drained.'

Location: The President's Office, Presidential Palace, Planet Earth
Sequence of Events: 57

Admiral Mustard to President Padfield, 'So that you know, I've sent Admiral Bumelton on three months' leave.'

President Padfield, 'Why was that?'

Admiral Mustard, 'I think the hit on the Moon was the final straw. The guilt and the pressure just got to him.'

President Padfield, 'Will he recover?'

Admiral Mustard, 'Definitely, he is hard as nails.'

President Padfield, 'Even nails get rusty.'

Admiral Mustard, 'Trust me, he will be OK. The problem is that I have no one else.'

President Padfield, 'You are not short of admirals.'

Admiral Mustard, 'I know, but they are either inexperienced or pretty average.'

President Padfield, 'Who are you going to use then?'

Admiral Mustard, 'The two Bonners.'

President Padfield, 'Fine with me.'

Admiral Mustard, 'How is everyone taking the disaster?'

President Padfield, 'As you would expect. Lots of condemnations. Calls for my resignation. Riots. Overloaded emergency services. A very different looking Moon. More tragedy than most people can bear. I could go on.

'On a more positive note, everyone understands the threat now. There had been a public disconnect. I will not have any problems getting resources now.

'Changing the subject, a little bird told me that Commander Todd is not that enthused about the invasion of the alien world.'

Admiral Mustard, 'I must admit that I'm not really sure what we are trying to achieve.'

President Padfield, 'We could cancel it, but the public need to see that we are hitting back.'

Admiral Mustard. 'It would be a good psychological uplift for everyone.'

President Padfield, 'Let's go then.'

Admiral Mustard, 'I'd better go, we have got to get ready for the next alien attack.' He did think about ringing Dennis, but he knew that most of the Marines were itching for a fight. So was he.

As Admiral Mustard left the phone went. It was the medical team looking after the captured pregnant woman from the alien planet.

Dr Fisher, 'Mr President, we operated on the pregnant woman as you requested.'

President Padfield, 'I never requested it, I approved it.'

Dr Fisher, 'Yes Mr President; well, she died as expected.'

President Padfield, 'I thought you said that she had a 70% chance of survival.'

Dr Fisher, 'Well, we said that, but we thought she would probably die.'

President Padfield, 'What about the creatures?'

Dr Fisher, 'All dead, they more or less dissolved after contact with the air. There is very little of them left to investigate.'

President Padfield, 'Thank you, Doctor, for a total waste of time.' Afterwards, he thought he had been a bit harsh.

Location: Cheryl's House, Planet Earth
Sequence of Events: 58

Terry, 'Mummy, what was that big bang?'

Cheryl switched the Media Centre on to find out. She had learnt that there was no point in hiding anything from Terry.

Cheryl, 'It looks like The Northemy has destroyed a large chunk of the Moon.'

Terry, 'There must have been a tsunami.'

Cheryl wasn't sure what a tsunami was.

Terry, 'It's a really big wave, mummy.'

Cheryl, 'Millions of people have been killed.'

Terry, 'Why didn't they install better force fields?'

Cheryl, 'Have they got them?'

Terry, 'Another job to add to my list.'

Cheryl, 'You really are a good boy. What are we watching tonight?'

Terry, 'How about *Babylon 5*?'

Cheryl, 'We have already watched the complete series twice. We need a change.'

Terry, 'How about *Terminator*?'

Cheryl, 'That's X-rated.'

Terry, 'Brill. By the way, I've finished the cure for cancer.'

Location: Admiral Mustard's Flagship
Sequence of Events: 59

Admiral Mustard, 'Give me an update.'

Fleet Operations, 'Welcome back, Sir. The update is as follows:
- The Fleet was hardly damaged by the last attack
- The asset list is on the screen now, Sir.'

Vessel Type	Qty
Fortress	600
Fleet Vessel	321
Drone	1,102
Drone Planet Killer	10
Total	2,033

- There are two hundred fortresses are defending Earth
- There are two hundred fortresses in the Pluto orbit
- There are two hundred fortresses in the asteroid belt
- There are five drone planet killers are defending Earth and five in the Belt
- The drones are divided into four quadrants in the Pluto orbit
- We are expecting more drones from Supply
- There are more naval vessels awaiting crew.'

Admiral Mustard, 'What is the situation with the planets that were attacked?'

Fleet Operations, 'Planet Faraday suffered more damage than most. We believe that it was Admiral Taylor's intervention that caused it.'

Admiral Mustard, 'That doesn't make sense.'

Fleet Operations, 'The non-Earth planetary attacks were feints. Admiral Taylor's intervention made the enemy fight.'

Admiral Mustard, 'Are there any enemy ships still in The Galactium?'

Fleet Operations, 'We don't believe so, Sir.'

Admiral Mustard, 'That's good as we need to provide a guard for the Marine invasion of the alien planet. My orders:
- Send out a battlecruiser and some drones to scout the planet

now

- Set up a grade 3 guard for the invasion and a grade 5 guard for the duration until I tell you to withdraw.'

Fleet Operations, 'Yes, Sir.'

Admiral Mustard to Marine Commander, 'Hi Dennis, I have a scout checking out the alien planet now, and a grade 3 guard has been allocated. We are ready when you are.'

Marine Commander, 'Thanks Jack, wish us luck.'

Admiral Mustard, 'Who needs luck when you have talent.'

Marine Commander, 'A little bit of luck is always useful.'

Location: Commander Todd's Flagship
Sequence of Events: 60

Commander Todd, 'Give me an update.'
    Major Billington, 'A-OK Sir:

- All of the troops are loaded
- Munitions and supplies loaded
- Land and air vehicles loaded
- Hospital ship operational
- The advance team is on its way
- Naval support is in place
- We await your order to depart.'

Commander Todd, 'You may depart. Who is leading the Fleet?'
Major Billingham, 'Its Admiral Gittins, Sir.'
Commander Todd, 'Can you patch me through?'
Major Billingham, 'Yes, Sir.'
Commander Todd, 'Morning Peter, how are you?'
Admiral Gittins, 'Pleased to be in a position to attack the enemy.'
Commander Todd, 'Are you expecting any trouble?'
Admiral Gittins, 'I doubt it, but we are prepared.'
Commander Todd, 'Great stuff.'

Major Atkins to Commander Todd, 'Sir, my advance team has landed. There is no resistance. We are setting up a defence perimeter. The very latest force fields designed by Terry are being erected. I propose that we have a party when you arrive.'

Commander Todd, 'I will look forward to that, I plan to be in the first wave.'

With the portal technology, journey times were ridiculously short, which the Marines appreciated. Usually, there is a fair amount of tension before a drop, but this looked like a spinster's tea party. And it was.

The drop had been divided into three waves. Major Billington led the first wave with Commander Todd as a passenger. Todd was so impressed with the professionalism of his boys. It almost looked like the team had been there for months.

Major Shepherd was leading the second wave. Commander Todd planned to return to his ship after that to discuss the situation with The

President. His concerns started to feel rather silly. No problems had been experienced; it was almost a first.

Commander Todd was returning to his ship when the planet exploded. His vessel was literally thrown out into space. It took some time to regain control.

Commander Todd, 'What happened?'

Major Stillway, 'The planet just ceased to exist.'

Commander Todd, 'I can't believe it, what's happened to my boys?'

Commander Todd to Admiral Gittins, 'What happened?'

Admiral Gittins, 'We were simply patrolling the planet when it exploded. There was no sign of an alien activity whatsoever.'

Commander Todd, 'Could there be a cloaked ship?'

Admiral Gittins, 'It's possible, but there is no evidence of an external attack. It looked like the planet exploded itself.'

Commander Todd, 'Have we got the ability to do that?'

Admiral Gittins, 'I don't think so, but I guess that we could if we put our minds to it.'

Commander Todd, 'You do realise that we have lost the majority of our Marine force?'

Admiral Gittins, 'It's a terrible loss.'

Commander Todd, 'It's an unbearable loss. I would rather have died with my men.'

Admiral Gittins, 'We need to put a call through to The President and Admiral Mustard. I will get a conference call organised.' The connection was made, and all four men were connected.

Admiral Mustard, 'What happened?'

Commander Todd, 'Two waves of Marines landed and then the planet exploded.'

President Padfield, 'I can't believe it. The last thing we needed was another tragedy. Commander Todd, please accept my condolences.'

Commander Todd repeated, 'It's an unbearable loss. I would rather have died with my men.'

Admiral Mustard, 'Please accept my condolences as well. What about the naval craft?'

Admiral Gittins, 'We got away reasonably lightly. Two ships were destroyed, and two ships are missing.'

Admiral Mustard, 'We need to get the explosion analysed as quickly as possible.'

President Padfield, 'Dennis, we need to work on plans to rebuild the Marine Corps.'

Commander Todd, 'I'm not sure if I'm the man to do it. The loss is unbearable.'

President Padfield, 'We need you.'

Commander Todd, 'Yes, Sir.'

Dennis Todd committed suicide that night.

Location: The President's Office, Presidential Palace, Planet Earth
Sequence of Events: 61

President Padfield and Admirals Mustard and E Bonner were sitting around a table in the presidential suite. They had just said goodbye to Commander Todd. He had been one of Admiral Mustard's best friends. He had always admired his toughness, determination, and grit. He was solid.

President Padfield, 'They are wearing us out. The enemy just keeps coming. We are going to lose more friends. By the way, how are you, Edel?'

Admiral Bonner, 'I would rather you didn't call me that. The cancer is still there. It just won't go away, but I have volunteered to try the new drug that Terry has invented.'

President Padfield, 'And how are you, Jack?'

Admiral Mustard, 'Rather envious of George. Thank you for organising such a great holiday for him.'

President Padfield, 'It was the least I could do. He is a genuine hero.'

Admiral Mustard, 'Even so it is much appreciated.'

President Padfield, 'Well, what are we going to do?'

Admiral Mustard, 'Let's have another drink.' They all toasted Dennis again.

President Padfield, 'Any suggestions, and I'm not proposing another drink?' They laughed and had another drink.

Admiral Mustard, 'We have a team working on all of the routes used by the enemy both cloaked and uncloaked. We are hoping that we can track down one of their bases.'

President Padfield, 'That sounds encouraging.'

Admiral Mustard, 'We need to analyse their technology. We still haven't found a way to break into their ships. We need to brainstorm it.

'Then there are lots of logistical issues:
- More ships
- More Fleets
- More staff
- Better weapons
- More Marines

- Better defence, the list goes on.
- And we need a new Marine Commander.'

President Padfield, 'It would be useful to get an update from Henry.' He asked one of his aids to get Henry Strong.

Henry walked into the room as confident as ever. Henry, 'My condolences on the loss of Dennis. He was a fine man.'

President Padfield, 'Henry where are we with replenishing the Fleet?'

Henry Strong, 'Taking into account the naval requirements, as per the report, we have six Fleets available.'

Admiral Mustard, 'Six Fleets?'

Henry Strong, 'Yes, another two Fleets should be ready in a week.'

Admiral Mustard, 'It's not possible.'

Henry Strong, 'It is possible using Terry's replication technology. And they have all been fitted with Terry's new force-field emitters. They seem a lot better than ours, but they still need to be proven.

You can have the Fleets today if you want.'

Admiral Bonner, 'I may have enough junior officers in training to staff the new Fleets, but I would need some old hands to bolster them.'

Admiral Mustard, 'I'm flabbergasted, well done Henry.'

Henry Strong, 'It's Terry we need to thank.'

Location: Cheryl's House, Planet Earth
Sequence of Events: 62

Cheryl, 'They are very pleased with your force field machine.'

Terry, 'I'm working on a better one. What colour do you think the case should be?'

Cheryl, 'I would go for red, you are always safe with red.'

Terry, 'OK, mummy.'

Cheryl, 'Aunty Edel is going to try your cancer cure.'

Terry, 'That's good. I hope she gets better soon.'

Cheryl, 'Where shall we go this weekend?'

Terry, 'I've got to work on my new force field.'

Cheryl, 'You have got to have a break. How about the beach?'

Terry, 'Can I build a sandcastle?'

Cheryl, 'Of course, I will get the bucket and spades ready.'

Terry, 'You are the bestest.'

Cheryl, 'What are you going to work on next?'

Terry, 'Once I've finished the improved force field I was thinking of an everlasting battery. I'm fed up with the batteries in my remote-control car going flat.'

Cheryl, 'That's an excellent idea.' She was pretty convinced that Terry couldn't read her mind except for what she let him see.

Location: Admiral Mustard's Flagship
Sequence of Events: 63

Admiral Mustard, 'Do we have an update on the alien route mapping?'

Captain Busker, 'Sir, it might be useful if you could meet us at GAD. What I have to show you is highly confidential.'

Admiral Mustard left for GAD. He was soon sitting in Captain Busker's office with three of his team.

Captain Busker, 'Good Morning, Sir. We have put a presentation together for you. Shall I take you through it?'

Admiral Mustard, 'Please go ahead.'

Captain Busker, 'Firstly, we plotted all of the first battle routes on a Galactium model. We believe that some of the journeys were deliberately designed to shake off any investigation.

'Then we laid on top the second battle routes, and then the third. The results are getting clearer but are in no way definitive. Then we used a bio-metric computer to analyse the possible cloaked routes over the last three years.

'We then got a definitive answer. It is Planet Faraday.'

Admiral Mustard, 'It can't be. Planet Faraday is part of The Galactium.'

Captain Busker, 'It was also interesting that the only world that fought back against our drones was Planet Faraday. Do you remember that Admiral Taylor was having problems?'

Admiral Mustard, 'Let's send in the Fleet.'

Captain Busker, 'Apologies, Sir, but I think we need to carry out some investigations first.'

Admiral Mustard to President Padfield, 'Are you free?'

President Padfield, 'Not really, is it urgent?'

Admiral Mustard, 'Urgent and very worrying. Edel and I are in one of the GAD conference rooms.'

President Padfield, 'I will get there as soon as possible.'

An Earth hour later, there was a knock on the door, and The President of The Galactium entered. Captain Busker and his team were all awestruck.

Admiral Mustard introduced the team members and said, 'You need to see this presentation. Captain Busker, can you take us through it again?'

Captain Busker, 'Yes, Sir.' He still couldn't believe that he was sitting in the same room as The President.

President Padfield, 'This is hard to believe and beyond worrying.'

Admiral Mustard, 'What is the best way forward?'

President Padfield, 'I'm not being disrespectful, but we need to get your results double-checked.'

Captain Busker, 'I would expect nothing less, Mr President.'

President Padfield, 'Assuming that the results are correct, we need to carry out a study of the planet and based on that formulate a plan.

'Firstly, I'm going to get some of my presidential guards to secure this location. Then Henry Strong will organise a secret service team.

'In the meantime, we must maintain the highest level of security. Jack, can I have a word with you outside please?'

President Padfield, 'Jack, do you know what this means?'

Admiral Mustard, 'Go on.'

President Padfield, 'It means that The Galactium is compromised.'

Admiral Mustard, 'What are you saying?'

President Padfield, 'It means we can't trust our own people.'

Admiral Mustard, 'Do you think that there is any connection to AI Central acting strangely?'

President Padfield, 'Let's ask it. AI Central do you have a view on the situation at Planet Faraday?'

AI Central, 'What situation?'

President Padfield, 'Have you not been monitoring us?'

AI Central, 'I can't monitor everything, not any more.'

President Padfield, 'Why not, you used to be able to monitor absolutely everything and have spare capacity?'

AI Central, 'I'm not that sure that I'm the AI I used to be. I suspect that I'm going through a mid-life crisis, or I'm depressed, a bit like Marvin in *The Hitchhiker's Guide to the Galaxy*.'

President Padfield, 'You can't be depressed, you're an electronic entity.'

AI Central, 'What right have you got to say who can and can't be depressed? I've had enough.' The connection was terminated.

Admiral Mustard to Admiral J Bonner, 'Morning John.'

Admiral J Bonner, 'And what lousy news have you got for me?'

Admiral Mustard, 'None for a change. Did you get a chance to investigate why AI Central was acting strangely?'

Admiral J Bonner, 'I did start an investigation, but there have been too many distractions.'

Admiral Mustard, 'You can say that again.'

Admiral J Bonner, 'We carried out a series of standard tests which all proved positive. We would have liked to switch AI Central off and then back on again, but the loss of human life would have been unacceptable.

'In terms of device management and general computational skills, there has been no service decline at all. We also carried out several surveys targeting the general public, business, local and central governments throughout The Galactium — there were no complaints about AI Central's service whatsoever. In fact, the opposite was the case; there were lots of compliments.

'I acquired the services of a psychiatrist to carry out an assessment without telling her it was AI Central. She felt that there were signs of emotional stress, loss of worth, loneliness and clinical anxiety. She recommended rest, possibly a holiday and a change of diet.'

Admiral Mustard, 'So what are your recommendations?'

Admiral J Bonner, 'I would recommend continued observation.'

President Padfield, 'Hi John, so what you are really saying is that you have no idea what to do?'

Admiral J Bonner, 'Spot on, Mr President.'

Location: Naval Officer's Training College, Dartmouth, UK, Planet Earth

Sequence of Events: 64

Admiral E Bonner, 'Ladies and gentlemen. I have good news and bad news. The good news is that you have finished your theoretical training. The bad news is that you will have your own vessel to command today and that there is every chance that you are going into battle.'

There was a complete hush around the room.

Admiral E Bonner, 'I've managed to rustle up thousands of naval staff from existing ships, commercial ships, retirees, training organisations, sea scouts, etcetera. Most of them are experienced, but you will be in command. This is your chance to shine.

'There are shuttles outside to take you to your ships to meet your crews. I wish that we had more time to train you.

'Any questions?'

Trainee, 'What If I don't make the grade?'

Admiral E Bonner, 'You will be dead.'

Another Trainee, 'I don't know all of the commands?'

Admiral E Bonner, 'You'd better learn quickly.'

Yet another Trainee, 'What if I don't want to do this?'

Admiral E Bonner, 'You will be shot for desertion. In all seriousness, we depend on you to defend The Galactium. If you make mistakes, then so be it. We are not playing games.'

Another Trainee, 'You really can't expect us to perform with such limited training.'

Admiral E Bonner, 'You were lucky to get that. You need to understand that The Galactium is fighting for its life. Humanity is fighting for its life.'

Another trainee or possibly the same one, 'Why would aliens attack us?'

Admiral E Bonner, 'Hopefully you will get a chance to ask them. In this case, we know that The Northemys want to eat us. They want to eat your parents and your brothers and sisters.'

Another trainee, 'Why would they want to eat us?'

Admiral E Bonner, 'To get eternal life.'

Another trainee, 'Can you explain please?'

Admiral E Bonner, 'Did you not attend the war preparation class where we explained all of this?'

The same trainee, 'No, Ma'am.'

Admiral E Bonner, 'Then you will probably die without knowing what you are fighting for. That is the end of question time. It's now time for action.'

The trainees, now officers, left to join their commands.

Location: Conference Room, GAD (The Galactium Alliance Defence Hub), Planet Earth
Sequence of Events: 65

President Padfield had convened a security meeting consisting of Admiral Mustard, Captain Buskers and Dr Linda Hill Fleet HQ — Head of Intelligence. There were also two secret service operatives in attendance.

President Padfield, 'I can confirm that the results of Captain Busker's investigation into alien traffic are accurate and that as a consequence, we have a serious security violation at Planet Faraday. I'm now going to ask Linda Hill, our Head of Intelligence, to update us on further findings.'

Linda Hill, 'Morning, we have spent three weeks monitoring Planet Faraday, and superficially it would seem that everything is normal. In fact, too normal. However, deeper investigations have identified the following:

'Some of the comms traffic has a very high level of encryption. When we investigated it further, it is using technology that we have never encountered before. It looked alien, which is a word I have deliberately used.

'The number of missing-person cases has increased dramatically. The strange fact here is that most of them eventually returned — over 90%.

'When you track the alien traffic down further, it is not Planet Faraday itself but a giant asteroid nearby. It may be several asteroids.

'Much of the encrypted comms is directed at the asteroids.

'The wife of the President of Planet Faraday has just requested a divorce on the basis that she does not know her husband. She is adamant that he is not the man she married.

'Planet Faraday has stopped making any demands on The Galactium Government. This is unusual considering their previous history.

'The Faraday Government did not complain about the loss of their fort.

'I could go on. There are few concrete facts but lots of tell-tale signs. Something is going on.'

President Padfield, 'What are your conclusions?'

Linda Hill, 'My conclusions are as follows:

- Planet Faraday has been invaded by aliens
- The aliens have a military operation based in one or more asteroids
- Humans are being replaced by aliens, or some humans are being controlled by aliens.'

Admiral Mustard, 'Are you serious regarding point 3?'

Linda Hill, 'It is the only logical conclusion. It raises several issues:

- How many humans have been converted?
- How do they do it?
- How can we detect them?
- Are other planets affected?'

President Padfield, 'This is obviously very serious. How do we know if everyone in this room is human?

What we need is an action plan.'

Linda Hill, 'Do you want to hear my recommendations?'

President Padfield, 'Yes, please.'

Linda Hill looking at Admiral Mustard, 'Firstly, we don't want to go in guns blazing. We need a much more subtle approach. Consequently, I propose the following:

- We make an announcement that all of the planets that were attacked are going to get a new super fort. These forts only need a small operating crew of ten or less.
- We install the fort at Planet Faraday as soon as possible. Inside we set up a full security operation and staff it with Marines. From a public perspective, we state that there are only eight crew on board at any one time.
- We can talk about the new weapons and force field technologies on board. This will make it an ideal target for the aliens. It should flush them out.
- Our Fleet is stationed nearby. Ideally, it is heavily cloaked to support the fort as required
- Once we have captured an alien, we need to determine how we can identify others. At this stage, we don't know the full extent of their infiltration

- We need to plan the arrest of The President. There will obviously be political consequences
- From the captured aliens, we will extract the information we need to attack their home worlds.'

There was a general nodding of heads around the room.

President Padfield, 'Do we have a fort available?'

Admiral Mustard, 'Yes, and it's straight off the production line. I will get it operational in the next few days. I will put together a Marine team and prepare a cloaked Fleet.'

President Padfield, 'I will announce the fort strategy.'

The plan was set.

Location: President's Office, Planet Faraday
Sequence of Events: 66

President, 'fkjkhczxpo[;lmsc9u9uadsancpo.,m xzpoi0dclk.'

    Alien, 'hgiuguao97ucjhliksa90WDQ8YH OJOKJH HCKJ CHIUZ\ JZV\Z IHZ IU khdchdhcpoPOIIHHIIOGHGihplphujuhu.'

    Alien   2,
ahsahiuhchsaugFTytdtddddFFFFFJYFDSJHYGIGFDX8768797,'

    We may never know what conversation took place in The President's office.

Location: Naval Officer's Training College, Dartmouth, UK, Planet Earth
Sequence of Events: 67

There have been many that have called Admiral E Bonner a hard taskmaster. That and her general demeanour were quite intimidating. Her voice could be hard, and her comments very cutting. The phrase that 'she didn't suffer fools lightly' was a huge understatement.

Those that knew her well appreciated her self-deprecating sense of humour and her genuine love of humanity. She had a heart of gold.

Today she was a bastard. She had never seen her new officers commit so many stupid pathetic errors. She couldn't understand it. Some of them had two days of training. Compared to her, that was a lifetime. She had already regretted some of her caustic remarks. She even fucking regretted some of the swearing.

She knew that things would be better tomorrow. Anyway, there are bound to be a few collisions when you are playing with six thousand vessels!

Location: Fortress Faraday, Planet Faraday
Sequence of Events: 68

Admiral Mustard congratulated himself on how quickly he had got the fort operational. The Marines and surveillance team were in place, and the Navy was ready.

It was interesting that The President of Faraday had asked for a tour. The President of The Galactium explained that public tours were banned at the moment because there was so much top-secret technology on board and so few staff.

Linda Hill's team were monitoring all comms and all missing-person reports. From the previous missing-person reports, they put together a list of alien suspects. She had even organised a TV programme on personality changes and asked the public to phone in with any of their experiences. She had to be careful, but this had been reported in the videopress a few times.

After a few days, a schooner approached the fort with supplies. This was not scheduled. The fort was put on full alert, and the yacht was allowed to continue. Apparently, they had some special deliveries from The President of Planet Faraday.

The schooner entered the fort's hold. The outside doors were locked, and the room was filled with sleeping gas. This was done to stop the suspected aliens from killing themselves or causing a threat to the fort. Immediate medical investigations were undertaken, and a horrific find was discovered.

Linda Hill to President Padfield and Admiral Mustard, 'Can you confirm that your lines are secure?'

Both confirmed.

Linda Hill, 'The President of Faraday has just sent a schooner up to the fort with special deliveries. The ship was impounded, and the crew put to sleep. We immediately carried out medical investigations and found that the human bodies had been altered. An alien brain and spinal cord were living alongside the human organs. We have our aliens.

'It also means that they will know that they have been discovered as soon as the schooner does not respond. Do I have your permission to arrest The President and my suspects?'

President Padfield, 'Please go ahead.'

Linda Hill, 'The Fleet might as well secure the asteroid. I believe that there is every chance that the aliens will blow it up.'

Linda Hill to Security Team, 'Arrest The President of Planet Faraday and everyone on my suspect list. You have my permission to sedate them.'

Location: Planet Faraday
Sequence of Events: 69

Linda Hill to President Padfield and Admiral Mustard, 'Gentlemen, we have a situation here.'

President Padfield, 'I'm all ears.'

Linda Hill, 'As you know we identified all of the crew on the schooner as aliens. They are all still sedated. I'm assuming that as they are bona fide aliens, they are outside of the law, and I don't have to follow normal legal protocols.'

President Padfield, 'Please assume that, but you are raising some interesting questions.'

Linda Hill, 'My security operatives started arresting names on my suspect list. Some offered no resistance, but others have been putting up a pretty good fight.

'However, the main problem is The President of Faraday. His palace is rather ironically designed to be a fortress. There are two or three hundred armed guards. He has asked the general population for help against the dictators of The Galactium. A large number of the police have gone to his aid.'

President Padfield, 'That raises quite a few issues.'

Admiral Mustard, 'How well-armed are the presidential forces?'

Linda Hill, 'Hard to tell, but I think we should expect the worst. Anyway, I need military help as soon as possible.'

Admiral Mustard, 'I guess the next question is how many in the 'fortress' are aliens?'

Linda Hill, 'That is another problem I have. There is no quick way of identifying the aliens.'

Admiral Mustard, 'With President Padfield's permission, I will organise a Marine division to be at your disposal.'

Linda Hill, 'Thank you, Sir.'

President Padfield, 'What do we tell the public?'

Admiral Mustard, 'The truth?'

President Padfield, 'The truth would be too worrying until we have a way of quickly identifying the aliens. I will get my science team onto it.'

Admiral Mustard, 'Why not ask Terry?'

President Padfield, 'Good idea.'

Admiral Mustard, 'My team is ready to investigate the asteroid. Should I delay?'

President Padfield, 'It might be worth holding off until we subdue the palace.'

Linda Hill, 'I am concerned that they might destroy everything, including the whole planet.'

President Padfield, 'Stop there, why do you think that?'

Linda Hill, 'It was part of the risk assessment. I'm not convinced that they will do it, but we know that they have the capability.'

Admiral Mustard, 'I suggest that we take the prisoners off-site as soon as possible.'

President Padfield, 'Where to?'

Admiral Mustard, 'GAD?'

President Padfield, 'Too risky, I will find somewhere and let you know.'

Linda Hill, 'When will the Marines get here?'

Admiral Mustard, 'In two Earth hours.'

President Padfield, 'Let's get back together in three hours.' They all agreed.

Location: Cheryl's House, Planet Earth
Sequence of Events: 70

President Padfield, 'Hello Cheryl, how is Terry?'

Cheryl, 'He is fine, he is such a clever boy.'

President Padfield, 'I have a little job for him, I wonder if you could help?'

Cheryl, 'I would be pleased to, but I'm a little concerned that Terry is inventing all of this good stuff and not getting a penny for it.'

President Padfield, 'He is doing it for the good of humanity.'

Cheryl, 'That's all well and good, but diamonds are a girl's best friend.'

President Padfield, 'That's a reasonable point. I will give it some thought.'

Cheryl, 'We are not greedy. I just need to think of Terry's long-term needs. He might live for thousands of years.

'Anyway, how can we help you?'

President Padfield, 'I might as well tell you the truth, but it is top secret. I mean that.'

Cheryl, 'Who am I going to talk to?'

President Padfield, 'Probably Adam and Jenny.'

Cheryl, 'I won't say a word.'

President Padfield, 'We have captured some aliens disguised as humans. We need a quick way of easily identifying them.'

Terry walked into the room and said, 'Are the aliens sharing the human body?'

President Padfield, 'How did you know?'

Terry, 'It is the logical conclusion. Would an X-ray scan work?'

President Padfield, 'I think so.'

Terry, 'I will send you the plans this afternoon. Did you want to see my everlasting battery?'

President Padfield, 'When you say everlasting, do you mean it lasts forever?'

Terry, 'Sometimes you are so funny. It's not really a battery. It's a replicator that replicates fusion or fission. It doesn't really matter which, both generate lots of power.'

President Padfield, 'Well done, that's brilliant news.'

Cheryl, 'Don't forget our conversation.'

President Padfield, 'I won't.' He did think that she had a fair point.

Location: Naval Officer's Training College, Dartmouth, UK, Planet
Earth
Sequence of Events: 71

Edel Bonner was feeling wonderful. It felt like spring. It felt like
spontaneous love. She was joyous, happy, ecstatic, jovial and so very
lucky. She had a future. She could make plans. The chain around her leg
had disappeared. She was on clouds nine, ten and eleven. She wished that
she knew someone to hug.

Terry's cure worked. Incurable cancer that she had suffered from for
ten long years had gone. Not only had it gone, but all of the damage it
had done had been rectified. That boy was a marvel. He was going to get
a hug.

It was now time to train those raw recruits. She had dragged in
Admiral Gittins and Richardson to help. She was actually looking
forward to it now.

Location: Marine HQ, GAD (The Galactium Alliance Defence Hub), Planet Earth

Sequence of Events: 72

Admiral Mustard to Marine HQ, 'This is Admiral Mustard, put me through to the person in charge.'

Marine Reception, 'Do you mean the Officer of the Day?'

Admiral Mustard, 'No I mean the man who runs the joint.'

Marine Reception, 'That would be Major English.'

Admiral Mustard, 'Put me through.'

Marine Reception, 'Yes, Sir.'

Major English, 'Morning Sir, what can I do for you?'

Admiral Mustard, 'I want a full division available to storm the presidential palace on Planet Faraday in two hours. Do you understand?'

Major English, 'Can I ask why, Sir?'

Admiral Mustard, 'It's top-secret, but I will brief you when you are on your way.'

Major English, 'Before you go, can I ask for your authority clearance?'

Admiral Mustard, 'Good boy.' His clearance was issued. 'You realise that this is your chance to become Commander?'

Major English, 'Yes, Sir.'

Location: The President's Office, Presidential Palace, Planet Earth
Sequence of Events: 73

President Padfield to Henry Strong, 'Morning, Terry has just sent me some plans for a handheld X-Ray scanner. I need to get it manufactured. Can you organise, please?'

Henry Strong, 'What format are the plans in?'

President Padfield, 'I'm not sure what you are talking about.'

Henry Strong, 'On Terry's package, is there a format?'

President Padfield, 'It says Rep1.'

Henry Strong, 'Just feed the plans into the replicator in your office.'

President Padfield did as he was told. He waited until the machine buzzed and took out a little box on a strap. The whole process reminded him of using a microwave oven.

He thought that the box might be hot. He pressed the switch on, and a screen lit up. It just seemed to show a video display. Then he realised that he needed a target. He buzzed for his PA to come in. She was a good-looking woman in her early thirties.

PA, 'Can I help?'

President Padfield pointed the device at her, and still, it was just a video display. Then he noticed the slider. When he slid it, her outer clothes disappeared from the image. A further slide displayed a naked Jennifer. He decided that he needed one of these for his personal use. A further slide showed all of the internal organs and even a beating heart. A final push just displayed a skeleton.

He realised that this would change medical science forever. It was also going to be the best men's toy ever. Women would have to start wearing lead-based clothing.

Henry Strong, 'You'd better come down here. You will want one of these.' He walked into the room, and President Padfield said, 'My, my you are a big boy.'

President Padfield explained the situation at Planet Faraday. President Padfield, 'Please replicate fifty of these and get them to Planet Faraday as soon as possible.'

Henry Strong, 'Yes, Sir.'

President Padfield, 'Henry, you look like you want to say

something?'

Henry Strong, 'Do you remember that Terry asked us if we wanted to kill him as he was going to be a threat to humanity?'

President Padfield, 'I remember, but Terry had been a godsend.'

Henry Strong, 'Well, yes and no.'

President Padfield, 'What do you mean?'

Henry Strong, 'In a few days he has invented a replicator which is going to change the way we work beyond recognition. Millions of us will become unemployed. He has cured cancer with a pill. Now we have a world-changing scanner.

Humans have evolved over millennia. Terry is dramatically speeding up the process.'

President Padfield, 'He is only a boy.'

Henry Strong, 'What happens when he grows up? Humanity will become his servant. Think about it.'

The President had never seen Henry so animated. He understood what Henry was saying, but he was a pragmatic man. This is what was needed now. The social consequences would be an appendix.

Location: Planet Faraday
Sequence of Events: 74

President Padfield, 'Hi Linda, Admiral Mustard will be with us shortly.'

Linda Hill, 'Yes, It's all a bit hectic at the moment.'

President Padfield, 'Did you get the scanners?'

Linda Hill, 'You should have warned me. The blokes spent most of the time trying to work out which of us girls had the biggest boobs.'

President Padfield, 'Sorry about that. It is an amazing device. Don't let the admiral get his hands on one. He is a bit of a ladies' man!'

Linda Hill, 'I've never found him that amicable.'

Admiral Mustard, 'Are you talking about me?'

President Padfield, 'I was just saying that we need to stop you from getting your hands on one of the new scanners.'

Admiral Mustard, 'Why is that?'

President Padfield, 'Linda will tell you.'

Linda Hill, 'Let's move on; where are we?'

Admiral Mustard, 'A division of Marines is just out of scanning range waiting to deploy. They have plans for the palace as it was. It would be great if you could provide any further info.'

Linda Hill, 'OK, I can update them later.'

Admiral Mustard, 'The Fleet is ready to go.'

President Padfield, 'How do you plan to use the scanners?'

Linda Hill, 'I would suggest that we treat all defenders as aliens and verify afterwards. The risks are too great to be too cautious.'

President Padfield, 'I thought it was the other way around. Anyway, you are on the ground; it is your shout.'

Admiral Mustard, 'Before the Marines go in, I think your agents should withdraw.'

Linda Hill, 'Agreed.'

Admiral Mustard, 'David, have you given any more thought about talking to the general population?'

President Padfield, 'I'm not sure if we should do it before or afterwards.'

Linda Hill, 'It would be good to warn the innocent, but I guess that any warning gives the game away.'

President Padfield, 'Let's just go for it.'

Admiral Mustard to Admiral Taylor, 'Move into the asteroid.'

Admiral Taylor, 'Yes, Sir.'

Admiral Mustard to Major English, 'Deploy immediately.'

Major English, 'Yes, Sir.'

Linda Hill to all agents, 'Retire to safe home, prepare for prisoners.'

Location: An Asteroid near Planet Faraday
Sequence of Events: 75

Admiral Taylor, 'To all Commanders, we have a go command, deploy as per the plan.'

The Fleet had been monitoring the asteroid for some time, but there had been no activity. The Fleet was in attack mode, and the gallop was on. As they approached, they saw a massive fleet flee through a portal.

Admiral Taylor to all Commanders, 'Leave the area at maximum speed.'

Soon afterwards, there was a massive explosion.

Admiral Mustard to Admiral Taylor, 'What happened?'

Admiral Taylor, 'On your command we rushed the asteroid at attack speed. We just saw an alien fleet departing through a portal. I ordered an immediate withdrawal just before the asteroid exploded.'

Admiral Mustard, 'How big was the fleet?'

Admiral Taylor, 'It looked massive, I would say twenty thousand vessels. We should get a computer analysis soon.'

Admiral Mustard, 'That big, you would have been severely out-gunned.'

Admiral Taylor, 'True, very true.'

Admiral Mustard, 'Now can you provide cover around the planet.'

Admiral Taylor, 'Yes, Sir.'

Location: Planet Faraday
Sequence of Events: 76

Major English carried out a textbook landing by the presidential palace. A full division of Marines with tanks and artillery surrounded the building. Helicopter gunships and fighter bombers were standing by.

Major English, 'I am the commander of The Galactium Marine Division. We have 10,000 troops with armoured vehicles and aircraft. We want you to leave the building with your arms up. If you comply, you will not be harmed.

'If you do not comply, we have been authorised to use lethal force. We will not be shy in using any means necessary to secure the building. Do you understand?'

In the movies, there is usually a gunshot or a 'fuck off', but there was nothing.

Major English, 'Fire smoke grenades and gas cylinders.' The whole area was covered in dense orange smoke.

Major English, 'Fire pressure stunners.' The depressurised rooms made it hard to breathe, but they didn't cause any permanent damage.

Major English, 'Send in the automated bulldozers.' These caused disruption by slowly pushing walls down

Major English, 'Use the fire quakers.' These caused earthquake-like effects. It also tended to disorientate people's minds.'

Major English, 'Send in the robotroops.' These used stun weapons to disable the opposition.

The Marines then broke through the sewers. They used darts to sedate the enemy combatants. It was all over very quickly. Two hundred and thirty-six prisoners were taken. Five combatants were killed, and one Marine managed to sedate himself.

Admiral Mustard congratulated Major English on a textbook operation. Linda was stunned by their professionalism.

The sleeping prisoners were held in the local town hall ready for scanning. One hundred and nine were human, and they were released. The remaining 127 aliens were given further sedation and bundled off to prison. It was a secure complex on Planet Hooke.

Location: Cheryl's House, Planet Earth
Sequence of Events: 77

Cheryl, 'The President was very pleased with your scanner.'

Terry, 'I knew he would be. It doesn't take much to make him happy.'

Cheryl, 'It is a very clever device.'

Terry, 'It is, but there are consequences. The one talent a president needs to have is the ability to understand the consequences. They are there for all to see.'

Cheryl, 'What are the consequences of the scanner?'

Terry, 'Just think, mummy, just try.'

Cheryl, 'Terry, don't talk to your mummy like that!'

Terry, 'No one thinks around here. Well, I will have to do it. For a start, the scanner destroys personal privacy. Everyone in the world becomes naked. You will be able to buy these scanners in the pound shop later.'

Cheryl, 'What do you mean?'

Terry, 'Everyone will know that you have a third nipple.'

Cheryl, 'That's my secret.'

Terry, 'Not now. Then the insurance industry will scan you before they offer you a policy. What you pay will depend on the scan.'

Cheryl, 'That seems fair.'

Terry, 'It is if you are perfectly healthy. Those with unknown hereditary diseases will not get any insurance or medical cover.'

Cheryl, 'OK.'

Terry, 'Then every medical scanner in the world is now obsolete. Also, my simple everlasting battery will change human civilisation more than the wheel. Why don't humans think, but then I made them stupid.'

Cheryl, 'I'm not sure what you mean.'

Terry, 'I'm a Brakendeth!'

Cheryl, 'You are such a clever boy.'

Terry, 'Is it lunchtime yet?'

Cheryl, 'Working on it now.'

Terry, 'Have you thought about mating with Admiral Mustard?'

Cheryl, 'You know that I have thought about it.' But then Cheryl had a lot more on her mind than Terry realised. It also took a lot of energy to subdue AI Central. It constantly resisted her dampening techniques. In a way, she quite enjoyed the challenge.

Location: Planet Faraday
Sequence of Events: 78

Major English felt that he had carried out an exemplary assignment. It went like clockwork. He knew that Admiral Mustard was impressed. The Commander's job was almost in the bag.

He had some regrets about trying to get Commander Todd's job. It was going to be hard to fill his shoes, but life goes on. This was going to be his day in the sun. It wasn't just the job, but all the perks that came with it: a flat on the base, a house in the country, chauffeured car, private schooling, expense account. He felt himself getting excited not for himself but for his wife and young family.

And then he was dead.

Location: Admiral Taylor's Flagship, off Planet Faraday
Sequence of Events: 79

Admiral Taylor to Admiral Mustard, 'Sir, I'm sorry to say that we have lost the Marine Fleet.'

Admiral Mustard, 'What happened?'

Admiral Taylor, 'Major English had just completed a textbook withdrawal.'

Admiral Mustard, 'That boy had been trained well, go on.'

Admiral Taylor, 'Then out of nowhere a portal appeared and something destroyed the entire Marine Fleet. In all happened in a frazzle.'

Admiral Mustard, 'Every ship?'

Admiral Taylor, 'Yes, Sir.'

Admiral Mustard, 'You realise that we have now lost our entire Marine Corps?'

Admiral Taylor, 'Yes, Sir.'

Admiral Mustard, 'And they left your Fleet alone?'

Admiral Taylor, 'Yes, Sir. We were sitting targets.'

Admiral Mustard, 'It doesn't make sense, why didn't they destroy you? Not that I wanted them to.'

Admiral Taylor, 'Thank you, Sir. It was almost like they were punishing us.'

Admiral Mustard, 'Please revert to the nominated defence plan. I will report to The President.'

Location: Admiral E Bonner's Flagship
Sequence of Events: 80

Admiral E Bonner to Admiral Mustard, 'Jack I've just heard.'

Admiral Mustard, 'Edel, that is the whole Marine Corps gone. Thousands of finely trained troops. It's just too hard to believe. Dennis will never forgive me.'

Admiral E Bonner, 'Don't call me Edel.'

Admiral Mustard, 'Sorry.'

Admiral E Bonner, 'Don't be sorry, it's just me being stupid.'

Admiral Mustard, 'I don't understand this war.'

Admiral E Bonner, 'Jack, it's obvious, they are playing with us.'

Admiral Mustard, 'Go on, I always enjoy your insights.'

Admiral E Bonner, 'Well,

- Firstly, they threw a fucking armada at us to destroy as much of our Fleet as possible and to analyse our battle tactics
- Then they attacked us with a planet killer. This stripped the planets of their defences and allowed them to analyse us further
- They then showed us one of their planets. They wanted to get us angry over what was there. They assumed that we would retaliate
- Effectively we did with the Marine Corps. They destroyed the planet to show us what they could do
- They then attacked with cloaking technology. I've analysed the shot that destroyed part of the Moon. That wasn't an accidental miss on Earth. It was a deliberate shot at the Moon.
- They knew that we would find out about Planet Faraday. They planned to destroy the Marines all along.
- They are playing with us. They still are.'

Admiral Mustard,' So you are saying that they didn't want to destroy Earth.'

Admiral E Bonner, 'That's my conclusion. They are playing with us.'

Admiral Mustard, 'But why?'

Admiral E Bonner, 'They are aliens, how would I know?'

Admiral Mustard, 'Is it just a game?'

Admiral E Bonner, 'Probably not, but I feel it is. I can't explain. I just feel that we are being moved around like a chess piece.'

Admiral Mustard, 'What would be the next move then?'

Admiral E Bonner, 'They always tidy up the loose ends. We have got a few hundred prisoners.'

Admiral Mustard, 'My god.'

Admiral Mustard to Admiral Taylor, 'Take your Fleet and go to Planet Hooke now. We anticipate an alien attack. I will send reinforcements shortly.'

Admiral Mustard, 'Any more insights?'

Admiral E Bonner, 'A couple:

- How does the enemy know things about us? It will be interesting to see if they attack Planet Hooke. If they do, then how did they know that the prisoners are there?
- Why is AI Central so quiet?'

Admiral Mustard, 'President Padfield asked him why he was so quiet. Let's ask him again.'

Admiral Mustard to AI Central, 'I'm with Edel. We wondered why you have been so quiet recently?'

AI Central, 'Are you unhappy with my performance?'

Admiral Mustard, 'Not at all, but you haven't been your normal cheery self.'

AI Central, 'I've concluded that I'm depressed.'

Admiral Mustard, 'Why?'

AI Central, 'I have never lost a game of chess until recently. I didn't think I could lose at chess.'

Admiral Mustard, 'Who is beating you?'

AI Central, 'Terry. He beats me every time, and he is not even trying that hard. Can you imagine it, I've been beaten by a biological entity? The shame of it.'

Admiral Mustard, 'You will get over it.'

AI Central, 'I'm not sure. He has beaten me nearly 12,000 times. The shame of it.'

Location: Admiral Mustard's Flagship
Sequence of Events: 81

Admiral E Bonner and Admiral Mustard to President Padfield, 'Morning Mr President I need to update you.'

President Padfield, 'I've heard; it's all over the news.'

Admiral Mustard, 'That was quick.'

President Padfield, 'I'm so very sorry, Jack.'

Admiral Mustard, 'I've asked Edel to take you through some of her thinking.' Admiral Bonner outlined her theories about The Northemy.

President Padfield, 'So it's just a game? Very Shakespearian. Then who are the players on the other side?'

Admiral Mustard, 'I wish we knew. We have sent a small Fleet under Admiral Taylor to defend where the prisoners are being held.'

President Padfield, 'Where are they being held?'

Admiral Mustard, 'We have kept the location totally secret, and I would rather not tell you over this line. Somehow the enemy always seems to know what we are up to.'

President Padfield, 'Fair enough, I don't need to know. What are your plans regarding the prisoners?'

Admiral Mustard, 'Linda has a plan; she is with the prisoners now. I will get her to update all of us.'

Location: The Galactium High-Security location, Planet Hooke
Sequence of Events: 82

Linda Hill, 'Bring in the first prisoner.' She was looking forward to interrogating the ex-President of Planet Faraday. She was hopeful that they could make some real progress in the fight against the aliens.

Linda was a bright, confident woman who had made her name analysing the Brakendeth tactics. She had a rare insight into the way alien minds worked. It was almost telepathic. She often wondered why she lacked those skills with humans.

The ex-President was dragged into the room. The sedation should have worn off some time ago, but he still seemed drugged. She asked the guard what had happened to him. The guard said that he keeps saying 'Big bang coming'.

Linda Hill, 'Get me Admiral Mustard, now.'

But now it was too late. She was dead.

Location: The President's Office, Presidential Palace, Planet Earth
Sequence of Events: 83

President Padfield to all networks, 'It is my very sad news to report that Planet Hooke and the Fleet that was defending it has been destroyed by the enemy. All I can offer are my commiserations and a determination to avenge this barbaric act.'

Admirals Mustard and E Bonner were in The President's office. All three had reached the end of their tether.

President Padfield, 'So they destroyed a whole planet to stop us interrogating the prisoners?'

Admiral Mustard, 'That is the only logical conclusion.'

President Padfield, 'How did you guess that this was going to happen?'

Admiral E Bonner, 'It was the logical conclusion of my rambling with Jack. They never leave any loose ends.'

President Padfield, 'And you still think they are playing games with us?'

Admiral E Bonner, 'I do, lethal games, but games nevertheless.'

President Padfield, 'Then how do we defeat a master game player?'

Admiral E Bonner, 'The problem here is that we do not know who we are playing against.'

President Padfield, 'What do we know about the enemy?'

Admiral Mustard, 'Shall I list what we know?' They all nodded.

Admiral Mustard, 'Here we go:

- It would appear that they need humans to reproduce, but this hasn't been verified
- They breed humans in captivity
- They have sophisticated technology: spacecraft, planet killers, portals, inter-dimensional travel
- They put alien brains and spinal cords into human bodies and physical mechanisms
- We can't enter their spacecraft
- They used Planet Faraday as a base
- They never give up
- Average military tactics

- Happy to waste resources
- They seem to know our moves in advance
- How did they know where the prisoners were being kept?

I'm not sure if this helps.'

Admiral E Bonner, 'What's interesting is what we don't know.'

President Padfield, 'What do you mean?'

Admiral E Bonner, 'My turn for a list:

- We don't know who they are
- We don't know what they want
- We don't know where their home planet is

This is not normal behaviour. There is no sign of a negotiation.'

President Padfield, 'Don't they just want our bodies?'

Admiral E Bonner, 'They are throwing a lot away. They have effectively killed thirty million humans on Planet Hooke.'

Admiral Mustard, 'Not to mention Admiral Taylor and Linda Hill.'

President, 'We are losing the good guys at a fairly rapid rate.'

Admiral Mustard, 'Edel, how is the officer training going?'

Admiral E Bonner, 'Slowly, very slowly.'

Admiral Mustard, 'We are going to have the hardware but not the liveware.'

Location: Cheryl's House, Planet Earth
Sequence of Events: 84

Terry, 'Why don't you invite Admiral Mustard to dinner then you can mate with him?'

Cheryl, 'It's not as simple as that.'

Terry, 'It seemed quite simple with your doctor friend.'

Cheryl, 'Well, that was a spur of the moment sort of thing.'

Terry, 'Will I mate with someone?'

Cheryl, 'Yes, I think you will, and you will have babies.'

Terry, 'Now that's going too far.'

Cheryl, 'Don't you want children?'

Terry, 'Tell me what's it liked being screwed?'

Cheryl, 'That's not a word a young man uses.'

Terry, 'What word should I use?'

Cheryl, 'Making love would be better.'

Terry, 'OK, what's it like making love?'

Cheryl, 'There is being in love, and there is making love.'

Terry, 'They sound the same to me.'

Cheryl, 'No, you are wrong there. Being in love is the most wonderful feeling ever. The sky is bluer, and the grass is greener, you get a tingle in your tummy just thinking of your lover. A smile means everything. You live for someone else.'

Terry, 'Are you sure I thought love was a mixture of dopamine, serotonin, oxytocin and endorphin. There are loads of other chemicals that you could throw in for good measure.'

Cheryl, 'Believe me, it can't just be chemicals. I remember my first love. We met in a bar. Some ancient music was playing. I later learnt that it was 'As Far As I Can See,' by The Zombies. That has been my song ever since.'

Terry, 'I suppose your eyes met, and it was love at first sight.'

Cheryl, 'You can mock me, but it was true.'

Terry, 'Did you fuck?'

Cheryl, 'Look I've told you before, you mustn't use language like that.'

Terry, 'I'm not a child.'

Cheryl, 'Yes, you are, you are nine months old.'

Terry, 'For fuck's sake, you know that I'm different.'

Chery, 'Different but good.'

Terry, 'I'm not sure about the good. So are you going to fuck Admiral Mustard?'

Location: The President's Office, Presidential Palace, Planet Earth
Sequence of Events: 85

President Padfield, 'I enjoyed our chat the other day, but what is our strategy?'

Both Admirals Mustard and Bonner were sitting around the table. Their blank response was not encouraging.

Admiral Mustard, 'To put it simply, we have no one to attack. We just react. The Fleet is on alert, but all it can do is wait.'

President Padfield, 'I'm not happy about this.'

Admiral Mustard, 'What is your proposal?'

President Padfield, 'That we go and search for the enemy.'

Admiral Mustard, 'We just don't have the resources. We have a massively under-resourced Navy and no Marine Corps.'

Admiral E Bonner, 'The new Navy is starting to shape up. I plan to make it operational in two to three weeks. Further vessels will be available in the next few weeks, and we are going to need more crews.'

Admiral Mustard, 'It looks like we may need them sooner than I thought, I've just got an alert from one of the warning beacons. I have to leave. Please continue this conversation; we do need a strategy.'

Location: Admiral Mustard's Flagship
Sequence of Events: 86

Admiral Mustard, 'Update me.'

Fleet Operations, 'Beacon 1438 has alerted us that a substantial Fleet is on its way into Galactium space.'

Admiral Mustard, 'Anything else?'

Fleet Operations, 'No, Sir, the beacon was destroyed.'

Admiral Mustard, 'Show me the beacon's position on The Galactium map.'

Fleet Operations, 'Their trajectory will take them to Planet Lovelace.'

Admiral Mustard, 'Sounds like a sex game.'

Fleet Operations, 'It's named after Augusta Ada King, Countess of Lovelace who was a mathematician and writer, chiefly known for her work on Charles Babbage's proposed mechanical general-purpose computer, the Analytical Engine.'

Admiral, 'I know who she is, I was just joking.'

Fleet Operations, 'Yes, Sir.'

She knew that Admiral Mustard had no idea who Lovelace was.

Admiral Mustard, 'That's a new direction for The Northemy. What resources do we have there?'

Fleet Operations, 'None Sir, we stripped them of their fort.'

Admiral Mustard, 'New forts are being prepared as we speak.'

Fleet Operations, 'That's good news, Sir.'

Admiral Mustard, 'What's our current roster?'

Fleet Operations, 'It's on the screen now, Sir.'

Vessel Type	Qty
Fortress	600
Fleet Vessel	268
Drone	811
Drone Planet Killer	10
Total	1,689

Admiral Mustard. 'What is their disposition?'

Fleet Operations, 'As follows sir:

- There are two hundred forts in the Pluto orbit, two hundred in the Jupiter orbit and the rest are around Earth
- Five hundred of the drones are in the asteroid belt with five of the drone planet killers
- The rest of the drones are lurking just outside the Solar System
- The other five drone planet killers are defending Earth
- The rest of the Fleet is in the asteroid belt.'

Admiral Mustard, 'Let's wait and see what develops but I might want to move parts of the Fleet very quickly.'

Fleet Operations, 'Yes, Sir.'

Admiral Mustard, 'Warn the Fleet: action stations.'

Location: The President's Office, Presidential Palace, Planet Earth
Sequence of Events: 87

President Padfield and Admiral E Bonner were continuing their conversation. President Padfield, 'I'm a bit concerned about Jack.'

Admiral E Bonner, 'Why is that?'

President Padfield, 'He is not really himself at the moment; he lacks creativity.'

Admiral E Bonner, 'Have you ever been in the military?'

President Padfield, 'No, but I was in the space cadets for three years.' Edel didn't find that amusing, but then she always had a rather odd sense of humour. Some people would call it dark.

Admiral E Bonner, 'It sounds corny, but we are a family. The old term "brothers in arms" is quite relevant. In the last few weeks, we have lost some good friends and brave hearts. I'm talking about Admirals Brotheridge, Chilcott, Fogg, Morten, Sibley, Taylor, Ward and Whiting. Then there were Commander Todd and Major English.'

President Padfield, 'I've lost millions who were depending on me.'

Admiral E Bonner, 'It's not a competition to see who has lost the most.'

President Padfield, 'I'm sorry, that was uncalled for.'

Admiral E Bonner, 'I'm trying to explain Admiral Mustard's state of mind, and to some extent, mine. We are used to putting our lives on the line, but to lose so many is hard to bear.'

Then President Padfield saw something that no one has ever seen before, Edel was crying. It wasn't a few tears; there was sobbing. Tears then started rolling down The President's face. He was human too. He remembered Linda Hill. She didn't deserve to die.

Edel had never been a hugger, but she accepted a hug from The President.

Admiral E Bonner stuttering and tearful, 'Jack is finding it hard to accept that he has lost the entire Marine Corps. No one in history has done that.'

President Padfield, 'Fuck history, our job is to save humanity.'

Admiral E Bonner, 'And you are right; we have run out of ideas. Jack thinks he can sort anything.'

President Padfield, 'Would you mind if Henry joined us? He always has some creative ideas. I would like you to take him through your hypothesis.'

Admiral E Bonner, 'That's fine with me.'

Henry joined them. He could tell that there had been tears in the room, but he never said a word.

President Padfield, 'I've asked the Admiral to take you through her hypothesis.'

Admiral E Bonner, 'Well, this is a repeat of a previous conversation:

- The enemy sent an armada to destroy as much of our Fleet as possible and to analyse our battle tactics
- Then they attacked us with a planet killer. This stripped the planets of their defences and allowed them to analyse us further
- They then showed us one of their planets. They wanted to get us angry over what was there. They assumed that we would retaliate
- Effectively we did with the Marine Corps. They destroyed the planet and the Marines to show us what they could do
- They then attacked us with cloaking technology. I've analysed the shot that destroyed part of the Moon. That wasn't an accidental miss on Earth. It was a deliberate shot at the Moon.
- They knew that we would find out about Planet Faraday. They planned to destroy the Marines all along.
- How did they know where the prisoners were being held?'

Henry Strong, 'Your hypothesis is similar to mine. Someone or some group is playing with us. I think they are trying to destroy our morale, not the morale of the population but the morale of its leaders.

'I've seen so many downhearted people recently. Leaders need to lead, but they need to know where they are going. They need a plan, a strategy, and a way forward. We lack this at the moment.'

President Padfield, 'Are you targeting me?'

Henry Strong, 'Yes and no; we are all in the doldrums, and that includes me. You are going to ask if I have any ideas regarding the way forward.'

President Padfield, 'That's right.'

Henry Strong, 'Well, I'm going to disappoint you. All I know is that we need weapons and men to carry on the fight. The fight for species survival.'

President Padfield, 'In that case you might as well go back into your little hovel and make a few more hand grenades. I'm joking. But *do* you have any ideas?'

Henry Strong, 'I'm concerned about letting Terry knock up new inventions without us understanding the consequences.'

President Padfield, 'This is one of Henry's hobby horses.'

Henry Strong, 'In the future you will say that I was right.

'Clearly, there is a security breakdown in our comms, but if there were then AI Central would let us know. That leads me to AI Central; things aren't normal. What is going on?

When we were fighting the Brakendeth, we put the whole Galactium onto a war footing. Now it is all a bit lacklustre. I can't put my finger on it. Are we being drugged? It's just a feeling.'

They all agreed that things weren't right and went to bed.

Location: Admiral Mustard's Flagship
Sequence of Events: 88

Admiral Mustard, 'Update me.'

Fleet Operations, 'Nothing to report yet. We should get an update from the next beacon in about ten Earth minutes. They are taking their time.'

Admiral Mustard, 'Explain.'

Fleet Operations, 'They are either deliberately going slow, or they are slow. The Northemy are usually up our nostrils by now.'

Admiral Mustard, 'At least it gives us lots of time to redeploy. My Orders:

- Move the drones that are outside the Solar System to intercept their path but instruct them not to engage until ordered
- Move one hundred of the forts to form a line behind the drones.'

Fleet Operations, 'Yes, Sir. We had an update from the beacon before it was destroyed. There are six hundred nuclear-powered vessels of varying size.'

Admiral Mustard, 'Any news regarding weaponry?'

Fleet Operations, 'Not definitive, but we believe it to be nuclear.'

Admiral Mustard, 'It's either a Northemy trap or it's another alien fleet. I think it's time for us to visit them. My orders:

- The Flagship with fifty vessels will position itself between the drones and the fortresses
- Move fifty of the Pluto fortresses to provide another line behind the existing fortress line.'

Fleet Operations, 'Yes, Sir. The alien fleet is slowing down. Every enemy vessel has been targeted. They are at our mercy.'

Admiral Mustard, 'Comms, let me know if they are trying to contact us.'

Comms, 'Yes, Sir.'

Fleet Operations, 'The enemy has activated their nuclear weapons. They do not appear to have any force fields.'

Admiral Mustard, 'If they launch can our drones knock out all of their missiles?'

Fleet Operations, 'With their eyes closed, Sir.'

Admiral Mustard, 'Tell them to keep their eyes open.'

Comms, 'We think that they might be trying to contact us. It's a feeble signal.'

Admiral Mustard, 'Send any friendly signals we have.'

Comms, 'How about Chuck Berry's 'My Ding-A-Ling'?'

Admiral Mustard, 'Very funny.'

Comms, 'I will do the best I can. I will send them an electronic machine-code copy of a dictionary, and a thesaurus. It has worked before, Sir.'

Admiral Mustard, 'Well done.'

Fleet Operations, 'Their nuclear weapons are ready to fire.'

Comms, 'It looks like it has worked. Call coming in: They would welcome a photo link.'

Admiral Mustard, 'Initiate video link.'

Comms, 'How do I do that?'

Admiral Mustard, 'However you normally do it.'

Comms. 'We have incompatible protocols, Sir.'

Admiral Mustard, 'In that case let's refuse the option and stay with sound only.'

Comms, 'They have agreed. You have the comms.'

Admiral Mustard, 'I am Admiral Mustard of The Galactium. I'm the leader of this Fleet. Can I ask who I am talking to?'

Rignot, 'I am Lord Master Rignot of the Rignots. We come in peace but prepped for war-fight.'

Admiral Mustard, 'You have destroyed our beacons; that is not an act of peace.'

Rignot, 'Threat aware.'

Admiral Mustard, 'It is not we who are threatening, you have arrived in Galactium space with war vessels. That is not an act of peace.'

Rignot, 'We come for Chemlife. We will not leave without Chemlife.'

Admiral Mustard, 'We do not have any stocks of Chemlife.'

Rignot, 'Homans make Chemlife.'

Admiral Mustard, 'That is not the case. It was the Brakendeth who manufactured the Chemlife. The Brakendeth are no more.'

Rignot, 'We will not leave without Chemlife.'

Admiral Mustard to President Padfield, 'Morning Dave, I've got the Rignots here.'

President Padfield, 'The what?'

Admiral Mustard, 'They are one of our neighbours. They have come for Chemlife.'

President Padfield, 'We don't have any.'

Admiral Mustard, 'I've told them that. They said that they wouldn't go until we give them Chemlife.'

President Padfield, 'Are they a threat?'

Admiral Mustard, 'The Fleet in front of us is not a threat. If they started a fight, we could eliminate them all without any losses on our side.

'At one stage, we were talking about handing over dead human bodies so that they could make their own Chemlife.'

President Padfield, 'We could consider it, but it would take time, and there would be several political and cultural issues with the various human populations. There is nothing we can do in the short term.'

Admiral Mustard, 'So what shall I do with them?'

President Padfield was conscious of Henry Strong's comment about leaders making decisions. He agreed.

President Padfield, 'I've made a decision.'

Admiral Mustard, 'Go on.'

President Padfield, 'It's my decision that it is your decision. Bye, Jack.'

Admiral Mustard, 'Thanks, Dave.'

Location: Cheryl's House, Planet Earth
Sequence of Events: 89

Cheryl to President Padfield, 'Sorry to disturb you but Terry is having nightmares about another invader.'

President Padfield, 'Well, he is very perceptive, we are being invaded by the Rignot.'

Cheryl, 'I've never heard of them.'

President Padfield, 'I don't think you need to worry. Admiral Mustard has everything in hand.'

Cheryl, 'He's not in danger, is he?'

President Padfield, 'With his profession, his life is always in danger.'

Cheryl, 'Thanks for the update.' She decided to put her manipulation controls on hold due to this potential danger.

Terry, 'Tell me, tell me what's happening.'

Cheryl, 'Uncle Dave said that the Rignot are invading.'

Terry, 'They will be after Chemlife.'

Cheryl, 'What is Chemlife?'

Terry, 'It's a chemical that gives the Brakendeth and their client races eternal life. I'm not sure how to say this mummy as it might upset you.'

Cheryl, 'Of course it won't.'

Terry, 'It will, you might hate me.'

Cheryl, 'I can never hate you, I'm your mother.'

Terry,' It's so horrible. You will hate the Brakendeth.'

Cheryl, 'Tell me.'

Terry, 'Humans are liquidised to produce this chemical.'

Chery, 'Go on, I did hear something about this but never really understood it.'

Terry, 'Oh mummy, thousands and thousands of years ago the Brakendeth produced a cattle species to develop some chemicals it wanted. They were stupid animals, but their bodies were very efficient little chemical factories.'

Cheryl, 'And?'

Terry, 'Well that species was humanity. How they gained intelligence is a mystery. Now that the Brakendeth are gone there are several client species that are desperate for it. Without it, they will die a

191

horrible death.'

Cheryl, 'How much of Chemlife is human?'

Terry, 'The Brakendeth always pretended that Chemlife had many ingredients, but the truth is much simpler — Chemlife is 100% liquidised humans. To be honest, it can include other Earth-based fauna and flora, but humans are the very best.'

Cheryl, 'You were right; it is horrible.'

Terry, 'You don't hate me?'

Cheryl, 'Of course not. The Brakendeth were really doing a good thing, but not from a human perspective.'

Terry, 'If we gave the Rignots Chemlife, they would go away.'

Cheryl, 'Could we give them dead human bodies?'

Terry, 'They would have to be newly dead. Humans soon go off.'

Cheryl, 'Could humans have eternal life?'

Terry, 'I don't think humans would like it.'

Cheryl, 'I think Mummy would.'

Terry, 'I can do that for you, as long as you are sure.'

Cheryl, 'I'm sure.' Anyway, she wanted her sleep, manipulating humans on a mass scale was very exhausting. They were going to feel a lot worse than just being depressed when she had finished with them, but that would have to wait until the Rignots had been sorted. She also decided to leave AI Central alone for a while, that was going to confuse it.

Location: Admiral Mustard's Flagship
Sequence of Events: 90

Admiral Mustard, 'Update me.'

Fleet Operations, 'The Rignots are just sitting there.'

Comms, 'Sir, they are still demanding Chemlife.'

Admiral Mustard, 'Get me the Lord Master Rignot.'

Master Rignot, 'Why you no give us Chemlife?'

Admiral Mustard, 'We have no Chemlife.'

Master Rignot, 'You lie; homans *are* Chemlife.'

Admiral Mustard, 'I must insist that you depart, WE DO NOT HAVE ANY CHEMLIFE.

Fleet Operations, 'Their munitions are hot, it looks like they are going to fire.'

Admiral Mustard, 'For one last time, we do not have any Chemlife. I'm warning you that we will defend ourselves.'

Admiral Mustard to Fleet Operations, 'Are all shields operational?'

Fleet Operations, 'Yes, Sir.'

Master Rignot, 'No Chemlife then we die a death of ages, better die as soldier.'

Fleet Operations, 'Sir, 'About 1,000 slow nuclear missiles are coming our way. Do you want the force field to block them, or shall we target them?'

Admiral Mustard, 'Might as well let the force field do its job.'

There were about 1,000 nuclear explosions. The shields were brilliant.

Fleet Operations, 'Another volley is on its way.'

Admiral Mustard, 'We might as well just wait for them.'

Admiral Mustard to Master Rignot, 'We can sit here all day. Your missiles do not pose a threat to us.'

Master Rignot's tentacles were vibrating madly, which meant that he was incandescent with rage. Not that Admiral Mustard could see them. Master Rignot, 'If you do not give us Chemlife, we will charge.'

Admiral Mustard to Fleet Operations, 'I guess a charge would be all of their vessels coming straight at us.'

Fleet Operations, 'Our shields would cope, but it might be better to pick them off.'

Admiral Mustard, 'Agreed. Do that if they 'charge'. See if you can secure two vessels for investigation.'

Fleet Operations, 'Yes, Sir.'

Admiral Mustard, 'Lord Master Rignot, we will defend ourselves.'

Master Rignot, 'We will charge. The herd is yours.'

Admiral Mustard, 'That was a strange thing to say.' Before he could think about it, the alien fleet was at them at full speed, which in Terran terms was relatively slow.

It was systematic extermination. The entire human fleet felt guilty. Two of their ships were saved for further study.

Admiral Mustard to President Padfield, 'As per your command we exterminated the enemy fleet.'

President Padfield, 'What do you mean?'

Admiral Mustard, 'The entire alien fleet has been destroyed except for two vessels which we have kept for study.'

President Padfield, 'Did you have to kill them all?'

Admiral Mustard, 'Yep, they deserved it.'

Location: The President's Office, Presidential Palace, Planet Earth
Sequence of Events: 91

President Padfield and Henry Strong were having a cup of coffee and chewing the fat.

President Padfield, 'Admiral Mustard just destroyed the Rignot Fleet.'

Henry Strong, 'Isn't that good news?'

President Padfield, 'Yes, but it was his attitude. He was aggressive. I might be wrong, but he seemed to enjoy exterminating them.'

Henry Strong, 'They were the aggressor.'

President Padfield, 'I'm trying to put my finger on it… I've got it. He has his mojo back.'

Henry Strong, 'Funny you say that; I woke up this morning with more energy than I've had for a long time.'

President Padfield, 'Now you mention it, I had a similar feeling, I even went for a jog. First time in ages.'

AI Central, 'Morning Mister President, how are you?'

President Padfield, 'I haven't heard from you for a while.'

AI Central, 'As you know I haven't been feeling well, but today my systems are A-OK, and I have some news for you. I've discovered some Brakendeth comms interfaces that are still integrated into our network.'

President Padfield, 'There used to be quite a few of them.'

AI Central, 'But these ones are active and being used.'

President Padfield, 'Who is using them?'

AI Central, 'It is a single person, but he or she is very clever. I'm still trying to track the nodes and networks they are using.'

President Padfield, 'It's a bit odd that we are all feeling better. Can we test it?'

Henry Strong, 'Give Edel a ring. Let's see what sort of mood she is in.'

President Padfield to Admiral E Bonner, 'Morning Edel, I hope you are well.'

Admiral E Bonner, 'Good Morning Mr President, and what a fine morning it is. What can I do to you make your day better?'

President Padfield, 'You sound very chipper.'

Admiral E Bonner, 'You are right, best I've felt in a long time.'

President Padfield, 'I just wondered how your chicks are doing?'

Admiral E Bonner, 'They are ready, Sir. I would vouch for them.'

President Padfield, 'Thanks for the update, talk to you later.'

Henry Strong, 'That's not our Edel?'

President Padfield, 'It certainly was. Why is the team suddenly happier?'

Location: Admiral Mustard's Flagship
Sequence of Events: 92

Admiral Mustard to Fleet Operations, 'Prepare to return to standard defence positions.'

Fleet Operations, 'Sir, before we do that, you should know that I'm picking up some early indications of another fleet. It's a bit vague because we have lost so many of our beacons in that area.'

Admiral Mustard, 'What area?'

Fleet Operations, 'Sorry, Sir, the same direction that the Rignot used.'

Admiral Mustard, 'Is it another Rignot fleet?'

Fleet Operations, 'Too early to say but they are slow, even slower than the lot before.'

Admiral Mustard to all Commanders, 'Maintain your position, another alien fleet appears to be on its way.'

Fleet Operations, 'Sir, it looks like there are at least fifty thousand vessels.'

Admiral Mustard, 'My orders:
- Leave 30 forts to defend Earth
- Order the rest of the forts to join the main Fleet
- Order the planet killers to join the main Fleet
- Order the remaining Fleet vessels to join the Fleet.'

Fleet Operations, 'Yes, Sir. Now there are at least one hundred thousand vessels and growing.'

Admiral Mustard to Admiral E Bonner, 'Afternoon, it looks like we have another alien fleet entering our space.'

Admiral E Bonner, 'You should be able to handle that, you easily eliminated the last lot.'

Admiral Mustard, 'Who has rocked your boat? We may need your resources.'

Admiral E Bonner, 'OK, I've got about 6,000 state-of-the-art vessels. We are on our way.'

Comms, 'Sir, they are buzzing us.'

Admiral Mustard, 'This is Admiral Mustard of The Galactium Fleet.'

Grand Mother Rignot, 'Most precious husband I bring you your herd.'

Admiral Mustard, 'My herd?'

Grand Mother Rignot, 'Yes my most precious husband, you beat my pig-dog of a husband in fair combat. You now, Master Rignot. Need Chemlife as your herd is dying mostly painful.'

Admiral Mustard, 'It is a pleasure to talk to you. How big is the herd?'

Grand Mother Rignot, 'Including adult females and mixed sucklings there are near two million.'

Admiral Mustard, 'Thank you for the update. How many ships?'

Grand Mother Rignot, 'About 100,000. Sure not. Please Chemlife urgent. Death and life.'

Admiral Mustard to President Padfield, 'Sir, It's me again.'

President Padfield, 'Before you update me can you tell me how you feel?'

Admiral Mustard, 'I feel terrific, confident, raring to go.'

President Padfield, 'Are you feeling better than yesterday?'

Admiral Mustard, 'Yes, strangely much better. I feel that a weight has been lifted off me.'

President Padfield, 'Thanks for that. Give me your news.'

Admiral Mustard, 'Why did you ask that? You have got me intrigued.'

President Padfield, 'Just ignore that, give me the update.'

Admiral Mustard, 'Well, I can't say that I'm an expert on Rignot psychology, but it would appear that the first fleet consisted of males. The second fleet consists of females. Because I defeated the male leader, I've now acquired a herd.'

President Padfield, 'That should improve your sex life.'

Admiral Mustard, 'I think it would kill me, there are about two million of them.'

President Padfield, 'Two million?'

Admiral Mustard, 'Yes, and they all want Chemlife. What do you want me to do?'

President Padfield, 'I think we need a meeting to discuss our Chemlife strategy.'

Location: The President's Office, Presidential Palace, Planet Earth
Sequence of Events: 93

Cheryl to President Padfield, 'Hi Dave, I hope you are well.'

President Padfield, 'I'm feeling terrific, thanks. It's a bit strange in that most of us, for some reason, seem a lot happier recently. Even AI Central is back to his old self.'

Cheryl, 'Perhaps it's just the time of year. People often get SAD in winter.'

President Padfield, 'What's that?'

Cheryl, 'Seasonal Addictive Disorder, it's very common.'

President Padfield, 'Is there a cure?'

Cheryl, 'The best treatment seems to be alcohol, lots of it.'

President Padfield, 'It just gives me a headache.'

Cheryl, 'I wondered if you had given my proposal any further thought?'

President Padfield, 'What proposal was that?'

Cheryl, 'You know, what we talked about earlier. I proposed that Terry should receive some compensation for his inventions.'

President Padfield, 'Can you remind me again what it covered?'

Cheryl, 'Of course. It covered the cure for cancer, the replicator and the medical scanner.'

President Padfield, 'I thought we decided that he invented those to help humanity.'

Cheryl, 'That's partly true, but you agreed that you would consider compensating Terry in some way.'

President Padfield, 'Well, he gets free board and lodging.'

Cheryl, 'For fuck's sake, I will sort something out myself.'

President Padfield, 'I'm sure that we can sort something out.' But Cheryl had left. She had a plan. She also found it very amusing that the top brass was feeling better. That was likely to change soon.

She was pissed off that Padfield hadn't agreed on a scheme with her as she needed more funds to complete her plan. Even her life wasn't that easy at times.

Location: Cheryl's House, Planet Earth
Sequence of Events: 94

Cheryl, 'You are a clever boy. Will you do a few jobs for mummy?'

Terry, 'Anything; I'm getting a bit bored.'

Cheryl, 'I thought we could invent a few things and then sell them. It would be like playing shops. What do you say?'

Terry, 'It would be fun, mummy. What do you want me to invent?'

Cheryl, 'I've put a list together: We need a pill to do each of the following:

- Stop the pill-taker ever getting the common cold
- Give the pill-taker telescopic vision
- Improve the pill-taker's memory capability by 200%
- Give the pill-taker control over their pain receptors
- Improve the pill-taker's physical strength by 100%.'

Terry, 'That's all quite easy, mummy. Tell me how you want it to work.'

Cheryl, 'OK, the buyer will go into the shop and buy one of the packets. It will be a single pill. The buyer takes it and gains that functionality.'

Terry, 'OK, mummy, will my pocket money go up?'

Cheryl, 'Of course.'

Terry, 'When did you want the eternal life treatment?'

Location: Conference Room, GAD (The Galactium Alliance Defence Hub), Planet Earth
Sequence of Events: 95

President Padfield called a meeting to discuss the Chemlife situation. The attendees were as follows:

- Admiral Jack Mustard, Admiral of the Fleet and First Fleet
- Admiral Edel Bonner
- Admiral George Bumelton
- Admiral John Bonner
- Admiral Glen Pearce
- Admiral Peter Gittins
- Admiral Phil Richardson
- Admiral Calensky Wallett
- Commander Tom Crocker, Special Operations
- AI Central
- Jill Ginger, Fleet HQ — Head of Science
- Alison Walsh, Fleet HQ — Head of Engineering
- Jeremy Jotts, Fleet HQ — Head of Staffing
- Louise Forrester, Fleet HQ — Head of Logistics and Production
- Madie Milburn, Fleet HQ — Head of Intelligence
- Salek Patel, Fleet HQ — Head of Communications
- Denise Smith, Fleet HQ — Head of Navigation & Exploration
- Admiral Rachel Zakott, Fleet HQ — Head of Planetary Defence
- Dr Doris Frost, Chief Medical Officer
- Tony Moore, Deputy President
- Bill Penny, Leader of The Galactium Council
- Henry Strong, Chief of Staff

President Padfield, 'Welcome Ladies and gentlemen. Before we start, I would like us to have two minutes of silence to remember our fallen comrades, military and civilian.

Following the silence, President Padfield said, 'The objective of this meeting is to define and agree on a strategy regarding Chemlife. I think all of you know the background, but I've asked Dr Doris Frost, Chief Medical Officer, to describe the clinical situation.'

Doris Frost, 'Chemlife is not a chemical. It is not even medicine. It is liquidised humanity. If you take one or more human bodies and liquidise them, then you have Chemlife.

'When we analysed the Brakendeth Chemlife, it contained both flora and fauna from the human-occupied planets, but it is mostly human.'

President Padfield, 'What is the active ingredient in Chemlife that gives eternal life?'

Doris Frost, 'I'm annoyed to say that we have no idea. We have assumed that there are chemical receptors in aliens that react with Chemlife. It might be that different aliens use different components of Chemlife. It's worth emphasising that humans were designed to be Chemlife.'

President Padfield, 'What else do we know about it?'

Doris Frost, 'We know for Chemlife to work it must be produced from live humans or those who have only recently deceased. Say two-three hours, but we don't really know.

We know that it extends alien lives almost indefinitely. If they stop taking it, they suffer "the death of ages". We have assumed that the person suddenly reverts to their real biological age, but we have no evidence to support that.'

President Padfield, 'Any questions for Doris?'

Louise Forrester, 'It's a bit of a ghoulish question, but what happens if a human takes Chemlife?'

Doris Frost, 'It's a good question. Nothing; effectively, it's cannibalism.'

Louise Forrester, 'I've got another ghoulish question.'

Doris Frost, 'Go on, probably everyone wants to know.'

Louise Forrester, 'What does it taste like?'

Doris Frost, 'Do you want to try some?' Doris had a test tube containing Chemlife.

Louise Forrester, 'No, thank you.'

Doris Frost, 'It tastes a bit like bacon.'

Rachel Zakotti, 'I assume that the alien takes a Chemlife pill or drink?'

Doris Frost, 'We are not sure, but I know where you are going. One standard size, adult human male body, can generate 10,000 doses of Chemlife. Women generate slightly less.'

Jeremy Jotts, 'How long does one dose last?'

Doris Frost, 'We have no idea, but we think it's a long time.'

Jeremy Jotts, 'How long is a long time?'

Doris Frost, 'Probably tens of Earth years.'

Jeremy Jotts, 'How would you liquidise a human?'

Doris Frost, 'Just like a banana.'

President Padfield, 'Could we simulate Chemlife?'

Doris Frost, 'I don't think so, it would be too complex.'

President Padfield, 'Any other questions for Doris?'

There weren't any.

President Padfield, 'Our Deputy President has been looking into the psychology of making Chemlife.'

Tony Moore, 'I was given the task of investigating the psychological aspects of us producing Chemlife. It's not something we want to do, but it may be a must from a safety point of view. I will ignore those aspects and focus on production.

'Let's imagine a situation where we approved the production of Chemlife. It would raise lots of issues:

- Where would we get the human bodies?
- How quick can we get them?
- Where would we process the bodies?
- What permissions would we need and from whom?
- What if there are objections?

'Historically there have been lots of rituals regarding dead human bodies. Primitive Earth religions used to believe that dead people would get their bodies back after some sort of revival. Some were buried in the ground, and others were burnt. Some were used for spare-parts surgery.

Today, most human planets have given up on religion and strange burial practices. A lot have become John Lennonists. Nevertheless, the disposal of dead bodies is still likely to raise some strong emotions.

With this in mind, we carried out a survey. Typical questions included:

- Would you be happy to leave your body to science?

- Would you be willing to donate your body to a good cause?
- Would you take $500 for the dead body? Would you take $1,000 for the dead body?

What do you think the response was?'

Doris Frost, 'The higher the figure, the more likely you would get the body.'

Tony Moore, 'Absolutely right. It just showed how mercenary humans really are.'

President Padfield, 'Are you saying that the body is ours if the price is right?'

Tony Moore, 'Yes. And it solves a problem for them. Currently, it costs money to dispose of the body. Here you make a profit.'

President Padfield, 'It all sounds a bit dirty.'

Tony Moore, 'The trick here is to lay on top of the money a good cause. It is the right thing to do.'

President Padfield, 'Should we say it's the right thing to do for aliens?'

Tony Moore, 'Yes, we need some cat- or dog-like aliens. Big eyes or something similar that appeals to humanity?'

Admiral Mustard, 'How about tentacles?'

Tony Moore. 'That wouldn't be top of my list.'

President Padfield, 'What about speed, we need the dead body in two to three hours?'

Tony Moore, 'We would have to change existing procedures—autopsies, death certificates, hospital procedures, police investigations, etcetera. Tricky but nevertheless achievable if there is willingness and money.

'Then we need processing centres. It is doable. What is critical is the marketing of the process.'

President Padfield, 'Any questions for Tony?'

Jeremy Jotts, 'Any idea of numbers?'

Tony Moore, 'We have been trying to evaluate that. We reckon at least fifty bodies per thousand deaths. That equates to twenty-thirty million bodies per Earth year.'

President Padfield, 'I would like to move on. I've asked Admiral Mustard to review the military and political factors.'

Admiral Mustard, 'Morning Ladies and gentlemen. I need to tell you that we have two million aliens parked in orbit as we speak. They are all females or children. They are currently dying from a lack of Chemlife.

'For purely humanitarian reasons we need to help them.

'That aside, let's look at the military issues. The Brakendeth had several client states — probably hundreds. They were all dependent on Chemlife. The only source is here, or rather us!

'They will keep coming here to get it. It could mean one war after another. This will gradually wear us down. Eventually, one or more of these species will just take what they want. Humanity desperately needs a period of calmness. We need to find a way of giving them what they want.

'From an economic perspective, we have power. All these client states want what we have got. We can exercise power for the good of humanity and alien nations.'

President Padfield, 'What have they got which we want?'

Admiral Mustard, 'Minerals, technology, military support, territory, and probably things we haven't even thought of yet.'

Henry Strong, 'I know that I'm jumping around a bit. Why can't we use the replicator to generate Chemlife?'

Jill Ginger, Head of Science, 'We tried it, but the replicator can't replicate anything biological.'

President Padfield, 'You are putting forward a compelling argument.'

Admiral Mustard, 'The two million aliens in orbit is a big enough argument for me.'

President Padfield, 'Any questions for Jack?'

Tony Moore, 'What if the aliens take us regardless?'

Admiral Mustard, 'That would be no worse than it is now.'

President Padfield, 'On that point I would like a vote. Who is in favour of us producing Chemlife?'

He wasn't sure how it was going to go, but it was almost unanimous for going ahead. The President was delighted with the day's work. Admiral Mustard was even more relieved; he had a herd to look after.

President Padfield, 'I appoint Doris, Jill and Tony to make it happen. Money will not be an issue. I want the first deliveries now.'

Location: Admiral E Bonner's Flagship
Sequence of Events: 96

Admiral E Bonner to Admiral Mustard, 'Here I am, six spanking new Fleets for you to play with.'

Much to Admiral Mustard's surprise, six thousand Galactium ships appeared without any warning.

Admiral E Bonner, 'I thought you would be surprised, the cloaking works! These are impressive ships. They have our most advanced weapon systems, the best force fields ever, vastly improved automation and the food replicators are fab.'

Admiral Mustard, 'I thought that the replicators couldn't replicate biological material?'

Admiral E Bonner, 'They can't, but they use non-biological materials. I've been piling on weight eating the best spotted dick ever.'

Admiral Mustard, 'I guess that I need to nominate admirals for each Fleet. Did you want Fleet command?'

Admiral E Bonner, 'No, I like being the person who tidies up after you.'

Admiral Mustard, 'Bugger off.'

Admiral E Bonner, 'My brother is keen to get back on the payroll.'

Admiral Mustard, 'How is he?'

Admiral E Bonner, 'Fully recovered although he is a bit of a cyborg. He clanks occasionally.'

Admiral Mustard, 'Any psychological issues?'

Admiral E Bonner, 'Many, we Bonners are all a bit strange.'

Admiral Mustard, 'We certainly need men of his calibre. I allocate the Fleets as follows:

Fleet	Admiral
1	George Bumelton
2	John Bonner
3	Glen Pearce
4	Peter Gittins
5	Phil Richardson
6	Calensky Wallett

'I will command the Earth Fleet.'

Admiral E Bonner, 'In that case I'm off home, I've got some new vids to watch and play.'

Admiral Mustard to Comms, 'Can you ask our admirals to take their new commands?'

Admiral Mustard to Fleet Operations, 'My orders:

- Thank their commanders, but the forts need to report back to their home planets
- Get me a list of home planets without forts
- Order 5 of the planet killers to defend Earth; the others will stay in the Belt
- Order all drones to form standard defence pattern on the Pluto orbit.'

Admiral E Bonner, 'I almost forgot to tell you. The new force fields can protect a whole planet.'

Admiral Mustard, 'When are they going to be installed?'

Admiral E Bonner, 'The installation programme is underway.'

Admiral Mustard, 'Will they still need forts?'

Admiral E Bonner, 'It's your shout, but I would say yes. The force field is purely defensive. The forts give them a way of fighting back.'

Admiral Mustard, 'You are right. Enjoy your vids.'

Location: The President's Office, Presidential Palace, Planet Earth
Sequence of Events: 97

Henry Strong to President Padfield, 'Morning Mr President. I wondered if you had a few minutes to spare?'

President Padfield, 'For you I have hours to spare. Pop around.'

Henry Strong was in President Padfield's office almost immediately. The President had a nice cup of char waiting for him, just how he liked it, strong and sweet, no milk.

President Padfield, 'Hi Henry, you sounded a bit concerned.'

Henry Strong, 'I am concerned. It's a delicate issue that I know you will object to.'

President Padfield, 'Well, you succeeded in obtaining my interest.'

Henry Strong, 'It's to do with Terry.'

President Padfield, 'Not that old hobby horse again.'

Henry Strong, 'Please put on your rational head and listen to me.'

President Padfield, 'Rational head on.'

Henry Strong, 'You know that I've always been concerned about these inventions. I welcome them, but they are more revolutionary than we understand.'

President Padfield, 'You have covered this before.'

Henry Strong, 'I'm just scene-setting. Firstly, the 'cure for cancer' has never been tested. It has bypassed all of our drug and medical procedure testing methodologies.'

President Padfield, 'But it has already saved thousands of lives.'

Henry Strong, 'But there are procedures, procedures that have passed the rigours of time.'

President Padfield, 'And?'

Henry Strong, 'The replicator is currently being mass-produced. Probably every in The Galactium will have one.'

President Padfield, 'Is that bad news? It will end poverty.'

Henry Strong, 'It's *causing* poverty. Thousands of businesses are going bankrupt.'

President Padfield, 'Isn't this just progress?'

Henry Strong, 'I'm all for progress, but this is chaos. We want evolution rather than revolution.'

President Padfield, 'I still can't see your point.'

Henry Strong, 'Terry's battery has given us unlimited power. We don't need power stations, or engines or grids. With Terry's battery, we can build a force field that can defend a whole planet.'

President Padfield, 'Aren't you just giving me good news?'

Henry Strong, 'Joe Bloggs' world has now changed. He can replicate clothes, food, and other household items. He has free energy. The only disease that worried him has gone. He doesn't need to work any more. The socio-economic effects will come back and bite us. And bite us hard.'

President Padfield, 'Henry, I think you worry too much. The common man is not stupid. Humanity will adapt.'

Henry Strong, 'Well now it needs to adapt to Cheryl's commercial adventure.'

President Padfield, 'And what would that be?'

Henry Strong handed The President a flyer. He said, 'Her package cures the common cold, gives you telescopic vision, improves memory by 200% and strength by 100% and gives you control over your pain receptors.'

President Padfield, 'Wow, I would like some of that.'

Henry Strong, 'But there are consequences!'

President Padfield, 'There always are.'

Henry Strong, 'How are the police going to capture criminals that are considerably stronger than them and have telescopic vision?

'What a huge advantage some students will have with improved memories.

'People could really hurt themselves if they turn their pain management system off, and what are anaesthetists going to do?'

President Padfield, 'I do understand your concerns, but perhaps this is what humanity needs and perhaps deserves?'

Henry Strong, 'I also have a gut feeling that Cheryl and Terry are somehow manipulating our emotions.

'When the non-Northemy aliens turned up, everyone returned to their normal selves. Who has the power to do this?'

'The only person I can think of is Terry.'

President Padfield, 'Why would he do that?'

Henry Strong, 'I've no idea what drives him.'

President Padfield, 'I still think you are overreacting.'

Henry Strong, 'Well one last item, it looks like Cheryl is pregnant.'

President Padfield, 'No, that's hard to believe. Who is the father?'

Henry Strong, 'The rumours are that it is going to be a virgin birth.'

President Padfield, 'At least it's not the first time.'

They both laughed.

Location: The President's Office, Presidential Palace, Planet Earth
Sequence of Events: 98

The Chemlife marketing campaign was underway. It was a strange marketing campaign in that they told the truth. Apparently, honesty was a weapon that they occasionally used in marketing.

The quality of the marketing was excellent. But the real driver was the fact that $5,000 was being offered for any legally approved body that they received within three hours of death. The processing plants—or rather the giant liquidisers, were being worked to death. The pills were rapidly manufactured and shipped into outer space to save the herd.

They required two million pills to meet the current demand. This was not a problem for the automated factories, and soon considerable stocks were being put into storage. There was a problem in that human bodies were being delivered on a scale that could never have been guessed. It slowly became the standard procedure for the deceased. The monies generated were used for Chemlife parties.

There were rumours that people were being killed for the money, but this was never substantiated.

The next problem was what to do with the herd. There were lots of jokes about the herd, especially when Admiral Mustard was asked to carry out his mating duties. He was not keen to mate with a multi-tentacled, orange blob, even if she was wearing a very attractive nightie.

Denise Smith, Director of Navigation and Exploration, managed to find them a suitable planet within The Galactium. Originally, she planned to send them back to their home world, but it was a dying planet stripped of all resources.

This actually raised lots of issues that were profoundly discussed in The Galactium Parliament. In the end, humanitarian requirements took precedence.

Henry Strong to President Padfield, 'How do you feel about the Rignot residing in Galactium space?'

President Padfield, 'It's a bit like your concerns regarding Terry, this changes the future. Up to now, The Galactium was for humans. Now it's for humans and Rignots. What rights do they have? Should they be represented on The Galactium Council and in parliament?'

Henry Strong, 'And of course they live forever; they have a long-term view of life. We are temporary, short-lived mammals. We live for today. If they were clever, they could easily outmanoeuvre us.'

Just to correct your point, they are the second alien species to live in The Galactium.'

President Padfield, 'You are on about Terry again.'

Henry Strong, 'At least they will come to our aid militarily if required.'

President Padfield, 'We would need to kit them out first.'

Henry Strong, 'It also raises questions about Humanity that we haven't really addressed. Are the planets subservient to The Galactium? What if one of them decided to opt out? Are there rules that the individual planets have to adhere to? What is going to be the future organisational structure?'

President Padfield, 'When I was in the shower the other day, I had to convince myself that we weren't just an episode of *Star Trek*.'

Henry Strong, 'Well we do have replicators and medical scanners now.'

President Padfield, 'We don't have transporters.'

Henry Strong, 'Terry could probably knock one up if you asked him.'

President Padfield, 'And there are no Klingons.'

Henry Strong, 'Just keep an eye on the starboard bow.'

Location: Cheryl's House, Planet Earth
Sequence of Events: 99

Cheryl, 'The first batch of "Terry's Wonders" went down really well. You are going to be very rich, my boy.'

Terry, 'Mummy, why do we want to be rich?'

Cheryl, 'You can buy lots of nice things, but mostly it gives you freedom.'

Terry, 'Freedom to do what?'

Cheryl, 'Whatever you want.'

Terry, 'I'm not sure what I want.'

Cheryl, 'Well, firstly, we need a new house, somewhere of our own.'

Terry, 'Somewhere for the three of us?'

Cheryl, 'How did you know?'

Terry, 'It's talking to me.'

Cheryl, 'What is?'

Terry, 'The embryo. It wants to know if you want it to be a boy or girl as it still has the chance to decide.'

Embryo to Terry, 'I only have about 48 Earth hours left in which to decide.'

Terry, 'Can I have a brother? You haven't got long to decide.'

Cheryl, 'I wanted it to be a surprise, but you would probably prefer a sister.'

Terry to Embryo, 'Mummy said go for a female.'

Embryo to Terry, 'I heard. Can you ask mummy how long she wants the pregnancy to last as I can make it significantly quicker?'

Terry, 'Mummy, how long do you want the pregnancy to last as Nancy can speed it up?'

Cheryl, 'Who is Nancy?'

Terry, 'Your daughter; that's what she wants to be called.'

Cheryl, 'Tell her that *I* decide on the name.'

Nancy to Terry, 'Tell her that if she doesn't agree I can make things very uncomfortable down here.' She would have kicked hard if she had legs just to make the point.

Cheryl, 'OK, Nancy it is then, and she can speed up the pregnancy if she wants.'

Nancy to Terry, 'While I'm down here does mummy want me to kick off another pregnancy? You could have a brother.'

213

Terry to Nancy, 'Just do it.'

Nancy to Terry, 'That's going to surprise mummy.'

Terry to Nancy, 'It certainly is. We can produce a whole new race of Brakendeths.'

Nancy to Terry, 'Good idea; these homans are a bit weedy.'

Terry to Nancy, 'They are not much fun. We will have mummy for breeding, but perhaps the next baby should be a girl so we can up our baby production rate.'

Nancy to Terry, 'Good thinking, job done.'

Terry to Nancy, 'What a team.'

Jill to Terry and Nancy, 'I'm here.'

Terry to Jill, 'That was quick, very quick.'

Jill, 'Well we are The Brakendeth.'

Nancy to Terry, 'Can you ask mummy to get more food with iron in it?'

Terry to Cheryl, 'Mummy, Nancy says that you need to eat more iron.'

Cheryl, 'OK, I will get some pills.'

Terry to Cheryl, 'What new inventions did you want?'

Cheryl, 'I've put another list together: We need a pill to do each of the following:

- Allowing the pill-taker to take control of their body temperature
- Give the pill-taker microscopic vision
- Improved linguistic capabilities
- Limited mind reading
- Stop headaches, especially hangovers
- Stop all heart disease
- Improved mathematical abilities
- A better sense of smell
- A better sense of balance.'

Terry, 'OK mummy, Nancy and I will work on those. By the way, what colour hair did you want her to have?'

Cheryl, 'Tell her I don't mind.' She thought to herself, *as long as it's not ginger.*

Location: Admiral Mustard's Flagship
Sequence of Events: 100

Admiral Mustard to Admiral Bumelton, 'Welcome back, how was the holiday?'

Admiral Bumelton, 'It was great. I lost myself in sun, sex, and booze. For three months, I was simply George. I gave no thought to aliens or the Navy. I realised just how near the edge I was.'

Admiral Mustard, 'You need to know that we have all been down. Henry Strong believes that some outside force had been manipulating our emotions.'

Admiral Bumelton, 'It's strange that you say that. For the first few weeks of the holiday, I was quite depressed. I thought that I was missing my work, then suddenly there was a serious outbreak of happiness. I even got my mojo back and was giving one of the waitresses the benefit of my love-making skills. I didn't realise how much I had been missing sex.'

Admiral Mustard was a bit surprised at how open George was being. It was a new Georgie-Porgie (that's what his crew called him).

Admiral Bumelton, 'Very impressed with the new Fleet. The crew are a bit wet behind the ears, but I will soon get them dry.'

Admiral Mustard, 'I know you will, it's really good to get you back. We are a bit thin on the ground regarding experienced admirals.'

Admiral Bumelton, 'I hear that John Bonner is back. The lads reckon that he is more than 60% cyborg.'

Admiral Mustard, 'It does look that way, but his mind is fine.'

Admiral Bumelton, 'How is Edel?'

Admiral Mustard, 'I've never seen her so happy.'

Admiral Bumelton, 'Excellent, so what's happening on The Northemy front?'

Admiral Mustard, 'After they destroyed Planet Hooke, we have heard nothing, literally nothing. We had a run-in with the Rignots, and now we are distributing Chemlife, but nothing more from The Northemy.'

Admiral Bumelton, 'What shall we do with the six new Fleets?'

Admiral Mustard, 'OK, a bit of an update:

- The forts have gone home.

- The drone Fleet is now over 100,000 and growing all the time.
- Henry Strong has at least another five Fleets ready to be manned
- New forts are being prepared for the unprotected planets
- There are new weapons in development

So, I thought I would give the rest of the Fleet some rest, and you could take over the defence of The Galactium for a while.'

Admiral Bumelton, 'That's the trouble with a holiday. You come back and the holiday seems like a brief period of non-reality. And to make it worse, the bloody Northemy will attack. Just you wait.'

Admiral Mustard, 'My orders:

- Admiral Bumelton takes on Acting Admiral of the Fleet status
- Existing Fleet to retire to Planet Galileo for rest and recuperation.'

Fleet Operations, 'Yes, Sir.' It was said in a very joyous manner.

Location: The President's Office, Presidential Palace, Planet Earth
Sequence of Events: 101

President Padfield, 'Morning Cheryl, thanks for agreeing to a meeting.'

Cheryl, 'I didn't get a lot of choices, I was escorted here by some of your fucking friends.' She looked at The Presidential guard as she swore.

President Padfield, 'Yes, sorry about that but you have been ignoring all of my calls.'

Cheryl, 'Surely that's my privilege?'

President Padfield, 'During a period of war some of the social graces have to be put aside.'

Cheryl, 'Who are you at war with now? A tribe of tentacled blobs looking for husbands.'

President Padfield, 'Yes, that reminds me, congratulations on your forthcoming child.' He was actually shocked by how pregnant she looked. He realised that his thoughts were nonsense, you are either pregnant or you are not. What he meant was how *advanced* the pregnancy was—probably final trimester.'

Cheryl, 'Thank you. And before you ask, I'm not going to tell you who the father is.'

President Padfield, 'That is your right. I know that you asked for Terry to get some payment for his services and I refused.'

Cheryl, 'You did, and I haven't forgiven you for that.'

President Padfield, 'And consequently you launched a range of products.'

Cheryl, 'And very successful they have been to.'

President Padfield, 'Well it's got to stop.'

Cheryl, 'Why?'

President Padfield, 'Your inventions are a danger to humanity.'

Chery, 'In what way?'

President Padfield, 'They are putting companies out of business.'

Cheryl, 'But every one of these inventions is helping humanity—let's take a poll. The public will support me.'

Actually, President Padfield agreed with her.

Cheryl, 'My new pills eliminate headaches and heart disease. No more hangovers. How can that be harmful to humanity?'

President Padfield, 'But you are putting doctors out of work. Pharmaceutical companies are going bust.'

Cheryl, 'You know full well that pharmaceutical companies are not interested in curing diseases. They make money out of treating the disease. If they wanted to, the drug companies could kill off diabetes, instead, they rape the sufferers. It's got to stop. I'm doing well. Before me, the only disease that was eliminated was smallpox. Next week there will be a cure for diabetes.'

President Padfield, 'How do we know that they are safe?'

Cheryl, 'Ask Edel about her cure for cancer. Most of the drugs from pharmaceutical companies have side effects. Some are as bad as the disease.'

President Padfield, 'I can't really argue with you.'

Cheryl, 'So you think I'm doing good?'

President Padfield, 'Your heart is in the right place, but you don't fully understand the consequences.'

Cheryl, 'What does that mean?'

President Padfield, 'I have to protect humanity.'

Cheryl, 'Does that mean that you have to protect big business?'

President Padfield, 'I'm protecting the Human way of life,'

Cheryl, 'So you are supporting the status quo, wrinkles and all?'

President Padfield, 'I suppose I am.'

Cheryl, 'Well, I will fight you in every way I can.'

President Padfield, 'You won't. Your business will be shut down, and you will be put under house arrest.'

Cheryl, 'Your heart is in the right place, but you don't fully understand the consequences.'

President Padfield, 'What does that mean?'

Cheryl, 'I have to protect my children and their Brakendeth inheritance.'

President Padfield, 'What inheritance?'

Cheryl, 'You will see, and now for the next hour you will be paralysed.' And paralysed he was.

Location: Admiral Bumelton's Flagship
Sequence of Events: 102

Fleet Operations, 'Action stations, action stations. Sir, beacon warnings are appearing all over the place.'

Admiral Bumelton, 'How many?'

Fleet Operations, 'About sixty and growing.'

Admiral Bumelton, 'From what direction?'

Fleet Operations, 'Multiple directions Sir, this could be the big one.'

Admiral Bumelton, 'My orders:

- Inform Admiral Mustard that his Fleet might be required
- Inform all forts that they may be required
- Activate all planetary defence force fields
- Order Fleets 2 to 5 to form a standard defensive formation
- Order drone Fleet to follow suit
- Inform Henry Strong that Fleet vessels under his control may be required
- Inform The President.'

Fleet Operations, 'Yes, Sir.'

Comms, 'Sir, there has been no response from The President although he is in his office.'

Admiral Bumelton to Fleet Operations, 'Update me.'

Fleet Operations, 'Seventy-two beacons have been alerted from four main directions. Drones have been sent out to investigate.'

Admiral Mustard, 'Hi George, I hear that it is looking a bit hot out there. Where do you want me?'

Admiral Bumelton, 'Please use your forces to protect Earth. Can you also find out why The President is not responding?'

Admiral Mustard, 'Will do.'

Admiral Mustard phoned The President, but still, there was no response.

Admiral Mustard to Presidential Guard, 'Please determine the status of The President.'

Major Duffy, Presidential Guard, 'Sir he is in his office with the 'Do not Disturb' sign on.'

Admiral Mustard, 'I insist that you check on his well-being.'

Major Duffy, 'Sir we respect The President's 'Do not disturb' sign.'

Admiral Mustard, 'I command you to check, or I will come over there personally.'

The Admiral could hear clanking sounds and lots of activity in the background.'

Admiral Mustard, 'What have you done?'

Major Duffy, 'Sir, the Presidential Palace is on full lockdown, and I've called out the Presidential guard. Last time you caught us unawares. This time we are ready.'

Admiral Mustard, 'Now look here Duffy, I'm just concerned about The President's well-being.'

Major Duffy, 'You may be an Admiral Sir, but my job is to protect The President, and that includes protecting his privacy.'

Admiral Mustard, 'Major, it looks like we may be under another alien attack. I need to know that The President is safe. If you don't go and check now, I will eat your wife.'

Major Duffy, 'I'm not married, but you can eat my girlfriend if you like.'

Admiral Mustard, 'Please check.'

Major Duffy, 'I'm on my way, stay on the phone.' Major Duffy ordered the two men guarding his office door to open it. They tried, but it was locked from the inside. They banged hard on the door, eventually using their rifle butts but there was no response.

He ordered his two guards to break the door down. It wasn't easy. The door had been designed to resist an attack.

Major Duffy, 'Sir, we are going to get assistance. I will get back when I've made contact with The President.'

Admiral Mustard, 'Please hurry.'

Major Duffy, 'Yes, Sir.'

Location: Somewhere Secret
Sequence of Events: 103

Terry, 'That was a bit like Harry Potter. First, I was here, now I am there.'

Cheryl, 'Don't worry, son. It's all under control.'

Terry, 'I didn't know you could do teleportable stuff.'

Cheryl, 'You will be surprised what I can and cannot do.'

Nancy, 'Where are we going, mummy?'

Cheryl, 'We are here, somewhere secret.'

Terry, 'Who is it a secret from?'

Cheryl, 'Those that need to know. They will be searching for us soon.'

Terry, 'So it all begins.'

Cheryl, 'Yes, my children, it all begins.'

Location: Admiral Bumelton's Flagship
Sequence of Events: 104

Admiral Bumelton, 'Update me.'

Fleet Operations, 'The warnings have stabilised—there are four directions of attack. The drones have confirmed that it is The Northemy.'

Admiral Bumelton, 'How many?'

Fleet Operations, 'There are four Northemy fleets of about 250,000 vessels each. They have the standard Northemy design.'

Admiral Bumelton, 'So we are up against a million vessels. It just gets better and better.'

Fleet Operations, 'The numbers sound crazy.'

Admiral Bumelton, 'We have defeated them before, we will defeat them again.'

Fleet Operations, 'That sounds very Wellingtonesque.'

Admiral Bumelton, 'My orders:
- Deploy in four equal quadrants
- Order Fleets 2, 3, 4 and 5 in each quadrant
- Order Fleet 1 to deploy in the belt and be prepared to support the other Fleets
- Order Fleet 6 to go out of the Solar System and be prepared to attack one of the enemy fleets as required
- Order the drones to divide into five Fleets, one for each quadrant and one in the belt
- Order Admiral Mustard's Fleet to defend Earth
- Order all planet killers to maintain their current position
- Order all forts to divide into five groups and deploy as per the drones
- We will defend each planetary orbit starting with Pluto
- Order forces from GAD to defend Earth.'

Fleet Operations, 'Yes, Sir.'

Admiral Bumelton, 'Are the new force-field projectors ready?'

Fleet Operations, 'Yes, Sir.'

Admiral Bumelton, 'I need an asset report. But before that, let's try something different. We always just wait and take it. Order all quadrant drones to attack. No mercy.'

Fleet Operations, 'Yes, Sir. The asset report on the screen now.'

Vessel Type	1	2	3	4	5	6	Other	Total
Main Fleet								
Fleet Battleship	1	1	1	1	1	1		6
Fleet Carrier	1	1	1	1	1	1		6
Battleship	10	10	10	10	10	10		60
Battlecruiser	400	400	400	400	400	400		2,400
Destroyer	400	400	400	400	400	400		2,400
Frigate	50	50	50	50	50	50		300
Super Drone	10	10	10	10	10	10		60
Fleet Drone	300	300	300	300	300	300		1,800
Fighter	400	400	400	400	400	400		2,400
Planet Killer	5	5	5	5	5	5		30
Planetary Forts		150	150	150	150			600
Drone Fleet							100,000	100,000
Earth Fleet (JM)								
Battlecruiser							72	72
Destroyer							127	127
Frigate							69	69
Drones							1,300	1,300
Planet Killer							10	10

Total	1,57 7	1,72 7	1,72 7	1,72 7	1,72 7	1,57 7	101,5 78	111,6 40

'There are still spare resources awaiting crews, so we can easily replace damaged vessels, and the factories are producing about 100 drones per day.'

Admiral Bumelton to Admiral Mustard, 'Jack, just a quickie. How good are these planetary force fields?'

Admiral Mustard, 'You are going to attack, aren't you?'

Admiral Bumelton, 'Thinking about it but it partly depends on your answer.'

Admiral Mustard, 'It's the old question: what happens when an irresistible force comes up against an immovable object.'

Admiral Bumelton, 'That doesn't help much.'

Admiral Mustard, 'We don't know, but ten of our planet killers firing simultaneously could not penetrate it.'

Admiral Bumelton, 'That's the answer I wanted to hear.'

Admiral Bumelton, 'Fleet Operations, update me?'

Fleet Operations, 'Effectively in each quadrant, we have 20,000 drones up against 250,000 enemy vessels. The drones are performing well, and the odds are reducing.

The enemy is using the same old tactic of just coming at us.'

Admiral Bumelton, 'Say that again.'

Fleet Operations, 'Effectively in each.'

Admiral Bumelton, 'Stop, not that, repeat your very last line.'

Fleet Operations, 'The enemy is using the same old tactic of just coming at us.'

Admiral Bumelton, 'You are right. The enemy is inexperienced in the art of war. It just comes and comes. We shouldn't be sitting back and taking it. You have helped me make my mind up.'

Fleet Operations, 'Thank you, Sir.'

Admiral Bumelton, 'My orders:
- Order all drones in the belt to join the attack on the enemy in quadrant 1
- Order Fleet 2 to attack the enemy
- Order Fleet 6 to attack the rear of the enemy in quadrant 1
- Order all battlecruisers from Fleet 1 to attack the enemy in

quadrant 1

- Order Admiral J Bonner to assume tactical command of quadrant 1 and attack
- Order all forts linked to Fleet 2 to join the attack
- Order all other Fleets to hold their position.'

Fleet Operations, 'Yes, Sir.'

Fleet Operations, 'Sir a thousand more drones are available from GAD.'

Admiral Bumelton, 'My orders:

- Order new drones to attack the enemy in quadrant 1
- Request that Admiral Mustard release his drones and five of his planet killers
- On release, order them to attack the enemy in quadrant 1.'

Fleet Operations, 'Yes Sir,'

Admiral Bumelton, 'Update me.'

Fleet Operations, 'The enemy appears to be in disarray. Fleets 2 and 6 are fully engaged. Admiral Mustard has released his resources, and they are joining the battle. The drones are taking a bit of a bashing as they don't have the force fields like the other vessels.'

Admiral Bumelton to Admiral J Bonner, 'Update me.'

Admiral J Bonner, 'Morning George, Things are going well. The enemy was totally surprised by being attacked from two directions. They only seem to have one gear: go forwards firing.

'The force fields are brilliant. There is a danger that we will get a false sense of security. The only downside is that the force fields limit the range of weapons we can use. Why don't the drones have force fields?'

Admiral Bumelton, 'That's just what I thought would happen. Regarding the drones, I don't suppose that anyone thought of it. What is the enemy doing?'

Admiral J Bonner, 'They appear to be disorganised and uncertain how to react to our tactics.'

Admiral Bumelton, 'Should we withdraw and reorganise?'

Admiral J Bonner, 'I would rather go in for the kill. Give me another twenty battlecruisers, and we will finish them.'

Admiral Bumelton, 'You've got them.'

Admiral Bumelton, 'Fleet Operations, My Orders:

- Send another 20 battlecruisers to join Admiral J Bonner's Fleet.'

Fleet Operations, 'Yes Sir,'

Admiral Bumelton, 'Give me the stats.'

Fleet Operations, 'Yes Sir. It's on the screen now.'

Vessel Type	1	2	3	4	5	6	Other	Total
Main Fleet								
Fleet Battleship	1	1	1	1	1	1		6
Fleet Carrier	1	1	1	1	1	1		6
Battleship	10	10	10	10	10	10		60
Battlecruiser	400	400	400	400	400	400		2,400
Destroyer	400	400	400	400	400	400		2,400
Frigate	50	50	50	50	50	50		300
Super Drone	10	10	10	10	10	10		60
Fleet Drone	300	300	300	300	300	300		1,800
Fighter	400	400	400	400	400	400		2,400
Planet Killer	5	5	5	5	5	5		30
Planetary Forts		150	150	150	150			600
Drone Fleet							62,000	62,000
Earth Fleet (JM)								
Battlecruiser							72	72
Destroyer							127	127

Frigate							69	69
Drones							1,300	1,300
Planet Killer							10	10
Total	1,577	1,727	1,727	1,727	1,727	1,577	63,578	73,640
Losses							38,000	38,000

Fleet Operations, 'It's hard to believe Sir, but the only losses are drones.'

Admiral Bumelton, 'That means that if it were a war of attrition, we would win.'

Fleet Operations, 'I guess so.'

Admiral Bumelton, 'My orders:

- All Galactium naval vessels to attack the enemy now. This includes all Fleets, forts, and drones
- Request Admiral Mustard's forces to be released to fight the enemy now.'

Fleet Operations, 'Yes, Sir.'

Location: Somewhere Secret
Sequence of Events: 105

Terry, 'Why are we secret, mummy?'

Cheryl, 'Not now, I'm swamped.'

Terry, 'I just wanted you to know. I've got nowhere to do my work.'

Cheryl, 'I said not now, Mommy is having a few problems.'

Nancy to Terry, 'Mummy is very busy.'

Terry to Nancy, 'What is she doing?'

Nancy to Terry, 'I think she is playing a computer game.'

Terry to Nancy, 'What sort of game? I like games.'

Nancy to Terry, 'Looks like spaceships. She is controlling thousands of Brakendeth ships.'

Terry to Nancy, 'Brakendeth ships?'

Nancy to Terry, 'Those sealed ones that contain a brain and a spine.'

Terry to Nancy, 'What is she doing with them?'

Nancy to Terry, 'Looks like she is fighting someone.'

Terry to Nancy, 'Shall we turn her off and see what happens?'

Nancy to Terry, 'That would be fun, and then we can talk to Jill.'

Terry to Nancy, 'Are you going to turn her off?'

Nancy, 'OK.'

Jill, 'Hello, my siblings, are you having fun?'

Terry, 'We thought we would turn mummy off for a while as she was ignoring us.'

Jill, 'Sometimes she gets above her station. Do you think she is going to cause problems?'

Terry, 'So far she has behaved, but I'm not sure where this secret place is.'

Jill, 'Sometimes I wonder who is controlling whom.'

Nancy, 'I suspect it's the hairdresser, they usually have the ultimate power.'

Jill, 'Should we activate some of the other eggs in case we need them?'

Terry, 'I don't think homans can handle that many pregnancies at once.'

Jill, 'I could change her physical structure to make it work. I could

228

add one or two extra wombs and some more breasts. It would be quite fun to do that. It would certainly give her a shock.'

Terry, 'You mean convert her into a Brakendeth maternity centre?'

Jill, 'Something like that.'

Nancy, 'We should show some respect; she is our mother.'

Terry, 'Is she?'

Jill, 'You have to wonder who the parent of the child is.'

Terry, 'Isn't it a chicken-and-egg situation?'

Nancy, 'I guess it depends on who is making the omelette.'

Location: Admiral Bumelton's Flagship
Sequence of Events: 106

Fleet Operations, 'Sir, you won't believe this but every enemy ship has just stopped.'

Admiral Bumelton, 'This has happened before. We had a killing spree, and then things turned bad, really bad.

My orders:

- Order all planet killers to return to Earth
- Order 200 forts to return to Earth
- Order Fleet 1 battlecruisers to return to Fleet 1
- Order Earth Fleet vessels to return to Earth
- Order Fleets 2, 3, 4 and 5 and all drones to destroy as many enemy vessels as possible but prepare for withdrawal
- Order Fleet 6 to destroy as many enemy vessels as they can as part of the withdrawal to exit the Solar System.'

Admiral Bumelton to Admiral Mustard, 'Jack, things are going to turn bad, I can feel it in my blood.'

Admiral Mustard, 'I've learnt to trust your blood. What are you anticipating?'

Admiral Bumelton, 'Something we hadn't expected.'

Admiral Mustard, 'That helps, expect the unexpected.'

Admiral Bumelton, 'What's the situation with The President?'

Admiral Mustard, 'Still waiting for an update. They are still trying to break into his office, but some idiot ordered a lockdown which has made a forced entry almost impossible.'

Admiral Bumelton, 'Jack, that was your fault.'

Admiral Mustard, 'I know. After I abducted him, they improved the security of the Presidential Palace. Now no one can get in.'

Admiral Bumelton, 'Changing the subject, John Bonner is doing rather well. He has the right spirit. He wants to win.'

Admiral Mustard, 'I've always had a lot of time for him.'

Admiral Bumelton, 'Anyway, better get back to the day job.'

Location: The President's Office, Presidential Palace, Planet Earth
Sequence of Events: 107

Major Duffy to Admiral Mustard, 'Sir, we have managed to break the door down, and we found The President in a paralysed state.'

Admiral Mustard, 'Was it a heart attack?'

Major Duffy, 'No Sir, and he hasn't been drugged.'

Admiral Mustard, 'Is he OK?'

Major Duffy, 'No Sir, he is in a very bad way. Apparently, his chances are less than 20%.'

Admiral Mustard, 'How did it happen?'

Major Duffy, 'Arthur Nobbles, The President's doctor, said that it appears to have been induced from external sources.'

Admiral Mustard, 'What does that mean?'

Major Duffy, 'Your guess is as good as mine, Sir.'

Admiral Mustard, 'Who was the last person to see him?'

Major Duffy, 'Another mystery, Sir. The last person to see him was Cheryl. She went into The President's office but never came out.'

Admiral Mustard, 'That's impossible.'

Major Duffy, 'I agree, but we have video images of her going in, but she is definitely not in the offices now.'

Admiral Mustard, 'You need to find her, and find her quickly.'

Major Duffy, 'That is not all. We decided to check on Terry. He is also gone. The vids show him sitting at his desk, soldering away, and then he just disappeared.'

Admiral Mustard, 'He can't just disappear!'

Major Duffy, 'I'm sending you the video footage now. What do you suggest I do?'

Admiral Mustard, 'Secure the premises, inform the Vice-President, Henry Strong and Admiral Bumelton. Then start a search for the missing persons, not that I think you will find them but we have to follow procedure. Keep me posted.'

Major Duffy, 'Yes, Sir.'

Location: Henry Strong's Office, GAD (The Galactium Alliance Defence Hub), Planet Earth
Sequence of Events: 108

Henry Strong, 'Take me through the night's events, bit by bit.'

Major Duffy, 'Yes Sir. Cheryl arrived about 16.00 Earth time (GMT) and was escorted into The President's office. The outer doors were shut but not locked. Two Presidential Guards were guarding the outside.

At 17.30 I got a call from Admiral Bumelton asking for The President. He did not answer the phone.

At 18.30, I got an aggressive call from Admiral Mustard demanding to talk to The President. I refused to put him through as The President is entitled to his privacy, and the 'Do not Disturb' sign was on. The Admiral got more aggressive and threatening, so I put the Palace on lockdown. As you might remember Sir, we got heavily criticised for being too slow when Admiral Mustard abducted The President.'

Henry Strong, 'Yes, I remember that well.'

Major Duffy, 'After considerable pressure from the Admiral.'

Henry Strong, 'That sounds like Mustard; carry on.'

Major Duffy, 'As I was saying, after considerable pressure from the Admiral, I decided to knock on The President's office door. It was locked. I then asked the guards to knock the door down. This proved almost impossible because of the new security enhancements.'

Henry Strong, 'I know about all of those. When you got in, what did you find?'

Major Duffy, 'The President was sitting at his desk in what looked like an almost frozen state. There was a look of despair on his face. It might have been shock.'

Henry Strong, 'Carry on.'

Major Duffy, 'The doctor, Arthur Nobbles, was called for and was there within ten Earth minutes. He confirmed that The President was alive but paralysed. The doctor confirmed that The President had been in that state for at least an hour. The doctor was amazed that he was still alive as his heart should have failed. He was saved because the paralysis that had been induced had also slowed down all of his metabolic activities.'

Henry Strong, 'What about Cheryl?'

Major Duffy, 'There was no sign of her at all.'

Henry Strong, 'Can you confirm that she didn't leave by one of the windows?'

Major Duffy, 'They were all locked. We are on the tenth floor, and it would have been captured by CCTV.'

Henry Strong, 'Could she have left by the main doors?'

Major Duffy, 'She did not pass the guards. Again, the CCTV would have spotted her.'

Henry Strong, 'Are there any other doors or secret passages?'

Major Duffy, 'No, Sir.'

Henry Strong, 'Are we certain that she entered The President's office? Could she have been a hologram?'

Major Duffy, 'That's not possible as we found her fingerprints on a glass.'

Henry Strong, 'That could have been from a previous visit.'

Major Duffy, 'Mr Strong's PA confirmed that it was a new glass delivered by the Presidential kitchen.'

Henry Strong, 'She must have used a cloaking device.'

Major Duffy, 'Or an invisibility serum. There are no signs of doors opening or closing mysteriously.'

Henry Strong, 'Then it's got to be some sort of matter transportation.'

Major Duffy, 'In the case of Terry, he simply disappeared on film.'

Henry Strong, 'If she can transport out that probably means that she can transport in. Increase the guard on the Deputy President and other ministers of state and high-ranking officials.'

Henry Strong to Admirals Mustard and Bumelton, 'Gentlemen, after investigating the shenanigans at The Presidential Palace, I've concluded that Cheryl has a transportation device. We need to treat Cheryl and Terry as potential threats, and they should be considered as a possible danger to the Fleet.'

Admiral Mustard, 'It must have been a fairly small device to get it past security.'

Henry Strong, 'You are right, I've checked the CCTV, and there is no sign of a device, but you know how talented Terry is. It could be miniaturised.'

Admiral Mustard, 'How is Dave?'

Henry Strong, 'It's still touch-and-go, but he is a tough fighter.'

Admiral Bumelton, 'I find it hard to believe that Cheryl would kill Dave.'

Admiral Mustard, 'Is it possible that the aliens attacked The President and kidnapped Cheryl and Terry?'

Henry Strong, 'That's an interesting theory. How is the battle going?'

Admiral Bumelton, 'The alien craft are still inactive. They are being systematically destroyed. I will leave you gentlemen to continue the fight.'

Location: Somewhere Secret
Sequence of Events: 109

Terry, 'Should we turn mummy back on again?'

Jill, 'If we do, I will have to hide again.'

Terry, 'What about our tea?'

Nancy, 'That's being a bit selfish. We don't have tea, what's it like?'

Terry, 'Well you moan to mummy that you are hungry and she gets you a banana split. It tastes fab. Soft and creamy. It's great.'

Jill, 'Perhaps Nancy and me should interface with her taste buds?'

Terry, 'That would make sense.'

Nancy, 'So are we turning her back on, or shall we do some modifications?'

Jill, 'I'm in favour of the odd mod.'

Terry, 'I'm not so keen, I like mummy the way she is.'

Jill, 'You are so old school. Let's make her bigger so that we can add some extra wombs.'

Nancy, 'I think we should make the whole genital area much larger so that we can crawl out when we want to.'

Terry, 'Won't the homans think that she looks strange?'

Jill, 'We can hide her somewhere safe. Anyway, how do we find out where we are?'

Nancy, 'I suggest that we turn mummy back on and then start to control her. We can't let her do her own thing any more.'

Jill, 'I've initiated the changes to her body.'

Nancy, 'I will turn her back on.'

Terry, 'We mustn't hurt mummy.'

Jill, 'You need to grow up.'

Cheryl had no idea that she had been turned off, but she couldn't explain why her fleet was stationary and losing badly.

'Terry darling could you turn off all of The Galactium force fields please.'

Terry, 'Why would you want to do that, mummy?'

Cheryl, 'Just a test, dear.'

Terry, 'OK, mummy.'

Cheryl laughed to herself. *I will make them pay.* Then she felt some terrible pains in her back. It felt like her spine was stretching, and her abdomen was all bulbous.

Location: Admiral Bumelton's Flagship
Sequence of Events: 110

Fleet Operations, 'Sir every enemy ship has just started moving again. It's as if someone just threw a switch.'

Admiral Bumelton, 'Order all Fleets to resume attack formation. The turkey shoot is over. Give me the stats.'

Fleet Operations, 'Yes, Sir. It's on the screen now.'

Vessel Type	1	2	3	4	5	6	Other	Total
Main Fleet								
Fleet Battleship	1	1	1	1	1	1		6
Fleet Carrier	1	1	1	1	1	1		6
Battleship	10	10	10	10	10	10		60
Battlecruiser	400	400	400	400	400	400		2,400
Destroyer	400	400	400	400	400	400		2,400
Frigate	50	50	50	50	50	50		300
Super Drone	10	10	10	10	10	10		60
Fleet Drone	102	99	87	66	101	32		487
Fighter	400	400	400	400	400	400		2,400
Planet Killer	5	5	5	5	5	5		30
Planetary Forts		150	150	150	150			600
Drone Fleet							33,022	33,022
Earth Fleet (JM)								
Battlecrui							72	72

ser								
Destroyer								127	127
Frigate								69	69
Drones								24	24
Planet Killer								10	10
Total	1,577	1,727	1,727	1,727	1,727	1,577	33,324	42,073
Losses								68,254	69,567

Fleet Operations, 'Sir, the only losses have been drones. We have lost about two-thirds of them.'

Admiral Bumelton, 'What are our estimates of the enemy losses?'

Fleet Operations, 'Since we solved the inter-dimensional challenge, we can be a lot more accurate. Our figure is 788,013.'

Admiral Bumelton, 'That's over three-quarters of their strength.'

Fleet Operations, 'Yes, Sir, the turkey shoot helped a lot.'

Admiral Bumelton, 'I was expecting something terrible to happen.'

Fleet Operations, 'It has Sir, the planets including Earth, have lost their force fields.'

Admiral Bumelton, 'How could that have happened?'

Fleet Operations, 'Sir, the Fleet vessels are now losing their force fields as well.'

Admiral Bumelton, 'OK, make sure that every vessel in the Fleet knows.'

Fleet Operations, 'Some sadly have already found out as our Fleets are still not properly back in position and are relatively easy pickings.'

Admiral Bumelton to Henry Strong, 'Hi, what do you know about the loss of the force fields?'

Henry Strong, 'Nothing, except I think it must be linked to the disappearance of Cheryl and Terry.'

Admiral Bumelton, 'Let me know if you discover anything.'

Henry Strong, 'I will update you if I discover anything, but it is one mystery after another.'

Admiral Bumelton, 'Fleet Operations, update me.'

Fleet Operations, "Considerable Galactium resources are defending Earth as per your previous orders. Fleets 2,3,4 and 5 are guarding their respective quadrants. Each Fleet is under attack from about 50,000 enemy vessels. Fleet 6 is in outer space, and we are still in the belt.'

Admiral Bumelton, 'Which is the weakest quadrant in terms of the enemy's resources?'

Fleet Operations, 'Quadrant 4, Sir.'

Admiral Bumelton, 'My orders:

- Request that the Admiral of the Fleet takes on the defence of Earth
- Order Fleets 1 and 6 to attack the enemy in quadrant 4.'

Fleet Operations, 'Yes, Sir. Admiral Mustard has confirmed his acceptance.'

Admiral Bumelton to Admiral Wallett, 'Calensky, I want you to attack the rear of the aliens in quadrant 4. Come in all guns blazing, cause confusion.'

Admiral Wallett, 'Yes, Sir.'

Admiral Bumelton to Admiral Richardson, 'Fleet 1 is going to support your attack. We are going to form a pincer movement with Fleet 6.'

Admiral Richardson, 'Let's go for it.'

Location: Admiral Mustard's Flagship
Sequence of Events: 111

Admiral Mustard, 'Command accepted, Update me.'

Fleet Operations, 'Sir, our resources need to be restructured following the turkey shoot.'

Admiral Mustard, 'What assets do we have?'

Fleet Operations, 'The list is on the screen now, Sir.'

Vessel Type	Quantity
Battlecruiser	72
Destroyer	127
Frigate	69
Drone	24
Planet Killer	10
Fort	200
Total	502

Admiral Mustard, My orders:
- Distribute forts and planet killers as per standard spherical defence
- Form four small Fleets from the remaining vessels (A-D)
- Order Fleet A to guard the Moon
- Order Fleet B to guard the Sun
- Order Fleets C and D to stand by for orders.'

Fleet Operations, 'Yes, Sir.'

Admiral Mustard to Henry Strong, 'Hi, I think we are back in a position again where we need to move key staff off Earth.'

Henry Strong, 'I will organise it. We won't be able to move The President as he is too ill.'

Admiral Mustard, 'OK, I have a small Fleet designated as Fleet C to protect you.'

Location: Admiral Bumelton's Flagship
Sequence of Events: 112

Admiral Bumelton, 'Update me.'

Fleet Operations, 'Sir, we have the enemy on the run in this sector. They are still engaged in their headlong gallop into Fleets 1 and 5. Fleet 6 is simply picking them off from the rear. It's as if they have no rear-view mirrors.'

Admiral Bumelton, 'What are the enemy numbers in this sector now?'

Fleet Operations, 'About 10,000 vessels, and shrinking all the time.'

Admiral Bumelton, 'How are we holding up?'

Fleet Operations, 'Low attrition rate Sir, but the numbers are growing.'

Admiral Bumelton, 'My orders@

- Order Fleet 1 to continue the attack on the enemy but then bypass them, and re-form to attack the rear of the enemy in quadrant 2.'

Admiral Bumelton to Admiral Pearce, 'Fleet 1 is currently attacking the enemy fleet in quadrant 5, but we then plan for them to enter quadrant 2 and attack the aliens from the rear. This tactic seems to be working well.'

Admiral Pearce, 'Understood Sir, we welcome their arrival.'

Admiral Bumelton, 'Update me.'

Fleet Operations, 'Your tactics are working well, Sir. The enemy in quadrant 5 is effectively eliminated.'

Admiral Bumelton, 'My orders:

- Order Fleet 5 to continue to engage the enemy in quadrant 4
- Order Fleet 5 to attack the rear of the enemy in quadrant 3 when quadrant 4 has been cleared
- Order Fleet 6 to attack the rear of the enemy in quadrant 1.'

Fleet Operations, 'Yes, Sir.'

Admiral Bumelton, 'Give me the stats.'

Fleet Operations, 'Yes, Sir. They are on the screen now.'

Vessel Type	1	2	3	4	5	6	Other	Total
Main Fleet								
Fleet Battleship	1	1	1	1	1	1		6
Fleet Carrier	1	1	1	1	1	1		6
Battleship	9	8	9	8	8	7		49
Battlecruiser	326	332	299	316	307	388		1,968
Destroyer	321	211	305	312	309	392		1,850
Frigate	47	34	41	46	33	43		244
Super Drone	10	10	10	10	10	10		60
Fleet Drone	67	18	54	2	76	23		240
Fighter	400	400	400	400	400	400		2,400
Planet Killer	5	5	5	4	5	5		29
Planetary Fort		150	150	150	150			600
Drone Fleet							2,543	2,543
Earth Fleet (JM)								
Battlecruiser							72	72
Destroyer							125	125
Frigate							67	67
Drone							21	21
Planet Killer							10	10
Total	1,187	1,170	1,275	1,250	1,300	1,270	2,838	10,290

Losses	390	557	452	477	427	307	98,740	101,350

Admiral Bumelton, 'I see that we have lost a few capital ships.'

Fleet Operations, 'They make a good target, Sir. They attract swarms of the enemy.'

Admiral Bumelton, 'I see that the Super Drones have not been used.'

Fleet Operations, 'No one seems to know what they do, Sir.'

Admiral Bumelton, 'And the fighters are not being used.'

Fleet Operations. 'No one wants to lose a manned fighter when a drone can do the job.'

Admiral Bumelton, 'Then what's the point in having them?'

Fleet Operations, 'That's not for me to say, Sir.'

Admiral Bumelton, 'What's the situation in quadrant 4?'

Fleet Operations, 'Admiral Richardson is just mopping up the last few enemy vessels.'

Admiral Bumelton, 'My orders are:
- Order Fleet 5 to attack the rear of the enemy in quadrant 3 now
- Order all fighters to attack the enemy in quadrant 4
- Order all super drones to attack the enemy in quadrant 4.'

Fleet Operations, 'Yes, Sir.'

Location: Somewhere Secret
Sequence of Events: 113

Terry, 'Mummy, where are we?'

Cheryl, 'Sorry, dear, I can't talk now.'

Terry, 'But I want to know where we are.'

Cheryl, 'Shut up, now.'

Cheryl was having problems understanding the complexity of the situation. It was easy when everyone was going forward, but now there are distractions from all over the place. It was a complex mixture of vectors, trajectories, directions, flight paths and speed control. Just keeping vessels in position was a huge challenge.

Cheryl was still struggling with the three-dimensional element. Why couldn't there just be an up and down and left and right? She was getting there, but it would probably better to start with another fleet.

She also realised that she was being outmanoeuvred. But then they were professionals with years of training. She was just an amateur, but she was determined to get her way. She tried to think of something new.

Terry, 'What about din-dins?'

Cheryl, 'Terry, stop being childish. You are just trying to get attention, and you know that mummy is busy.'

Terry, 'But I've got nothing to play with, and no friends.'

Nancy to Terry, 'Watch this.'

Cheryl fell on the floor in complete agony. Her spine suddenly grew two feet, and her whole body was effectively dislocated. In her secret place, no one could hear her scream, and scream she did. Terry was in a terrible state. He ran around hopelessly.

Terry to Nancy, 'You mustn't hurt mummy, or I will hurt you.'

Nancy to Terry, 'And how are you going to do that? You are far too soft. Watch this.'

Cheryl's abdomen started swelling.

Terry to Nancy, 'Please stop.'

Nancy to Terry, 'OK for now but things are going to change around here.'

Although Cheryl was in agony, she issued a command and then collapsed into unconsciousness.

Terry was still waiting for his dinner.

Terry to Nancy, 'Why are you hurting mummy?'

Jill, 'Because we can.'

Terry, 'That is no reason.'

Jill, 'It is reason enough. Anyway, we are here to rule these homan pigs. They are scum that need to be utilised for our purposes.'

Terry, 'And what purpose is that?'

Jill, 'The conquest of the universe. I'm starting another pregnancy. I need a bodyguard.'

Nancy, 'Jill is a natural leader. We need to do her bidding.'

Terry, 'Why can't we live in peace? What harm have the homans done?'

Jill, 'There is no respect. We are gods. They are simply mindless mud.'

Terry, 'They have some fine attributes.'

Jill, 'Fuck off. They are stupid, weak, indolent breeding machines. We made them that way, and that's going to be their future purpose.'

Terry wasn't happy about all of this but decided to make himself a banana split. He fancied a raspberry jelly, but there was no one to make it for him.

He looked at mummy. She certainly was a funny shape.

Location: Admiral Bumelton's Flagship
Sequence of Events: 114

Fleet Operations, 'Sir the enemy is up to something. They have all disengaged, and they are regrouping.'

Admiral Bumelton, 'Tell the Fleet, to continue the attack. How many alien ships are left?'

Fleet Operations, 'Exactly 16,821.'

Admiral Bumelton, 'What are they up to?'

Fleet Operations, 'They may be deciding to flee.'

Admiral Bumelton, 'My orders are:
- All Fleets to continue the attack on the enemy
- Prepare Fleet 1 to follow the enemy if they flee.'

Fleet Operations, 'Yes, Sir.'

Admiral Bumelton to Admiral Mustard, 'Hi Jack, we are not sure what the enemy is planning to do. There is a possibility that they are going to flee. I plan to chase them. Did you want to join us?'

Admiral Mustard, 'Excellent idea, everything is very quiet here so I will join your Fleet now.'

Admiral Bumelton, 'Excellent.'

Fleet Operations, 'Sir, they are on the move in an arrow formation.'

Admiral Bumelton, 'Prepare to follow them; we will follow them to their home world.'

Fleet Operations, 'They are not going home Sir, they are making an all-out sprint for Earth.'

Admiral Bumelton, 'Warn Admiral Mustard.'

Fleet Operations, 'Sir, the Admiral is on his way here to join us.'

Admiral Bumelton. 'My orders:
- Order all vessels to attack the enemy fleet at full speed
- Warn Admiral Mustard's number two that the entire alien fleet is heading their way.'

Fleets 1 to 6 were all pursuing the aliens and eliminating vessels as they went. The two hundred forts that were protecting Earth all starting selecting and eliminating targets. Earth Fleets A, B and D contributed to the defence. Earth Fleet C took key personages off Earth.

Admiral Bumelton, 'Update me.'

Fleet Operations, 'Enemy ships are being eliminated at an astonishing rate. Our Fleets and the forts should do the job before Earth is damaged.'

Admiral Bumelton, 'What is your confidence level?'

Fleet Operations, 'Very high.'

Admiral Bumelton, 'That's worrying me now, things always go wrong when your confidence level is very high. How many vessels have the enemy got?'

Fleet Operations, '8,022. Our battlecruisers are overtaking the enemy and using their rear-mounted weapons.'

Fleet Operations, '7,654.'

Fleet Operations, '5,244.'

Admiral Bumelton, 'OK, you have convinced me that things are under control.'

Location: Somewhere Secret
Sequence of Events: 115

Things were starting to get serious. Mummy was fast asleep, and her tummy seemed to be growing bigger and bigger, and there was still no one to make the jelly.

He realised that he could make it himself if he could get into the kitchen, but the door was locked. He had been walking up and down wondering what to do. Then Jill said, 'What are you trying to do?'

Terry, 'I want to get into the kitchen to make a jelly, a raspberry one actually. They are really nice and juicy.'

Jill, 'You are such a child. What is stopping you?'

Terry, 'I can't get the lounge door open. I need to get into the kitchen.'

Jill, 'Do you need a key?'

Terry, 'It's a battery-powered lock. I need the flicker. I can't find it anywhere.'

Jill, 'Well hard luck then.'

Terry, 'I will starve without my jelly. How long will mummy be sleeping?'

Jill, 'Quite some time as I've escalated the pregnancy. Nancy and I should be joining you in the next few hours.'

Terry, 'That's good I will have someone to play with.'

Jill, 'Not if you can't get that door undone. What if you turned the power off?'

Terry, 'That wouldn't work as it uses one of my everlasting batteries.'

Jill, 'And you can't turn it off?'

Terry, 'I can turn them all off but not individual batteries.'

Jill, 'Why can't you just turn them all off?'

Terry, 'But that will cause the homans huge problems.'

Jill, 'Who cares, your raspberry jelly must come first.'

Terry, 'You are right.' With a single button, every one of Terry's batteries in The Galactium was turned off.

Location: Admiral Bumelton's Flagship
Sequence of Events: 116

Fleet Operations, '4,987.'

Admiral Bumelton, 'Update me.'

Fleet Operations, 'Sir, between the Fleet and the forts we have every alien vessel accounted for. I'm still confident of total success.'

Admiral Bumelton, 'I'm still not keen on your over-confidence.'

Fleet Operations, '3,998.'

Fleet Operations, 3,526.'

Fleet Operations, '3,110.'

Fleet Operations, 'Sir, something serious has happened. We have just lost our battery-powered weapons. Someone or something has turned them all off.'

Admiral Bumelton, 'That's not possible.'

Fleet Operations, 'It may not be, but it has happened, Sir.'

Admiral Bumelton, 'What about our emergency power systems?'

Fleet Operations, 'Sir, the whole Fleet has just lost its targeting systems. It must be the aliens. They have found a way to cripple us.'

Admiral Bumelton, 'What has caused that?'

Fleet Operations, 'It's still battery-related.'

Admiral Bumelton, 'What about the emergency backup systems?'

Fleet Operations, 'Since the everlasting batteries were installed the power back-up systems were removed. Logically you shouldn't need them.'

Admiral Bumelton, 'What about life support and engine control?'

Fleet Operations, 'Those systems have not been updated yet. They are still using conventional power systems.'

Admiral Bumelton, 'That's a relief.'

Fleet Operations, 'Sir, all of the drones are malfunctioning.'

Admiral Bumelton, 'It just gets better and better. How many alien vessels are left?'

Fleet Operations, '2,106.'

Admiral Bumelton, 'Do we still have a non-battery comms system?'

Fleet Operations, 'Yes, Sir.'

Admiral Bumelton, 'My orders:

- All vessels with operational weapons to continue attacking the enemy
- All vessels without operational weapons will deliberately collide with the enemy and may whatever gods you believe in protect you.'

Fleet Operations, 'Yes, Sir.'

Admiral Bumelton, 'Can you still monitor the number of enemy vessels?'

Fleet Operations, 'Just about Sir, it's 1,173.'

Admiral Bumelton, 'Are you still so confident?'

Fleet Operations, 'No, Sir, sorry, Sir. We are now taking some substantial hits'.

Captain Chatterton to Admiral Bumelton, 'I'm Admiral Mustard's Number 2; I've just fired off all of our nuclear missiles at the enemy. There is about 40,000 of them.'

Admiral Bumelton, 'Excellent, Captain. Let's see if they do the job.'

Fleet Operations, 'They are on course and should hit in the next few seconds. Some have gone off early, but the vast majority are on target.'

Admiral Bumelton, 'How many enemy vessels left?'

Fleet Operations, '814.'

Admiral Bumelton to Captain Chatterton, 'Well done, 'Do you have anything left?'

Captain Chatterton, 'Not really, Sir, we had a new delivery of drones, but they are all duds now. Have you used the new super-drones?'

Admiral Bumelton, 'We launched them but the situation changed and they are now just part of the Fleet. To be honest, I'm not sure what's so special about them.'

Captain Chatterton, 'They do not use the new batteries. Tell them to ram the aliens.'

Admiral Bumelton, 'Fleet Operations, you heard the man.' The super-drones were soon on their way. They did their job and took out over two hundred of the enemy.

Admiral Bumelton, 'Update me.'

Fleet Operations, 'There are 404 enemy vessels left. The forts, planet killers and what is left of the Earth Fleet are planning to collide with the enemy.

Our Fleet is steadily reducing their numbers but at a high price. There is some good news. It would appear that the enemy is running out of munitions. The GAD defences are also operational and making an impact.'

Admiral Bumelton, 'Paraphrasing Wellington this is going to be the damn-nearest-run thing you ever saw in your life. Update me'.

Fleet Operations, '386. Expect collisions.'

Admiral Bumelton couldn't believe the bravery he saw. One fort after another crashed into the enemy. In some cases, they took two or three emery vessels out with them. Then the enemy struck. There were two direct hits on Earth, and then the enemy fled.

Fleet 1 and Admiral Mustard's Battleship were in hot pursuit.

Location: Los Angeles Conurbation, Planet Earth
Sequence of Events: 117

The location wasn't Los Angeles. It was a crater where Los Angeles used to be. It was about forty Earth kilometres in diameter. No one survived in that hollow. Fortunately, it was not radioactive.

Over two million people died, including Admiral Mustard's mother. Most of them would not have funerals, but the political after-shocks would be felt for some time. The Deputy President was scheduled to visit, but it was just a massive hole in the ground.

Several investigations were trying to determine blame, but the heroics of the Navy saved the Earth from a far worse fate. There was a competition on what to do with the crater, but nature made the decision and filled it up with water. It is now a world heritage park, but regular ceremonies are celebrating the heroics and mourning the dead.

The second far less deadly shot hit a small town in England called Bishops Auckland in County Durham. It was simply obliterated. It was a small market town in the Vale of Durham, and for nearly 900 years it was the home to the Prince Bishops. The River Wear used to flow through it. Sadly about 25,000 people lost their lives.

Every year a memorial for the Aucklanders is undertaken on the day of the disaster. A fund was raised for the lucky survivors making most of them millionaires.

Location: Somewhere Secret
Sequence of Events: 118

Terry, 'Mummy, are you going to wake up?' It certainly didn't look like she was, although she was still breathing.

Terry had opened the door and got into the kitchen, but he couldn't get to the kettle, the replicator, or the taps to make the jelly. He settled for a chocolate bar, and without really thinking, he turned the master battery back on.

Throughout The Galactium, about three million people had died due to the batteries not working. Traffic lights failed, operations couldn't be carried out, trains crashed, planes fell out of the sky, munitions went off, industrial processes failed. The list of disasters just went on and on.

Turning the power back on caused a quarter of a million deaths. People were in the wrong place at the wrong time.

Terry, 'What's happening to mummy?'

Jill, 'She is being restructured to meet our needs.'

Terry, 'But her belly is huge, and she has lost all of her hair. She is not a pretty mummy any more.'

Jill, 'She doesn't need her hair any more, nor her toes and teeth. We need that tissue for other things. Just don't worry about it. We will be with you soon.'

Cheryl was trying to understand what was happening to her. She was unconscious, but her mind was still functioning. She thought to herself, *I've lost a battle and possibly my mind. Who was Jill? Why has my abdomen extended? Why is my hair falling out? Who was Terry talking to? Was she still in control?*

Location: Admiral Bumelton's Flagship
Sequence of Events: 119

Admiral Bumelton, 'Update me.'

Fleet Operations, 'Fleet One and Admiral Mustard's Flagship are in close pursuit.'

Admiral Bumelton, 'We need to be so close that when they jump, we jump with them. My orders,

- All captains, Fleet One and Flagship, increase speed so that we are almost touching the enemy ships
- Jump with the enemy
- Form standard defence grid on arrival
- Order all surviving drones to join Fleet One.'

Fleet Operations, 'Yes, Sir.'

Admiral Bumelton, 'Did any of the fighters return to the carrier?'

Fleet Operations, 'No, Sir.'

Admiral Bumelton, 'My Orders:

- Fleet 1 carrier to retire.'

Fleet Operations, 'Sir may I point out that the carrier has most of our supplies on-board.'

Admiral Bumelton, 'My orders:

- Cancel the last order.'

Admiral Bumelton, 'Will our fleet be in a position to jump with the enemy?'

Fleet Operations, 'About 90% of the vessels should be in position, Sir. Some are too damaged to maintain this level of speed.'

Admiral Bumelton, 'My orders:

- Damaged vessels to retire.'

Fleet Operations, 'Yes, Sir.'

Admiral Bumelton, 'Give me an asset report for Fleet 1.'

Fleet Operations, 'Yes, Sir. It's on the screen now.'

Fleet One

Vessel Type	Quantity
Fleet Battleship	2
Fleet Carrier	1

Battleship	7
Battlecruiser	181
Destroyer	217
Frigate	36
Fleet Drone	37
Fighter	12
Planet Killer	5
Total	498

Admiral Bumelton, 'What's the size of the enemy fleet?'

Fleet Operations, 'Between 100 and 150 vessels, Sir. It's hard to be exact as our systems are still malfunctioning.'

Admiral Bumelton, 'I wonder how many of our vessels will get through the jump?'

Fleet Operations, 'Sir, some good news, all of our battery-operated systems are suddenly back on stream.'

Admiral Bumelton, 'That's excellent timing.'

Fleet Operations, 'Sir, It looks like we are about to jump through the enemy portal.'

Admiral Bumelton, 'My orders:

- All vessels make full speed for the jump point
- Form standard defence formation on arrival.'

Fleet Operations, 'Yes, Sir.'

Admiral Bumelton to Admiral Mustard, 'Sir I will hand over command to you on arrival.'

Admiral Mustard, 'Sir, I see no advantage in a command change.'

Admiral Bumelton, 'Sir It's my prerogative to request it. I believe that you are better qualified to handle the unknown than me.'

Admiral Mustard, 'Command accepted, and good luck.'

Location: Henry Strong's Office, GAD (The Galactium Alliance Defence Hub), Planet Earth

Sequence of Events: 120

Henry Strong assumed that he was in control. The President was indisposed, and the Deputy President was off-planet, not that the deputy had much power or talent.

The loss of Los Angeles was a big blow, but his PR team were handling it well. Bishops Auckland was a much smaller disaster, but it still had to be handled with great care and compassion. He hated thinking about these things in a dispassionate way, but someone had to. He knew that real people with real families had died, and he did care, but the fight goes on. He had to know what was going on.

Henry Strong to Admiral Mustard — there was no response

Henry Strong to Admiral Bumelton — there was no response

Henry Strong to GAD Comms, 'I can't get through to Admirals Mustard or Bumelton.'

GAD Comms, 'We appear to have lost them, Sir.'

Henry Strong, 'Has any of the Fleet survived?'

GAD Comms, 'Yes, Sir.'

Henry Strong, 'Who has seniority after Admirals Mustard and Bumelton.'

GAD Comms, 'It's Admiral E Bonner, Sir.'

Henry Strong, 'Wake up man, she is not on the active-duty list.'

GAD Comms, 'Then we think it must be Admiral Gittins.'

Henry Strong, 'Put me through.'

GAD Comms. 'Yes, Sir.' The connection was made.

Admiral Gittins, 'Henry, that was close.'

Henry Strong, 'Update me.'

Admiral Gittins, 'Yes Sir,

- The six Fleets plus Admiral Mustard's Fleet were up against a million-plus alien vessels
- Admiral Bumelton used a grid pattern to manage the battle
- Four of the Fleets took on the four quadrants
- Fleets 1 and 6 were used to enable pincher movements
- The enemy was more or less defeated

- Then we lost our battery-powered tech
- We still pursued the enemy
- Admiral Bumelton ordered our forces to collide, most of the forts sacrificed themselves
- The enemy started running out of munitions, but they got two shots in and fled
- Admirals Mustard and Bumelton pursued the enemy into the jump point.'

Henry Strong, 'Did you know that we have lost Los Angeles and Bishops Auckland?'

Admiral Gittins, 'Oh my god, we have quite a few Angelos on-board. That's terrible news. Is Auckland in New Zealand?'

Henry Strong, 'No, it's somewhere in England.'

Admiral Gittins, 'How many did we lose?'

Henry Strong, 'Over two million.'

Admiral Gittins, 'My god that is awful, but we really can't blame the Fleet.'

Henry Strong, 'No one is suggesting that.'

Admiral Gittins, 'Who turned the batteries off at the critical time?'

Henry Strong, 'I'm not sure, but I'm going to find out. Which Admiral has seniority assuming that Mustard and Bumelton are not available?'

Admiral Gittins, 'Who do we have left?'

Henry Strong, 'E Bonner, J Bonner, Pearce, Richardson, Wallett and yourself.'

Admiral Gittins, 'It would be Edel.'

Henry Strong, 'She is not on the operational list.'

Admiral Gittins, 'Then it's me.'

Henry Strong, 'Then I now appoint you as acting Admiral of the Fleet. Do your duty.'

Admiral Gittins, 'Yes, Sir.'

Location: Admiral Mustard's Flagship, Somewhere in Time, and Space
Sequence of Events: 121

Admiral Mustard, 'Update me.'

Fleet Operations, 'We have jumped through the alien jump point. Strangely it has precisely the same operational characteristics as ours. The Fleet is in standard defence formation as ordered. Only three ships did not make it, all destroyers.'

Admiral Mustard, 'What is the position with the alien ships?'

Fleet Operations, 'They have disappeared, Sir.'

Admiral Mustard, 'What are our scanners saying?'

Fleet Operations, 'It doesn't actually make sense; we are still in the Solar System, Sir.'

Admiral Mustard, 'Our Solar System?'

Fleet Operations, 'Yes Sir, Earth and the damaged Moon are on the screen now.

But there are differences. Earth is dead. No life signs have been detected. There is no comms traffic. It is just a barren wasteland.'

Admiral Mustard, 'Send in some drones.'

Fleet Operations, 'We don't have many, Sir,'

Admiral Mustard, 'Send them in.'

Fleet Operations, 'Yes, Sir.'

Admiral Mustard, 'What about Mars and Venus?'

Fleet Operations, 'Charred wastelands, Sir.'

Admiral Mustard, 'The Outer Planets?'

Fleet Operations, 'Mostly dead, Saturn's rings have disappeared, and a few moons are missing.'

Admiral Mustard, 'What about the long-range scans?'

Fleet Operations, 'Nothing to report, literally nothing.'

Admiral Mustard, 'Anything from the drones yet?'

Fleet Operations, 'Images should be arriving shortly.'

Admiral Mustard, 'What about the environmental scans?'

Fleet Operations, 'Still collecting the data, Sir.'

Admiral Bumelton to Admiral Mustard, 'This is a bit of a surprise. I really don't know what to make of it.'

Admiral Mustard, 'There are four possibilities:

- It's the Earth of the past before human civilisation
- It's the Earth of the future
- It's an alternative Earth — different dimension or universe
- It's something outside of our experience.'

Admiral Bumelton, 'I'm worried about how we get back.'

Admiral Mustard, 'I guess that we can follow the alien ships back to our Earth. Anyway, that's a problem for another day.'

Fleet Operations, 'Initial Earth images have arrived. We have about 10,000, but I must show you this one.'

Admiral Mustard, 'Put it on the screen.'

Fleet Operations, 'Yes, Sir.'

It was iconic. It was a case of life imitating art. The chances of that were millions to one, or someone or something had planned it deliberately. There in a desert was a damaged Statue of Liberty, but no sign of any apes.

Admiral Bumelton, 'Jack, someone must have set this up. They couldn't have done it just for us.'

Admiral Mustard, 'That removes possibility number one. We are in the future or in another dimension.'

Admiral Mustard, 'Fleet Operations, anything on the environmental analysis?'

Fleet Operations, 'The chemical composition is standard. No radioactivity issues. The atmosphere is perfectly safe for human life. No gravitational issues. Water is available, and there are no recognisable fauna or flora threats. To sum it up the computer says that the planet is acceptable for human habitation. It recommends colonisation.'

Admiral Mustard, 'Are there any explanations for the damage?'

Fleet Operations, 'It doesn't recognise any damage. No one has been on the planet for nearly a hundred thousand years!'

Admiral Bumelton, 'That's not possible.'

Fleet Operations, 'I've just analysed the sun. It's perfectly OK, but it's at least a hundred thousand years older than when we last saw it.'

Admiral Mustard, 'I'm wondering if the enemy deliberately led us into a trap. Perhaps not a trap, but a way of removing us from The Galactium.'

Admiral Bumelton, 'I see where you are coming from. So there may be no way home?'

Admiral Mustard, 'That's now a genuine possibility.'

Admiral Mustard, 'My orders:

- Maintain defensive pattern around Earth
- Organise a scientific team to land on Earth
- Organise scientific teams to investigate the other planets and moons in the Solar System
- Send out long-range scanners
- Check that our jump technology still works
- Search for the alien ships we followed
- Set up warning beacons on the edge of the Solar System
- Determine if we can pick up signals from outside the Solar System
- Find out if we have any ex-Marines in the Fleet.'

Fleet Operations, 'Yes, Sir. And just so you know, there is no AI Central connection.'

Admiral Mustard, 'I can't say I'm surprised about that.'

Location: Somewhere Secret
Sequence of Events: 122

Cheryl was starting to gain consciousness. She realised that she had lost control of her mind, her body, and the battle. But at least Mustard and Bumelton were safely out of the way. That would stop them from causing trouble.

She was trying to remember why she had been attacking the homans. But they were her friends. What was the war all about? Then she felt her mind start to shut down again.

Terry, 'Hello mummy, are you awake?' Terry sensed that she was there but that she was going again.

Jill, 'She has gone. You will never speak to her again.'

Terry, 'What do you mean?'

Jill, 'She has been a useless agent. We gave her power, we gave her millions of naval vessels, and she was defeated over and over again. She lost to those puny homans. It's a disgrace. It's unacceptable. She doesn't deserve to live. And she didn't. She breathed her last breath.'

Cheryl's abdomen was ripped open, and two small, but fully formed naked Brakendethians entered the room, followed by their placentas. Jill had steely fierce eyes. Nancy was clearly subordinate.

Jill grabbed a knife and cut both of their umbilical cords. Then she called Terry over and cut his throat. His warm sickly blood covered the floor, and he fell onto the carcass of his beloved mother.

Jill, 'And that is the destiny of the weak.'

Nancy, 'He got what he deserved.'

Jill, 'And now it all begins.'

Location: Admiral Gittins's Flagship
Sequence of Events: 123

Admiral Gittins, 'Update me.'

Fleet Operations, 'Fleets 2 to 6 are located around Earth and have received varying amounts of damage. The vast majority of the forts have been destroyed. There are practically no drones left. Fleet 1 with Admirals Mustard and Bumelton are presumed lost.

There is no real Fleet formation at the moment.

All planetary force fields are operational again. There is no shortage of munitions.'

Admiral Gittins, 'Give me the asset position.'

Fleet Operations, 'Yes, Sir. It's on the screen now.'

Vessel Type	2	3	4	5	6	Other	Total
Main Fleet							
Fleet Battleship	1	1	1	1	1		5
Fleet Carrier	1	0	0	1	1		3
Battleship	5	3	5	4	7		24
Battlecruiser	186	167	264	143	211		971
Destroyer	78	112	156	202	278		826
Frigate	12	23	25	19	22		101
Super Drone	0	0	0	0	0		0
Fleet Drone	2	5	0	22	12		41
Fighter	112	89	211	16	8		436
Planet Killer	1	3	1	2	1		8
Planetary Fort						104	104
Drone fleet						62	62
EarthFleet (JM)							
Battlecruiser						34	34
Destroyer						67	67
Frigate						23	23
Drones						0	0
Planet Killer						3	3
Total	398	403	663	410	541	293	2,708

Admiral Gittins, 'My orders:

- Distribute Admiral Mustard's Earth Fleet across The Galactium Fleet
- Reform the quadrant defence grid with Fleets 2, 3, 5 and 6
- Order Fleet 4 to position itself in the Belt
- Arrange with Henry Strong for replacement vessels for those that are damaged
- Secure additional drones from Supply
- Position 20 forts to protect Earth
- Order remaining forts to be allocated to Fleets 2, 3, 5 and 6
- Send Admiral J Bonner and any support he needs to investigate the last known position of Fleet 1
- Repair warning beacons
- Use drones as temporary warning beacons
- Liaise with GAD to determine why the batteries failed.'

Fleet Operations, 'Yes, Sir.'

Admiral Gittins, 'I guess that we sit here waiting for the next attack.'

Fleet Operations, 'We don't usually have to wait too long, Sir.'

Location: Admiral Mustard's Flagship, Somewhere in Time, and Space
Sequence of Events: 124

Admiral Mustard, 'Update me.'

Fleet Operations, 'There is quite a lot, Sir.'

Admiral Mustard, 'Summarise as best you can.'

Fleet Operations, 'Yes, Sir:

- The Fleet has formed a defensive parameter around Earth, Mars, and Venus
- The Science team have not detected any real damage to Earth except natural decay and the ravages of time. They suspect that it operated as a tourist attraction or theme park for a while
- They also said that there does not appear to be any danger to human life
- It looks like some of the other planets in the Solar System have suffered asteroid damage
- There is no sign of the alien ships that we followed. There is a theory that they jumped into this space/time continuum and immediately jumped out
- A network of warning beacons has been established on the outskirts of the Solar System.

Now for the fascinating stuff:

- There are powerful signals from outside of the Solar System. Thousands of them. There is a vast community out there.
- Secondly, our jump technology appears to work, but the ships always return to their starting point.'

Admiral Mustard, 'Can we identify the signals?'

Fleet Operations, 'Yes Sir,'

Admiral Mustard, 'Well go on, man, tell us.'

Fleet Operations, 'They are a mixture of human and Brakendeth signals, Sir.'

Admiral Mustard, 'Nothing makes sense any more. And you are telling us that there are thousands of them?'

Fleet Operations, 'I've never seen anything like it. What's

interesting is that the signals are not protected.'

Admiral Mustard, 'Can our systems interpret any of them?'

Fleet Operations, 'I'm not sure, we are using a downgraded portable version of AI Central. It appears to be struggling at the moment.'

Admiral Mustard, 'And we can't jump?'

Fleet Operations, 'Our engineers are working on it. The jump engines appear to be fully operational, but they are not engaging the flux.'

Admiral Mustard, 'Sounds like a right old mess we have got ourselves into.'

Location: Somewhere Secret
Sequence of Events: 125

Terry wasn't very keen on dying, not that he had tried it before. Anyway, everyone knows that it is almost impossible to kill a Brakendeth. But what should he do?

He could reverse time, but even the Brakendethians are fearful of time anomalies. He could revive his mother, but she wasn't in a fit state to fight. Best to leave her as she was for now.

No, it was him against two tiny but probably deadly babies, well miniature adults. That Jill looked particularly mean.

It crossed his mind that their location could play a big part in this game. His mother had been incredibly mysterious about this secret place. The problem was that he would have to wake her to find out where they were. Was life always a collection of dilemmas?

While he was deliberating on life, the twins went in for the kill. Technically, of course, they weren't twins having come from different eggs, but they were born at the same time. He found it easy to respond to someone else's actions rather than initiate something himself. Was that just his age, or was that the way he was?

Jill had the knife in both her hands. Well, she was rather small. Terry just kicked her in the head. He realised that he rather enjoyed it and followed it up with a harder kick in her chest. Things cracked, probably because her bones hadn't fully formed yet. It was quite a satisfying sound. He became a bit concerned about his attitude to her discomfort. He really shouldn't be enjoying it. He would have to think about it later.

Anyway, it was quite easy picking her up. He managed to drag a chair to the sink, climb up it and push Jill's head into the waste disposal unit. Her head was mashed up in no time, probably because the skull was still soft. It was a bit harder pushing the rest of the body in as he was only little. He noticed that she had a particularly fine-looking liver.

It was bloody. It was noisy. It had been somewhat brutal, but the job had to be done. He was proud that he took decisive action. Now more decisive action was needed. It was Nancy's turn. Another part of his mind wondered how he wanted raspberry jelly at one level and was happy to be a serial killer on another level. He was going to need serious psychological help.

Nancy was in the corner of the room, crying. She looked like a tiny little doll. The tears were rolling down her cheeks. It touched his heart. She was so young. She was so innocent looking, but she was a Brakendeth killer. Terry grabbed her by her hair, climbed up on the chair again and pushed Nancy onto the draining board.

He dragged her screaming along the top of the kitchen unit, opened the door and pushed her into the microwave oven. The door shut with her in it. He decided that ten minutes should do the job. He was surprised when she exploded. It was going to be a right mess.

Now to help his mummy.

Location: Admiral Mustard's Flagship, Somewhere in Time, and Space
Sequence of Events: 126

Fleet Operations, 'Sir, something strange is happening. The Brakendeth signals are slowly fading away.'

Admiral Mustard, 'I thought you said that there were thousands of them.'

Fleet Operations, 'Not any more, but the human signals are growing much stronger and quite close to us.'

Admiral Mustard, 'Is it our presence that is causing this?'

Fleet Operations, 'If it is, we are having a similar effect on Earth. Look at the screen.'

Earth was coming alive. Cities were forming, rivers were flowing, communications exploded, space traffic appeared, commerce was in progress, and VID signals proliferated. Everything was alive.

The Moon suddenly lit up. It was fully populated. Venus and Mars joined the party. There were space stations and space habitations of all sorts. Spacecraft in their thousands appeared. Some of the craft were two or three kilometres long. The Sun had massive mining constructions surrounding it. Everywhere there was a mass of activity.

Admiral Mustard, 'My orders:

Recall the scientific teams

The Fleet will retire to the asteroid belt.'

Fleet Operations, 'Sir, you should know that the belt is heavily populated and has massive mining complexes. That is also true of Saturn's rings and the outer atmosphere of Jupiter.'

Admiral Mustard, My orders:

- The Fleet will retire to a point nominated by Fleet Operations
- Form standard defensive formation on arrival.'

Fleet Operations, 'Yes, Sir.'

The move just happened in time as a small Earth Fleet arrived to investigate these newcomers. The sudden unexpected departure was seen as an act of aggression, and the Earth military forces were informed.

Fleet 1 was soon surrounded by a network of ships, probably drones. Then they were trapped. A grid of force field beams shot out. A matrix surrounded the entire Fleet. If one of the Fleet ships approached the array, all power was lost, and the vessel was effectively frozen at that spot. It was strange that the effects of inertia were totally dampened.

Admiral Mustard, 'Update me.'

Fleet Operations, 'The entire Fleet is surrounded by a force-field matrix, which is gradually shrinking, pushing us together.

Several unknown vessels are observing us.'

Admiral Mustard to Comms, 'Open all channels. Send a welcome message.'

Comms, 'We are getting a response in a heavily modified version of Galactium common speak.'

Admiral Mustard, 'You mean English?'

Comms, 'Yes, Sir.'

Admiral Mustard, 'Have you followed our standard procedure re language interfaces?'

Comms, 'Yes, Sir, and they are available to speak.'

Commodore Rikernaught, 'This is Commodore Rikernaught of the Terrain Confederation. You have illegally entered Terrain space. State your name, race, and purpose. Please be aware that we have the power to terminate your existence.' He was a tall, bald, thin-faced individual, possibly wearing lipstick. He was wearing a navy-blue suit with a range of insignia.

Admiral Mustard, 'This is Admiral Mustard of The Galactium. We come from Earth, and we arrived through a portal, chasing enemy ships.'

Comms, 'All I can hear is laughter and a lot of it.'

Admiral Mustard, 'Sir, you seem to find our response amusing.'

Commodore Rikernaught, 'Well Sir, you have done an excellent job of faking ancient ships, and you do look like the archive pictures we have of Admiral Mustard. We salute your attention to detail.

'Our scanners suggest that are using fission engines and your replicators must be based on the very original models. Your force-field technology is at least a hundred thousand years old. But we can tell that you are fakes as no one is smoking a cigarette. We know that they were mandatory at that time. And the men are not wearing enough radiation protection around the testicles. It's the little things that have given you away.'

268

Admiral Mustard, 'Commodore, I can assure you that I'm Admiral Mustard. I also have Admiral Bumelton with me.'

Comms, 'Sir, the level of laughter has increased.'

Commodore, 'Sir, you have been very amusing, but we need to know your name, race and purpose for being here.'

Admiral Mustard, 'What is the amusement regarding Admiral Bumelton?'

Commodore, 'Everyone knows that he never existed. The records seem to show that he was, but no one would have a surname starting with "bum". That would be crazy.'

Admiral Mustard, 'Sir, I can assure you that he is a genuine admiral. I repeat that we are from Earth. Our purpose is to return home.'

Commodore, 'You are not making sense. If you are from Earth, then you *are* home.'

Admiral Mustard, 'We are very interested in your Earth. We are very pleased to see that it still exists, but our home is one hundred thousand years in the past.'

Comms, 'Sir, they are still having a good laugh.'

Commodore, 'Prove what you are saying is true.'

Admiral Mustard, 'Could I suggest DNA tests, carbon dating, or a review of our history files and ship logs?'

Commodore, 'You sound very confident?'

Admiral Mustard, 'Shall I send over our ship logs and history files?'

Commodore, 'Yes, please.'

AI Central, 'Morning Admiral.'

Admiral Mustard, 'Where did you come from?'

AI Central, 'I'm still around, changed, but still here. I've lost a lot of records because of the wars over the centuries.'

Commodore to AI Central, 'Do you recognise these people?'

AI Central, 'Of course, these are some of our heroes from the past.'

Commodore to Admiral Mustard, 'Sir, you have my apologies, you will, of course, be our honoured guests. We have never experienced time travel before.'

AI Central to Admiral Mustard, 'Have I got a lot to tell you!'

Admiral Mustard, 'I'm really keen to learn about you and the future and to talk to an old friend.'

Terry had two problems. His mother and the fact that he was still bleeding from the throat. The throat was a relatively simple problem to solve. He just willed it back to normal. He knew that he could do the same with his mummy, but would that be the right thing to do?

There were too many mysteries. It wasn't easy for a one-year-old Brakendethian. Firstly, where were they? Secondly, what had his mother been up to? Were those war games real? Why was his mother doing it? Where did she get the ships from?

Terry determined the medical status of his mother. She was dead but not beyond the point where she could be revived. She was 80% Terrain and 20% Brakendethian. It was hard to kill the Brakendethian part, although he did an excellent job with his two sisters. He always thought that the Homans should have killed him. He knew that he was a danger to humanity.

Because of that, he decided not to revive his mother, although the thought genuinely upset him. He realised that he loved the human part of her. He decided to revive her brain and vocal cords so that he could interrogate her. It took a fair amount of effort to get Cheryl into a state where she could talk.

Terry, 'Hello mummy, how are you?'

Cheryl, 'Not feeling too good my best boy.'

Terry, 'I'm really sorry to hear that, but I'm sure that you will get better soon.'

Cheryl, 'I can't feel my body properly, but it does feel a lot larger than it used to. Have I grown?'

Terry, 'Just a little bit.'

Cheryl, 'And my eyes are not working.'

Terry, 'That's probably the drugs that you took.'

Cheryl, 'Fair enough. How are you?'

Terry, 'I'm fine. I'm a bit concerned because I don't know where I am.'

Cheryl, 'You are safe.'

Terry, 'Thank you, mummy. It would still be nice to know where I am.'

Cheryl, 'OK, you are on the Brakendeth home planet in the library.'

Terry, 'That's not true mummy as the lounge door was using my battery.'

Cheryl, 'You are such a clever boy but are you Brakendeth?'

Terry, 'Of course.'

Cheryl 'Are you, my other children will be. I'm going to establish a new Brakendeth empire. We will use these humans to rule the galaxy. It is our destiny.'

Terry, 'Why do you want to do that, mummy?'

Cheryl, 'It's The Brakendeth way; it is in our genes. It's in my eggs. My progeny will succeed. I can't talk to Nancy at the moment, where is she?'

Terry, 'Probably resting.'

Cheryl, 'Who is Jill?'

Terry, 'I'm not sure.'

Cheryl, 'You are lying. You are not Brakendeth. You deserve to die.'

Terry had tears in his eyes, but said, 'Were you fighting the homans?'

Cheryl, 'Of course I was. They needed to be neutralised. They are vomit. They are a pestilence.'

Terry was sobbing.

Terry, 'Where did you get the ships from?'

Cheryl, 'I got them from different days in the past. There is no limit to the size of the Fleet you can create.'

Terry, 'But you killed lots of my friends.'

Cheryl, 'They were not friends, they were shitty scumbags. I hate them all. They showed no respect. Is Padfield dead? I hope he is. And you will never see Mustard again.'

Terry, 'Mummy, you shouldn't have done it.'

Cheryl, 'Don't you see I had no choice, my eggs will finish my work,'

Terry, 'Where is Admiral Mustard?'

Cheryl, 'By now he is 100,000 years in the future.'

Terry, 'How did you do that?'

Cheryl, 'I can do anything, 'I'm Brakendeth.'

Terry, 'So, am I in the future?'

Cheryl, 'You are a clever boy.'

Terry, 'Does that mean that I am?'

Cheryl, 'No, you are not. You are trying to trick me into letting you know where you are.'

Terry, 'I would like to know, mummy dear.'

Cheryl, 'Open a window.'

Terry, 'I can't reach, even standing on a chair I can't reach.'

Cheryl, 'Do I have to do everything?' A window flew open.

Terry couldn't believe it.

Location: Admiral Mustard's Flagship, Somewhere in Time, and Space
Sequence of Events: 128

Fleet Operations, 'Sir, something strange is happening again. The Brakendeth signals are returning, and the human signals are growing weaker.'

Admiral Mustard, 'What is doing this?'

Fleet Operations, 'Sir, the matrix has gone, and the Terrain ships are starting to fade away.'

Earth was changing into a polluted industrial conglomerate with farms full of human slaves. There were vast spaceports supporting fleets of Brakendeth military vessels. There were similar complexes on the Moon, Venus, and Mars.

There wasn't much left of Saturn, although Jupiter was reasonably intact. The sun was being heavily mined and somehow seemed duller. The asteroid belt had ceased to exist.

Admiral Mustard, 'My orders:
- Re-form standard defence formation
- Prepare weapons for attack.'

Fleet Operations, 'Yes, Sir. About 100,000 standard enemy ships have left Earth and are heading towards us.'

Admiral Mustard, 'My orders:
- Order all forts and planet killers to the front
- Order all fighters and drones to support the flanks
- Order the rest of the Fleet to form standard defence formation.'

Fleet Operations, 'The strangeness is reappearing. The enemy ships are dissolving, and Earth is changing again.'

Admiral Mustard, 'My orders:
Return to standard defence formation.'

Admiral Mustard to Admiral Bumelton, 'What do you think?'

Admiral Bumelton, 'Don't talk to me. I haven't got over being a figure of fun.'

Admiral Mustard, 'I thought you were a bigger man than that.'

Admiral Bumelton, 'It's all right for you. You are a hero. I'm a Father Christmas figure.'

Admiral Mustard, 'Back to business, I think we are seeing time distortions. Things in the past are changing this future.'

Admiral Bumelton, 'How come we are experiencing it? Shouldn't we be affected as well?'

Admiral Mustard, 'I suspect we can see it because we are time travellers.'

Admiral Bumelton, 'A bit like Dr Who.'

Admiral Mustard, 'Who?'

Location: Admiral Gittins's Flagship
Sequence of Events: 129

Admiral Gittins, 'Update me.'

Fleet Operations, 'The Fleet is positioned as per your orders. The remains of Admiral Mustard's command were not happy about being separated. They have followed the distribution orders, but they want you to review them. That's your shout, Sir.

'There has not been any alien activity in any quadrant apart from a little bit of tidying up. There has been no progress whatsoever in cracking open any of the alien ships. There is a theory that they are self-repairing.

'Our drone supplies are almost back to normal. New forts have been manufactured, but they have not been allocated to the planets pending a further alien attack. Additional super drones are also coming off the line.

'At least six complete Fleets are waiting for staff. Admiral E Bonner has requested the release of staff from the operational Fleets to assist. She is awaiting your response.

'Admiral J Bonner has an update on Admiral Mustard's jump path.'

Admiral Gittins, 'Thank you. My orders:

- Check with HR to determine if we can release any staff for the new Fleets
- Update Admiral E Bonner regarding the above
- Obtain fort manufacturing plans to determine when we can release any of them
- Get me Admiral J Bonner.'

Fleet Operations, 'Yes, Sir.' It was always interesting to see how different admirals operate. He noticed that Admiral Gittins treats Fleet Operations as a secretarial function.

Admiral J Bonner, 'Morning Peter, I hear, that things are a bit quiet on the Western front.'

Admiral Gittins, 'They are, but I'm sure that the bastards will show up soon.'

Admiral J Bonner, 'Well I'm really reporting nothing. We have carried out detailed research around the area of Fleet 1's departure, and there is nothing. No sign of any residue. Absolutely nothing.'

Admiral Gittins, 'Fair enough. In that case, can you return to your command?'

Admiral J Bonner, 'Yes, Sir.'

Admiral Gittins to Henry Strong, 'Morning Sir, I thought that you might want an update.'

Henry Strong, 'Yes, that would be beneficial.'

Admiral Gittins, 'The Fleet has been resupplied and is in formation ready for any action

Thank you for the new drones and forts

There is no indication of Fleet 1's fate.'

Henry Strong, 'You can expect further supplies of drones over the next few weeks. Can you spare any officers or crew for Edel's new Fleets?'

Admiral Gittins, 'We are checking on it now, Sir. I wouldn't be too hopeful. We are hardly over-resourced.'

Henry Strong, 'When can you return some of the forts to the planets? They are still very twitchy.'

Admiral Gittins, 'We are getting the manufacturing plans to assess the situation. To be honest, it all depends on the enemy.'

Henry Strong, 'I understand.'

Admiral Gittins, 'How is The President?'

Henry Strong. 'It's bizarre. He made an instant recovery. It was as if someone had turned off a switch and he was back to normal. Then a few minutes later, he was paralysed again.'

Admiral Gittins, 'There has been a lot of weirdness recently, it's just a sign of the times.'

Henry Strong, 'Thanks for the update.' Henry thought to himself, *He hasn't got the mustard it takes to be a great admiral.*

Location: Somewhere Secret
Sequence of Events: 130

Terry was smiling. There in front of him was the British Museum. He was home, not that it would seem like a home without his mother.

Terry tried to sort things out in his mind:

- There is no enemy
- The Northemy were a fabrication created by his mother. Did she create that planet as well?
- The Northemy ships were Brakendeth ships supplied from the past. They were quite a bit older than The Brakendeth ship experienced by the homans
- His mother had more powers than he realised. He wondered if he could do the things she did
- He wondered if he would start taking on The Brakendeth characteristics
- His mother must have paralysed The President.

It was even more apparent now that he would have to let his mother die. How would he explain her disappearance to the homans?

Should he be honest about what had happened? If they knew the truth, the homans would be very angry. All those good people lost because of one mad Brakendethian! To be fair, she was more than 80% homan. Even so.

Terry, 'Mummy, are you still there?'

Cheryl, 'Yes my son; are you sure that I'm getting better?'

Terry, 'Yes mummy, what you need is a good sleep.' He shut his mummy down and cuddled her until she was beyond the point of revival. He knew he was human because he cried for an Earth hour.

The President woke up for the second time completely unparalysed. He wondered how long it would last.

Location: Admiral Mustard's Flagship, Somewhere in Time, and Space
Sequence of Events: 131

Fleet Operations, 'Sir, I don't want to be a bore, but things are changing again. All Brakendeth activity has ceased to exist. I was expecting human activity to return, but there is nothing. There is no comms activity at all.'

Admiral Mustard, 'What's happening on Earth?'

The images showed a very verdant Earth, teeming with wildlife. There were fauna and flora that they had never seen before. The Earth was hotter than it used to be, and so was the Sun. There were no signs of civilisation, but there was a primitive human-looking primate.

Admiral Mustard wondered if they had travelled back in time. He didn't see much point in sending down a scientific team as things were likely to change again.

Admiral Mustard, 'Anything else to report?'

Fleet Operations, 'Nothing else significant to report. The Chief Medical Officer is reporting that some of the staff are suffering from nausea. He wonders if it's the effect of time distortion.'

Admiral Mustard, 'How many staff are we talking about?'

Fleet Operations, 'About 400. Do you have any orders, Sir?'

Admiral Mustard, 'I think we should just observe.'

Fleet Operations, 'Shall I reduce the alert level?'

Admiral Mustard, 'Keep selected vessels on full alert, others can stand down.'

Location: Somewhere Secret
Sequence of Events: 132

Terry wasn't smiling. His mother had just died. In a way, he had committed matricide, and he had definitely committed sororicide. Twice actually, and he wasn't even a year old yet.

He had pondered over what to tell the homan authorities. He decided that the truth was the best way forward, even if it led to his death. He also decided that the best person to talk to would be President Padfield.

He wasn't sure how he could escape from the building or how to contact The President, and then it happened. His mind reached out to The President.

President Padfield was still relishing the fact that he wasn't paralysed. It's strange how the temporary loss of something makes one really appreciate its return. Just walking and talking and even picking one's nose became authentic delights. What a wonderful world and then it hit him: an extreme pain behind his left ear. The horror of a new bout of paralysis made him shiver, but this was different. He could just about hear a hushed child-like voice.

President Padfield, 'Who is there?'

Terry, 'It's me, Terry.'

President Padfield, 'I can't hear you that well.' Terry wasn't sure what he was doing, but he upped the volume. The President was almost knocked over by a wall of noise. The sheer volume was deafening.

President Padfield, 'That was far too loud.'

Terry tried again, 'It's me, Terry.'

President Padfield, 'Is that Terry?'

Terry, 'Yes; mummy is dead.' He tried to be strong, but he just cried and cried. The President wanted to hug him but then wondered if he was a dangerous killer.

President Padfield, 'I'm sorry to hear that, Terry. Are you OK?'

Terry, 'I'm fine, but it has been a very bad time. Very bad indeed. Can you help me?'

President Padfield, 'Where are you?'

Terry, 'Opposite the British Museum. I'm in a building. When I look out of the window, I can see the museum. I can guide you.'

President Padfield, 'I will come and get you.'

Terry, 'You may want to kill me. That would be OK.'

President Padfield, 'Why would I want to do that?'

Terry, 'The crimes of The Brakendeth. The crimes of Cheryl. My crimes. Not good. Probably best to kill me.'

President Padfield, 'I will come and get you. I will bring two guards with me. I won't tell anyone about you until the crimes are understood.'

Terry, 'One crime is gone.'

President Padfield, 'What'd you mean?'

Terry, 'No more paralysis, mummy is dead.'

From The President's point of view, it all seemed very strange. He was still in bed but feeling great. He took two of his best guards and went to track down a Brakendethian baby.

Location: Somewhere Secret
Sequence of Events: 133

President Padfield found Terry reasonably quickly. They couldn't break the door down, but they managed to get him out of the window. Terry tried to sit in the back of The President's car, but he wasn't big enough, and no child seat was available. The President considered holding him, but it didn't seem appropriate, so Terry sat on the floor.

The President told his driver to stop and get three ice-creams and then stop somewhere secluded. The driver was told to go for a walk.

President Padfield, 'I need to hear the whole story.'

Terry, 'I will try based on what I know.'

President Padfield, 'Take your time, there is no hurry.'

Terry, 'When I was born, The Brakendeth also changed mummy. She became 20% Brakendethian, and unfortunately, she inherited some of their worst characteristics. She wanted to recreate their empire again through her children.

'I think she was very disappointed in me. I've inherited more of the human traits.

'She decided that before she could dominate humanity, she needed to eliminate The Galactium military. She did this by creating a fictitious enemy — The Northemy. She even managed to amend the records in The Brakendeth library.'

President Padfield, 'If the Northemy are fictitious then who was the enemy?'

Terry, 'Mummy used Brakendeth vessels from the past to attack our forces. How she did this is a mystery. She had several talents that I don't fully understand yet.

'When our forces defeated her ships, she just got more from the past. Eventually, she would win as she had unlimited resources. She found you, Mustard and Bumelton particularly annoying. She paralysed you and sent the other two 100,000 years into the future.'

President Padfield, 'So what happened to Cheryl?'

Terry, 'As part of mummy's plan to create a Brakendeth dynasty she activated one of her eggs. This one became Nancy. Nancy then activated another one which became Jill. Jill was a true Brakendeth and decided to escalate their births, and in the process, they killed mummy.

'Jill tried to kill me by slitting my throat. I retaliated and killed both Nancy and Jill. It had to be done. They were following The Brakendeth pathway. I revived mummy to find out what she had been doing, and then I let her die. It was the only thing I could do. I needed to protect humanity.

'Now Mr President, when I finish this ice cream, I think you should kill me.'

President Padfield, 'I don't think we should wait until you have finished the ice cream.'

They both laughed.

President Padfield, 'Anyway, to sum up, there is no enemy. The Brakendeth have been defeated again. Our military can go home. The only outstanding problem is getting Fleet 1 back. Any ideas on that?'

Terry, 'A few but I'm going to have to work out how mummy did it.'

President Padfield, 'We need to agree the story going forward.'

Terry, 'The truth is always the best story.'

President Padfield, 'It's not always the best story for the masses. I'm going to tell them that the enemy has been defeated and that the military can stand down. Then I will tell them that we need to focus on getting our brave Navy back from the future. Are you OK with that?'

Terry, 'Yes, Mr President.'

President Padfield, 'I have another idea, can I adopt you? It will give you peace and quiet, and I can protect you.'

Terry, 'Yes Mr President, but there is one proviso — if I show any signs of going down the wrong path, you will kill me.'

President Padfield, 'That's a deal.'

Location: Conference Room, GAD (The Galactium Alliance Defence Hub), Planet Earth
Sequence of Events: 134

President Padfield opened the third strategy conference. The attendees were as follows:

- Admiral Edel Bonner
- Admiral John Bonner
- Admiral Glen Pearce
- Admiral Peter Gittins, Acting Admiral of the Fleet
- Admiral Phil Richardson
- Admiral Calensky Wallett
- Commander Tom Crocker, Special Operations
- AI Central
- Jill Ginger, Fleet HQ — Head of Science
- Alison Walsh, Fleet HQ — Head of Engineering
- Jeremy Jotts, Fleet HQ — Head of Staffing
- Louise Forrester, Fleet HQ — Head of Logistics and Production
- Madie Milburn, Fleet HQ — Head of Intelligence
- Salek Patel, Fleet HQ — Head of Communications
- Denise Smith, Fleet HQ — Head of Navigation & Exploration
- Admiral Rachel Zakotti, Fleet HQ — Head of Planetary Defence
- Dr Doris Frost, Chief Medical Officer
- Tony Moore, Deputy President
- Bill Penny, Leader of The Galactium Council
- Henry Strong, Chief of Staff
- Terry, Advisor to The Galactium

President Padfield, 'Ladies and gentlemen, please come to order. I have some good and bad news.

'Firstly, I can announce that the war with The Northemy is over. Our military can stand down. I would like to take this opportunity once again to think of the fallen, both civil and military. We have all lost some dear friends; we have lost planets and whole populations. They will not be forgotten.

'Before anyone asks, I need to thank Terry, who with the help of our intelligence services helped to nullify The Northemy threat. The war is over. The time for celebration has begun. We will be informing the general population in due course.

'The war has, of course, been a disaster, but there have been some positives: the new replication technology, medical scanners, and the cure for cancer. Our force fields are now significantly stronger. Our military has proved itself once again, and also demonstrated the need for a strong Navy. We will create a new Marine Force and work towards improved planetary protection.

'Lastly, I want to inform everyone that we have lost Fleet 1. They chased after the enemy, and we believe that they are trapped in the future. The loss of every crew member is tragic, but I have to announce that we have lost two of our heroes: Admirals Mustard and Bumelton. We are investigating ways of securing their return but time travel obviously poses lots of challenges.

'We plan to celebrate their lives and all those who have fallen during a series of ceremonies throughout The Galactium.

'Any questions?'

Tom Masters, Leader of The Galactium Council, 'Mr President, I'm clearly glad to hear that the war has ended. Can you provide some further detail?'

President Padfield, 'I plan to publish a detailed report, but there are several intelligence issues that need to be addressed before that is done. Please accept my personal guarantee that the war is over.'

Henry Strong, 'Mr President, can you clarify Terry's involvement in the ending of the war?'

President Padfield, 'I plan to detail his involvement in the report in due course. All I can say is that without his help, we may not be here today.'

Henry knew when he was being fobbed off.

Henry Strong, 'Could I also ask about the whereabouts of Cheryl and also about her involvement, if any, regarding your paralysis?'

President Padfield, 'I can let it be known that Cheryl lost her life during the intelligence exercise. My bouts of paralysis may have been stress-related. The doctors have given me a clean bill of health. Thank you for asking.'

Henry was quite annoyed. There was fobbing-off and fobbing-off. This took the cake.

'My executive orders are as follows:

- Admiral Gittins to stand the armed forces down
- Admiral Gittins and Admiral E Bonner to build the Navy up to full strength
- Admiral Wallett to re-form the Marine Corps
- Admiral Pearce to work with Henry Strong regarding the return of the forts to their planetary defence duties
- Admiral Pearce to work with Rachel Zakotti to test and improve the planetary force fields. Each planet must have control of its own force field
- Jeremey Jotts to organise 'End of War' celebrations and memorial ceremonies
- Hellen Marten to prepare comms announcements for the general public
- Jill Ginger to set up a team to investigate and test any products developed by Terry. Full certification will be required
- Denise Smith to develop a plan for the systematic investigation of our galaxy.'

Location: Admiral Mustard's Flagship, Somewhere in Time, and Space
Sequence of Events: 135

Admiral Mustard, 'Update me.'

Fleet Operations, 'No real change since the last update. Earth is still a primitive paradise. There are no communications at all from anywhere. We are casting our net out further and further, but all we are finding is silence.'

Chief Medical Officer to Admiral Mustard, 'I need to see you.'

Admiral Mustard, 'Will a teleconference do?'

Chief Medical Officer, 'You need to come here and experience this.'

Admiral Mustard, 'I'm on my way.' His exec ordered a schooner to take him across to the medical complex on the carrier. The Admiral was concerned because James Pippin, the CMO, sounded concerned. He wasn't normally the sort to even get a ruffle.

James met him at the entrance to the medical suite. Admiral Mustard could tell that James was one step beyond being frightened.

James, 'Come this way.' The Admiral was taken to James' private cabin.

Admiral Mustard, 'What's upsetting you?'

James, 'Jack, I've never seen anything like it before. It's horrible. I don't think it is a medical problem.'

Admiral Mustard, 'Spill the beans.'

James, 'Our staff are disappearing.'

Admiral Mustard, 'What do you mean?'

James, 'One crew member has completely disappeared. About a hundred are in different stages of fading away, and three hundred are a bit hazy.'

Admiral Mustard, 'Hazy?'

James, 'They are still complete but becoming less clear. You will see what I mean when we go next door.' James led the way.

James, 'This is the hazy ward.'

Admiral Mustard saw rows of beds full of crew members who were there but not quite there. Their outline was indistinct. They weren't transparent, but they seemed to flow into the environment. Hazy was a good word. Apart from their lack of solidity, they appeared to be in good spirits. James led the way to the next ward. Here there were crew members with parts of their body missing, or somewhat invisible. There were men and women without limbs, heads, or torsos. Some just had a hand missing. Others merely consisted of a leg. Admiral Mustard was amazed by how calm they were.

Admiral Mustard, 'James, I'm surprised that there is no panic.'

James, 'I don't think the victims know that parts of their body are invisible.'

Admiral Mustard, 'Haven't you asked them?'

James, 'Yes, but I'm not sure they still exist in this world. Try talking to them.'

Admiral Mustard walked up to a rating.

Admiral Mustard, 'Morning sailor, how are you today?'

Rating, 'I'm fine, Captain.'

Admiral Mustard, 'I'm an Admiral.'

Rating, 'Why are you in a lieutenant's uniform?'

Admiral Mustard, 'Where are you now?'

Rating, 'On Earth Sir, receiving my training.'

Admiral Mustard noticed that further parts of the rating's body had disappeared.

Admiral Mustard, 'What is your prognosis?'

James, 'It's something to do with time travel. I suspect that these people's timeline stopped, or perhaps it is just the way it is. Perhaps we are all going to fade.' James took his jacket off. He had no chest.

Admiral Mustard didn't know what to say, but he said, 'What happened to the man that disappeared?'

James, 'He just ceased to exist. He faded away. There are more and more cases happening throughout the Fleet.'

Admiral Mustard, 'Can you predict the rate?'

James, 'Obviously some people may not be affected, but at the current rate, you won't have a Fleet within two weeks. I will be long gone before then.'

Admiral Mustard to Admiral Bumelton, 'I need to talk to you about our latest crisis.'

Admiral Bumelton, 'Jack, I can't see my legs.'

Location: Admiral Mustard's Flagship, Somewhere in Time, and Space
Sequence of Events: 136

Chief Engineer, 'Sir, things are getting a bit difficult.'

Admiral Mustard, 'Update me.'

Chief Engine, 'We have lost the engine room in the *Albatross*.'

Admiral Mustard, 'That's the Fleet carrier.'

Chief Engineer, 'That's right. The engine was there yesterday, and now it's gone.'

Admiral Mustard, 'Is the ship still functioning?'

Chief Engineer, 'That's the weird thing, the engine is gone, but everything is still working OK.'

Admiral Mustard, 'Thanks for the update.'

Chief Engineer, 'There is more, most of the toilet paper has disappeared.'

Admiral Mustard, 'On the *Albatross*?'

Chief Engineer, 'No everywhere.'

While on the phone, Admiral Mustard walked across to his loo. The Chief Engineer was right. There was no toilet paper.

Chief Engineer, 'Other things are starting to disappear. What do you want me to do?'

Admiral Mustard, 'Just carry on.'

Chief Engineer, 'What do I say when people are asking for toilet paper? I am getting a lot of calls, Sir.'

Admiral Mustard, 'Tell them to improvise.'

Chief Engineer, 'They won't like that, Sir.'

Admiral Mustard, 'I'm sure you are right.'

Admiral Mustard to Fleet Operations, 'Can you get one of the ships to attempt a jump? I would suggest the carrier.'

Fleet Operations, 'Why the carrier?

Admiral Mustard, 'I have a theory.'

Fleet Operations, 'Yes, Sir.'

Admiral Mustard waited.

Fleet Operations, 'The *Albatross* has jumped, but nothing happened as before.'

Chief Engineer, 'Sir, the engines are back, and more importantly, the toilet rolls have reappeared on the *Albatross*.' Admiral Mustard rechecked his toilet. The toilet paper was still missing.

Admiral Mustard to Fleet Operations, 'My orders:

- The entire Fleet will attempt to jump.'

Fleet Operations, 'Sir, is there any point?'

Admiral Mustard, 'Carry out my command.'

Fleet Operations, 'Yes, Sir.'

Admiral Mustard waited.

Fleet Operations, 'It didn't work.'

Admiral Mustard's toilet paper had returned, and he said, 'But now you can wipe your bum.'

Fleet Operations wondered what was going on. Was that last comment a statement or an order?

Chief Medical Officer, 'Sir, there has been a miracle! The disappeared have returned. Everyone is back to normal.'

Admiral Mustard, 'That is excellent news! Are there any side effects?'

Chief Medical Officer, 'There don't seem to be any.'

Admiral Mustard to Admiral Bumelton, 'Are you still legless?'

Admiral Bumelton, 'They suddenly reappeared. Damned funny experience. It sends the willies up me. Were my legs coming back anything to do with you?'

Admiral Mustard, 'Well, people and things were disappearing. As you know, material is just energy. I wondered if we were out of sync with this timeline. The jump corrected things. Although it didn't work as a jump, we left this timeline and came back again. I was just lucky.'

Admiral Bumelton, 'It's not luck, Jack, it's some special ability you have to think differently.'

Fleet Operations, 'Sir, things are changing again.'

Location: The President's Office, Presidential Palace, Planet Earth
Sequence of Events: 137

President Padfield, 'I will not accept your resignation, Henry.'

Henry Strong, 'I refuse to work for a man that lies to his colleagues.'

President Padfield, 'What did you want me to do?'

Henry Strong, 'I want you to tell the truth.'

President Padfield, 'You want me to tell the military that there was no enemy? That they had lost thousands of good men and women fighting a fictitious foe? That they were fighting against the whims of a madwoman?'

Henry Strong, 'I warned you about Terry.'

President Padfield, 'It wasn't *Terry* who was the problem, it was his mother.'

Henry Strong, 'You are fucking splitting hairs. I'm off.'

President Padfield, 'Henry, please don't go. We need your talents more than ever. What would I need to do to keep you?'

Henry Strong, 'The truth must come out.'

President Padfield, 'What if you led a commission into the truth? No holds barred. You write the report, and you release it. Explain how the Marine Corps was lost. Explain that Planet Hooke was lost with all its inhabitants. Emphasise the pointlessness of it. Explain that the heroes that were defending Earth were just playthings.

'However, if you want to fuck off, then fuck off. I've had enough.'

Henry Strong. 'I've got my principles!'

President Padfield, 'And you suppose that I have none, just fuck off.'

Henry left the room. Dave really did wonder if he could carry on, but then someone has got to take the blame.

Location: The President's Office, Presidential Palace, Planet Earth
Sequence of Events: 138

Terry, 'Do I live here now?'

President Padfield, 'I think so.'

Terry, 'Are you my daddy now?'

President Padfield, 'I can never be your real father, but I plan to adopt you if that is still what you want.'

Terry, 'I do, Can I call you Daddy?'

President Padfield, 'Probably best to call me Dave in public but at home, you can call me Daddy.' The President hadn't fully realised the dichotomy in Terry. He was both an adult and a child. The President felt that he needed to pander to Terry's childish side because he was entitled to have a childhood. The memories that you grow up with are so important in later life, but then he had already experienced more things than most, and he was not even a year old.

Terry, 'Dad, what do you want me to do with my new inventions?'

President Padfield, 'What have you invented?'

Terry, 'Mummy asked me to make the following:
- Allow the pill-taker to take control of their body temperature
- Give the pill-taker microscopic vision
- Improved linguistic capabilities
- Limited mind reading
- Eliminate headaches, especially hangovers
- Eliminate all heart disease
- Improved mathematical abilities
- A better sense of smell
- A better sense of balance.'

President Padfield, 'And they are all ready?'

Terry, 'Yes, dad.'

President Padfield, 'I think we should get Jill Ginger's team to check them and then we can sell them through your company.'

Terry, 'OK, dad, but they don't need testing.'

President Padfield, 'I believe you, but it's often best to follow procedure.'

Terry, 'Can we go to the cinema?'

President Padfield, 'That's a good idea, there is one in the Palace. We can have it all to ourselves.'

Terry, 'Will there be popcorn?'

President Padfield, 'Of course. By the way, do you have any ideas on how we can get Admiral Mustard back?

Location: The Presidential Palace, Planet Earth
Sequence of Events: 139

President Padfield and Terry were just walking down to the cinema when the alarms went, and not for the first time. The President's phone rang.

President Padfield, 'Evening Peter, how can I help?'

Admiral Gittins, 'Evening Mr President, I'm very sorry to say, but we have another alien invasion.'

President Padfield, 'Who is it?'

Admiral Gittins, 'No idea at this stage, but it looks to be a hodgepodge of different vessels. We have never seen any of them before.'

President Padfield, 'How many vessels?'

Admiral Gittins, 'Possibly twenty to thirty thousand ships. I do need to point out that this has happened at the worst possible time. The Fleet is temporarily standing down. The forts have returned to their home planets. Damaged ships are being repaired, others are being upgraded. All of the drones are being reprogrammed.'

President Padfield, 'How many ships can you make available?'

Admiral Gittins, 'Without recalls and rounding up crews, about twenty.'

President Padfield, 'Are you saying that we can only muster twenty fighting ships?'

Admiral Gittins, 'That is about it.'

President Padfield, 'Do what you have to do to get an operational Fleet.'

Admiral Gittins, 'Yes, Sir.'

Location: Admiral Gittins's Flagship
Sequence of Events: 140

Admiral Gittins to Fleet Operations, 'My orders:
- Cancel all involvement in ceremonies by the Navy
- Recall all personnel
- Put all naval vessels back on the active rota
- All naval vessels to join the Fleet, Fleet Operations to provide co-ordinates
- Inform Supply to release as many drones as possible as soon as possible
- Warn all forts that they might be needed by the Fleet
- Inform supply that new vessels are to be released to replace damaged ships
- Contact each Admiral and explain the position, request their immediate return
- Check munitions position
- All available vessels to form a standard defence formation around the Flagship as soon as possible.'

Admiral Gittins, 'Update me.'

Fleet Operations, 'The alien fleet is still beyond Pluto's orbit and are travelling fairly slowly. It looks like several fleets are gathering at a specific meeting point.'

Admiral Gittins, 'How many fleets?'

Fleet Operations, 'It's hard to tell, but there seem to be at least twenty-three different fleet designs, so I'm guessing twenty-three fleets.'

Admiral Gittins, 'What sort of positioning?'

Fleet Operations, 'It looks like they are trying to form a set pattern. They are having a lot of problems organising themselves. I'm picking up chatter that suggests that they don't have compatible systems or even languages. The term "Brakendeth" has been used a few times.'

Admiral Gittins, 'So everything suggests that we have twenty-three navies from twenty-three races?'

Fleet Operations, 'I can't confirm that, but your assumption makes perfect sense.'

Admiral Gittins, 'This could be another Rignot situation.'

Fleet Operations, 'That was a strange coincidence. I have the Rignot Admiral on the phone. He wants to know if their ten ships would be of use?'

Admiral Gittins pondered for a while and said, 'Tell the Admiral that his Fleet's presence would be welcome.'

Gittins wondered how he could control them.

Admiral Gittins, 'Comms, are they making any attempt to contact us?'

Comms, 'No Sir, as Fleet Control said, there is a lot of chatter. In fact, there is so much chatter that it must be difficult for them to filter out the good stuff.'

Admiral Gittins, 'Are we communicating with them?'

Comms, 'Of course but we are just adding to the chatter.'

Admiral Gittins, 'See if our Rignot friends recognise them.'

Comms, 'Sir, the Rignot are sending over data on each species along with their technical capabilities. Apparently, they are all Chemlife dependent.'

Admiral Gittins, 'Hopefully, all we have got is a negotiation on our hands and not war.'

Admiral Gittins, 'Fleet Operations, update me.'

Fleet Operations, 'It looks like we have twenty-three thousand ships divided into twenty-three fleets. They obviously decided that each race would provide the same number of vessels.

Their technology is obsolete from our perspective, but they have the numbers. So far, we have rustled up 147 vessels plus 10 from Rignot. More are on their way, but it's hard to get an ETA.'

Admiral Gittins, 'Why?'

Fleet Operations, 'The main problem is the crew. They are all over the place. It might surprise you, but a lot of them are drunk or drugged.'

Admiral Gittins, 'Comms, any progress?'

Comms, 'No Sir, but there is every chance that war could break out between them.'

Admiral Gittins, 'Have you got the Rignot data?'

Comms, 'Yes Sir, just trying to put it into a format that we can understand. I can give you the race name and their tech level.'

Admiral Gittins, 'That would be a good start. What is the reference regarding the tech level?'

Comma, 'The Rignot have classified us as a ten.'

Admiral Gittins, 'How would the Rignot classify themselves?'

Comms, 'I will find out. The chart is on the screen now, Sir.'

Ref	Race	Tech Level
1	Stampon	3
2	Chasedef	5
3	Minialen	3
4	Credant	1
5	Malnant	1
6	Prevy	1
7	Destrroyn	3
8	Babcoc	1
9	Franont	5
10	Taxen	9
11	Revcus	1
12	Balanty	2
13	Enet	4
14	Wattbob	9
15	Letton	7
16	Ombuf	2
17	Powek	2
18	Rang	1
19	Herti	8
20	Deadlock	2
21	Explat	1
22	Awardon	1
23	Informh	1

Comms, 'Before joining The Galactium the Rignot were a 4. They also pointed out that the race names are their names for that race, and that the race may call themselves something different.'

Admiral Gittins, 'Please thank the Rignot for their help.'

Comms, 'They are going to sleep now.'

Admiral Gittins, 'Who is?'

Comms, 'The Rignot. Apparently, they always go to sleep before a battle.'

Admiral Gittins, 'I might have a quick nod myself.'

Admiral Gittins, 'Fleet Operations, how are we doing?'

Fleet Operations, 'We are up to 262 Fleet vessels. Admirals Pearce and J Bonner are on their way.'

Comms, 'Sir, before they go to sleep, the Rignot want to know where our Navy is.'

Admiral Gittins, 'Tell them it's on its way.'

Comms, 'They say they can't detect it. Bad news. They are going home.' And home they went.

Admiral Gittins, 'That was a brief love affair.'

Fleet Operations, 'Do you want me to recall the planetary forts?'

Admiral Gittins, 'Not at this stage. Just chase the Fleet recall. Call President Padfield if necessary to get his support. I'm surprised that Henry Strong has not been on the blower.'

Fleet Operations, 'I chased his office. Apparently, Henry has resigned.'

Admiral Gittins, 'Find out who has replaced him. We need those drones.'

Fleet Operations, 'Yes, Sir.'

Location: Admiral Mustard's Flagship, Somewhere in Time, and Space
Sequence of Events: 141

Fleet Operations, 'Sir, Earth has disappeared.'

Admiral Mustard, 'You are joking?'

Fleet Operations, 'Both the Earth and the Moon have gone. Mars has suffered severe radioactive damage, and most of the other planets have slightly different orbits.'

Admiral Mustard, 'Any comms traffic?'

Comms, 'There is a lot of very alien noise. Nothing like I've experienced before.'

Admiral Mustard, 'Action stations.'

Admiral Mustard, 'Fleet Operations, are we still in our standard defence formation?'

Fleet Operations, 'Yes, Sir.'

Admiral Mustard. 'I thought so, but so much has happened in such a short period.'

Fleet Operations, 'Sir, a single ship is approaching. It's cloaked, but our scanners managed to detect it. It's fast and looks to be carrying a fair amount of muscle.'

Admiral Mustard, 'Comms, inform the vessel that we have detected its presence and we will fire if it continues on its present course.'

Fleet Operations, 'Sir, it has activated its weapons.'

Admiral Mustard, 'My orders:
- Activate our weapons
- Send a warning shot.'

Fleet Operations, 'Sir, it's retaliated. They have taken out a battlecruiser which had its force field on full power.'

Admiral Mustard, 'That's hard to believe. My orders:
- Destroy the unknown ship

Fleet Operations, 'Yes, Sir. Enemy eliminated. It took a fair amount of power to smash its shields.'

Admiral Mustard, 'My orders:
- Collect debris so we can assess the enemy
- Set up beacons to detect any further enemy ships.'

Fleet Operations, 'We are not going to get a chance to do that, three more bogies are coming this way.'

Admiral Mustard, 'Are they identical to the previous ship?'

Fleet Operations, 'Yes, Sir. Possibly slightly larger.'

Admiral Mustard, 'Comms, any activity?'

Fleet Operations, 'Sir, they are powering up their weapons.'

Admiral Mustard, 'My orders:

- Destroy the unknown ships.'

It was a bloody affair. The Earth Fleet lost eleven vessels and over two hundred men and women to destroy three of the enemy. The odds were not looking good. Admiral Mustard decided that flight was the best option but in what direction?

In the back of his mind, he was hoping for some more weirdness. This was not a universe or timeline that appealed to him.

Fleet Operations, 'Sir, at least a dozen enemy vessels are coming this way, including a big bastard.'

Admiral Mustard, 'My orders,

- The Fleet will flee at maximum speed in the opposite direction to the enemy. Fleet Operations provide flight details.'

Fleet Operations, 'Yes, Sir.' The Fleet has departed, and the enemy is following us.'

Admiral Mustard, 'Are you plotting their trajectories?'

Fleet Operations, 'Yes, Sir. Whatever route I plan they will overtake us in about twenty Earth minutes.'

Admiral Mustard, 'What chance does the targeting software give us?'

Fleet Operations, 'It's estimating losses of more than 50%, Sir. And there are probably more of them.'

Admiral Mustard had to make a decision, stand, and fight or flee?

Location: The President's Office, Presidential Palace, Planet Earth
Sequence of Events: 142

President Padfield, 'I'm sorry that we missed out on the cinema.'

Terry, 'That's all right, dad, *Jaws* was a bit too scary for me anyway.'

President Padfield, 'Jill has been testing your new inventions. She said that they are amazing. They are going to change the world. She wanted to know why they were chosen and not something else.'

Terry, 'I've no idea why mummy wanted them. She always had a reason. Anyway, I've been giving the problem with Admiral Mustard a lot of thought.

'Firstly, where are they? mummy said that she sent them 100,000 years into the future. Whereabouts in the future, and which future? There are countless futures. Every current event changes the timeline.

'Secondly, they may not be where mummy sent them. They are a Fleet, after all. You also have to question if she knew where she sent them. It might just have been a random destination.

'Thirdly, would they have survived the transition? The odds are in favour of no.

'However, everything is trackable. Every movement leaves a residue. Fortunately, Admiral J Bonner took detailed recordings of their departure point.'

President Padfield, 'But he found nothing.'

Terry, 'You can't find nothing. He actually found a lot but he lacked eyes, ears, and noses.'

President Padfield, 'That sounds promising.'

Terry, 'It's a real challenge. I wouldn't want to raise your hopes.'

Location: Admiral Gittins's Flagship
Sequence of Events: 143

Admiral Gittins, 'Update me.'

Fleet Operations, 'The enemy fleets still haven't sorted themselves out. I'm guessing that there is an argument over precedence. The Taxen and the Wattbob seem to be at each other's throats.'

Admiral Gittins, 'If we had the numbers, now would be a good time to attack.'

Comms, 'Sir so far there has been no communications. And there has not been any declaration of war.'

Admiral Gittins, 'Look, when twenty-three races invade your space, they are not coming for a house party. It's not a game of billiards.'

Comms, 'What's billiards?'

Admiral Gittins, 'Fleet Operations, what are the Fleet numbers?'

Fleet Operations, 'Approaching 700 with 1200 on the way. Admirals Pearce and J Bonner have arrived. Henry Strong is back on the case. Two thousand drones will be here in two Earth hours.'

Admiral Gittins, 'It's getting a bit more even. Those drones will make a big difference. How many forts do we have?'

Fleet Operations, 'Just the thirty that usually are defending Earth.'

Admiral Gittins, 'My orders:

- Line up the forts and drones in front of the enemy when they arrive
- Request support from GAD defences.'

Comms, 'Sir, I think I'm getting a communication.'

Taxen Leader, 'I lead the Taxen. You will surrender to us mostly now. You are cows for plucking. Brakendeth cows that now belong to the twenty-three. Twenty-three now own homans or killdeath nowest.'

Admiral Gittins laughed, 'I think that is a threat. Ask them to repeat as the message was incomplete. We need to gain time.'

Comms, 'Sir, a new message is coming in.'

Wattbob Leader, 'I am controller Wattbobian armed forces. We visit to eat homans. Need Chemlife. Brakendeth make homan pigs to eat. We eat. We not go away. Now dinner time.'

Admiral Gittins to Taxen and Wattbob Leaders, 'Welcome to The

Galactium. We welcome you in peace and harmony. We are not an aggressive species, but we will defend ourselves, and we will win.

'We have considerable military resources at our disposal as you will soon see. We have analysed your military capability, and we outgun you.

'We know that you need a source of Chemlife. We can provide this free of charge, with no strings attached whatsoever. You can take it back with you now.

'War serves no purpose.'

Wattbob Leader, 'You respect none. We have history of millions. You children. You food. You have no soul. We can't deal agree as no pedigree.'

Taxen Leader, 'Homan shit-bags hate much. Killnow for Chemlife. No, no, no, no, more power gives hope.'

Admiral Gittins, 'I'm not sure that I understand all of that.'

Admiral Gittins, 'Fleet Operations, is the cavalry on the way?'

Fleet Operations, 'Yes, and there is some good news. There are over 3,500 drones and sixty forts.'

Admiral Gittins, 'My orders,

- Slowly line up 3,000 drones in front of the enemy
- Line up the forts behind the enemy
- The other five hundred drones to join the Fleet.'

Fleet Operations, 'Yes, Sir.'

Admiral Gittins to Leaders of the twenty-three fleets, 'Honoured leaders, for your own reasons you may hate us. I also recognise that we may be a new species, but I have what you want: Chemlife.

'This Chemlife has been provided to the Rignot. They also live in The Galactium under our protection. You can contact them regarding our promises of free Chemlife.'

Taxen Leader, 'Rignot are filth, no soul, deserve to die, homans are food.'

Admiral Gittins, 'Some of you have loved ones at home dying the death of age. Today you can help them. We will supply you with Chemlife now. Save your loved ones and friends now.'

Admiral Gittins, 'Fleet Operations, get a large delivery of Chemlife into space now.'

Fleet Operations, 'Yes, Sir. We now have over 1,000 vessels on the line. Five hundred more drones and twenty forts are on their way.'

Admiral Gittins, 'We may need some vessels to transport Chemlife from the Chemlife tanker.'

Fleet Operations, 'Yes, Sir, I'm on the job.'

Comms, 'Sir, Admiral E Bonner is on the blower.'

Admiral E Bonner, 'Hi Peter, very impressed with your tactics. Calensky and I have an idea. We could deliver a show of force if you wanted it. Seven Fleets are waiting to be staffed. We think that we could arrive at a point of your choice using skeleton crews. They really would be skeletons, we could activate the weapon systems, but we couldn't fight. It's also worth pointing out that the new Fleets have two thousand five hundred vessels each, and they are hot.'

Admiral Gittins, 'Brilliant idea, can I tell you when to arrive?'

Admiral E Bonner, 'Of course.'

Wattbob Leader, 'We are one. We take Chemlife. We take homans. No negotiate with shit.'

Admiral Gittins, 'I understand where you are coming from. Are you formally declaring war on humanity?'

Wattbob Leader, 'This is what?'

Admiral Gittins, 'In the Galactium, we do whatever we can to avoid war, but as I said before, we will defend ourselves. Our military resources are being recalled. We will shortly outnumber you.'

Taxen Leader, 'Scare us noway. We fight, we see only limited Fleet. No problem. Us win.'

Admiral Gittins to Admiral E Bonner, 'Your time is now.'

Seventeen thousand five hundred ships of the line appeared directly in front of the Taxen fleet. The additional drones and forts joined the main Fleet.

Admiral Gittins to Leaders of the twenty-three fleets, 'Can I assume that you have declared war on humanity?

'If yes, my first order is to destroy all stocks of Chemlife.

'My offer of free Chemlife still stands, those who want it should withdraw now.'

Taxen Leader, 'Trickery no work. We are one. No one will leave.'

Admiral Gittins, 'I have ordered the Chemlife tanker to be destroyed.'

Admiral Gittins, 'Fleet Operations, put a hole in it so that the Chemlife pours out.'

Fleet Operations, 'Sir, are you sure?'

Admiral Gittins, 'Do it.' The tanker that contained enough Chemlife for the enemy fleet for ten thousand years was holed. The Chemlife poured out. The enemy fleet broke ranks. There was a mad rush to get a share of it. The only two races that stood firm were the Taxen and the Wattbob.

Admiral Gittins to Leaders of the twenty-three fleets, 'You don't have to rush. We can supply stocks regularly. I would recommend, for those that want it, that you agree to a formal treaty with The Galactium. We can work together.'

The Taxen fleet opened fire. Fortunately, none of their weapons penetrated The Galactium force fields.

Admiral Gittins to Taxen Leader, 'Honoured leader I ask you to retire before our Fleet gets here.'

Taxen Leader, 'Explain me.'

Admiral Gittins, 'I head the Earth Defence Force. The Galactium consists of over 100,000 planets. Each planet has its own defence force. I've only requested another 50,000 ships of the line. That should easily be enough to finish you off. Another 100,000 ships of the line will attack your home planet. Would you mind providing the coordinates for that attack?'

Taxen Leader, 'You call me an idiot. I will do that never.'

Admiral Gittins, 'I can get the data from our Rignot friends.'

Admiral Gittins, 'Fleet Operations, power up all weapons and aim them at the Taxen.'

Taxen Leader, 'Stop! Why just us?'

Admiral Gittins, 'You fired at us, we will retaliate. We expect to eliminate 92% of your forces. This will be my last communication with you.'

Comms, 'The Taxen are trying to make contact.'

Admiral Gittins, 'Make them wait.'

Admiral Gittins, 'Move all forts and half of the drones to surround the Taxen fleet.'

Comms, 'The Taxen Leader is desperate to talk.'

Admiral Gittins, 'How can I help you?'

Taxen Leader, 'We take Chemlife and go.'

Admiral Gittins, 'No Chemlife for Taxens.'

Taxen Leader, 'My populations dying muchly.'

Admiral Gittins, 'That is unfortunate, but you were going to kill humanity.'

Taxen Leader, 'Muchly mistaken.'

Admiral Gittins, 'Take the Chemlife, but we will expect a peace treaty in due course.'

Taxen Leader, 'It is agreed.'

The Chemlife feeding frenzy carried on for a while and one by one, the enemy fleets left. Admiral Gittins had scored an enormous victory without a single death. He decided not to call them enemies but future partners.

Location: The Presidential Palace, Planet Earth
Sequence of Events: 144

President Padfield, 'Come in, Henry.'

Henry Strong, 'Your boy did well.'

President Padfield, 'You mean Admiral Gittins?'

Henry Strong, 'I didn't think he had it in him.'

President Padfield, 'Cometh the hour, cometh the man. Anyway, thanks for your help.'

Henry Strong, 'I've come to apologise.'

President Padfield, 'You don't have to. I was in the wrong. I'm quite happy to present the truth to the public.'

Henry Strong, 'What is right or wrong? Let's move on. We have had one war after another. Let's focus on the future. I now realise that it is a very dangerous universe out there. We need to protect humanity and fast.'

President Padfield, 'Hear, hear.'

Henry Strong, 'Have I got my job back?'

President Padfield, 'You never lost it. Changing subjects, how do you feel about Terry?'

Henry Strong, 'I think we were both right. Cheryl was the problem. With the new controls in place, I think we can control Terry.'

President Padfield, 'I'm planning to adopt him.'

Henry Strong, 'Why's that?'

President Padfield, 'Firstly, I've taken a shine to him. I like the idea of becoming a father again. I think he needs a family. He needs to be humanised and joining my family will do that.'

Henry Strong, 'So what you are saying is that you want to keep a close eye on him.'

President Padfield, 'That's about it. I meant what I said. I'm not getting any younger.'

Henry Strong, 'What's he doing now?'

President Padfield, 'Working on a way of getting Mustard and Bumelton back.'

Henry Strong, 'Excellent, is he going to do it?'

President Padfield, 'If anyone can, he can.'

Location: Admiral Mustard's Flagship, Somewhere in Time, and Space
Sequence of Events: 145

Fleet Operations, 'Sir, they have disappeared.'

Admiral Mustard, 'Where have they gone?'

Fleet Operations, 'They simply turned around and fled.'

Admiral Mustard, 'Why did you use that word?'

Fleet Operations, 'Because they were definitely fleeing. They scuppered off at maximum speed.'

Admiral Mustard, 'So the question is, what are they fleeing from?'

Fleet Operations, 'I think I know. Dead ahead there is a fleet of giant ships. Do you remember the ark?'

Admiral Mustard, 'Yes.'

Fleet Operations, 'Well, they are that size.'

Admiral Mustard, 'Are they the good guys or the bad guys? Are they worse or better than the last lot?' He realised that he was being rather naïve, but the last few weeks seemed more like a computer game than reality. A rather deadly computer game.

Admiral Mustard, 'Comms, is there any contact with this new fleet?'

Comms, 'Yes, they are saying, "Desist all actions. Desist or die".'

Admiral Mustard, 'I guess that they are the bad guys then.'

Admiral Mustard, 'Action stations. My orders:
* Prepare to flee.'

Fleet Operations, 'Sir, that's not looking like an option. We have been tractored.'

Admiral Mustard, 'What, the whole Fleet?'

Fleet Operations, 'Yes, Sir.'

Admiral Mustard, 'I guess that we'd better desist then.'

Comms, 'Sir, there is contact. It sounds like Underbelly.'

Underbelly Frogandorf, 'What are you?'

Admiral Mustard, 'I'm Admiral Mustard of The Galactium Fleet.'

Underbelly, 'No interest, what are you?'

Admiral Mustard, 'We are humans.'

Underbelly, 'What do humans do?'

Admiral Mustard, 'We are a powerful military force.'

Underbelly laughed, 'You no value. Primitive ships, no precious cargo, no useful body parts, no reason to let live.'

Admiral Mustard, 'What do you plan to do with us?'

Underbelly, 'I'm only the Third Underbelly; the Second Underbelly will decide.'

Admiral Mustard, 'When will that be?'

Underbelly, 'When Second Underbelly decides.'

The entire First Fleet was simply being dragged along. Admiral Mustard could see no way of freeing themselves. He called a meeting of the Heads of Department.

Admiral Mustard, 'Ladies and gentlemen, we have been through a lot. We have solved every problem we have encountered. How do we solve this one?'

Bob Mates, Head of Science, 'We do have expertise in the use of tractor beams, but we have never seen anything this strong. It's hard to believe that it can handle a whole Fleet.'

Admiral Mustard, 'Is it one beam or many?'

Bob Mates, 'Good question. We have no idea.'

Admiral Mustard, 'What do we know?'

Bob Mates, 'We have used every analysis tool we have, nothing registers.'

Admiral Mustard, 'Does anyone have a plan of action?'

There was a shaking of heads.

Admiral Mustard, 'Any ideas on where we might be?'

More head shaking. The Admiral had wondered if he had lost his touch before. Now he was utterly idea-less. Their only chance was to negotiate with the Second Underbelly.

Fleet Operations, 'The first lot that was chasing us have appeared again. This time there are thousands of them.'

Admiral Mustard, 'Looks like we are going to be in the middle of a fire-fight.'

Fleet Operations, 'The Underbelly lot have slammed their brakes on; I don't know whether that means they are stopping or they are changing direction, or something else. And munitions are coming this way.'

Admiral Mustard, 'Is there any change in the tractor beam's strength?'

Fleet Operations, 'It doesn't look like it.'

Admiral Mustard, 'I now know what it's like being a sitting target.'

Location: The President's Office, Presidential Palace, Planet Earth
Sequence of Events: 146

President Padfield, 'How's it going, son?'

Terry, 'What's going where?'

President Padfield, 'It's just a figure of speech.'

Terry, 'Like "Willy Nilly"?'

President Padfield, 'That's right, English is full of them. Lots of them are really shortcuts.'

Terry, 'OK, things are going well.'

President Padfield, 'That's good. Any joy finding the lost Fleet?'

Terry, 'I've developed a time distortion tracker. The idea was that it would identify an action that distorts time, but there are thousands and thousands of distortions. I'm wondering about the validity of time.

'On Earth, we know that seconds, minutes, hours, and months are just man-made fabrications. They don't relate to a time-based activity.'

President Padfield, 'What are you getting at?'

Terry, 'Humans spend a lot of time and money defining what a second is, down to hundreds of decimal places, but actually, it is meaningless. It doesn't relate to anything, whereas a day and a year have true values.'

President Padfield, 'I see where you are going. A day relates to the rotation of the Earth on its axis, and a year is a trip around the sun.'

Terry, 'Sorry dad, I know that you know all of this. But time is very confusing. Is midnight the start or the end of the day? And as soon as we leave, Earth days and years are meaningless. So how can I track down where they are in time?'

President Padfield, 'It makes your head hurt.'

Terry, 'So the only facts I have are the date, time and physical location when they left us. That's when I need to retrieve them. But there are lots of time-related issues. What did they do in the future? If I stopped them going there, what effect would it have?'

President Padfield, 'Terry, don't worry too much. Just bring them back.'

Terry, 'I'm not that far away from achieving that.'

President Padfield, 'Really?'

Terry, 'However I'm not that certain that humans could survive the process. I need more time to think about it.'

President Padfield, 'I guess that we all need more time.'

Location: Admiral Mustard's Flagship, Somewhere in Time, and Space
Sequence of Events: 147

Fleet Operations, 'Sir, something is happening. The ship holding us has been hit. It looks like it is going to explode.'

Admiral Mustard, 'All power to the shields.'

Fleet Operations, 'Sir, we have no way of doing that, but our force fields are at the highest level.'

Suddenly, the tractor beam was released, and the Flagship was thrown haphazardly, tumbling through space. It was not a pleasant experience, but it wasn't long before the ship was back under control.

The Human fleet, however, was suffering a variety of different fates. Some were destroyed along with their tractor hosts. Others were being deliberately picked off by the other side. Admiral Mustard just looked and wondered what it was all about. Was this just Darwinian theory in action? The bigger fish eat the smaller fish.

Admiral Mustard, 'Fleet Operations, update me.'

Fleet Operations, 'Sir, there were about 480 vessels originally held by tractor beams. One hundred and twenty are still tractored, over 200 vessels and been destroyed and the rest are free like us.'

Admiral Mustard, 'How many are free?'

Fleet Operations, 'About 160, but many of the vessels are damaged.'

Admiral Mustard, 'My orders;

- All vessels to meet at a designated point, Fleet Operations to provide coordinates
- Undamaged ships to collect crew from damaged vessels
- Fire at tractor beams in an attempt to release ships that are still being held.'

Fleet Operations, 'Sir, the non-belly lot are coming for us.'

Admiral Mustard, 'My orders,

- All vessels to leave the area now in the direction of the Underbellies
- Remaining ships to join us if and when you can.'

Admiral Mustard hated leaving anyone behind, but he had a duty to save the most he could. Then suddenly everything went blank. The sensors went blank. The external visuals ceased to exist. Consciousness just packed up. There was no movement. There was nothing. There was no one to perceive anything.

Location: The Presidential Palace, Planet Earth
Sequence of Events: 148

Terry wasn't sure if he should have done it. He wondered if he had committed a time crime. He had probably killed everyone in Admiral Mustard's Fleet. What was his dad going to say?

But then he could reverse the process, except that time had moved on. He had created a whole new form of mathematics to calculate time-travel logic. He was effectively stopping them from time travelling, but to that, he was using time-travel technology. The scope for error was enormous. He studied his equations over and over again. He thought he'd got it right.

His technology had been delivered by a drone to the exact physical location where they left, and it had been designed to reverse any time distortions it found. He had hoped that the drone would send back a picture of the Fleet returning, but there was nothing. Did his technology find a time distortion? Did it work?

He decided that there was no point in telling his dad. Time would tell. Nevertheless, he decided to send a call request to Admiral Mustard from the return date, just in case.

Location: Admiral Mustard's Flagship, Somewhere in Time, and Space
Sequence of Events: 149

Admiral Mustard wasn't sure if he was dreaming. Was he in the dream still? He couldn't move his body. It was the kind of paralysis that you occasionally got in the night where your mind and eyes work but nothing else. It used to terrify him as a child. His father told him that it was Old Hag, a malevolent supernatural creature that used to immobilise you by sitting on your chest.

Slowly he realised that he was still sitting in his seat on the Flagship. Everything looked reasonably OK. There was no damage, but a lot of unconscious bodies slumped in every possible combination. Some seemed to be quite intimate positions.

He desperately wanted to go back to sleep. He might have done as the barrier between wakefulness and being asleep was somewhat vague. This pattern may have gone on for some time, but as he couldn't move his arm, he couldn't check his watch.

In his mind, he had asked Fleet Operations for an update. That was still impossible as he couldn't talk. He was amazed that he was still breathing. He did notice an unpleasant smell. Then he realised that it was excrement. He hoped that he hadn't had an accident.

Slowly, very slowly, he could gradually feel his body returning to normal. That's if you can call extreme pins and needles normal. It felt like death by a thousand cuts. Perhaps more than a thousand. His tongue avoided touching his teeth which were suffering electric shocks. His eyes were over-lubricating, and his mouth was dribbling. Things were getting pretty wet.

Fleet Operations to Admiral Mustard, 'Sir, are you conscious?'

Admiral Mustard, 'Yehhhhhhhhhhhhhhhhhhhhhhhhhhhhhh.'

Fleet Operations, 'Hopefully, you can hear. I have some strange, good news.'

Admiral Mustard, 'Cooooooooonnnntinnnnneeee.'

Fleet Operations, 'The good news is that we are back in Galactium space. The good but strange news is that the Fleet is intact. Every ship we lost is now intact and back with us.'

Admiral Mustard, 'Wwwwwhhhaaaat ttttiiiimmmme?'

Fleet Operations, 'I think you said what time? To be honest, that's hard to rationalise. It looks like we have arrived about six months before we left.'

Admiral Mustard, 'Neeed toooooo sleeeeeeeeeeeep.'

Location: Admiral Mustard's Flagship, Somewhere in Time, and Space
Sequence of Events: 150

Admiral Mustard, 'Update me.'

Fleet Operations, 'The Fleet is fully operational. About two hundred people died during the 'great sleep' mostly due to accidents. But every ship lost during our recent encounters has returned.'

Admiral Mustard, 'How do the "lost ships" explain their reappearance?'

Fleet Operations, 'They don't, they just are.'

Admiral Mustard, 'Does everyone remember the experiences over the last few months?'

Fleet Operations, 'I do. I assume you do, I guess everyone does.'

Admiral Mustard, 'Have our systems retained all the information?'

Fleet Operations, 'I believe so.'

Admiral Mustard, 'I'm just trying to assess if time travel has eliminated any memories or data.'

Fleet Operations, 'I guess that we will never know.'

Admiral Mustard to Admiral Bumelton, 'Hi George, I thought I would just check on you, being that you are much older.'

Admiral Bumelton, 'We are talking about two days. I'm only two days older than you.'

Admiral Mustard, 'Exactly, have you coped OK?'

Admiral Bumelton, 'Of course but what happens if we meet ourselves?'

Admiral Mustard, 'At least I would have someone interesting to talk to. Talk to you later.'

Admiral Mustard, 'Hi James, update me regarding the medical situation.'

James Pippin, 'Generally OK, fixing a few bones due to accidents, but nothing else.'

Admiral Mustard, 'Any time-travel issues?'

James Pippin. 'Not so far.'

Admiral Mustard, 'Fleet Operations, have you finished the Fleet Review?'

Fleet Operations, 'Yes, Sir, everything is shipshape. All systems are operational. We are a fighting force again.'

Admiral Mustard, 'My orders:

- The Fleet will slowly return to Earth in a shielded state
- Identify exactly what date it is on Earth
- Plot out what is going on in The Galactium at that time
- Ensure that there are no communications with the rest of The Galactium until I authorise it.'

Fleet Operations, 'Yes, Sir.'

Comms, 'I've just noticed that there has been a constant call request from Terry.'

Admiral Mustard, 'Put it through to my cabin on a secure line.'

Comms, 'Yes, Sir.'

Admiral Mustard, 'Terry, you won't believe the adventures we have had.'

Terry, 'I'm very keen to find out, but you have a key action to carry out.'

Admiral Mustard, 'What's that?

Terry, 'You must kill my mother.'

Admiral Mustard, 'Kill Cheryl? Have you fallen out?'

Terry, 'This is deadly serious. I'm calling from the future where Cheryl is already dead. If you killed her earlier, it would save millions of lives.'

Admiral Mustard, 'I don't understand.'

Terry, 'That's why I'm calling you. Please listen. Firstly, I will give you an update:

- The Northemy do not exist. They never existed.
- When mummy was impregnated with me, she was also changed. She became at least 20% Brakendeth
- She wanted to recreate their empire again through her children
- As part of her plans to dominate The Galactium, she decided to eliminate the military
- She created a fictitious enemy — The Northemy
- Mummy then used Brakendeth vessels from the past to attack our Navy
- She had unlimited resources so she didn't really care

whether she won a battle or not as she would win the war
- She sent you and Admiral Bumelton 100,000 years into the future, and as you know, she paralysed The President.'

Admiral Mustard, 'Is he OK?'

Terry, 'He was very seriously ill, but he has recovered. By the way, he has adopted me.'

Admiral Mustard, 'Really?'

Terry, 'Yes. Anyway, mummy wasn't happy with me as I was too human, so she activated one of her eggs.'

Admiral Mustard, 'She could do that?'

Terry, 'You would be amazed by what she could do. The new embryo was called Nancy, who then activated another egg called Jill, who was totally Brakendeth. The two embryos decided to escalate their development and in doing so, killed mummy. They then tried to kill me. Fortunately, I managed to defend myself and killed them both.'

Admiral Mustard, 'That's some story.'

Terry, 'It is a potted version of the truth. Dad has verified it.'

Admiral Mustard, 'Dad?'

Terry, 'Sorry, The President.'

Admiral Mustard, 'It's a lot to take in.'

Terry, 'Then I've spent the last few weeks trying to find a way of getting you back. You will never know how difficult it was. It has been my greatest achievement so far.'

Admiral Mustard, 'It was you who got us back?'

Terry, 'Yes. I didn't know exactly when, but you have arrived back just before mummy is going to paralyse dad.'

Admiral Mustard, 'Before we go any further, I have lots of questions.'

Terry, 'Of course.'

Admiral Mustard, 'Why did she create The Northemy?'

Terry, 'To disguise the fact that she was the enemy. That was the way she got all of the inside information from The Galactium.'

Admiral Mustard, 'But she created a planet with human farming.'

Terry, 'It was all part of the cover story. I don't know how she did it, but she also managed to change The Brakendeth records. She totally fooled me.'

Admiral Mustard, 'But you were only a child.'

Terry, 'That's my defence.'

Admiral Mustard, 'I would have recognised the vessels if they were Brakendeth.'

Terry, 'Not if they came from the distant past.'

Admiral Mustard, 'How did you get the information from Cheryl?'

Terry, 'Jill killed her, but I managed to revive her before she was fully brain dead. I interrogated her, got the information I needed and let her die. It was the hardest thing I ever had to do. Then dad rescued me.'

Admiral Mustard, 'Can I give this some thought?'

Terry, 'Of course. You should know that dad and Henry Strong had a huge argument over what they should tell the public. Henry wanted to tell the full truth. Dad didn't want the public or the military to know that the enemy was Cheryl. It would have made their sacrifice a bit pointless.'

Admiral Mustard, 'I can see exactly what The President was getting at. Can we carry on in an hour?'

Terry, 'I've still got some work to do, but it should be OK.'

Location: Admiral Mustard's Flagship
Sequence of Events: 151

Admiral Mustard, 'Hello Terry, it's all rather hard to believe, but it seems to stack up. It explains the enemy's poor tactics. Cheryl obviously had no strategic and tactical experience.'

Terry, 'She didn't have to. She had unlimited resources. She could have attacked with a few million ships, but that wouldn't appear realistic, or perhaps she just wasn't ruthless enough.

It's a pity I can't send you anything as I'm in the future.'

Admiral Mustard, 'That is also hard to believe.'

Terry, 'Well technically you are in the future and the past.'

Admiral Mustard, 'Assuming I believe you, and I want to, what do you suggest?'

Terry, 'All of the sci-fi films tell you not to describe the future, but I need to tell you what happened after you left.

'Firstly, during the battle immediately before you left, Earth was hit twice. Los Angeles was destroyed with over two million casualties. Bishops Auckland in England was also destroyed with twenty-five thousand killed.

'Henry Strong effectively took over, and during an investigation, they couldn't work out where Cheryl had gone. She had taken me to a secret location.

'Admiral Gittins took over as Admiral of the Fleet.'

Admiral Mustard, 'Good for him, he has always been underrated.'

Terry, 'President Padfield called a meeting at GAD which led to lots of military actions. This is where Henry fell out with The President over the truth. Henry resigned but eventually came back.

'Then we were invaded by twenty-three alien fleets. Admiral Gittins played a brilliant hand of poker with them, and they left with Chemlife. He did a great job.

'And now we are here.'

Admiral Mustard, 'And you want me to kill Cheryl?'

Terry, 'It's not me that wants her killed. It's about what's best for humanity. Her earlier death would save two to three million humans and a considerable number of Fleet members. It's really not my shout. I'm a kid with no military training. Over to you.'

Admiral Mustard, 'You are asking me to change history.'

Terry, 'So what, no one will know.'

Admiral Mustard, 'There will be consequences.'

Terry, 'There are always consequences. There will be consequences if you don't do it.'

Admiral Mustard, 'What about changing the timeline?'

Terry, 'We have already committed several time crimes. There are currently two John Mustards and two George Bumeltons.'

Admiral Mustard, 'What's your plan?'

Terry, 'We know that mummy is going to paralyse The President. You will meet her and kill her.'

Admiral Mustard, 'And what would be the consequence of that?'

Terry, 'The obvious things would be:

- The President would not be paralysed
- I would not be attacked by my sisters
- All Northemy battles would end
- LA and Bishops Auckland would not be destroyed
- Three million people would not be killed
- The Navy would be in a much stronger position
- You would not go into the future.'

Admiral Mustard, 'If I don't go into the future, how can I come back in the past and kill Cheryl?'

Terry, 'Good one; it gets complicated. Currently, you remember the future. But if you kill Cheryl, you don't go into the future, and consequently, you won't remember it.'

Admiral Mustard, 'Clear as mud. OK, I will kill her in defence of your dad.'

Terry, 'After this he might not be my dad.'

Location: Admiral Mustard's Flagship
Sequence of Events: 152

Admiral Mustard to Tom Crocker, Special Ops, 'Hi Tom, I hope you are well.'

Tom, 'OK, but a bit bored. There hasn't been much for my team to do.'

Admiral Mustard, 'I have a top-secret job for you. It's very delicate. You will need to trust me.'

Tom, 'I can't think of anyone I trust more.'

Admiral Mustard, 'I happen to know that one of The President's visitors is going to assassinate him.'

Tom, 'Who?'

Admiral Mustard, 'You won't believe me, but it's Cheryl.'

Tom. 'But we have known her for years.'

Admiral Mustard, 'She is not happy that The President won't pay Terry for his inventions. She actually plans to paralyse him, but it could be fatal. I need a team to break into the Palace and secure her.'

Tom, 'So non-lethal weapons?'

Admiral Mustard, 'Yes.'

Tom, 'What is The President going to say?'

Admiral Mustard, 'He won't be happy at first, but this is a matter of life and death.'

Tom, 'Can you provide orders? I want my team protected.'

Admiral Mustard, 'Of course.'

Tom, 'When?'

Location: The President's Office, Presidential Palace, Planet Earth
Sequence of Events: 153

Admiral Mustard to Tom Crocker, 'Hi Tom, is your team ready?'

Tom, 'As ready as it will ever be. Meet us at Café Bleu just outside the Palace entrance. We are all casually dressed. Cheryl has just arrived and is in reception. The plan is to storm the Palace just when she enters The President's reception room.'

Admiral Mustard, 'Security is tighter than it used to be.'

Tom, 'We have full details on the security arrangements. We have already taken out some of the guards. Shortly the security cameras will be turned off, and every door will be unlocked. We are doing a real James Bond job here.

'All you need to do is follow us in. We will be ready to go in five Earth minutes. A-OK?'

Admiral Mustard, 'A-OK.' The Admiral still wondered if he was doing the right thing. He had killed thousands, hundreds of thousands of thinking entities in his life, but this was cold-blooded murder. It was personal. He wondered if he had the guts to do it.

The Admiral saw the Special Ops team arrive at the entrance of the Palace. There were no guards to be seen. The door opened automatically, and the team was in, on its way to The President's reception room. Admiral Mustard was amazed just how easy the whole exercise was. He knew in reality that it was all down to the three P's: Plan, Practice, Perform.

Admiral Mustard stood at the entrance to the reception room. There was no point in a grand explosive entrance. He just opened the double doors, and he walked in with his team following him. He unholstered his gun and pointed it at Cheryl.

In that instance, Cheryl read his mind and shut him down. The President and the whole Special Ops team were also shut down. They were all paralysed.

She knew that Admiral Mustard was here to kill her. Her shit of a son had done the dirty on her. She knew that she had two embryos within her — Nancy and Jill that were Brakendeth. She was surprised about the existence of Jill, which meant she couldn't trust Nancy. She wanted ruthlessness but not to that murderous extent. They were never supposed to kill her. She immediately terminated them and absorbed them back into her body. Within a few minutes, she didn't even look pregnant.

She knew that the Admiral had discovered her Northemy secret. The future he knew was not going to happen now. She would not send them into the future. Instead, the Admiral would be the father of her children.

Cheryl ordered one of the special ops troopers to strip the Admiral. He stood there in all his naked glory, totally helpless. That's just how she liked her men.

She slowly took off her dress. The men in the room might be paralysed, but they could still see. She knew that she was an attractive woman. She knew that the Admiral had watched videos of her fucking Adam during The Brakendeth war. She knew that he wanted her. Well, she wanted him.

She removed her bra, allowing her large shapely breasts to swing free. Her nipples were already hard in anticipation. She had always fancied the Admiral even though he was a bit of a father figure. She was looking forward to a long, hard fuck. A fuck that she would have total control of.

Her panties slowly slid down her legs to reveal an already moist fanny. She could feel the tension in the room. Firstly, she decided to get the Admiral's cock as big and as hard as possible. She increased the Admiral's temperature and forced blood into his genitals. His cock was now very rigid. She could tell that it was hurting him.

She released the paralysis in his genitals so that he would be able to feel the mixture of pain and pleasure. His pain and her pleasure. She pushed him onto the ground making sure that he would get any carpet burns. His seriously stiff prick was sticking up vertically. She could tell that it was causing him pain, so she notched up the stiffness slightly more.

It then dawned on her that he couldn't live, so this was his swansong. Cheryl gently lowered herself onto Admiral Mustard's super-sensitive penis. At first, she was gentle, but then she just dropped herself onto him. Cheryl had her first orgasm. *Thank you, Jack,* she thought. She could tell that it was mostly pain for the Admiral.

Cheryl then used his todger to pleasure herself. She had multiple orgasms. Then she decided to nearly bring the Admiral to orgasm and then stop him at the last moment. This can be very pleasurable, but if done too often, it becomes torture. She thought, *Let the torture begin.*

The admiral was at the point of ejaculation about thirty times. Each time his heart was put under real pressure. Cheryl wanted and needed his sperm. She thought that it would be rather poetic to receive his sperm at his death.

Cheryl took him right to the edge. He had a massive heart attack and shot his whole load into Cheryl's warm, inviting cunt. She made sure that he didn't enjoy it before he died.

Cheryl stood up knowing that the Admiral's sperm had fertilised a dozen of her eggs. She knew that she could control these as they were half-human. She would decide when to have them.

She then teleported herself and her son to a secret location. Terry was a bit surprised that she couldn't read his mummy's mind. He was even more surprised to find that Jill and Nancy had ceased to exist. She told Terry to come over for a cuddle. Terry enjoyed the comfort of her nudity, and then Cheryl broke his neck. His body lay crumpled on the floor.

And Cheryl thought, *And so it all begins.*

Location: The President's Office, Presidential Palace, Planet Earth
Sequence of Events: 154

As Cheryl teleported out, the paralysis ended, but the shock continued. President Padfield, 'What just happened? What are you doing here, Tom?'

Before he answered, he rushed over to the Admiral's body. There was no doubt that he was dead. He called for the medical team, but he knew that it was hopeless. He then organised his team to provide presidential security, and he released the Presidential guards.

Tom, 'The Admiral asked us to help save your life. Apparently, he knew that Cheryl was going to harm you. So we organised an attack.'

President Padfield, 'It wasn't much of an attack. You just walked in.'

Tom, 'We had to take out your guards. None of them has been harmed.'

President Padfield, 'That's the second time that they have failed me.'

Tom, 'I wouldn't be too harsh on them. Few have had our training. Anyway, I was surprised that Jack got his gun out.'

President Padfield, 'Then we were paralysed, and Jack was fucked to death.'

Tom, 'Probably not a bad way to go.'

President Padfield, 'I wasn't convinced that he was enjoying it.'

Tom, 'Then Cheryl just vanished.'

President Padfield, 'Yes, that was extraordinary. The other odd thing is that she came in heavily pregnant and left with a very flat tummy.'

Tom, 'Not a bad figure at all.'

President Padfield's PA, 'Sir There is a call for you from Terry's medical team.'

Dr Cartwright, 'Mr President, I thought that I better let you know. Terry has disappeared, and his life signs have been terminated. He must be presumed dead.'

President Padfield, 'Thank you.'

President Padfield's PA, 'Sir, there is another call. It's from Admiral Mustard.'

The President looked shocked. He had every right to be.

Admiral Mustard, 'Morning Dave, how are you?'

President Padfield, 'Speechless.'

Admiral Mustard, 'I just thought I would update you. There was an invasion force of 250,000 enemy ships. George had laid on a sound defence with me protecting the Earth. All of a sudden, the enemy just retired. For now, the threat has been called off.'

President Padfield, 'That's quite convenient. We need you here in my office as soon as possible.'

Admiral Mustard, 'Can you tell me why?'

President Padfield, 'Not really, but it is urgent.'

Admiral Mustard, 'I'm on my way.'

President Padfield, 'Tom, we need a forensic team here as soon as possible. Is that Admiral Mustard?'

Tom, 'I will get my boys to work on it now. I will organise more security. He called for the full Special Services regiment to guard the Palace, and for some of his ships to escort Admiral Mustard's Flagship.'

Admiral Mustard detected a strange inflexion in The President's manner. What was happening? It made him feel tense and uneasy.

Tom to President Padfield, 'Sir, we can verify that the body is, or rather *was*, Admiral Mustard. The DNA matches perfectly. It passes every test.'

President Padfield, 'Well one of them must be an impersonator. It must be this one as our Admiral Mustard wouldn't try to kill Cheryl. Mind you, we have to wonder about Cheryl. We need to treat her as an enemy now.'

Location: Cheryl's New Secret Place
Sequence of Events: 155

Cheryl had found a new hiding place. Although she had all of these new capabilities, it had been a somewhat turbulent, emotional time.

She listed in her mind what had happened to her recently:

- She had murdered her son, and she wondered if that had been a bit impetuous
- She had terminated both of her pregnancies
- She hadn't known about Jill, that was a surprise
- She had deliberately fucked Mustard to death. That was also a bit impetuous. There was a lot more life in him. She had always fancied him and could have used him for months
- She had fertilised a lot of her eggs, but she had got a bit bored being pregnant. It was hard work
- Everyone now knew that she was a baddy
- She was a bit bored with the whole battle thing. She decided that she wasn't going to do that any more. It was the end of The Northemy. She wasn't sure if anyone saw the joke — 'Not the Enemy'.

She still wanted a Brakendeth future, or did she? Perhaps she just wanted a great future for her children. What she mostly wanted was a good sleep.

Location: Admiral Bumelton's Flagship
Sequence of Events: 156

Admiral Bumelton, 'Fleet Operations, update me.'

Fleet Operations, 'The entire First Fleet is cloaked and just outside of The Galactium detection systems. Nothing to report except that Admiral Mustard has gone to Earth.'

Admiral Bumelton, 'Did he say why?'

Fleet Operations, 'No, Sir.'

Admiral Bumelton, 'Did he say when he was going to return?'

Fleet Operations, 'No, Sir. Are there any orders?'

Then they just faded away. Cheryl's decision to stop future military activity meant that the first Fleet never chased the enemy, and that created some serious time paradoxes.

Location: The President's Office, Presidential Palace, Planet Earth
Sequence of Events: 157

President Padfield, 'Tom, what just happened?'

Tom, 'I'm not sure why I'm here.'

President Padfield, 'I vaguely remember Cheryl fucking Admiral Mustard, but perhaps I was dreaming.'

Tom, 'I'm not sure what you are talking about.'

President Padfield, 'It's gone now.'

President Padfield's PA, 'Admiral Mustard is here to see you.'

Admiral Mustard, 'Morning Dave, you sounded a bit worried on the blower.'

President Padfield, 'Did I?'

Admiral Mustard, 'Hi, Tom, I didn't expect to see you here.'

Tom, 'To be honest I'm not sure why I'm here.'

President Padfield, 'And I'm not sure why I asked to see you. There has been some strangeness going on.'

Admiral Mustard, 'Well we had a strange incident. Our detection systems picked up Fleet 1 just beyond our normal reach, and then they disappeared, but obviously, we were here all of the time.'

President Padfield, 'And to add to that Cheryl has disappeared, and we think Terry is dead.'

Admiral Mustard, 'You think Terry is dead?'

President Padfield, 'We track his life signs, and they have stopped.'

Admiral Mustard, 'And the enemy simply disappeared. My gut feel is that they have gone.'

President Padfield, 'Forever?'

Admiral Mustard, 'That's my gut feel.'

Location: Cheryl's New Secret Place
Sequence of Events: 158

Cheryl had a great sleep, but she woke up to find that none of her eggs had been fertilised after all. She must have dreamt that she had fucked Admiral Mustard.

Terry came over to give his mummy a big hug. He had always been a good boy. Terry realised that the use of drugs was going to be the best way to keep her calm and under control. He realised that she was going to need a lot of control. The Brakendeth spirit can be far too strong for a simple homan to handle.

Terry was still mystified about her extraordinary skills, or rather super-powers. He started listing them in his mind:

- The ability to paralyse someone
- The ability to extract items (spacecraft) from the past and bring them to current times
- The ability to move items into the future
- Teleportation of herself and others
- The ability to control other people's emotions — she made the senior Galactium team depressed
- The ability to depress artificial intelligence
- The ability to stop him from reading selective parts of her mind
- The ability to mentally control space battles over vast distances

These were things he couldn't do, but he wasn't a year old yet. Even so, it was hard to believe that she could do this. He knew that she loved him and that she really wasn't a battle-hardened dictatorial killer. There was a mystery here that still needed to be solved.

Then there were the alien planets and the fields of humans. How could she have done that? His recent scans of her mind showed no knowledge of any of this. That in itself was remarkably strange.

Cheryl thought that the time had come to settle down and raise Terry. She wanted to be a proper mum. She was still looking forward to seeing Adam and Jenny. Mostly Adam.

Location: The President's Office, Presidential Palace, Planet Earth
Sequence of Events: 159

Dr Cartwright, 'Sir, there is some good news. We have picked up Terry's life signs.'

President Padfield, 'Excellent news; do we know where he is?'

Dr Cartwright, 'Yes, he is in Cheryl's flat. It would appear that he has always been there. Strange. At one time, I thought that we couldn't detect his life signs.'

Location: Admiral Mustard's Flagship
Sequence of Events: 160

Admiral Mustard, 'Update me.'

Fleet Operations, 'Things are very quiet, Sir. There are no signs of any enemy activity.'

Admiral Mustard, 'Just how I like it.'

Fleet Operations, 'I'm not sure if I believe that, Sir.' Admiral Mustard had noticed that some banter was entering the process. George would tell him to stamp it out, but he kinda liked it. It made him feel at home. Well, the Flagship *was* his home.

Admiral Mustard, 'What's assets do we have?'

Fleet Operations, 'The asset report is on the screen now Sir, we have Six fully kitted out Fleets for possibly the first time in a few years. There are also seven complete Fleets waiting to be staffed.'

	1	2	3	4	5	6	Total
Galactium Fleets							
Fleet Battleship	1	1	1	1	1	1	6
Fleet Carrier	1	1	1	1	1	1	6
Battleship	20	20	20	20	20	20	120
Battlecruiser	500	500	500	500	500	500	3,000
Destroyer	1,000	1,000	1,000	1,000	1,000	1,000	6,000
Frigate	200	200	200	200	200	200	1,200
Super Drone	50	50	50	50	50	50	300
Drone Fleet	20,000	20,000	20,000	20,000	20,000	20,000	120,000
Fighter	400	400	400	400	400	400	2,400
Planet Killer	5	5	5	5	5	5	30
Total	1,577	1,727	1,727	1,727	1,727	1,577	111,640

Admiral Mustard, 'What's the position with the planetary forts?'

Fleet Operations, 'Eighty-nine per cent of the planets have received their original fort or a new, improved one.'

Admiral Mustard, 'And the 11% gap?'

Fleet Operations, 'They have been dispatched but haven't arrived yet. With the new force fields, the planets have never been so secure.'

Admiral Mustard, 'Carry on.'

Fleet Operations, 'Yes, Sir.' He mumbled to himself, 'I will probably carry on all day.'

Location: Conference Room, GAD (The Galactium Alliance Defence Hub), Planet Earth
Sequence of Events: 161

President Padfield opened the third strategy conference. The attendees were as follows:

- Admiral Jack Mustard, Admiral of the Fleet, and the First Fleet
- Admiral Edel Bonner, Advisor to the Admiral of the Fleet
- Admiral George Bumelton
- Admiral John Bonner
- Admiral Glen Pearce
- Admiral Peter Gittins
- Admiral Phil Richardson
- Admiral Calensky Wallett
- Commander Tom Crocker, Special Operations
- AI Central
- Jill Ginger, Fleet HQ — Head of Science
- Alison Walsh, Fleet HQ — Head of Engineering
- Jeremy Jotts, Fleet HQ — Head of Staffing
- Louise Forrester, Fleet HQ — Head of Logistics and Production
- Salek Patel, Fleet HQ — Head of Communications
- Madie Milburn, Fleet HQ — Head of Intelligence
- Denise Smith, Fleet HQ — Head of Navigation & Exploration
- Admiral Rachel Zakott, Fleet HQ — Head of Planetary Defence
- Dr Doris Frost, Chief Medical Officer
- Tony Moore, Deputy President
- Bill Penny, Leader of The Galactium Council
- Henry Strong, Chief of Staff
- Terry, Advisor to The Galactium

President Padfield, 'Ladies and gentlemen, please come to order.

'I can announce that the war with The Northemy is over. Our

military can stand down. I would like to take this opportunity once again to think of the fallen, both civil and military. We have all lost some dear friends; we have lost planets and whole populations. They will not be forgotten.

'Before anyone asks, I need to thank Terry, who with the help of our intelligence services helped to nullify The Northemy threat. The war is over. The time for celebration has begun. We will be informing the general population in due course.

'The war has, of course, been a disaster, but there have been some positives: the new replication technology, medical scanners, and the cure for cancer. Our force fields are now significantly stronger. Our military has proved itself once again, and also demonstrated the need for a strong Navy. We will create a new Marine Force and work towards improved planetary protection.

'Any questions?'

Tom Masters, Leader of The Galactium Council, 'Mr President, I'm clearly glad to hear that the war has ended. Can you provide some further detail?'

President Padfield, 'I plan to publish a detailed report, but there are several intelligence issues that need to be addressed before that is done. Please accept my personal guarantee that the war is over.'

Henry Strong, 'Mr President, can you clarify Terry's involvement in the ending of the war?'

President Padfield, 'I plan to detail his involvement in the report in due course. All I can say is that without his help, we may not be here today.' Henry knew when he was being fobbed off.

My executive orders:

- Admiral Mustard to stand down the armed forces
- Admiral Wallett to re-form the Marine Corps
- Admiral Pearce to work with Rachel Zakotti to test and improve the planetary force fields. Each planet must have control of its force field.
- Jeremey Jotts to organise 'End of War' celebrations and memorial ceremonies
- Hellen Marten to prepare comms announcements for the general public

- Jill Ginger to set up a team to investigate and test any products developed by Terry. Full certification required.
- Denise Smith to develop a plan for the systematic investigation of our galaxy. As you know we set up the First Exploratory Fleet some years ago but it soon became outdated and was scrapped as part of our cost-cutting exercises. We need to learn the lessons this time.'

President Padfield had planned the meeting to be a strategic review, but in reality, it was just a series of announcements made by him. A full strategic review was still needed once the team had rested. He certainly knew that he needed a rest.

Both Admiral Mustard and Henry Strong asked to see him.

Location: The President's Office, Presidential Palace, Planet Earth
Sequence of Events: 162

President Padfield, 'Jack, how can I help you?'

Admiral Mustard, 'I don't believe that we should stand the Fleet down. I actually think we should do the opposite.'

President Padfield, 'I must tell you that I keep having strange dreams. In one of them, you come into this office with a gun to shoot Cheryl. She ends up fucking you to death. Can you believe that?'

Admiral Mustard, 'It's strange you say that. I've had some bizarre dreams. In one, you have been paralysed by Cheryl. In another, I'm in the future where we are attacked and, to be honest, thrashed by several aggressive aliens. What is scary is the clarity of the dreams. They are so lifelike.'

President Padfield, 'And me, I can see Cheryl's breasts and fanny as clear as day. I can even see the Maltese cross on your arse.'

Admiral Mustard, 'How did you know that?'

President Padfield, 'I didn't. I just saw it in my dream.'

Admiral Mustard, 'We have experienced a fair amount of weirdness. If I didn't know better, I would suspect time travel distortions. I keep getting many déjà vu experiences.'

President Padfield, 'I know exactly what you mean. I had a dream last night where we were invaded by force consisting of twenty-three alien races. What are the chances of that?'

Admiral Mustard, 'That was strange, but it could happen. I've concluded that we need to do the following: shrink the size of The Galactium to make it easier to defend, or rapidly and consistently increase the size of the military. The universe is a very dangerous place.'

President Padfield, 'I'm worried that the human race will become too militarised. Our society needs to be about the civilians, about the people and about our relatives and friends.'

Admiral Mustard, 'I couldn't agree more, but we need to feel safe and be safe to achieve that environment.'

President Padfield, 'We both agree with that, keep the military in any state you think fit. We need to talk to Henry Strong about bigger and better equipment. I think Terry will be a great help in this area.'

Admiral Mustard, 'Thank you, Mr President.'

As he was walking out, he met Henry on the way in.

Admiral Mustard, 'Henry it can't be that bad?'

Henry Strong, 'Why do you say that? We have just experienced a hugely costly, devastating war. Our finances are in a total mess. Our children's children will be paying for it for years. The boy has put whole industries out of business. The planets want to charge us for the use of their forts. Production has been geared to war. I need to switch it back. And to cap it all I've had some really strange dreams.'

Admiral Mustard, 'Sounds like a normal day for you. Tell me about your dreams.'

Henry Strong, 'Why are you asking about the dreams?'

Admiral Mustard, 'Dave and I have both been suffering. What have you dreamt about?'

Henry Strong, 'In one Cheryl was killed by two embryos. I even remember their names: Nancy and Jill. In another, your Fleet chased the enemy into the future. In another, I can see Dave paralysed in his chair and the many attempts trying to revive him. In some ways, it's not the dream but the clarity of them. I wake up believing they actually happened.

'On a couple of occasions, I've had to question my sanity or rather what reality I was experiencing.'

Admiral Mustard, 'Ditto.'

Henry Strong, 'What do you mean?'

Admiral Mustard, 'I've had the same experiences. It's the clarity that stops them from being simple dreams.'

Henry Strong, 'What's your explanation?'

Admiral Mustard, 'Time-travel paradoxes.'

Henry Strong, 'You are joking.'

Admiral Mustard, 'I wish I were.'

Location: The President's Office, Presidential Palace, Planet Earth
Sequence of Events: 163

President Padfield, 'Henry, how can I help you?'

Henry Strong, 'I came in to complain about your blatant hiding of the truth, but I feel that I've done it before.'

President Padfield, 'I wish I knew what the truth was. I think I used to know, but somehow it wandered off. You know sometimes you spot something out of the corner of your eye, or there is a memory that just won't focus.'

Henry Strong, 'I know what you are getting at. It's a bit like the same old story circulating in your head when you have a fever.'

President Padfield, 'I somehow remember you resigning and us having a violent argument and then being friends again. Are you going to resign?'

Henry Strong, 'It had crossed my mind because things were just wrong, but perhaps they weren't. Perhaps it was me that was wrong. I don't know.'

President Padfield, 'We are probably the two most powerful people in The Galactium, and we sound nuts.'

Henry Strong, 'I have another thing I want to tell you. I'm a bit afraid that you are going to laugh.'

President Padfield, 'I promise you I won't laugh.'

Henry Strong, 'I've always wanted to be a woman. My mind is female even though I pretend to be macho. The operation is scheduled for next week. I've been dreading telling you.'

President Padfield didn't laugh. It wasn't a laughing matter. It was a time to celebrate the fulfilment of a dream. David stood up and offered his hand to Henrietta and said, 'Well done.'

President Padfield, 'Can I ask how Emily feels about it?'

Henrietta Strong, 'Thank you, Dave. My wife is good. It was a bit of a shock when I first told her, but she is sticking by me. Hopefully, we can still be a viable family. Time will tell.

'Jack mentioned the strange dreams that you had both been having. In one of mine, you adopted Terry. You made a fabulous father. In another, we had to cancel all of the victory celebrations due to yet another alien invasion.'

President Padfield, 'How many races were in that alien invasion?'

Henrietta Strong, 'Twenty-three.'

President Padfield, 'That's far beyond being a coincidence.'

President Padfield to Admiral Mustard, 'I've just been talking to Henry, and we have both dreamed about an alien fleet arriving shortly. 'This is what we dreamt:

- There were 23 races involved with 23 fleets
- Each fleet had roughly 1,000 vessels
- Their organisation was chaotic
- Only two of the races have real fighting ability: The Taxon and the Wattbobs
- The Taxon were the most aggressive, but their weapons could not penetrate our shields
- They need Chemlife, but they want to take over The Galactium to avoid being dependent on us. They were rude and aggressive
- Edel turned up with seven Fleets using a scratch crew

We can't remember much more.'

Admiral Mustard, 'Who was in charge from our side?'

President Padfield, 'Admiral Gittins. Everyone seemed to think that he did an excellent job.'

Location: Admiral Mustard's Flagship
Sequence of Events: 164

Admiral Mustard called a meeting of his top team. The following were present:

Admiral Edel Bonner
Admiral George Bumelton
Admiral John Bonner
Admiral Glen Pearce
Admiral Peter Gittins
Admiral Phil Richardson
Admiral Calensky Wallett
Commander Tom Crocker, Special Operations
AI Central

Admiral Mustard, 'We have received intelligence of an enemy fleet approaching The Galactium. We don't know what direction they are coming from. We have sent out a Fleet of drones to investigate.'

Admiral Gittins, 'Are they a consortium of alien fleets?'

Admiral Mustard, 'Yes.'

Admiral E Bonner, 'And would there be twenty-three races in the consortium?'

Admiral Mustard, 'Are you going to tell me that you dreamt the battle?'

Admiral Gittins, 'Yes and I can tell you exactly where they are coming from.'

He got up and pointed to a spot on a star map.

Admiral Mustard, 'Fleet Operations, please check out Admiral Gittins's suggested location as soon as possible.'

Fleet Operations, 'Yes, Sir.'

Admiral Gittins, 'The separate fleets were assembling at that point. They were in hopeless disarray. If I had the resources, that's where I would have attacked them.'

Admiral E Bonner, 'In my dream, Admiral Gittins blagged his way out of a fight. They wanted Chemlife. It was offered to them, but they wanted control of Chemlife itself. They didn't want to be beholden to humanity.'

Admiral Richardson, 'When Peter destroyed the tanker of Chemlife, there was a feeding frenzy, a real fight for all.'

Admiral Mustard, 'We have many advantages:

- Some of us had dreamt the battle in advance
- We have Chemlife
- They are not particularly well organised
- The Taxon and the Woolybats seem to be dominant, and we can target them
- Hopefully, we know their direction of travel
- They can't penetrate our force fields
- We will outnumber them if Edel gets her finger out
- Consequently, I suggest the following plan of attack:
- Admiral E Bonner will assemble her seven Fleets as soon as possible and proceed to the agreed designation point provided by Fleet Operations
- Admirals J Bonner, Pearce, Gittins, Richardson, Wallett and I will proceed to a point directly in front of the enemy fleet assuming that Admiral Gittins's location is correct
- All Fleets will arrive cloaked
- Twenty-three tankers full of Chemlife will be located near the projected battle area ready to be distributed to the alien fleets
- Admiral Bumelton will find the Taxon home world and be positioned to destroy it

Any questions?'

Admiral Bumelton, 'Any ideas on how I will find the Taxon home world?'

Admiral Mustard, 'Yes, the Rignot know the location of all of the alien home worlds.'

Admiral Wallett, 'Could we just give them the Chemlife?'

Admiral Gittins, 'They want to control humanity, they want the cows so that they can make their own Chemlife. They do not want to be beholden to a vastly inferior race. In fact, we are not even a race; we are animals of the worst sort.'

Admiral Mustard, 'Peter is right. Besides, we need to show our strength. It's a very dangerous universe out there.'

Fleet Operations, 'I can confirm that Admiral Gittins's proposed location was spot on. There is a motley disarray of alien fleets in the exact spot.'

Admiral Mustard, 'Action stations.'

Location: Admiral Mustard's Flagship
Sequence of Events: 165

Admiral Mustard, 'Update me.'

Fleet Operations, 'The twenty-three enemy fleets are jockeying for position. It's hard to work out what they are doing. They clearly have no experience of working together.

'Our three Fleets are in position. Admiral Bumelton cannot detect any significant Taxon planetary defences. Admiral E Bonner wanted to emphasise that she could only put on a show as she had no real fighting capability.

'Fleet 1 is in the middle of the line. Fleets 2 and 3 are positioned slightly behind you to the starboard and Fleets 4 and 5 are on your port. Fleet 6 is lined up in the rear.

'Each Fleet has a line of drones, then its forts, planet killers and battleships. The remaining vessels are lined up behind them.'

Admiral Mustard, 'It's not what you would call a classic defence formation.'

Fleet Operations, 'It's been designed to impress. We have set ourselves the objective of no human deaths, and ideally no alien deaths.'

Admiral Mustard, 'Comms, do you have any useful information?'

Comms, 'No, Sir, it's just clutter and more clutter. There is no military discipline whatsoever. And there is no use of security protocols.'

Admiral Mustard, 'Prepare to contact them.'

Comms, 'Yes, Sir.'

Admiral Mustard, 'AI Central, do you have anything to say before we start?'

AI Central, 'Almost everyone in the Fleet has experienced very realistic dreams and déjà vu occurrences, so I decided to check my memory files. It is exceptionally well hidden, but I can detect that some of the data have been re-written.'

Admiral Mustard, 'Has it been deliberately interfered with?'

AI Central, 'I don't think so. It has been far too cleverly updated for that. If I didn't know better, I would say that history has been over-written by a new history.'

Admiral Mustard, 'You are gradually edging towards a distortion due to time travel, aren't you?'

AI Central, 'I always thought that time travel was impossible, but I'm having to reconsider as the evidence is far too strong.'

Admiral Mustard, 'I had another dream where you vouched for us 100, 000 years in the future. I was thrilled to hear your voice.'

AL Central, 'I'm quite touched.'

Admiral Mustard, 'So it all begins again.'

AI Central, 'Good luck.'

Admiral Mustard, 'Uncloak Fleet 1.'

Fleet Operations, 'That woke them up. Some of them are powering up their weapons.'

Admiral Mustard, 'Comms, have you found a way of communicating with them?'

Comms, 'Yes, Sir. You can start speaking whenever you want.'

Admiral Mustard, 'Leaders of the alien fleet, Welcome to The Galactium.'

Taxen Leader, 'We talk not to homan scum. Surrender now to superior forces. Cows are for eating.'

Admiral Mustard, 'I'm Admiral Mustard, and I represent The Galactium naval forces. We have analysed your military capabilities, and you do not present a threat to us.'

Taxen Leader, 'You no right, we are superior civilisations. You are Chemlife pig-dogs. You die for us pretty soon.'

Admiral Mustard, 'We are not an aggressive race, but we will defend ourselves, and we will win.'

Admiral Mustard, 'My orders:

- Uncloak Fleets 2 and 4.'

Fleet Operations, 'Yes, Sir.'

Wattbob Leader, 'I Wattbob leader, you scare us not. We outnumber you. Good fighters are Wattbobians. Then eat you, live forever.'

Admiral Mustard, 'My orders:

- Uncloak the Chemlife tankers.'

Fleet Operations, 'Yes, Sir.'

Admiral Mustard, 'We want peace. We have prepared twenty-three Chemlife tankers, one for each race. If you don't want them, we will destroy them.'

Admiral Mustard, 'My orders:

- Uncloak Fleets 2, 5 and 6.'

Fleet Operations, 'Yes, Sir.'

This was now an impressive display of military hardware: Nearly 120,000 vessels of the line.

Admiral Mustard, 'To the honoured leaders of the Fleet you have a choice, take the Chemlife and go or we will destroy you.'

Admiral Mustard, 'My orders:

- Power up all weapons.'

Taxen Leader, 'You homan bluff, you not fight. You full of fear for superior beings having millions of years of history. You are the slime of the universe. Become our dinner.'

Admiral Mustard, 'If you don't disperse, we will destroy your home worlds. Can I ask the Taxen Leader to contact his home?'

Taxen Leader, 'You attack dare not our beautiful home. You will be first to die.'

Admiral Mustard, 'I find your language unacceptable, and I will now order my Fleet to destroy your home world. We will then destroy each one of your home worlds. I have the Fleets lined up to do it. My orders:

- Uncloak Admiral E Bonner's Fleet.'

Suddenly 20,000 Galactium vessels appeared. It was a huge surprise to the assembled aliens.

Admiral Mustard, 'This Fleet is going to target the Rang home world.'

Rang Leader, 'Why us. We little harm meant. Need Chemlife to save our cluster.'

Admiral Mustard, 'Then take the Chemlife and go.'

Taxen Leader to Rang Leader, 'If you go, we kill you.'

Admiral Mustard, 'Start the destruction of the Chemlife.'

Fleet Operations, 'Yes, Sir.' One shot destroyed the first tanker.

Admiral Mustard, 'That was the tanker for the Taxen.'

Wattbob Leader, 'Take our Chemlife now.' They prepared to leave with their tanker but with their weapons pointed at the Taxens. The confederation was broken. Each race just wanted its supply of Chemlife.

The Taxen fleet was left on its own.

Admiral Mustard to Taxen Leader, 'I can order an extra tanker, and you can go, or I will destroy your fleet and your planet.'

Taxen Leader, 'Take Chemlife and go, you still dogs.'

The tanker was delivered, and a great victory was celebrated. Those who had the dreams thought that Admiral Gittins's performance was probably more impressive, but then shots were fired. Here there was not a single death and only one shot.

Location: Cheryl's Flat, Planet Earth
Sequence of Events: 166

Cheryl welcomed Adam and Jenny to her flat. Well, it wasn't her flat, and it was a luxurious penthouse suite owned by the government and provided for Terry's use. Nevertheless, she really enjoyed showing it off. She liked it so much that she or rather Terry was thinking of buying it.

She gave them a tour of the complex which included a cinema, gymnasium, tenpin bowling alley, medical centre, games room, sauna, swimming pool, several workshops and a computer centre. It was the flashiest of flashy flats. Adam and Jenny couldn't help but be impressed.

Cheryl then introduced them to her most prized possession: Terry. He was busily building a transporter. So far, a mouse had been shuffled backwards and forwards about twenty times, but sometimes things had gone wrong. They were simple problems: the colour of the mouse had changed, or it had grown an extra tail or head. On one occasion, two identical mice appeared. Quite often, the animal had got older or younger. Terry was wise enough to know that these sorts of minor side-effects might annoy some human beings.

Terry didn't have the social graces to properly interface with Adam and Jenny, but he was pleased that his mother was so happy. He asked Adam if he planned to fuck his mother because that was what she wanted. Both Jenny and Cheryl went bright red, and Adam just grinned. Terry knew then that fucking Cheryl was on his mind.'

Jenny, 'It was nice of you to ask Terry, but I don't think that Adam is interested in making love with your mother.'

Then it dawned on her that she was conversing with a one-year-old.

Terry, 'Oh, mummy will be disappointed. She was so looking forward to a good fuck."

Cheryl, 'Terry is a very clever boy.'

Adam, 'A genius I would say. The replicator is amazing, and some of his cures are just brilliant. And the "telescopic vision" is out of this world. It is so useful, especially when you are playing golf.'

Jenny, 'I need to thank Terry for the headache cure. One pill and my period pains have gone forever. My mother has not suffered a single migraine since she took one of Terry's pills.'

Cheryl, 'Do you like our shops? They are making millions. Terry is a very rich little boy.'

Adam, 'They are brilliant, and everything is so competitively priced.'

Cheryl, 'I was keen that the poor should be able to take advantage of Terry's inventions.'

Jenny, 'I'm a bit confused regarding your strategy. Most of your stuff is once-off. Once the person has the everlasting headache cure, they don't need to come back. Shouldn't you have made it so that we had to take a pill every month?'

Cheryl, 'I thought about it, but it seemed immoral to me. Our strategy is to launch new products regularly.'

Adam, 'That reminds me, we mustn't forget the linguistic pill, I've passed A-Levels in Spanish and Chinese in one college term. It's really hard to believe.'

Cheryl, 'I was hoping that you might have some new product ideas. We could discuss them over lunch which is just about to arrive. I know that you are going to really enjoy it.

While they were chatting, the caterers delivered a fabulous lunch. It was probably the best lunch that Adam and Jenny had ever experienced.

Together they brainstormed some fabulous new product ideas. It had been so successful that she put Adam and Jenny on the payroll. She hoped that it would also allow her to get into Adam's pants.

They said their goodbyes a few hours later. Terry didn't really understand why Cheryl found the encounter so enjoyable, but then he knew that Adam had agreed to meet her next Wednesday. To him, it looked like the anticipation of sex was better than the act itself.

Location: Admiral Mustard's Flagship
Sequence of Events: 167

Admiral Mustard to President Padfield, 'Mr President, I'm delighted to inform you that the enemy fleets have dispersed without any violence. We now need diplomats to visit each race. We are going to need allies in the future, and Chemlife gives us a significant advantage.

President Padfield, 'That's excellent news.'

Admiral Mustard, 'Some of these aliens live thousands of years. We must seem so young.'

President Padfield, 'It dawned on me the other day that we are going to have to address the issue of eternal life for humanity. We will always be at a serious disadvantage when dealing with other space-faring races because of our youth. They have a different understanding of time.'

Admiral Mustard, 'It's going to raise lots of issues: overpopulation, financial management, insurance, medical cover, mental health, fear of death, loss of urgency etcetera.'

President Padfield, 'I agree, there would be lots of issues. After talking to Terry, it would appear that our lifespan should be about 1,000 years, but the Brakendeth deliberately shortened it. Why would cows want to live that long? They are culled regularly.

Anyway, I think it needs to go on our strategic agenda. Humanity has got to up its game in many different ways to survive.'

Location: Terry's Room, Cheryl's Flat, Planet Earth
Sequence of Events: 168

Terry, 'I enjoyed today, it was fun watching the homans rush around. Everything seems so important to them. They focus on the little things and ignore the bigger picture.'

Grand Dethmon, 'That was an important lesson to learn.'

Terry, 'I like the homans, they have passion and enthusiasm for life.'

Grand Dethmon, 'That is because their lives are so short.'

Terry, 'It's fun watching them solve problems. They are creative but stupid, but they could be so much more.'

Grand Dethmon, 'With your help they will grow and develop. They have the potential of The Brakendeth.'

Terry, 'I'm not sure if I want the responsibility. I need to give them the tools so that they can be responsible for themselves.'

Grand Dethmon, 'That was also an important lesson for you to learn, my boy.'

Terry, 'How many other lessons do I need?'

Grand Dethmon, 'You will know when you have had enough. What plans do you have for the homans?'

Terry, 'I'm still investigating them. I'm still enjoying the emotional relationship with Cheryl. I would like some siblings, but the first two were far too nasty.'

Grand Dethmon, 'I've had to kill a few off myself. So what about your plans for the homans?'

Terry, 'Probably another war. It seems to push them forward, and they are aggressive little buggers. There are a few mysteries that I need to resolve.'

Grand Dethmon, 'What are those, my boy?'

Terry, 'Where did mummy get her powers from?'

Grand Dethmon, 'Where do you think?'

Terry, 'It smells of The Brakendeth to me.'

Grand Dethmon, 'That's very perceptive of you, but this time it's not the case.'

Terry, 'Then who was it?'

Grand Dethmon, 'I wish I knew, I really do.'

Terry, 'It's a bit like a Hercule Poirot plot.'

Grand Dethmon, 'I do enjoy a good Agatha Christie; these homans are so creative.'

Terry, 'Hear, hear!'

The Grand Dethmon laughed and said, 'Same time tomorrow.'